Winning the Covert Lady's Heart

A LADIES COVERT ACADEMY NOVEL
BOOK THREE

BY JENNY HARTWELL

Dragonblade Publishing, Inc. is an imprint of Kathryn Le Veque Novels, Inc.
P.O. Box 23
Moreno Valley, CA 92556
ceo@dragonbladepublishing.com

Produced in the United States of America

First Edition July 2023
Trade Paperback Edition

ARE YOU SIGNED UP FOR DRAGONBLADE'S BLOG?

You'll get the latest news and information on exclusive giveaways, exclusive excerpts, coming releases, sales, free books, cover reveals and more.

Check out our complete list of authors, too!

No spam, no junk. That's a promise!

Sign Up Here

www.dragonbladepublishing.com

Dearest Reader;

Thank you for your support of a small press. At Dragonblade Publishing, we strive to bring you the highest quality Historical Romance from some of the best authors in the business. Without your support, there is no 'us', so we sincerely hope you adore these stories and find some new favorite authors along the way.

Happy Reading!

CEO, Dragonblade Publishing

DEDICATION

To my sisters and BFs for life, Sharon and Coco

Chapter One

London, 1819

T HE BARD, LADY Lydia Dashwood reflected, had a knack for capturing complicated emotions with simple lines. Parting *was* such sweet sorrow.

"I'll miss you," Lydia said into her brother's shoulder as she hugged him tightly.

Servants bustled about them in the gleaming foyer, carting trunks and valises to the carriage waiting outside their Mayfair home.

"I'll miss you too," Jack murmured.

There was a note of surprise in his voice, and Lydia felt surprised too. Not that long ago, they'd been rather indifferent toward one another. It wasn't that she hadn't loved her brother. Of course, she did. But he'd been aloof and stiff with his overwhelming sense of duty for so many years, and when one added in her own sneaking about and secret life of political writing, their familial bonding had been rather stunted.

But all that had changed when Pippa came along. Lydia's friend had slid into his heart with the smoothness of her epee's blade, and Jack was a much better man—and brother—because of it.

Lydia released Jack and turned to her recently acquired sister-in-law. "And I'll miss you even more," she said to Pippa.

"Hey," her brother protested.

Pippa's eyes danced with mirth. "It's just my fencing lessons that she'll miss, darling," she said, patting her husband on the arm. "No need to feel second best."

Lydia and Pippa embraced. "I know you'll only be gone two weeks, but for some reason, it feels much longer," Lydia said.

Pippa pulled back, her dark eyebrows furrowing in concern. "Have we left you with too much responsibility? I know the timing to check on the estate up north is bad with Jane also away, but the reports Jack has received from his land agent sounded rather urgent."

Jane was the third member of their merry band of friends and had recently left London on her honeymoon.

Lydia adjusted her expression before waving her hand through the air as if brushing aside Pippa's worry. She hadn't meant to reveal any trepidation.

"It will be fine," Lydia said. "We've became accustomed to running the Academy as a trio, but I'm certain I can manage for a couple weeks on my own."

Polite society knew of the LCA as the Ladies Charitable Association where proper young women from fine households worked together to knit booties for orphans, sew bandages for soldiers, and raise funds for the poor. And all of that was true.

However, it wasn't the whole truth.

The LCA was actually the Ladies *Covert* Academy, a secret center for young women who chafed at the many restrictions placed on them by polite society. At the LCA, they could study botany, like Lydia's friend Jane, or become an expert fencer like Pippa. Others sculpted, trained horses, learned the inner workings of the shipping trade industry, and all sorts of other fields that were not open to women who wished to keep some semblance of a reputation.

It was as a Ladies Covert Academy member that Jane had begun writing articles critical of the House of Commons under the pseudonym *Democratium Liberum*—meaning, "free democracy" in Latin. Plus, she had basically given the world her initials in reverse order—DL, instead of LD, for Lydia Dashwood. She'd felt quite clever when she'd come up with that one, teasing at her true identity in the city's largest newspaper.

But that was all behind her now.

"Lydia," Jack said, pitching his voice low so that the servants wouldn't overhear. "If our trip is placing too much of a burden on you—"

Lydia touched her brother's arm. "It's fine. I can manage this." She used her most convincing voice.

Pippa and Jack exchanged a glance.

Oh dear. She must not have sounded that convincing. The newlyweds were having an entire conversation about her with their eyeballs. What would it be this time? *Avoid accidentally slicing your hand open during knife throwing practice while we're gone? Don't let anyone burgle the LCA? Try not to get kidnapped for writing incendiary articles again?*

Once more, all true. Unfortunately.

Lydia braced herself.

Her sister-in-law leaned in close. "We don't doubt you in the least, it's just…"

Lydia folded her arms across her chest. "It's just that I haven't been myself since the kidnapping and you're worried something is permanently wrong with me and you feel guilty for leaving me here alone even though it's most likely quite normal for someone to be skittish after a man woos her, convinces her to sneak away for a romantic, clandestine meeting, and then kidnaps her for a power-mad industrialist hell-bent on stopping her from writing any additional newspaper articles criticizing the House of Commons which he thought he had so neatly in his pocket?" Lydia finally paused to draw breath. "Is that what you were going to say?"

Pippa's mouth hung open.

Jack blinked at her.

Perhaps she'd gone a bit too far. It was just…if she couldn't poke fun at what had happened, then she would drown in a pit of despair. She'd lost all trust in men—except for her brother, of course—and realized that love was not in her future. It was too bleak to stare at directly.

Lydia reached out and grasped their hands. "I'm sorry. I don't mean to be grumpy and downplay what occurred." She worried at her lip trying to find the right words. Thankfully no servants were in the foyer at the moment. "I don't want what happened to define me though. I'm more than the anonymous, once-kidnapped author of fiery political essays published in the newspaper. I'm still me. And I'll be fine here for two very short weeks on my own. I promise."

Pippa blinked rapidly in an apparent effort to dispel tears while Jack cleared his throat.

"We know you're more than what happened to you," Jack said, his voice rough with emotion. "You are so strong and smart and capable, Lydia. I have no doubt of that whatsoever."

Ah, perhaps she'd gone a bit too far in the other direction now. Getting Pippa and Jack all emotional before they left had not been her intention.

Lydia didn't have many intentions lately. She hadn't written since the kidnapping, and although she yearned to put her latest thoughts about politics and the government onto paper, every time she actually contemplated writing her stomach felt full of bees. Her abrupt lack of purpose was rather a blow.

What she needed was a new writing project. That would give her purpose and help her out of this funk. She couldn't write about the House of Lords again though. No, after what had happened, that topic was closed to her. She needed something new, something important, a topic in which her thoughts and words could make a real difference.

But…she had no clue what that might be.

At least she had her family. And the LCA. Without the Academy, she didn't even know who she'd be.

She squeezed Jack's hand before releasing them both. "Thank you for that." She stepped back and eyed the carriage through the open door. Their luggage had been loaded and the footman stood beside the coach with his hand on the door handle. "Now, you'd best be off before those horses decide to leave without you."

Pippa donned her shawl and Jack tugged on his gloves. Lydia adopted a cheery smile as they prepared to leave.

"If that scamp Benedict shows up looking for breakfast," Jack said, "send him away. I don't trust him."

"What?" Lydia frowned. "He's your best friend. And he just helped us save Jane's new husband's title from his scheming relatives."

Benedict Southcott, Lord Lovell, had attended Eton with her brother, and he'd been a fixture in their household for years now. Apparently, the strawberry jam at his own residence was sub-par, so he often invited himself over for breakfast. Lydia pushed away the image of his laughing hazel eyes and his usual, lazy sprawl as the morning sunshine burnished his blond hair into a rather misleading halo.

Benedict was off limits. *All* men were off limits. And he was, in fact, a scamp, albeit a rather harmless one. Why, he was almost like a brother to her.

Something inside her rebelled at the thought, but Lydia shoved the feeling aside.

Jack huffed. "I don't mean I don't trust him in general. I just don't trust him with *you*."

He doesn't trust Benedict with me?

What in the world was that supposed to mean? Benedict might be a rake, but he'd never once been inappropriate around her. Other than a bit of delicious teasing that had left a warm feeling low in her belly. No, that wasn't right. His teasing was annoying. Like a buzzing fly. Yes. A fly. Benedict was a pesky insect.

"What you mean to say," Pippa said, directing her words to her husband through a smile that showed more teeth than usual, "is that you don't trust your very good friend not to eat us all out of house and home, right darling? With that big, hearty appetite of his. *For food.*"

Lydia wasn't certain, but it appeared that one of Pippa's elbows may have made accidental contact with his ribs.

Jack heaved a suffering sigh fit for the stage on Drury Lane. "Yes, that's what I meant."

The couple finally moved to the door, leaving Lydia standing in a puzzled silence in the middle of the foyer.

"See you in two weeks," Jack called as they left.

"Good luck with the LCA." Pippa gave a final wave.

Lydia drew a deep breath and straightened her shoulders. She could absolutely run the LCA on her own *and* hunt for a new writing project to give her life some purpose. After all, what could go wrong in just two weeks?

⇻⟫⟫⟪⟪⇺

BENEDICT SOUTHCOTT, VISCOUNT Lovell, strolled across the dewy grass in his back garden, his cheerful whistle matching the song of the morning birds as they chirped in welcome of a new day.

He'd always loved the morning. Even though others probably viewed him as a creature of the night, there was nothing he liked more than the crisp start of a day full of possibility.

"Good morning," he crooned to his bay once he entered the mews in the back yard. "Ready to ride?" He rubbed the horse's velvety nose, and his mount whinnied in reply. The bay seemed to be as eager for a good hard gallop along Rotten Row as Benedict was. He reached for the tack left out by the groom the night before. The man who tended the horses was getting on in years, and Benedict had started saddling his own mount for early morning rides so that the gent could get his sleep.

A noise sounded behind him, and Benedict swiveled, the tack still in his hands.

"Mother." He took a step forward. Had something terrible happened? "What has you up and about this early hour?"

His mother blinked at him, her brown eyes all innocence. "Why, whatever do you mean?" She gestured with her hand and his sister Emelia trudged into view from behind the thick trees in the center of the garden.

Benedict raised an eyebrow at his sister in silent question. She stifled a yawn before shrugging. Both she and their mother were dressed for the day with cloaks and bonnets as if setting out for an afternoon of shopping on Bond Street. At seven in the morning.

"You know Emelia and I love to take a stroll at this hour of the day!" His mother adjusted her gloves, avoiding direct eye contact. "Why, there's nothing we enjoy more than a bit of exercise in the fresh air."

Benedict stifled a sigh. "My apologies, Mother. How rude of me to forget all the morning walks you never take."

Emelia stifled a snicker. Benedict began inspecting his boots so he wouldn't accidentally make eye contact with his sister and end up laughing. He wouldn't wish to disrespect his mother in that way. Plus, he loved her, despite her predilection for Banbury tales when it suited her purpose.

"Do you need my assistance with anything?" Benedict asked, setting his tack back on the saddle rack. It seemed his early morning ride would have to wait.

"Certainly not, Benedict darling," his mother said, fluttering her hand to her chest as if the very question flummoxed her. "It's just a happy coincidence, running into you out here."

Benedict offered his mother a smile even as he began counting in his head. *One, two, three…*

"But since we *did* catch you here," his mother added in a rush, raising her eyes to meet his, "there is a small matter we could *perhaps* discuss before you head out on your ride."

Ever since his father's death a handful of years ago, Benedict had become accustomed to his mother's roundabout methods of requesting aid. Perhaps she felt embarrassed that her child was now the head of the household. He couldn't blame her for that. She was an adult full-grown, and yet had to rely on the son whose runny nose she'd once wiped to now provide her with money, her position in society, and even the roof over her head.

How lowering. If he was in her shoes, perhaps he too would contrive a coincidental early morning meeting to make a request feel more like an afterthought instead of asking permission from one's own offspring.

"What would you like to discuss?" Benedict asked, gentling his voice.

His mother straightened herself to her full height of five feet before answering. Unfortunately for her, this still left her a full foot plus several inches below him.

"Benedict," she began, the formal tone of her voice indicating that this was to be a Serious Talk. "As you know, your sister is getting on in years."

Benedict's eyebrows shot up, and Emelia made a choking noise.

Their mother whirled to face her second born. "Well, you know it's true!" she said, throwing her hands up in the air as if she were beyond exasperated to have to explain such an obvious thing.

"Mother, I'm only twenty years old. I am hardly an old maid, withering away on the shelf." Emelia rolled her eyes.

Benedict opened his mouth to back her up, but his mother was already speaking.

"You're not getting any younger, Emelia *dear*," she said. "*And you're not likely to receive any offers this season due to your brother's reputation.*"

Benedict stilled.

It couldn't be true. He'd sacrificed so much to protect his mother and sister from what had happened.

"Mother," Emelia said, her voice tinged with frustration. "I'm not pining away because no one has offered for me yet. I'm hoping for a love match as you well know. Plus, I've been enjoying the seasons since I came out, going to parties with my friends." She narrowed her eyes and placed her hands on her hips. "And what does Benny have to do with any of this?"

"Yes," Benedict said, leaning back against the wooden wall of the mews. "I too would be most interested to learn what *Benny* has to do with any of this."

He shot his sister a mock scowl at the old nickname. She stuck her tongue out at him in return, an impish gleam in her sherry brown eyes that were the same color as his own.

"I hate to speak of such things in front of delicate ears..." Their mother shot a telling glance in her daughter's direction.

"In that case," Emelia said after another yawn, "I'll just head back to bed and—"

"But," their mother interrupted, stalling her daughter's movements with a warning look, "it would be best if you knew what you're up against, my dear."

"Pray tell, what is she up against?" Benedict drawled. This should prove interesting.

"Why, your reputation, of course!" His mother pointed an accusatory finger at him. "Your carrying on. Your gallivanting! Everyone has heard it said that Lord Lovell is a rake." She folded her arms across her chest and somehow managed to stare down her nose at him despite her diminutive stature.

His blood turned cold in his veins. Benedict forced a chuckle. "Everyone knows, eh?"

Behind him, Benedict's horse neighed his support. It seemed even the bay had found this conversation rather unpleasant.

"Benedict, I'm being serious." His mother's bottom lip quivered. "Don't you want your sister to find a husband? After all, it's not as if you'll be giving me grandbabies anytime soon."

His chest squeezed, and he forced a calming breath into his lungs before pulling up from his casual slump against the wall.

"Emelia," Benedict said, striving for a casual tone. "Do you think that my behavior is causing you to lose out on suitors?"

Emelia shook her head.

Benedict felt his shoulders loosen, but then he noticed a bit of tightness around her eyes.

He rubbed his thumb and forefinger together. Perhaps a different question was in order.

"Do you think that my *reputation* is causing you to lose out on suitors?"

Emelia opened her mouth, but whatever she was going to say seemed to get stuck. Benedict let out a long slow breath of air.

His sister must've noticed a hint of his distress because she instantly stepped forward and seized his hand. "I know that you're not a rake. And whatever old stories they tell about you, well, I'm sure they've all been exaggerated. Your evenings are mostly spent in your study reading the newspaper."

Those old stories.

He tried to relax his clenched jaw. It wasn't important. What mattered was the present.

And it was true that he enjoyed reading the newspaper in the evenings. In fact, he'd become a bit obsessed with a series of articles in the paper a few months back. Penned by some anonymous political critic by the name of *Democratium Liberum*—meaning "free democracy" in Latin, Benedict had discovered after a bit of research—the articles uncovered corruption within the elections for the seats in the House of Commons. The articles had been brilliant. Then they'd gone sideways, with a complete change of tune. And then they'd stopped, all of a sudden. Benedict had scoured the newspaper for weeks afterward.

"Or," his sister continued, dragging him back to the conversation at hand, "you're visiting stodgy old White's with Jack to drink coffee and pretend that what you men talk about is something other than gossip. *I* know you're not a rake with a dissolute past. It's just that…" She bit her lip as if searching for the proper words. "Perhaps, it's possible, that other people…well, for some reason, *they* seem to think that you're a rake with a dissolute past."

Benedict swallowed and then swallowed again. This darn

lump in his throat that had suddenly appeared was making it difficult for him to speak or breathe normally.

He finally managed to answer. "I see."

A silence followed his words, the three of them standing in a triangle of increasing awkwardness which seemed to stretch on and on. But he couldn't be sure because his mind was spinning.

He knew how he was perceived by society. Everyone saw him as a jovial, happy-go-lucky fellow. Careless. Prone to grins and nonchalance. And to be fair, in his early years, he had been a bit wild during a few evenings out on the town. There had been drinking and women and perhaps a bit of youthful tomfoolery. But that was years ago.

He didn't do that anymore.

Not since…

He shook his head. In recent years, there had been no sowing of wild oats. He didn't gamble. He didn't take a mistress. He hadn't even drunk to excess in public. And yet everyone seemed to think he was a silly, empty-headed rake with a scandalous past.

Even his own family.

Benedict stepped away from the fetid air of the silence stretched taut between them. He offered a lazy shrug and a careless smile although the actions cost him. "I understand what you're saying, Mother. I shall make certain that none of my future words or actions cause any harm to the family's reputation. And now, if you don't mind, I shall excuse myself so that I might take my little ride about the park."

"Benedict," his sister began, reaching for him.

Benedict stepped farther away, shaking his head. "It's fine," he said, forcing a smile into even brighter levels. Perhaps they could use him to light up the dance floor at the next big ball. "You haven't said anything I don't already know. It's absolutely fine."

"Thank you, Benedict," his mother called as he slung the saddle onto his mount and rushed through the rest of the tack. "You're my favorite son."

"I'm your only son," he replied, the frequent words feeling

rote as he hurried out of the mews.

"Shall we expect you for breakfast?" Emelia called, her worry evident in her voice.

"My regrets." Benedict gave her a quick nod before he hurried his steed down the alleyway.

Although he would rather eat over-cooked kippers every morning for a year than allow his mother or sister to see it, their words had cut at him, nevertheless. And there was only one place to go when a fit of the blue devils came upon him. He needed some time with his best mate, Jack, whose deuced sense of duty always managed to make Benedict smile. He needed a spot of his favorite strawberry jam on a slice of buttered toast. And, if he was lucky, perhaps he would get what he needed most of all—a bit of time in the company of the one person who was guaranteed to ease the ache in his heart, even as she caused it to hurt anew.

Chapter Two

"GOOD MORNING, LORD Lovell," the butler at Benedict's friend's house greeted, his reserved expression belied by warm eyes crinkled at the corners. He gestured to a footman to see to Benedict's horse. "I do believe the crisp bacon you are so fond of is available in the breakfast room."

"What would I do without you and your bacon, Jameson?" Benedict smiled before handing the butler his hat. Then he walked the familiar route to the breakfast room of his friend, Jack Dashwood, Earl of Hartwick.

"I smell bacon," Benedict called as he entered the room, looking for the usual three people tucking into their breakfast.

But instead, there was only one person dining today.

And she was frowning at him most fiercely.

Benedict froze in the doorway, his heartbeat stuttering, before he offered her a lazy smile. "Good morning, Lydia." He strolled to the small buffet alongside the far wall with practiced nonchalance, his eyes not straying from the food. "Perhaps today is my lucky day. Am I so fortunate as to get both bacon *and* strawberry jam?"

"What are you doing here?" Lydia grumbled from behind him.

"Ah ah ah," he sang as he scooped some eggs onto his plate. "That's no way to speak to an honored guest."

"Oh? I wasn't aware one had arrived."

Benedict opened his mouth to give a saucy reply, but then recalled the new leaf he was attempting to turn over with his friend's sister. He was to be polite. Humble. Respectable. Plus, he'd already been quite properly put into his place by his mother earlier that morning. He was not prepared for a secondary offense from his most enjoyed verbal sparring partner.

And so instead of engaging in their usual banter from before, he asked, "Have Jack and Pippa come down yet? I hope to see them off this morning."

"They've already left."

Benedict dropped the serving spoon back into the bowl of eggs with a clank. "What?" He turned to face her.

"They left half an hour ago." Lydia shrugged, and in the ensuing silence, he let himself drink his fill of her.

Her soft, golden hair was piled atop her head with a few wispy strands framing her face. Clear blue eyes that missed absolutely nothing stared at him unflinchingly. And her lush lips that loved to narrow before delivering a clever remark or biting retort were, unsurprisingly, currently narrowed. Ah, his Lydia was the queen of a good biting retort. No one could put him in his place like she could.

His Lydia?

No no no. She was his friend's little sister, and Jack had made it abundantly clear to Benedict that she was off-limits.

Although that hadn't stopped Benedict from looking. And dreaming. And yearning.

What an absolute idiot he was, mooning after a lady he shouldn't want and couldn't have.

And yet here he was, staring at her in an increasingly awkward silence like some lecherous man who pinched the bottoms of his maids.

Unacceptable.

Both the hypothetical lecher and his own awkward staring.

Benedict cleared his throat before taking a chair several seats down the table from her.

"My apologies," he murmured, his eyes on a plate that was, sadly, only half full. "I was just surprised to learn I'd missed them."

"You shouldn't be here, you know."

But he belonged here.

Benedict shook the thought away. "Pardon?"

"It's not appropriate." Lydia stared at him over the rim of her teacup. "Not without Jack and Pippa here to chaperone. What will the servants think?"

Benedict set down his fork. *Damn.* Was his presence putting Lydia's reputation in danger? And what about his promise to his mother and sister to mind his own reputation? He hadn't even considered it. He'd spent most of more than half of his mornings in this very room in the past few years. This place felt more like home than his own residence.

Ah, that was a depressing realization.

"Should I leave?" Jack pushed back from the table. "My apologies, Lydia. I didn't mean to—"

"Ah, Lord Lovell!" Mrs. Smythe, the housekeeper, beamed at him from the doorway before she began tidying up the buffet. "We missed you yesterday. Oh no!"

She turned around and stared at Benedict, her eyes wide.

Had she just realized that he'd been in the breakfast room with Lydia unattended for all of three minutes? Was she about to announce he was a bounder, a scoundrel, and a rake to the breakfast room and then the world at large? Had Benedict forever destroyed Lydia's good name and his own sister's marriage prospects? The bite of eggs he'd consumed felt like lead in his stomach.

"We haven't set out your favorite strawberry jam!" Mrs. Smythe placed her hand over her stout chest. "I'm most sorry, my lord. Let me fetch some from the kitchen right away. I know how much you adore Cook's jam."

"Actually, he was just leaving," Lydia said, voice breezy, as she swirled her teacup.

He rose from his seat.

"Ach, no," Mrs. Smythe cried. "Jameson said you've only just got here. We can't send you off without a proper breakfast. A growing lad like you needs to keep up his strength."

And then, making *tsk*ing sounds all the while, Mrs. Smythe bustled around the table and motioned for Benedict to sit down before she straightened his fork and gave him a motherly pat on the shoulder. He was helpless in the face of such cheerful persistence.

"Back in a scooch with that jam," she tutted before whisking herself out of the room.

Benedict and Lydia both stared at the swinging door in silence.

"It seems your presence here is not a scandal at all," Lydia finally said, her tone morose. "And I think Mrs. Smythe likes you more than she likes me."

Well, I am much handsomer than you.

But Benedict did not give voice to the teasing rejoinder. He was reformed—polite, well-mannered, and not flirtatious in the least. And so instead, he replied, "I am quite certain that your housekeeper only permits my presence out of pity. Somehow, she must have discovered that my cook once put cinnamon on my kippers."

Lydia wrinkled her nose. Her whole face relaxed, her serious eyes softening and her tight mouth growing plump. Benedict tore his gaze away from those soft, pink lips and all they made him think of. It would be most unbecoming to have a bulge in his pants when Mrs. Smythe returned with the promised jam.

"So," Benedict said, turning the subject to something safe. "Jack and Pippa left quite early for their trip up north?"

"They wanted to get to the estate as quickly as they could as the land steward's letter was apparently quite alarming." Lydia pushed her breakfast dishes to the side and slid a stack of correspondence in front of her. "I'm sure they would have waited if they knew you were coming though."

Benedict shrugged. "It's my own fault. I decided to get a ride in at Rotten Row first. I imagined with them still being newly-weds and all that they'd spend the morning in bed."

Lydia's hand stilled on the mail in front of her.

Benedict replayed his words. "Oh, I do beg your pardon. I did not mean to insinuate…to say that they were engaging in—"

Lydia waved his words away, her expression nonchalant, but Benedict noticed how pink her cheeks had grown. They liked to pretend they didn't affect one another, but the proof was right there on her face.

"You aren't wrong," Lydia said. "But yes, perhaps we should not discuss such things when it is just the two of us."

Benedict held up his right hand as if taking a vow. "I shall be as proper as a vicar the rest of the meal, I swear."

Her lips twitched, and their gazes caught and held. Benedict stared into her eyes, his breath hitching in his lungs. Summoning self-restraint from some deep internal well he'd never bothered to explore before, Benedict ripped his gaze away and stared at his plate.

This woman.

What would it be like, to have breakfast with her—er, with someone *like* her—every morning? To playfully banter, to exchange sizzling glances, and to just feel a sense of belonging?

Mrs. Smythe returned with the promised jam, arranging the little pot of gooey goodness beside him just so. Benedict busied himself with a liberal application to his toast, the silence between him and Lydia not uncomfortable as she opened her mail.

Benedict was swallowing the last bite of jammy toast when she made a noise of aggravation in the back of her throat.

He looked up to find her blue eyes narrowed as she scanned a piece of correspondence.

"What's wrong?" Whatever it was, he would be her champion. If she was in any sort of danger, he would defend her. He didn't know the whole of it, but he'd gleaned that there'd been a bit of trouble a few months back. Some suitor who'd done her wrong or some such. His hand tightened on his napkin at the thought.

But no, suitors who deserved a solid punch to the gut were not the issue right now. His focus should be on whatever was in that letter that had caused such a look of annoyance on her face.

"It's the LCA," she said, finally looking up from the letter. "It seems some official at Westminster wants to ask the association's leadership a few questions."

⇶⇷

LYDIA HELD THE paper out in front of her, relaxing her grip on its crisp pages. This was nothing. Surely?

"You're being investigated? By the government?" Benedict's face was a map of confusion.

And no wonder. This made no sense at all. The Ladies Covert Academy members had been so careful with their secrets, making sure only those within their organization and their founder's household plus Lydia's brother knew what the LCA's true purpose was. Why would some official at Westminster—from the Office of Public Order no less!—wish to investigate them?

Lydia drew a deep breath, trying to push away the knot of anxiety that had taken up residence in her chest. Although she had no reason to believe their cover was blown, if the LCA's true purpose was discovered, the authorities would shut it down immediately.

There wouldn't even be an opportunity to save it.

And right now, the LCA was the only thing keeping her tethered to her life. She had no writing or political projects anymore. And she had little faith in herself after her terrible judgment with trusting a man. That decision had led to her kidnapping and the near murders of herself, her brother, and his love.

Without the LCA, she had nothing. Absolutely nothing.

"This is absurd," Benedict exclaimed. "Why would anyone in the government wish to investigate the Ladies Charitable Association? You're obviously a proper group of do-gooders."

Lydia bit her lip.

She couldn't tell him the truth, of course. She'd known Benedict far too long to think him trustworthy of a secret of this nature. It wasn't that she'd ever known him to be unkind or deceitful, but she'd heard whispers of an old scandal. Of his rakish ways. Of devil-may-care living without consequence. There was no way that she would allow him inside the inner sanctum of this most important of secrets.

Besides, even if she wanted to, she didn't trust *herself*. She didn't trust her own judgment. How could she after she had believed the lies of Andrew Aubrey, a charming solicitor who had wooed her with his kind words and sweet flattery? She had believed he loved her. And when he'd asked her to go on an evening carriage ride through the park to admire his new horses—without a chaperone, he'd explained so earnestly, so that they might have a bit of privacy to discuss something important—she had believed him. She'd believed that it was a safe adventure. She'd believed he'd meant to declare his love.

What a fool she'd been.

She wouldn't make that mistake again.

And so now, she lied. "I don't know what this could be about," she told Benedict, working to project the appropriate amount of confusion. "Of course, we're just a charity group. Perhaps they have us mixed up with some other organization. I've been reading in the paper about the recent crackdown on reform groups. Perhaps they think we're some group of radicals?"

"There's been quite a bit of debate in the House of Lords about the attacks on these groups since the Seditious Meetings Act was passed," Benedict said, scratching his chin. "More people are joining reform groups since the Corn Laws and new restrictions were instituted following the war with France. There have been crackdowns, but for officials to go so far as to investigate a charity organization of gently bred ladies is beyond the pale."

He lifted up the correspondence she'd received from Westminster, eyebrows raised as if asking permission to read it over.

Lydia nodded.

She moved the cutlery on the table with nervous movements, trying to get it exactly lined up so that the tines of the fork, the butter knife, and the spoon were at a ninety-degree angle to the edge of the table. She refolded her napkin, making the crisp edges of the linen as they'd been when it had been placed in her spot. She mentally recited her favorite lines from Shakespeare. By the time she was done setting at least this part of her world to rights, Benedict had finished reading the letter.

"The Office of Public Order," Benedict said, his brow furrowed. "I've heard plenty about the man in charge, Mr. Staines. He's known for being quite a bulldog with his investigations, often going far beyond acceptable behavior to win a victory for the Crown. Personally, I wouldn't trust him to investigate a missing sock, but I've heard that he's quite popular with the Prince Regent because he gets results."

Lydia pushed back from the table and surged to her feet. She began to pace the length of the dining room, worrying at her bottom lip all the while. This Mr. Staines wanted to question her about the LCA? What a disaster.

Her two fellow leaders of the Academy were out of town. Normally if any issue came up, she, Pippa, and Jane would put their heads together and solve it as a team. But Pippa had just left and Jane was on her honeymoon with her new groom, Dev.

She was alone in this. What was she going to do?

If her brother were here, he would have insight into how she should proceed in dealing with this Office of Public Order since he was a member of the House of Lords.

If only Jack was here.

"He's not," said Benedict from his seat at the table, where his usual leonine grace had transformed to a more tense posture once she had shared the letter with him.

She must've spoken the words about Jack aloud.

"You've overlooked something very important." Benedict watched her, his golden-brown eyes inscrutable. "*I am a member of the House of Lords.*"

Lydia's feet froze in their tracks.

"Did you forget?"

She had, in fact, forgotten. Benedict never spoke of politics when she was around. Although she knew he was an aristocrat, she had completely overlooked the fact that he too sat in the House of Lords because of his title. Would he be able to do for her what Jack could not with his absence?

He leaned back in his chair, crossing his hands behind his head. "Ask me."

She caught his eye, and the smug smile slid off his face.

Odd, but his expression had looked forced, as if he was playing a role which he thought was required of him. But that couldn't be right.

The moment stretched on as their gazes tangled together. Something strange and hot passed between them, and Lydia could no more name the sensation than she could decipher the book of Greek history that was upstairs in her room, waiting for her to have a spare year to begin studying that language as well.

"Lydia." Her name on his lips sounded dark and dangerous somehow. All the playfulness was gone. "Ask me."

Lydia sunk down onto the nearest chair, her legs no longer stable enough to hold her weight. She clenched her hands together.

Ask him.

She drew a deep breath. "Will you help me?"

"I will." His gaze was solemn as he studied her. He hesitated for a moment, and then added, his voice low and rough, "I would do anything you ask me to."

Despite the gravity of the situation, a little huff of laughter escaped Lydia. What a strange thing to jest about in the midst of this tense moment.

"Benedict, I know you like to joke, but I didn't take you for a fool."

He shook his head slowly. For a brief moment she wondered—*what if he actually meant it?*

"So," she said, forcing herself to lean back in her chair and unclench her fingers, "You can help me with this?"

He nodded.

"You can go with me to the Office of Public Order at Westminster and help me get this sorted out?"

For the first time since she'd broken the seal on the dratted letter and read its first words, she felt something other than anxiety pressing against her chest. Could it really be that easy? Benedict strolled into the office, waved his aristocratic wand, and *poof!* Everything was magically fixed?

"We could head to Westminster right now if you'd like and have this sorted out by teatime."

He must have sensed she needed a moment because he returned his attention to his breakfast plate.

Lydia's mind swirled as she considered the possibilities.

Perhaps it would be that easy, but was there a reason she had received this letter in the first place? Perhaps someone had brought the LCA to the office's attention. It made no sense for this investigation otherwise.

So, what did the office and its bulldog, Mr. Staines know, or at least *think* they knew about the LCA?

And she needed a little time to ponder all the implications before she charged in with her knight in shining armor. Or perhaps her knight in shining strawberry jam. He seemed to have acquired a smear of red at the corner of his mouth.

Lydia bit back a grin. How strange that even in the midst of this chaos, Benedict could bring a smile to her face.

"This afternoon," she told him, setting her hands decisively on top of the breakfast table. "I need a bit of time to get myself prepared for this meeting. After all, it would not do for me to show up without looking my best." She tried to inject a bit of humor into her voice, hoping that if they returned to the old back and forth they used to share, then it would lighten some of the tension in the room.

Instead, he looked her over and frowned. "I think you always look your best."

Lydia's heart fluttered.

"I'll pick you up today in my carriage at two o'clock." He pushed back from the table. "You'll find a chaperone?"

She nodded. Lydia had the perfect person in mind.

"We'll get you sorted out at Westminster then. And Lydia," he said, moving around the table to where she sat, taking her hand in his. He lowered his head and stared into her eyes. She shivered at both the warmth of his hand on hers, and the solemnity in his gaze. "I *will* help you until this is completely resolved."

The words sounded like a vow.

And then, with a cocky wink much more reminiscent of their old exchanges than the growing formality between them of late, he bid her farewell, leaving the room and taking that little bit of strawberry jam along with him.

Chapter Three

BENEDICT STARED AT the lovely lady across the carriage from him. He ran through several potential comments he might make to break the silence that had stretched between them since he'd picked Lydia and her chaperone up a few minutes earlier.

Mrs. Abbott, Lydia and Jack's housekeeper from their childhood, dozed in the corner of the carriage. Lydia had explained that Mrs. Abbott, although retired to a countryside cottage, was always willing to accompany Lydia to a house party or other event when she needed a companion, and luckily, the woman had been in town on an extended visit to see her daughter and new grandchild.

"She's always grateful for the bit of extra pay," Lydia had whispered once they'd first gotten settled into the carriage and Mrs. Abbott had promptly fallen asleep, "although I know Jack gave her a very generous pension once she retired. However," Lydia had added, her mouth quirking at the corners, "I think she's been staying up at night helping with her new grandbaby, so I'm not sure how much chaperoning she'll actually be doing."

A gentle snore from Mrs. Abbott's had punctuated Lydia's comment.

But now, in the close confines of the carriage, Benedict felt the need to make conversation with Lydia. It was different, spending time with her without Jack around.

This felt more…intimate.

He would not comment on her outfit, which made her look like a queen; the vivid royal blue of her gown perfectly matched her lovely eyes. And he would not say anything about her coiffure which she had changed since he'd seen her at breakfast. Her blond tresses were now pulled up in an elaborate series of twists and coils atop her head, as if she had her own golden crown. And he couldn't speak of her expression, which was fierce, like Boudicca about to charge onto the battlefield to defeat the Romans.

Instead, what he said was, "Beautiful weather we're having for this time of year."

Lydia swiveled from gazing out the window to face him, her eyebrows raised. "You are speaking to me of the weather?" she asked, voice incredulous.

"It's quite a proper thing to discuss you know," he said, attempting an affable smile. No, it was a *proper* smile. One given by a proper gentleman who was on his best behavior so as not to tarnish his reputation and destroy the prospects of his sister finding a good match. Plus, he wished to show Lydia that he was reliable. Sensible. A man one could count on… to make bland comments about the weather.

He grimaced.

"Have you heard anything from Jack and Pippa yet?" he decided to venture, hoping this line of questioning would be just as proper as the weather but perhaps less dull.

Lydia rolled her eyes. "They only left this morning. Do you expect me to have already received a letter from them?"

Benedict felt his cheeks warm. Proper conversation was apparently not his gift.

She narrowed her eyes at him. "Are you trying to antagonize me on purpose so that I won't be worried about this visit to Westminster?"

Benedict shifted on his side of the carriage while the muffled noises of other conveyances and people on the street filtered through the carriage walls.

"I'm just trying to converse. Isn't conversation a normal thing for two people to do when traveling together?"

Lydia's lips tightened until they matched her eyes, narrowed in disapproval. "Benedict, you once said that my embroidery looked like a tutorial on how *not* to embroider. It's not as if we don't know how to engage in frank conversation."

Benedict couldn't help his grin. "Well, the flowers on that pillow did resemble a collection of squashed bugs. Would you have me lie?"

Lydia huffed. He couldn't help but notice the way her eyes sparkled as she prepared her retort.

"At least I know how to embroider. My brother once told me that you were left to your own devices on your staff's half-day off and attempted to darn your own stocking. And you ended up with gloves for your feet." She smirked at him, obviously pleased at her comeback.

Benedict leaned forward on his seat. If it was a battle of re-membered transgressions she wanted, he was more than willing to enter the fray. "Well at least I never showed up to a musicale hosted by a duchess with ink stains on my gloves."

Lydia mimicked him, leaning forward in her seat as well. Their faces were a foot apart, and Benedict's gaze traced over the delicate arch of her eyebrow, the sweet curve of her cheek, and the pink fullness of her lips. His breath caught in his throat when her tongue darted out to quickly wet her lower lip. He felt an answering tug in his groin and dragged his gaze away to meet her eyes once more. There was something in her expression, a flare of surprise perhaps. Had she caught him staring at her mouth like a starving man spying his first meal in days?

Oh, the mortification of unrequited feelings.

"At least I know how to use a quill," Lydia finally retorted to his comment about her ink stains.

"Are you suggesting," Benedict asked, "that I am unable to write words?"

Lydia smirked. "If the shoe fits…"

Benedict barked out a laugh. "It's a wonder the shoe fits at all, what with my terrible darning."

Now it was Lydia's turn to laugh. "You know, if it really was your intention to take my mind off of this whole situation, you have succeeded." Lydia leaned back in her seat; a smile played at the corners of her mouth.

Benedict sat back in his seat as well, unable to look away from Lydia smiling at him without reserve or hesitation. How beautiful she was. How vibrant and full of light. There were so many elements that made up Lydia's appeal. The intelligence shining in her eyes, the air of mischief that always lurked at the edges of her expressions, and the happiness she displayed so readily when she wasn't on her guard—all these things about her tugged at his very heart.

And despite the fact that he had allowed himself to get caught up in the old familiar banter instead of working to remain a proper gentleman, he could not regret their interaction. There was something so freeing about speaking openly with Lydia.

The carriage slowed to a stop, and one of the grooms opened the door, announcing that they'd arrived at Westminster.

Mrs. Abbott continued to gently snore.

Lydia frowned. "Perhaps we should let her rest."

"Westminster is never empty. I'm sure we'll be properly chaperoned by agents of the Crown."

"It would be hard to find a more proper chaperone than that," Lydia replied.

Benedict hopped down from the carriage and then reached back to help her step down. He watched out of the corner of his eye while she smoothed the wrinkles out of her blue gown and pulled back her shoulders before she took in the sight of the looming brick building that was the seat of Britain's government.

"I've been here before of course, but always as a visitor," Lydia said. "Being here on business of my own?" She squeezed her hands at her side. "This is something different altogether."

Benedict wished he could take one of her hands in his and smooth open her tense fingers. He wished he could comfort her openly without reservation, but it wouldn't be proper. Instead he said, "I'll be with you the entire time. I'm sure this is just some mix-up."

She nodded, and they began to walk across the courtyard.

Along with several guards standing at attention and various clerks and officials hurrying this way and that, there was also a handful of women, dressed in white, standing at the edges of the courtyard, several of them with children. Perhaps they too had come to visit the Office of Public Order. Maybe Mr. Staines had called forth a whole host of people to visit him on this day. Was the man vying for some medal awarded to the government official who created the most paperwork in a single day?

Based on what he'd heard about the man in the House of Lords, Mr. Martin Staines seemed to possess the exact kind of ambition that would lead him to pursue such a meaningless trophy.

Benedict led the way inside the storied building. Several guards, armed with swords and suspicious stares, watched them enter. Benedict gave them a nod as they passed, and wondered what exactly they were on the lookout for.

"Lovell," called a voice, and Benedict turned to find an old classmate from Eton approaching from a side corridor. "I'm surprised to see you gallivanting about here when the Lords isn't in session."

Benedict grimaced. "Brutt," he greeted, wishing Lydia weren't with him. Gervase Brutt, second son to a baron, was loud, pompous, and crude...and not in a fun way.

"Aren't you going to ask what *I'm* doing here?" Brutt took great pains to adjust his cuff links as if wanting to draw their attention to the gold and jewels decorating them.

Benedict glanced at Lydia who was rolling her eyes. Brutt had yet to even acknowledge her. Truly, he was as gentlemanly as a pig rolling in the mud.

"What are you doing here, Brutt?" he asked, not even attempting to sound curious.

"I was elected to the House of Commons." Brutt puffed out his thin chest. "My old pater took care of it. You know how it is." He nudged his elbow toward Benedict as if they were cronies.

Benedict stepped back.

Lydia cleared her throat.

"Oh, my apologies," Brutt said, doing a terrible job of pretending to be surprised by her presence. "I didn't see you had a companion with you, Lovell. Just *one* this time?" Brutt guffawed and slapped his knee.

Benedict contemplated how best to murder him with so many armed guards about. "You are speaking," he growled, "to a *lady*."

"Oh, my pardons, my pardons." Brutt held his hands up as if remorseful, but a nasty gleam of satisfaction was visible in the cur's pale eyes. "Given what happened back at that house party all those years ago, I didn't expect to see you in the company of a fine lady ever again. Unless..." he paused, as if drawing out the suspense of whatever wretched comment he was about to make, "her maid was along for a bit of fun as well."

Everything turned red. Benedict stepped forward, his hands fisted at his side. It would be so easy to end this miserable man. Punch him in the face until bones crunched. Strangle him with his own cravat. Force him to eat Lydia's shoes until he choked.

Lydia. At the thought, he exhaled and stepped back.

"We'd best be on our way," Benedict managed to say through gritted teeth before taking Lydia by the arm and striding away.

Brutt's laughter echoed down the corridor after them.

"What was that all about?" Lydia asked, trotting beside him to keep up. "He was truly the most odious man. And was he implying that his father *bought* his seat in the Commons? I swear, the political corruption in Parliament never fails to astound—"

Lydia seemed to bite off her words, but Benedict didn't have the focus to contemplate why.

He turned a corner and stopped, leaning against a wall and breathing as if he'd just gone a few rounds in the ring at Gentleman Jack's.

The spectre of that scandal and its repercussions were never far from his thoughts. But for someone to speak of it so openly, and in front of a lady…

In front of *Lydia*.

"I apologize." Benedict ran his hand over his face. "He should not have spoken as he did with you present."

Lydia huffed. "He shouldn't have spoken that way at all. What was he talking about?"

He closed his eyes.

"Benedict?" Lydia's voice sounded tentative. He hated that this old, tawdry scandal was drawing her attention away from their purpose today—sorting things out for her charity group with the Office of Public Order.

"It was nothing," Benedict said after a deep breath. "I think he had me mixed up with someone else."

Lydia frowned but allowed Benedict to lead her through several hallways and staircases until they'd reached the correct office. They stood outside the door as Lydia shifted her weight from foot to foot.

"I'm rather surprised you knew your way around this place," she said. "It's a bit of a maze."

Now that the red haze of fury and shame had receded, Benedict assumed his usual posture, lazily leaning back against the wall beside the door with his arms crossed over his chest. "I spend quite a bit of time here."

Lydia arched a brow. "I'd assumed you were one of those House of Lords members who only showed up when it was convenient."

Benedict forced a grin, despite the way her words stung. "There's more to me than just a pretty face, Lydia."

She rolled her eyes before facing the door to the office once more.

"Are you nervous?" Benedict asked, a bit surprised to see her this ruffled.

She shot him a scathing look. "Of course not." With a seeming burst of energy, she flung open the door and marched into the office.

LYDIA PAUSED A few steps inside. The Office of Public Order had a large antechamber with a fleet of desks, all occupied by men with various levels of suspicion etched across their faces. Perhaps those who chose to pursue the enforcement of public order were a suspicious lot by nature.

A clerk with a thin face and even thinner lips approached. "May I help you?" he asked, directing his question to Benedict behind her.

Of course the clerk who looked as if he continually smelled something unpleasant would ignore the woman standing right in front of him.

Behind her was a warm wall of silence. She was uncertain if Benedict didn't respond because he was rattled by the run in with that odious man—there was so much to dissect about the interaction, but at a later time—or in deference to her, but she appreciated it, nonetheless.

Lydia cleared her throat, bringing the clerk's attention to her, and pulled the letter out of her reticule, holding it out as if presenting her credentials.

"I've been asked to see Mr. Staines about some questions he has regarding my organization, the Ladies Charitable Association."

The clerk's already tight face pinched even further after giving a cursory glance at the letter. Was the man sucking on the world's tiniest lemon?

"Follow me, please."

Lydia trailed behind the clerk, grateful for Benedict's quiet presence behind her. He'd not stepped in and spoken for her to the clerk, which was surprising.

As they wove their way through the desks, she questioned that thought. *Was* it surprising that Benedict had deferred to her? Had she ever actually witnessed Benedict speaking over a woman or treating her with disrespect?

She frowned as she searched her memory. *Hm.* Perhaps she'd been making an assumption or two about the man she'd thought she knew rather well.

The clerk stopped at a door and rapped on it.

"Enter." The voice from inside the office was sharp and clipped.

The clerk opened the door and gestured for them to enter. Lydia saw a man seated behind a massive desk lined with papers stacked in ruthlessly straight rows. His dark hair was clipped short, and his gray eyes were hard and assessing.

Lydia shivered.

"A response to a summons, sir," the clerk said before leaving the office and shutting the door behind him.

"And you are?" The man hadn't made the same mistake as his clerk and spoke directly to Lydia. Perhaps he recognized the document in her hands.

"I am Lady Lydia Dashwood of the Ladies Charitable Association."

"And who you might you be, sir?" Mr. Staines asked, directing his words to Benedict this time.

Lydia turned toward Benedict and opened her mouth to make the introduction, but he shot her a quick glance of warning.

"I am merely here as a friend of the family," Benedict said smoothly. His expression was affable and charming, but Lydia noticed a hardness in his eyes that hadn't been there when they were teasing one another in the carriage earlier.

What was his game?

Mr. Staines frowned his disapproval but gestured for them to sit in the two chairs in front of his desk then leaned back in his own seat and steepled his fingers together.

"I imagine you're wondering why I've summoned you here, Miss Dashwood." He stared at her, and Lydia felt a trickle of ice along the back of her neck.

"You are correct, sir," she replied, holding his gaze. She allowed a bit of her anger to seep through her expression. Perhaps it would do the man some good to know that she was no shrinking violet. "The Ladies Charitable Association is simply a charity group that I belong to and help run. I can see no reason why our organization should fall under your purview."

Mr. Martin Staines leaned forward in his seat and straightened out the already perfectly aligned stack of paper in front of him. "While all intelligence suggests that your group is benign," he said, "I would not be fulfilling my duty to the crown if I did not at least investigate your association. Perhaps you've heard about these *radical reform groups*"—he nearly spat the words—"that have been cropping up as quickly as baby bunnies in a meadow. They pose a serious threat to the Crown, and to England." His voice rose, and a vein pulsed in his neck.

Lydia instinctively leaned toward Benedict.

He was staring at the man, his hands in fists.

Mr. Staines seemed to realize he'd lost a portion of his self-control and smoothed a hand over his waistcoat as if that would erase his anger. "These reformers are a menace, as I'm sure you've read in the paper. And—" he continued, with a gleam in his eyes, "I've been tasked with destroying them all." The side of his mouth curled up as if the thought of crushing those who wished to petition the government for kinder, more humane laws was amusing to him.

Lydia read the newspapers every day. She knew about the goals of the reform groups. Reasonable taxes for workers and farmers who were already struggling to provide for their families. Repealing the Corn Laws so that grain could be imported into the country once more. As it stood, people without means were at risk of literal starvation. And perhaps most crucial of all—fair voting policies so that the people of England, and not just the wealthy and titled, could have a say in the laws of the land.

These people weren't a menace. They simply wanted to survive and have a voice in their own government.

Lydia fought to keep the look of disgust off her face. She could not afford to antagonize this man. The *LCA* could not afford it.

"Mr. Staines," she replied carefully, "we are not a radical reform group. In fact, our benefactress, the dowager Lady Rowling, started the Ladies Charitable Association over two years ago, and it is known for the good deeds that its members do."

"So you say," Mr. Staines replied, his cold gray eyes like granite.

Benedict leaned forward in his seat, and Lydia could feel the anger radiating off him like heat from the summer sun. "Now see here—"

Lydia reached out her hand and laid it on his arm. He started at her touch, and their gazes locked for a moment. She saw the outrage there in his expression, anger on her behalf that this man had insinuated she lied. It was a heady thing, seeing that blaze of anger in the golden-brown depths of Benedict's eyes. Anger for her sake. Anger that caused him to speak up for her. And sadly, anger that was not justified since she *was* lying to the head of the Office of Public Order.

But neither of these men could know that.

She raised an eyebrow in warning at Benedict. A muscle in his jaw pulsed as he seemed to struggle with his warring desires to both defend her and to also give her the support she silently asked for.

He gave a minute nod, and Lydia's breath came a touch easier knowing that Benedict was on her side in this. She returned her attention to the man behind the desk.

"Mr. Staines," Lydia said calmly, folding her hands together on top of her lap in what was meant to be a calm and proper pose. "I can see that you are an important man with much work before you." She gestured toward the stacks of papers on his desk. "I do not wish to waste anymore of your precious time. So, I shall speak plainly—the Ladies Charitable Association is exactly as the name suggests, a charity group for proper young ladies here in London. We knit booties for orphans, we sew bandages for our soldiers, and we bring warm meals to poor houses. We've also been known to throw the occasional ball to raise money for those in need. After all," she leaned forward to whisper conspiratorially, "young ladies enjoy their little parties, don't they?"

Lydia fluttered her eyelashes a few times and threw in a simpering smile for good measure.

Men like Mr. Staines always underestimated women. They thought women to be shallow, stupid, and concerned only with clothes, parties, and gossip. Although she was at risk of grinding her molars into dust even as she played into the stereotype, why shouldn't she use his own ignorance against him?

The rigid set of Mr. Staines's shoulders relaxed a degree, and he leaned back in his chair once more. "And you have people who can vouch for this work?"

Lydia nodded. "I can give you the address for the dowager Lady Rowling if you wish to write to her at her country estate. I have the names of the charities that have received aid from the LCA, as well as the names of our members if you wish to inquire with them directly."

He stared at her, his gaze assessing. Lydia stopped herself from squirming in her seat. Beside her, Benedict gripped the arm of his chair, and Lydia could see his fingers flexing against the wood. Would this officer of the crown take the investigation further?

Please, please, please…

Lydia held her breath.

After an endless moment, Mr. Staines scratched his chin before shaking his head. "That won't be necessary at this time, Miss

Dashwood, but if I do hear anything that arouses my suspicion, we will be speaking again."

Lydia longed to release a big sigh of relief, but instead she merely nodded an acknowledgment before rising from her seat.

Benedict followed suit, and after making their farewells, they left the office and made their way through the antechamber back into the hallway. By silent agreement, they continued down the hall and around the corner until they were out of sight of the miserable Office of Public Order. Lydia would rather give up all her quills and parchment than ever step foot in that place again.

They paused, and this time Lydia leaned against the wall, copying Benedict's stance from earlier. Perhaps she would exude some of his casual nonchalance if she perfected her wall-lean. After a slow exhale, she pressed her hand to her chest, where she felt her heart beating in a rapid staccato.

"My word," she breathed. "That man is as cold as a snake."

Benedict snorted. "About as charming as one, as well."

"I thought for a moment there that you might try to plant him a facer," Lydia said.

Benedict offered her a lazy grin, and her chest tightened.

It was just the aftereffects of the encounter with Staines, surely.

"Just say the word…" he drawled.

Lydia huffed in laughter. "He did have a rather punchable face…"

Benedict began to nod in agreement.

"… rather like yours," Lydia teased.

Benedict scowled in mock outrage and crossed his arms over his wide chest. Why did a man need such a big, brawny chest? Did Benedict wrestle bears or toss entire tree trunks for sport?

"I take great offense at that, Miss Dashwood. Perhaps we should meet up at Gentleman Jack's boxing club tomorrow to settle the matter?"

Lydia laughed. Her shoulders felt light, as if a weight had been cast off. It seemed that saving the LCA from some suspicious agent of the Crown had been far easier than anticipated. If someone had told her yesterday that having Benedict along would make the whole thing more bearable, she would've laughed at them. And here they were, smiling at each other like a pair of idiots in the hallway of Westminster Abbey while something strange happened in her chest.

"I appreciate you coming with me today," she said, feeling a bit shy for some reason. "With the others out of town, I would have gone by myself otherwise, and the thought of entering that viper pit with no one at my side was quite unpleasant."

"I'm glad to help you." The laughter slowly faded from Benedict's eyes, and instead a different expression—a *serious* expression—crept into his gaze. "I know I'm merely your brother's friend, but please know..." He hesitated for a moment as if he struggled whether to say something or not. He closed his eyes briefly before saying, "Please know that I am here for you as well. In whatever way you might need me."

His words hung between them. Lydia's pulse was fast once more, but for a reason other than fear this time.

Was he...was he feeling *romantic* toward her?

But that was absurd. Ludicrous. Wasn't it?

Determined to return their relationship to its usual teasing banter or—as of late—formal propriety, Lydia pulled away from the wall and gestured in the direction of the exit.

"Shall we?"

If she'd known what awaited them outside, she might not have been so eager to leave the dim, cozy hallway of Westminster.

Chapter Four

BENEDICT STRODE THROUGH the halls of Westminster with more emotions swirling through him than he had names for.

He felt frustrated beyond belief with the way that bounder Staines had spoken to Lydia, implying that she was a liar. If she had not warned Benedict off, he would have challenged the man to pistols at dawn.

And he was also feeling so damned proud of her for keeping a cool head. She had spoken up for herself and not once lost her composure. The LCA was important to her, that much was certain. And he knew there was more to the organization than he was supposed to know. A person didn't go on a covert mission with a group of determined women to the countryside, sabotage a house party, and poison one of the guests without sorting out that there was more going on than just charity work for this clever mix of ladies.

But the emotion that was perhaps the most pressing of all was his disappointment in himself.

She is not for the likes of you.

These words had echoed in his thoughts—in his *soul*—ever since Jack had warned him away from Lydia. What had he been thinking, gazing into her eyes with his heart on his sleeve, telling her that he would do anything for her like some lovesick swain.

But…wasn't that what he was?

He carried a torch for Lydia. He could admit to himself without embarrassment. He yearned for her. He dreamed of her. But everyone, including his best friend in the entire world who should know him best of all, thought him unworthy of her.

And so, he believed it.

But... not entirely.

For hadn't he just tried to woo her by being a helpful companion? That was the crux of the problem. All he had to offer her was his help. And if that was that was all that he could give and all that she could take, well then, he would give her the best damned help anyone had ever given. He'd give her the Hoby boots of help. The Manton pistols of help. The...silkiest of silk gowns of help. He'd lost sight of his point, but needless to say, he would help her with this investigation, no matter the cost or effort.

"We might have to walk a bit to the carriage," Benedict said as they approached the door to exit Westminster and head into the courtyard. "If everyone parked their carriage there, the entire place would reek of muck."

"So, you're saying that politicians, if left to their own devices, would be foul and putrid?" Lydia slid him a sly smile. "Sounds about right to me."

Benedict smiled. But as they approached the exit, he realized that the guards that had been stationed at the doors previously were no longer at their posts.

A cold trickle ran down his spine. "Let me peek outside before you—"

But Lydia—never one to take orders even in the best of circumstances—was already pushing through the doors into the courtyard. Benedict followed, close on her heels, but in the quick second that he'd glanced up and around the courtyard, he'd not noticed her abrupt stop.

"Eek," Lydia squeaked when he bumped into her from behind, nearly knocking her over.

He wrapped his arm around her waist to steady her. Her heat, her scent, and her nearness enveloped him.

My god.

The way she fit against him…it was like they'd been carved from the same piece of wood, each piece of her matching each piece of him. It was all he could do to not make an audible moan.

But her back turned rigid, and he moved his attention from the feel of her against him to the courtyard. As he took in the scene, he couldn't stop the curse that sprung to his lips.

"What's happening?" Lydia asked, stepping forward.

When they had arrived at Westminster, a small cluster of women dressed in white, many with children at their sides, had been loitering in the courtyard. Now the women's number had tripled in size. Many held babies or had small ones at their sides. A couple were visibly pregnant.

And they were chanting.

"Save England! Votes for all!"

This was one of the radical reform groups that Staines had spoken of with such disdain back in the office. And here they were, on his very doorstep, on both the House of Lords' and the House of Commons' doorstep. A place where only men of wealth and power had any say in the laws of the kingdom.

Ever since he'd become a student of Democratium Liberum's articles in the newspaper, Benedict knew that the House of Commons was much more corrupt than people could imagine. Although it was supposed to represent the common people of England, in truth, most of the seats were taken up by rich young lordlings, waiting for their fathers to pass before they could take their own seat in the House of Lords, or by second sons whose wealthy fathers had bought them a seat by bribing the tenants on his land. Other seats were taken up by the so-called rotten boroughs where large swaths of land in a voting district were uninhabitable and on which only a few people lived, and yet that parliament seat held as much sway as the one that represented the entirety of the city of London.

Parliament was unfathomable corrupt.

And apparently these women had come to the heart of the

corruption to shine a light on it for all to see.

And judging from the way the many guards in the courtyard had their hands on their swords, or their pistols out, the reformers would not be allowed to protest much longer.

"Lydia," Benedict said, voice low and urgent, "we need to get out of—"

But Lydia was already stepping away from him, moving faster than he would have assumed she was able. By the time he reached out to seize her hand, she was several paces ahead of him, approaching the women.

"Bollocks," Benedict muttered. He hurried after her, but already the guards were beginning to surround the protesters.

"Excuse me sir," one of the guards said, approaching Benedict with his hand on the hilt of his saber.

"Not now." Benedict tried to step around the man.

The guard shifted, blocking Benedict's path. Over the guard's shoulder, Benedict saw that Lydia had reached the group of women. She began to speak to one, a lady with bright red hair, who moved her hands in an animated fashion as they spoke.

Hell and damnation, but Lydia's curiosity was putting them right in the center of a potentially very dangerous situation.

"Lydia," he called, but the sound was swallowed up by the chanting from the protesters and the angry calls for them to cease from the guards.

Benedict's heart began to race as dread crept over his skin.

"Stop at once, by order of the Crown!" shouted one of the guards. The man raised his arm, pointed his pistol straight up into the air, and fired.

As the crack of the bullet rent the air, the protesters began to scream and scatter.

Benedict locked eyes with Lydia. He saw fear on her face, and he began to run, pushing aside the guard who had blocked him.

"Lydia!"

But guards were pouring in from all corners of the courtyard. The protesters and their children ran in every direction. It was chaos. It was madness. And Benedict felt the icy hand of fear clutch at his heart when he could no longer see Lydia.

He shouted her name over and over again as he ran to the area where he'd last seen her, but she was no longer there. Scores of guards attempted to round up the protesters. The women were shouting, and children cried, their eyes wide with fear.

What the hell had gone wrong?

The protesters had been peaceful. They had merely been chanting. There had been no threat of violence, no danger to anyone, until the guards had drawn their weapons. And now all around them it was madness, and Benedict could not find Lydia. He called her name out again but came to a halt when a guard stepped in front of him, a cocked pistol aimed directly up at Benedict's face.

"Sir!" The guard's hand trembled.

Benedict slowly raised his hands up. Fear was metallic in his mouth.

"I will comply," Benedict said, fighting to keep his voice calm and steady. "You have no cause to shoot me, or to shoot anyone here. I am Lord Lovell and a member of the House of Lords. Please lower your pistol." Benedict held his breath as the guard stared at him, his lips pressed in a tight, thin line as he seemed to consider Benedict's words.

"Member of the House of Lords, you say?" the guard asked.

Benedict nodded. "I'm a viscount. Will you release me? I must find my companion."

The guard lowered his pistol and looked around. "Good luck finding your companion in this madness. And good luck getting any of the other guards to let you by." With a shrug, the man left him and went to join his companions in rounding up the protesters.

A paddy wagon rolled into the courtyard, and the frightened-looking women were hurried over to the conveyance.

My God.

They were going to arrest the women, along with their babies and children. This was madness.

And where in heaven's name was Lydia?

Benedict felt feral as he continued to shout her name through the chaos. He couldn't find her anywhere. He looked back to the paddy wagon and saw a flash of blond hair and a bright blue gown as another group of women and children were ushered into the paddy wagon. He tried to shoulder his way through the thick crowd of guards to get to where he thought he'd seen her, but he couldn't get past them.

"Oi, enough of your pushing," one guard warned, brandishing his pistols.

Benedict wanted to howl up at the sky.

After a few deep breaths, he shouted, "Where are those women being taken?" to a guard standing nearby.

The guard's eyes looked wild, and if Benedict had to guess, the guards who worked here very rarely saw any action. It was most likely a job of standing around nodding at peers and parliamentarians and other officers as they entered Westminster. Perhaps this man had never even drawn his sword or pistol in the line of duty before today.

The men seemed to focus at last on Benedict's question. "Heard tell that they're taking the women radicals to Newgate."

Benedict's hands clenched into fists.

Newgate.

The most infamous prison in all of England. Lydia was about to be locked up with murderers, rapists, and the worst criminals the country had produced.

And it was all his fault.

Chapter Five

LYDIA SHIVERED AT the metallic sounds of the jail cell door banging shut and the guards turning the key in the lock.

She was in Newgate.

The past hour had been a blur. She and some of the protesters had been crammed into the back of a wagon and taken to London's largest prison, where they had given their names to an officer before the whole group was herded into one large holding cell.

She leaned her forehead against the cold stone wall and panted in short, quick breaths as fear churned her stomach. Throwing up would not improve her situation.

Being locked up in a prison cell was a terrifying echo of when she'd been locked inside a room in a remote country estate for days on end. The fear and terror of her kidnapping from months ago was upon her once more. Over the rushing through her ears, Lydia could just make out the murmurs of those around her along with the sound of crying.

She blinked. A hot tear trickled down her cheek as she continued to fight against the rising nausea.

A gentle hand pressed against her shoulder. "Are you all right, love?"

Lydia drew a shuddering breath and opened her eyes. A middle-aged woman whose brown hair held a few streaks of silver was watching her, her face tight with concern.

"What's your name, love?" the woman asked, her voice rich and strong.

Lydia could imagine her shouting across a village square to her friends, calling her children in for supper, or perhaps leading a group of reformers in chants outside Westminster.

"Lydia Dashwood," she finally answered.

The woman nodded. "I'm Agatha Sheppard from Stafford." She reached out a hand.

Lydia pulled away from the cold stone wall and wiped at her wet cheeks before rubbing the moisture off against her gown. "Pleased to meet you."

The two women shook hands, and Lydia noticed the calluses on Agatha's palms and fingers.

"Pleased to make your acquaintance as well, Miss Dashwood," Agatha said, a small smile crossing her face. "Although I'm sure both of us would wish for better conditions in which to meet."

The woman studied her for a moment, and Lydia became aware of their differences. Agatha, like the rest of the group, was dressed in white. It was the color of the suffrage movement. Her hair was styled in a simple, tight bun, and the toes of her boots looked scuffed and well-worn. Lydia wore a fine gown and her lady's maid had styled her hair into an intricate coiffure. These women and their families were from the countryside, perhaps living on farms or in villages. Perhaps Lydia, a daughter and sister of earls, was as foreign to them as they were to her. And yet here they were all together in this jail cell, equals in the eye of the law.

"I don't mean to make assumptions, love," Agatha continued, "but I do not think you are a member of the Stafford Female Reform Society."

Lydia dabbed her eyes one more time before shaking her head. "I've read about the creation of the Blackburn Female Reform Society in the newspaper. I take it the movement has spread to other areas?"

The Blackburn Female Reform Society was the first all-women's organization of working-class women demanding change for the betterment of their families. Their main argument was that the Prince Regent and Parliament were failing them, and thus the country as a whole. The passing of the Corn Laws, intended to protect English farmers, had led to a drastic increase in grain prices and in some places, even starvation. If working class men—and even women, they argued—had the power to vote, changes that would help regular English families would come to pass.

"Aye," Agatha said. "Things have gotten bad for us in the northwest of England. Our children's bellies are hungry. Our menfolk work hard in the mines, factories, and fields, but it's never quite enough." She ran a hand over her face and sighed. "We believe that all people of England, men and women alike, should be able to vote for parliament. It's not right that just fine rich folk have a say in the laws of our land." She looked Lydia over and grimaced. "No insult intended, Miss."

"Please, call me Lydia, and none taken. I agree with everything you just said. I myself am very interested in reform, especially in the House of Commons."

Lydia realized that her nausea had dissipated. Perhaps a rousing political discussion was just the thing to turn one's mind away from feeling trapped while imprisoned.

Agatha's eyes lit up. "Ah, I bet you've spent some time reading those Democratium Liberum articles from last year."

Lydia's heart jumped at hearing her pen name.

"Gave me and the others quite an education on what was really going on in Westminster," Agatha continued, "what with the corruption and all. That was part of why we came down to London to protest. Quite a journey from Stafford, and one we wouldn't take without good cause. Too bad Democratium Liberum isn't publishing articles in the newspaper anymore. What a voice he could be for change if he were to take up his quill again and write about our cause."

Lydia could only blink. Her own writing had been instrumental in this group of women creating their own reform society? In leaving behind their homes and traveling across the country to London to bravely stand in the Westminster courtyard against a battalion of armed guards and chant for change? Only to find themselves behind bars?

Her head spun.

"Ah, yes," she finally said, her voice faint. "I've heard of…him."

Agatha turned to the room. "Ladies, come meet Miss Lydia Dashwood. She knows about Democratium Liberum too."

The other protesters, who had been talking quietly amongst themselves or comforting crying children, gathered closer to Lydia and Agatha in the jail cell.

"This here is my daughter, Grace," Agatha said, gesturing to a young woman with hazel eyes and brown hair pulled back in a simple bun like her mother's. Grace was visibly pregnant and had a wide mouth that seemed to smile easily.

"Has my mother tried to recruit you yet?" Grace teased. "We could call your arrest with us your initiation into our reform society."

Lydia was surprised to find herself smiling despite the fact that she was locked up in Newgate. "She hasn't invited me to join yet, but I'm quite impressed with your group's politics."

"And who wouldn't be?" chimed in a woman with blue eyes and sandy hair, and with a little boy in tow. "'Tis the only way for a right-minded person to think." She nodded her head emphatically.

"And this one here is Harriet Wadham," Agatha introduced.

"And Timmy!" piped up the child at her side. "I'm eight."

The grin he offered Lydia was adorably gapped with his milk teeth. Like his mother, he had blue eyes, and his sandy hair stuck up in several directions as if he'd run sticky fingers through it. Given the eating habits of children, it was most likely a hairstyle created with a bit of jam and honey.

Lydia reached her hand down to the young child. "Pleased to make your acquaintance, Timmy. And how many times has a seasoned criminal like yourself been to jail?"

Timmy chortled. "This is my first time, but my daddy says I should be locked up on account of how I never stay in bed at night."

His mother Harriet raised her eyes heavenward. "Child, one of these days I might agree with your father and lock you up in your room. I'm much too tired to be woken up in the wee hours every night to give you another story and a glass of milk."

Timmy stuck out his lower lip. "But milk tastes better at night."

"How did you come to be arrested with us, Miss?" asked Grace, Agatha's daughter. "Not to be rude, but you don't exactly look like a reformer."

You'd be surprised.

Lydia sighed. "I was summoned to the Office of Public Order today by a Mr. Staines, and my companion and I were just leaving when the guards surrounded you."

Lydia recalled Benedict's panicked face across the courtyard when she'd been seized by the guards. He must be worried sick about her. She assumed he hadn't been arrested, otherwise he'd have been placed in the wagon with her and the protestors. Hopefully he hadn't gotten into an altercation with the guards.

"But why didn't you simply leave the courtyard?" asked Grace.

Lydia frowned. "It was my own curiosity that landed me here. I wanted to know more about your group, and I was just starting to ask someone a question, but then the officers swooped in. It seems that timing is not my strength."

"Mr. Martin Staines," Agatha spat. "That man has been a boil on the ass of the ladies reform societies since the very first day of our organization."

"Mother!" whisper-shouted Grace, pointing at little Timmy.

"Ach, never mind that," Harriet said waving a dismissive

hand through the air. "My Timmy has grown up on a farm. He's heard the word *ass* before, mark my words."

"Mr. Staines did strike me as rather a bit of a… *ahem*… backside boil." Lydia thought back on the man's cold, hard eyes and shivered. "Apparently, in his pursuit of rooting out all groups he views as radical, he is also investigating local London groups that he thinks might be associated with the female reform societies."

"And what group do you belong to, Miss?" asked Grace, her hand pressed to her pregnant belly.

"I'm a member of the Ladies Charitable Association," Lydia said, the lie springing easily to her lips despite the fact that she hated being dishonest with this kindhearted group. In order to keep the LCA safe, the circle of those who knew its true identity had to be kept small.

Agatha's eyebrows shot up. "I've heard of your association," she said. "Delivered a whole trunk of wool socks to an orphanage in Stafford. Might've saved the toes of many a young one that winter as it was particularly harsh."

The others murmured their assent.

Lydia swallowed. Had she honestly thought she had nothing else to offer the world after her Democratium Liberum articles ended? Here in this prison cell, she had learned not only that her essays had shaped the views and ongoing work of these protesters, but also that the charity work of the LCA actually benefited the children of their county. She had seen the group's good deeds in action before, but somehow hearing it from these ladies and learning about the children's little toes made it feel so much more real.

"I will look into which orphanage we helped in Stafford," Lydia said, feeling both powerful and humble at the same time. "We can be sure to send another trunk of clothing soon."

"That's quite kind of you," Agatha said, nodding her head. "Now if only the fates would see fit to send us a competent writer and a place to stay here in town, all our prayers would be answered."

"You don't have a place to stay?" Lydia asked. She decided to overlook the comment about a writer for the moment. She was finding the dual experience of prison and making new friends a bit overwhelming.

"The beds had bugs in them!" Timmy's eyes lit up with glee as he related this pertinent detail.

His mother Harriet shuddered. "The inn that had been recommended to us left much to be desired in the hygiene department."

"We left our luggage at that terrible inn before coming to Westminster," Agatha explained, "but we had decided to take the mail coach back home tonight as we could not find a place we could afford that was fit for beasts, let alone humans."

Lydia shook her head. "You can't take the mail carriage back on the same day you arrived!" She looked around at the group. In addition to several pregnant women and small children, there was also an elderly protester who looked as if a good jolt in one of those loaded-down coaches would snap her poor old bones. Lydia wouldn't wish the grueling back-to-back journeys on her worst enemy.

Then she recalled her wretched kidnappers and decided she'd have no qualms placing *them* on an endless carriage to Hades and back, seated next to a passenger who believed bathing to be bad for one's health.

"Well," said Grace, grimacing as she rubbed her pregnant belly again, "it likely doesn't matter what we prefer, as it seems the choice has been taken away from us. Instead of sleeping in an inn with bugs or on the mail coach, we'll be sleeping in a prison cell tonight."

Lydia patted her coiffure. Ever since her kidnapping, she'd asked her lady's maid to include hairpins in whatever style she chose for the day. After Lydia had returned home, she'd arranged with the previous head of the LCA for a talented thief to give her lessons on picking locks. Never again would a locked door keep her imprisoned.

Could she break them all out of jail with naught but some know-how, a sturdy hair pin, and a bit of luck?

Before she could formulate a plan, the sound of the heavy footsteps echoed through the cell. Again, came the metallic noise of keys on the metal and the door squeaking open.

"Dashwood?" barked the prison guard.

Lydia's heartbeat stuttered. "That's me." She tried to keep her nerves out of her voice.

"Come with me." The guard gestured for her to leave the cell.

"Where are you taking her?" demanded Agatha. "You're not to touch a hair on this girl's head, do you hear me?"

The guard merely sneered at the older woman. "What's that got to do with you? Anyway, it don't matter. She's being discharged."

"What about us?" called one of the reformers from the far side of the cell.

"Just her." The guard grabbed Lydia's arm when she didn't move fast enough and yanked her out into the dim hallway. He slammed the door shut, and it clanged with an ominous finality.

"Let them out too," Lydia said, pulling back against the man's tight grip. "They've done nothing wrong. Please, release all of them now as well."

"Just following orders," he grunted, tugging on Lydia's arm.

And before she could say any words of comfort or even say farewell to her new friends, Lydia was marched through the harrowing corridors of Newgate until at last she emerged into the courtyard of the prison.

Lydia drew in deep breaths of fresh air as she blinked against the bright light and tried to look around. Several guards milled about, all of them brawny and mean-looking. A doorway to the side opened and out stepped Benedict along with a man whose uniform looked more officious than the others.

Benedict.

Of course, he'd come for her. Despite her fear at being locked away, she must've known somewhere deep inside that he wouldn't allow her to languish in that prison for a minute longer than was necessary.

The official-looking man, his belt straining against the weight of a heavy keyring, jostled a coin purse in his hand. He spoke to Benedict before pointing in Lydia's direction.

Benedict turned and saw her. His cravat was askew, and his hair was mussed. He had a wild-eyed look about him, as if he'd just fought a swarm of ghosts.

He'd never looked so good.

"Benedict," she choked out, and in less time than she thought possible, he rushed to her and gathered her up in his arms.

"Lydia," he murmured. "Are you all right?"

She buried her face against his chest. He was clean and warm and strong, and he was here. He'd saved her. She was safe.

"Thank you," she choked out. "Thank you for coming for me. I'm so sorry I didn't stay with you in the courtyard. I—"

"Shh," he whispered, stroking her back as if reassuring himself that she was really here. "You don't have to apologize. I was just so scared. I'm so sorry I couldn't get to you in time, couldn't protect you."

Lydia felt a tremor pass through his body. This big, strong man was trembling…for her.

"I'm all right." She hoped he could hear her words, muffled as she continued to bury her face against his chest. Somehow this spot felt safer than any other in all of London at the moment. "It's all right now."

"Mrs. Abbott?"

"I had the carriage take her home," Benedict replied. "We weren't sure how long it would take to get you out, and her daughter needed her help with the baby."

"Thank you," Lydia whispered.

He pulled back slowly, as if reluctant to release her from his arms. Lydia wanted nothing more than to remain in his hold, her eyes closed against the harsh surroundings of Newgate, but his arms dropped away at last.

And…there was work to do.

She looked up at him, and their gazes caught and tangled. She'd never seen such a solemn expression on his face before. It was strange seeing this usually cheerful man with his devil-may-care attitude consumed by so much worry.

She drew a steadying breath. "Benedict?"

"Yes," he murmured, taking her hand in his.

"I hope you have more money on you than that single coin purse."

He blinked at her.

"Because we're going to need to pay the prison warden a much larger bribe."

❊

BENEDICT SLAPPED HIS last banknote into the prison warden's hand. "For that amount of money, I should've gotten all the women prisoners plus every other criminal locked up in Newgate," he grumbled.

The warden smirked. "Pleasure doing business with you, guv."

The man was a weasel. Despite the fact that those in Newgate were mostly hardened criminals, Benedict did not feel good about anyone's life or safety residing in this man's dirty hands. He would have to investigate prison reform before the next session of the House of Lords.

"They'd better be unharmed," Benedict warned.

"Not a hair on their sweet little heads has been harmed, guv," the prison warden assured him as he patted his stuffed pocket.

Benedict watched Lydia berate one of the prison guards who'd been standing at attention in the courtyard. Her scowl was at its most formidable, and she was gesturing out toward the street as she spoke. After bobbing his head in agreement for practically a full minute, the guard trotted off.

Benedict walked up to her. "What was that about?"

Hands on her hips, Lydia surveyed the remaining guards through narrowed eyes. "I despise this place and these horrid guards. I imagine it's the same for the reformers. I told that one that the least he could do after being such a despicable piece of refuse was to go and fetch a bunch of hackneys to transport all the ladies once they're released."

"I thought you were going to make the chap cry what with the horrific glares you were shooting him." Benedict kept his tone light and teasing, but there was still a knot of anxiety in his chest. Lydia should not have been there, standing in the courtyard of Newgate. Neither of them should have been there. The wrongness of this entire situation pushed on his shoulders as if he were pulling a wagon full of produce to market instead of some giant ox. Or some appropriate farming analogy. He didn't know how those things worked.

"It was lucky that glares were the only thing I gave that soldier." Lydia continued to mumble under her breath.

Benedict swore he heard the *knife* in there somewhere. Lydia could be quite ferocious when she was angry.

One hackney and then another rolled into the courtyard, and another was just visible pulling around the corner.

"Will you direct the hack drivers to take the reformers to the closest mail coaching inn?" He started to calculate the cost of the fares for so many hackneys. Would there be enough time for him to send a message home and have one of his footmen deliver more coins to him here? The corrupt warden had bled him dry, and he doubted Lydia had any coins on her. For the first time in his life, Benedict wondered how women carried their necessities, such as coins, when they didn't have pockets in their gowns. Ladies' fashion was not designed for practicality, it seemed. How deucedly unfair.

"I'm not sending them to the mail coaching inn," Lydia said, her tone distracted as she continued to watch more hackneys pull into the courtyard.

Benedict frowned. A troublesome possibility crossed his mind, and although it was absolutely preposterous, he couldn't seem to shake the thought. "If you're not sending them to the mail coaching station, then where are you sending—"

A commotion behind them had them both turning around before he could finish his question. Lydia's face lit up as a group of women, all dressed in white, along with several children were led out of the prison. She hurried over to them, and one, a middle-aged woman who seemed to be the leader of the group, clasped her hands.

"Thank you, love," the woman said to Lydia in a strong, clear voice.

The others gathered around her, also expressing their gratitude and thanks. One little boy with a gap-toothed grin tugged on Lydia's skirts.

"Now when my papa tells me he's going to lock me up for not staying in my bed at night, I'll just tell him I've already been to prison, and it wasn't that bad." The child snickered.

Lydia smiled and ruffled his hair.

Benedict approached her, the need to clarify one essential bit of information outweighing any thoughts of politeness or manners. "Lydia, what are you planning—"

Before he could finish his sentence, she'd seized his hand and dragged him into the center of the reformer's little circle. "Everyone, I would like to introduce to you Lord Lovell. He's the one who paid for your release. Isn't he just the most kind, generous, patient, and understanding man you've ever met?"

Lydia turned to face him, and her eyes twinkled in a way with which he was all too familiar.

Bloody hell.

If she was already trying to butter him up, then they were doomed.

He tried again, leaning to whisper in her ear. "Lydia—"

But she stepped away before he could tell her that whatever

she was planning was not possible. Not safe. Not even sane.

"All right," she said, clapping her hands to get everyone's attention. "Please get into the hackney carriages. Once we've dropped you off at your new accommodations, we'll send the carriages to that terrible inn to retrieve your luggage. You might have to squeeze in," she warned as the women and children began to clamber into the hackneys.

"Lydia," he tried again, knowing his voice was growing increasingly desperate, but he was not really caring about that at this point.

She didn't hear him—or at least gave a very good approximation of not hearing him—and approached the driver of the closest hackney. When she rattled off a familiar address, Benedict groaned.

"You can't." He grabbed her hand to catch her attention. "It will ruin you. It will ruin me too, and my sister…"

Lydia's eyebrows shot up. "Your sister? I don't understand."

Benedict swallowed. He'd promised his mother and sister that he would do nothing to bring scandal onto their family name so as not to jeopardize Emelia's chances of a good match, and what did he go out and do? The very day he made that promise, he got involved in a mass arrest at England's center of government and illegally bribed prison officials to get radical reformers out of Newgate.

And now *this*.

But he couldn't tell Lydia that. If he did, she would insist he leave and have no further part in this. And despite his promise and love for his family, that he could not do.

He would not leave Lydia alone in this. He *couldn't* leave Lydia alone. And so he closed his eyes and pinched the bridge of his nose before slowly exhaling.

"Where to, guv?" called out one of the hackneys that Lydia hadn't spoken to yet.

Lydia stared up into Benedict's eyes, her wide blue depths a combination of beseeching and fierce determination.

Benedict rattled off the address to the driver, and Lydia's shoulders dropped in relief.

"Thank you," she whispered, and gave his hand a squeeze.

Benedict merely nodded and went around to let all the drivers know the address. It was one he didn't have to think very hard to recall, as it was the address of his best friend Jack. The home Jack and his wife shared with Lydia.

In the course of a single day, the reformers' status was changing from prisoners at Newgate to guests in the home of an earl.

Chapter Six

"… AND WE'LL put Harriet and Timmy in the green room," Lydia instructed the housekeeper, "next to Agatha, who is in the purple room."

Mrs. Smythe nodded, and although she didn't utter the words *this is madness*, the message was there plain in her eyes for all to see.

The home that Lydia shared with her brother Jack and his bride Pippa was a large Mayfair house befitting an earl. However, Lydia doubted that the grand home had ever seen an influx of guests quite like this.

It was, in a word, chaos.

Timmy was leading several of the other children in a complicated game in which the only rules seemed to be sliding down the banister of the main staircase and making as much noise as possible. Meanwhile footmen shuffled in and out, carrying in the luggage that had been retrieved from the unacceptable inn. Maids dashed up and down the stairs as they readied rooms that had been unused for quite some time. Although they were generally kept clean, the curtains were drawn, the fireplaces were bare, and a bit of dust had settled.

Would everyone fit?

For the first time, Lydia felt an inkling of doubt about her impetuous plan. It had seemed so clear, back at Newgate: The protesters had traveled far in order to fight for reform. They had no place to stay. Meanwhile, Lydia had a gigantic house, and her brother was conveniently out of town. What could possibly go wrong?

"Miss Lydia," said Agatha, the practical woman seeming flustered for the first time since Lydia had made her acquaintance. And that included their stint in prison. "Are you sure it's all right for us all to stay here? This seems far too grand for the likes of us."

Lydia glanced around the home she'd lived in her entire life, trying to see it through the eyes of her new guests, who likely lived in simple cottages. Marble floors gleamed. A grand chandelier hung in the foyer from a high ceiling and light reflected off its many crystals, making it sparkle and gleam. Gilded frames adorned the wall, displaying priceless art.

And there were so many rooms. So many fireplaces. And so much furniture.

Embarrassment burned in Lydia's stomach.

She and Jack had so much, while most people had far too little. It was terribly unjust. She couldn't change the unequal distribution of wealth today, but she *could* give these brave women and their children a safe and certainly bed bug-free residence while they were in town.

"I won't hear of you staying anywhere else," Lydia said, voice firm. "And besides, we're friends now. When you're sent to Newgate with someone, you're bonded for life." She flashed Agatha a cheeky grin.

Thankfully, most of the older woman's expression of uncertainty faded and she chuckled. "Well, we are most grateful for your kindness, Miss."

"Please, call me Lydia."

Agatha frowned for a moment, then nodded her head. "All right then, Lydia. We are most grateful for your kindness. And we don't mind earning our keep by doing chores around the house."

Lydia glanced at Mrs. Smythe. The matronly housekeeper was within hearing distance, and given her current scowl, she'd overheard Agatha's offer.

Lydia cleared her throat. "Um, I don't think that would be necessary. I'm afraid the household staff would feel they have been usurped. But if any additional task should arise that are outside their normal duties, I shall be sure to let you know. But for now, please consider yourself a guest in my home."

A group of footmen entered with more luggage, and Lydia felt a shift in the air.

He was here.

She wasn't quite sure when it happened, but at some point during that day, her awareness of Benedict had shifted dramatically. Instead of just being her brother's friend who came over to gobble up all the strawberry jam, and perhaps exchange some pointed teasing, now she noticed him as…himself. Benedict. A man, entirely separate from her brother.

Why had this happened?

She watched him cross the foyer to her, the set of his jaw indicating he was still quite grumpy that she'd invited the protesters into her home.

Agatha looked back and forth between the two of them and then the brave leader of the reform group who'd stood strong against a squad of armed guards took the only sensible course of action. She excused herself.

"Look what you've done," Lydia said, watching the woman hurry away. She turned and frowned at Benedict. "You scared off Agatha. She's the leader of all these women, you know. It's important that she and I talk so that everyone can get situated."

Benedict's eyes swept the foyer, which was still in chaos with luggage, women in white, shrieking children, and bustling servants.

"I doubt there's anything anyone could do to get *this* situated." He gestured with his hand at the general melee. "And *we* need to talk." He leaned in closer, and Lydia found herself tantalized with his clean, masculine scent. "This isn't safe."

"What do you mean, it's not safe?" Lydia braced her hands on her hips.

"What I mean," he said through clenched teeth and in a voice meant only for her ears, "is that you don't know these people. You don't know who they are or what they've done. One of them could be a deranged murderer, for all we know."

"Oh yes," Lydia said dryly, nodding at Timmy whose whoops echoed in the foyer as he slid down the banister for the umpteenth time. "This one in particular looks quite dangerous. Or"—she continued, gesturing toward one of the mothers who sat with a toddler in her lap, softly singing to her wee one—"perhaps her? She looks like she'd strangle us all in our sleep. With her tot's blankie, no doubt."

Benedict's full lips tightened in apparent frustration.

Lydia blinked at the thought. His *full* lips? Why on earth would she take note of Benedict's lips? Of their general state of handsome fullness?

This was most strange. Perhaps she'd damaged her senses during her stint as a prisoner.

"I am serious," he gritted out.

Crossing the crowded foyer, footmen carrying several bags bumped into him, and Benedict cursed softly.

"We need a place with less chaos to have this conversation," he muttered, grabbing Lydia's hand. He started to walk down the hallway with her in tow.

"Where are we going?" Lydia asked, trotting behind him.

Benedict poked his head into several rooms, but apparently none of them met his criteria for they continued down the hallway. He tried a closed door; when he opened it, he nodded in satisfaction at what he saw inside. He stepped in, and Lydia shrieked in surprise when he tugged her into a linen closet.

Benedict shut the door behind them, and instantly the noise and chaos from the rest of the house disappeared. Perhaps the shelves of neatly stacked towels, sheets, and bedding muffled the noise. Or perhaps it was the darkness that engulfed them. Whatever the cause, the result was that they were alone, cocooned together in this dark, cozy space.

Then Lydia realized just how small the space actually was when she took a deep breath and felt her breasts brush against Benedict's firm chest. She tried to pull back to give them a bit of space but clocked her head on a shelf.

"Ow." She rubbed the back of her head.

"Careful," he warned and grasped her waist to pull her even closer to him. "Are you all right?" He gently brushed his hand against the back of her head as if searching for damage.

"I'm fine," she whispered, trying not to shiver at the sensation of his touch.

They both breathed into the silence. In addition to the clean scent of linens, Lydia could smell that tantalizing scent again. His light cologne. The fresh smell of his soap. And something that was just…him.

He broke the quiet. "I know it's tight in here, but we needed to speak privately."

Lydia cleared her throat. "Well, it seems you have found the only private space in the entire house. Just you, me, and the entire household's trove of towels."

Benedict cleared his throat as well, but then he didn't say anything. Perhaps he was trying to find the words. Or perhaps…perhaps…he was as distracted by her nearness as she was by his.

Each time they breathed their bodies pressed together. She was surrounded by his scent, his touch, his heat… Without being able to see, it was as if all her other senses were heightened. Her fingers twitched, and the temptation to reach out and pull him even closer than he already was almost overtook her good sense.

"What was it that you wish to say to me, Benedict?" Lydia finally asked. Best to get this conversation rolling. The sooner they finished talking, the sooner she could get out of there and away from the strange feelings his close proximity caused.

Benedict exhaled. "Lydia, you have such a big heart. I know you want to help these women in their wish to better society, and that's quite admirable. But isn't there some other way you could assist them?"

"What would you have me do?" Lydia demanded. "Send them off to some horrid inn where they will likely be robbed or taken advantage of? Cram them all into a mail coach for a grueling journey back to Stafford?"

"Exactly."

Even though they were in complete darkness, Lydia could perfectly envision Benedict's expression right now. The exasperation in his eyes. The sensual, almost lazy curve to his mouth, as if he were modeled on some classical sculpture of Bacchus. The slight cant to one eyebrow that hinted at teasing despite the serious tone of his voice.

"These women still have work to do," she replied. "And I can help them do it."

"But you don't even know them. What if this is some scheme to get invited into your home so they can rob you?"

Lydia scoffed. "You think they planned to get arrested by armed guards while they were accompanied by their *children?*" She let her incredulity ring out in her voice. "On the off chance that I or some other aristocratic member of the ton would be happening by at the *exact* moment of their arrest, and would feel some sort of connection to them and bring them into their home? I think," Lydia said gazing up to the darkness where his face would be, "with that sort of imagination you should consider writing a novel."

"Lydia," he growled, and she shivered at the vibrations his rough voice sent through her body.

"No, *you* listen," she interjected before he had the chance to speak his mind with whatever noble, cautious, or patronizing words of advice he felt it his duty to bestow upon her. "This is my house. These are my guests. And you, sir, have no say here."

Benedict sighed, the sound suggesting that she was the most

troublesome woman in all of England. "Perhaps I have no say here, but—" he paused, as if giving time for his words to sink in—"I'm certain your brother does."

Lydia gasped. "Are you threatening to tell Jack I won't do as you say? That's low, even for you Benedict."

She felt his body stiffen at her words, and Lydia felt an instantaneous regret. "I didn't mean—"

"Unfortunately," Benedict said, his voice tinged with hurt, "you meant exactly what you said. I suppose that's the price I must pay because of my wretched reputation, being considered less than a gentleman, even by my friends."

Lydia's cheeks burned with shame. And even as she grappled with what words could make this right, the analytical part of her brain noticed he didn't mention his *actions*, but instead his *reputation*, as if the two were unrelated. She would have to revisit that later.

Lydia reached up and laid her hand against Benedict's chest. She heard his breath catch at her touch.

"I'm so sorry," she said. "You've always been a good and loyal friend to Jack, and to me as well, in our own peculiar way. And how could I forget all that you did to help out Jane and Dev when his relative was trying to steal his title? You are a good man, Benedict Southcott, Viscount Lovell, and I won't have anyone saying otherwise, including myself."

He exhaled, his warm breath brushing Lydia's face. It made her imagine how they were positioned here in this dark linen closet. Their bodies pressed close together. Her face tilted up toward him. And his angled down toward her, as if they were to lovers about to kiss.

Her heart skipped a beat.

"Thank you for saying that." His voice was gravel.

Lydia felt a warm pressure against the back of her hand resting on his chest. He had laid his hand over hers. Her hand was surrounded by him—on one side his firm chest, the hard muscles apparent even through the many layers of clothing, and on the other, the large expanse of his hand sheltering hers.

What would it be like, to be truly held by a man such as Benedict? How would it feel to be cherished by him, to know he protected you and cared for you above all others?

"If you are intent on them staying here—"

"I am," she interrupted.

"Then we must take measures to ensure your safety."

Lydia considered his offer. "If I agree to these measures, you'll promise to not tell Jack?"

"He'll skin me alive if he finds out, but yes. I won't contact him about this."

Lydia smiled in satisfaction.

Despite the darkness, he seemed to sense her feeling of victory. "You haven't heard the measures yet," he warned.

"I'm sure it's fine."

He was silent.

Lydia frowned. "You wouldn't suggest anything too draconian, would you?"

Again, she felt a puff of his breath against her face but this time instead of a sigh, it was caused by a little huff of laughter. "It's not draconian, but it's not exactly proper either."

Lydia's hand flexed under his. "What is it?"

"As long as the reformers are residing here in your house," Benedict announced, "so shall I."

LYDIA GASPED AND stiffened against him.

Damn. He'd shocked her to her core.

"Lydia, I—"

He felt her shaking her head in the darkness. Perhaps she needed a moment to herself to process his outrageous request.

Truth be told, *he* needed a moment to process his outrageous request. Why had he said that? It was completely unthinkable for him, a bachelor, to sleep under the same roof as her, an unmarried lady of good reputation. Although, to be fair, the house was now full of an entire gaggle of chaperones.

He flashed back to the promise he made to his mother and to his sister Emelia that very morning in his stables. He was not to cause harm to the family's reputation. Emelia was counting on him. If he did anything that sullied his reputation—or *further* sullied his reputation as it had grown quite tarnished years ago without much help from him—her chances at making a favorable match dissipated like a bit of cigar smoke on a windy day.

Lydia trembled against him.

His arms wrapped around her of their own accord. He would give her whatever comfort he could, here in this dark, quiet linen closet.

"I'm sorry," he whispered.

His breath seized in his lungs when she rested her head against his chest. Despite the absolute darkness of the tiny space, Benedict closed his eyes so that he might savor this moment all the more. For years he dreamed of holding Lydia. Of her coming to him, untethered by expectation or misunderstanding. Of loving her in the open, instead of in the quiet stillness inside his own heart.

But in truth, he never expected this to actually happen.

He was holding Lydia Dashwood in his arms. She'd come to him of her own free will. He would savor this moment, here, now.

Benedict tipped his face down so that his cheek rested on the top of her head. Her hair was soft as silk against his face, and she smelled of fine soap and hothouse flowers. He inhaled a deep breath of her.

"Benedict," she whispered even as she nuzzled against him, as if she were a cat marking her territory with her scent.

"Yes, my darling," he replied and wondered if she could hear the loud thumping of his heart from where she pressed against his chest. Would she ask him for a kiss? Or would she ask him to come to her rooms that night after the house had grown still and quiet? But perhaps she was more traditional, and wished to wait until they'd spoken their vows in the church first.

"Benedict," she said again, and this time her voice sounded choked with emotion.

His sweet, sweet Lydia. She was so tough on the outside, but he knew beneath her prickly exterior was a tender heart. And it seemed she was getting just as emotional as he felt in this moment of their embrace.

"Anything you wish for, my darling," he vowed, his arms tightening around her lithe form.

She continued to nuzzle her head against his chest.

"My hair," she muttered.

Her hair?

"It's stuck on your button."

He lifted his head from her silky hair. "Erm, you…you're stuck to me?"

"Yes," she said with a huff. "Why else would I be moving my head to and fro against your chest like this? I'm trying to untangle my coiffure from your button."

Benedict's cheeks felt on fire. *Oh, hell and damnation.* He'd misread the entire situation. Instead of pressing against him in passion, she was merely trying to disentangle herself from his clothing. All while he had dreamed about entangling their entire lives together.

Truly, he was the stupidest man in all of England.

"My apologies." Benedict hated the formal tone in his voice, but he was helpless against it.

"Just help me," she demanded. She tugged her head away from him and hissed in pain. She must have yanked her scalp in the process.

"Hold still," he commanded. Feeling his way with gentle movements, he followed the curve of her head and found where her tresses had caught on his button. It was hard to figure out how to untangle them in the dark, but he didn't dare open the closet door and reveal their intimate pose to the rest of the household.

"Are you quite finished?"

Benedict could picture her eyebrows drawn tightly, and her mouth pouting and adorably grumpy in that way she had. If he were to move here—*could he actually move here?*—then he would doubtlessly see that expression every day.

He ignored the thrill the thought shot through him.

After moving a few more strands over the button, he said. "There, I think you're free of me now."

Lydia pulled back slowly. "I hope I haven't given myself a bald spot," she grumbled.

Benedict scooted back a scant inch until his back hit the shelves. He missed the warmth and closeness of her pressed up against him but touching her like that was far too dangerous. This close proximity had already caused him to issue one idiotic demand. If he was in here much longer with her, he'd be handing over his estate and title next.

He needed to fix this. Now.

Benedict cleared his throat. "About my staying here—"

Lydia interrupted him. "I've been considering the threat Staines poses to the LCA, and you were right to warn me. I've put myself and the LCA in danger by offering the women a place to stay."

Benedict breathed a sigh of relief. That had been much easier than he anticipated. Although he enjoyed his time with Lydia immensely, things were rarely easy with her.

"I'm so glad you've come to see things my—"

"But," she interrupted again, "I've already made the offer, and even though there is some element of risk, I can't cast these women out now. And so—" she drew a deep breath—"I agree to your terms."

Benedict's mouth dropped open. "You agree to my…"

He felt movement. She must be nodding in the darkness.

"Even though it comes with its own set of risks," Lydia said,

"I would feel better having you here while the reformers are my guests. You *are* a bit of a lummox—"

"A lummox?" This time he was the one doing the interrupting. "Stop or you'll turn my head."

"You *are* a bit of a lummox," she said, louder, "but I'd feel much better about the threat from Staines and the safety of the LCA if you were here."

Benedict wished he could see her face right now. She felt safe because of *his* presence? Their time in the linen closet had been nothing short of a revelation. But then he thought of his sister once more, and trepidation stirred in his stomach.

"I promised my family that I would rehabilitate my reputation," he blurted out.

The ensuing silence felt thick in the small space between them.

"Rehabilitate your reputation?" she repeated, as if the words were foreign and had no meaning to her.

"Yes," Benedict said, trying to keep any hint of bitterness out of his voice. "Apparently I am hurting Emelia's chances at landing a proper husband because I'm viewed as…" He couldn't finish the sentence. It was far too humiliating to say the words out loud, let alone to Lydia.

"Because the ton thinks you are a rake with some scandalous past?" Apparently, she had no such qualms.

"Er, yes?"

"Was this what that oaf was speaking of at Westminster?"

Benedict exhaled sharply.

"Yes."

Lydia gave a short hum to acknowledge his answer and then was quiet. He could sense that she was thinking. He didn't know what about her current activity told him this, but Lydia was the cleverest person he knew, and it had always been apparent to him when that talented brain of hers chewed over a problem.

At last, she replied. "I have a counterproposal."

Benedict was almost afraid to ask. "What is it?"

"In exchange for you staying here to help with the reformers and keep the threat of Staines away, I shall rehabilitate your reputation."

Benedict couldn't have been more surprised if she suddenly smacked him across the face with a lake trout.

Perhaps she sensed his discombobulation, because she continued to explain her idea seemingly without any response required from him. "We shall attend ton events together, and I can guide you in your interactions with the grand dames of the aristocracy. I'll help you be on your best behavior, and if people see us together, they'll assume you're completely reformed."

Benedict frowned. "Why would they assume that?"

"Have you met my brother?" she teased. "He's a stickler for duty and propriety and all that nonsense. When people see that you are my escort, they'll assume that Jack has given you his seal of approval as completely scandal-free."

"But Jack's out of town." Benedict felt like he was saying all the wrong things, but it was as if Lydia's brain had run laps around his own, and he couldn't keep up.

"You know that, and I know that, but the ton doesn't know that. Jack is rather private, so I doubt he's been telling people that he needed to head up north to oversee an estate in some trouble, or even that he was planning to leave town. So, we tell everyone that you have his approval as my escort, and we watch as your reputation receives a restoration of sorts. Everyone will see that your wild ways have been tamed, people will forget those old rumors, and your sister will have no trouble finding a respectable suitor. Although," she sniffed, "the whole idea of *respectability* is quite dull and outdated."

Benedict could think of no response. But it seemed, in this matter, that none was needed. His hand was taken up in hers and shaken most vigorously.

"There," she said, satisfaction evident in her voice. "We sealed the deal. You're stuck with me, and I'm stuck with you until this whole affair is behind us."

And then Lydia flung open the door and strode away, leaving Benedict blinking against the bright light streaming into the dark closet. Come to think of it, he often had to blink against the brightness when he was around dazzling Lydia Dashwood.

Chapter Seven

LYDIA USUALLY FOLLOWED her nose to the breakfast room, but today she followed the noise.

When she arrived, every seat was occupied, a sight she couldn't recall ever seeing before. The Stafford Female Reform Society was made up of early risers, it seemed. It shouldn't be surprising though. Unlike aristocrats who often slept the day away after a night of parties, dancing, and too much champagne, these women likely got up with the sun or the cock crowing to begin a day of work, either laboring at a job or caring for their family and home. Or both.

"Ah, good morning love," called Agatha from across the room. The older woman's smile was relaxed and easy.

Lydia gestured that she would fill a plate and join her shortly. As she walked toward the buffet, covered in copious trays and plates of breakfast food, she noticed a standoff happening.

"I'm sorry ma'am, but it's just not right." Mrs. Smythe, the housekeeper, had her hands on her hips. Her usually jolly face was twisted in a scowl.

"But we just want to be helpful," Harriet said in reply. She held an empty platter that looked as if it had once held eggs. "I can fry us up a new batch in a jiffy. Won't be any trouble at all."

Mrs. Smythe reached for the platter. "The kitchen servants are more than capable—"

"I *said*," retorted Harriet, tugging back on the platter, "that I could help."

Lydia gave her throat a vigorous clearing as she stepped forward.

Harriet and Mrs. Smythe froze, each one gripping a different end of the egg platter.

"Oh! Pardon me, my lady," the housekeeper said, bobbing her head as her cheeks grew even rosier than normal. She let go of the tray.

"I do beg your pardon, Miss." Harriet's face was turning a similar rosy shade.

"Perhaps I can help sort this out," Lydia said, even as she wondered how to solve this problem.

"My mum makes the best eggs!" crowed Timmy, popping up at her elbow. "And the mean lady won't let her."

Mrs. Smythe reared back, sputtering, even as Harriet began to chide her son.

"Perhaps," Lydia said gently tugging the egg dish out of Harriet's hands, "it would be best if we left the running of the household to the servants."

"I meant no disrespect," Harriet said, her gaze darting between Lydia, her indignant son, and the irate housekeeper. "Some of us in the group have been servants before and know what a burden it is with so many guests. I was just trying to help out. I didn't mean to insult you or your delicious eggs, I swear."

Mrs. Smythe stared at Harriet, gaze assessing.

"Well," the housekeeper said after a fraught moment. "It was most kind of you to offer. Most folks wouldn't have considered the toll on the help." She cast a baleful eye at Lydia.

Lydia blinked.

She had completely overlooked the fact that increasing the household by a few dozen guests would create quite a burden for the staff who already worked very hard at their jobs.

Lydia's cheeks burned. For all that she believed in equality for all, the truth of the matter was that she was a spoiled aristocrat.

She had never labored with her hands for a day in her life. Her guests had much more in common with Mrs. Smythe, the scullery maids, and the washer women than they did with her.

She was the one who was lacking. She was the one who hadn't seen.

"Mrs. Smythe, you have my sincere apologies." Lydia clasped her hands together, hoping Mrs. Smythe wouldn't think her a complete idiot. "Please hire however many servants you think we need to accommodate our guests. I shall be certain to add funds to the household account immediately."

Mrs. Smythe's fingers unclenched their tight grip around the egg tray. "Thank you, my lady. More servants while our guests are here would be most appreciated." She offered Harriet a civil nod before turning toward the door.

"And one more thing," Lydia called. "Please tell the regular servants that they shall receive a thirty percent increase in pay during the time that our guests remain."

Mrs. Smythe's face split into a jolly grin before she left the dining room.

"I didn't mean to cause any trouble," Harriet said. Her gaze followed Timmy as he grabbed a sweet roll from the food buffet.

"You were simply being thoughtful, which is more than I can say for myself." Lydia wrinkled her nose.

"Oh no, Miss," protested Harriet. "You have no cause to offer a group of strangers a place in your home, and yet here we are. That's as thoughtful as one could be, I would think." She flashed Lydia a smile and then dashed over to Timmy, who appeared to be stuffing three sweet rolls into his mouth at once.

Lydia filled her plate and joined Agatha at the far end of the table in a recently vacated seat.

"Looks like we caused a bit of trouble with your housekeeper," Agatha said, after dabbing at her mouth with a napkin.

"It was my fault." Lydia turned her plate so that the bacon was positioned closest to her. She had learned long ago to eat the tastiest things first, as Benedict was an infamous food snatcher.

Why, just a week ago, she'd rapped the back of his hand with her spoon when he'd attempted to snatch a slice of bacon off her plate. Although there was more at the buffet, he'd claimed that hers was the only truly *crispy* piece remaining and how could a growing boy like him be expected to reach his full potential with naught but soggy bacon to sustain him?

Lydia pictured his mischievous, lazy grin and something in her stomach flipped over.

"Are you suffering from a delayed flustering, perhaps?" Agatha eyed her over her teacup. "You've grown a bit pink around the cheeks just now, love."

"Ah," Lydia stammered. "I was just thinking about…"

Agatha's mouth curved up in a knowing grin. "In my experience, when a girl gets flushed from her own thoughts, she's thinking about one of two things."

Lydia toyed with her fork, but manners dictated she reply to the woman's statement. "Oh?"

"Either," Agatha said, a twinkle in her eye, "she's thinking about someone she's kissed…or she's thinking about someone she would *like* to kiss."

Lydia couldn't decide between laughing at Agatha's brazen commentary or hiding her flushed face in her breakfast plate. She settled for a well-practiced glare.

Agatha laughed. "I see how it is. You weren't exactly subtle when you snuck off down the hallway yesterday with that handsome, strapping man. There's no shame in finding a quiet corner to kiss your beau."

"He's not my beau," Lydia mumbled. Was her face on fire? It *felt* like it was on fire.

"Turns out," Agatha replied, "there's no shame in finding a quiet corner to kiss someone who's *not* your beau. Heaven knows I kissed more than my share of strapping village lads back in my youth."

Lydia lowered her fork from her mouth. No sense in risking choking.

Agatha continued. "In my opinion as a seasoned woman, before a woman enters into marriage and agrees to be kissing only one person for the rest of her life, she ought to sample the wares a bit, if you know what I mean." Agatha punctuated her relationship philosophy with a teasing eyebrow waggle.

Lydia did, in fact, know what Agatha meant. And she would rather eat only kippers for a week straight than continue this conversation.

"Did you all get settled in last night?" Lydia asked before taking a hearty bite of breakfast.

Agatha glanced around at the group of women and young children happily munching on eggs, pastries, bacon, and fruit. "We did at that, love. Truth of the matter is, we'd be a bit at sea if it weren't for you. Everyone was reunited with their luggage, which your footmen kindly fetched for us. The servants brought up a bit of warm water to wash off the taint of Newgate, as well as some supper, before everyone retired to nice—and clean!— warm beds. I have to admit, I've never slept on such a soft mattress nor on finer sheets. You've been most kind to us, love."

The older woman patted Lydia's hand, and Lydia's throat thickened at the maternal gesture. Her own parents had been dead since her childhood, and they hadn't been very present in her life before that. Aside from her brother Jack looking out for her, she was not used to having a parental figure in her life.

"I'm glad you've all gotten settled," Lydia said when she was able to swallow past the knot of emotion again. "I'm truly honored to be able to assist you in your cause. It's one that is important to me as well." She paused. Did she dare ask to aid their cause? But she didn't wish to be weak and meek, so she forged ahead with her offer. "Is there more that I could assist you with? You'd mentioned a need for a writer." She bit her lip as she waited for Agatha's reply.

What was she doing? *This was so reckless.*

"We *do* need a writer to help us spread our message to other families." Agatha frowned. "In the beginning, we tried to write our own pamphlets, but none of us have the gift of the quill. It's been a great disappointment that we don't have a writer in our midst. I've seen firsthand the power the written word can have in swaying minds and perhaps even votes." She sighed.

"Perhaps... I could help you?" Lydia's bones felt as wobbly as the jelly on her plate while she waited for Agatha to reply.

"Don't take this the wrong way, love, but we've had a go with novice writers, and it wasn't successful. We really need a professional, perhaps someone who's written political treatises before or has been published. But... I don't know how we could find that person."

Lydia stared at her plate. *Why was this so hard?* Either she should, or she shouldn't. It was so unlike her to dither over decisions. Usually, she saw so clearly what had to be done, and then she did it. Things had been so different for her since the kidnapping. She often felt that those wretched men had not only stolen her away from her home, but they had also stolen her confidence.

Lydia took a deep breath. It was suddenly clear what she needed to do to get that missing piece of herself back. "I know how we can find the perfect writer for you."

Agatha tilted her head. "What do you mean, love?"

"Well, it turns out that I have a connection to... Democratium Liberum."

Agatha gasped, and her eyes widened in shock. "You're connected to *Democratium Liberum?*"

The breakfast room grew silent. Lydia looked around to find all the women staring at her, their expressions similar to their leader's.

And there in the doorway, with an inscrutable look on his face, stood Benedict.

"GOOD MORNING, EVERYONE," Benedict greeted the women and children gathered around the breakfast table, trying to keep the shock out of his voice. *Lydia knew Democratium Liberum?* "I hope you left me some bacon and strawberry jam."

"You put strawberry jam *on* your bacon?" A young child somewhere between the age of three and thirteen regarded Benedict with a look that seemed to be one part disgust and one part admiration, as if the boy himself knew never try such a wretched combination but was rather impressed with Benedict's bravery.

"Timmy," said the woman at the boy's side, most likely his mother based on their similar coloring and her freedom to scold. "It isn't polite to comment on other people's food."

"Heaven's child, he doesn't eat them together!" Mrs. Smythe rushed over to Benedict with a plate of breakfast in hand. "I served you up myself, my lord, with all your favorites."

He offered her a lazy smile as he took the plate. "You have my eternal gratitude. When will you make an honest man out of me and accept my proposal?"

Mrs. Smythe twittered. "Oh, you cheeky scamp," she said before leaving the breakfast room.

"Are you Mrs. Smythe's sweetheart, or Miss Lydia's?" Timmy again, with the impertinence. Oh, and now the scamp was grinning, showing off the gaps in his smile where he'd lost teeth.

"Oh, hush now!" His mother chided.

"He's not either of our sweethearts," Lydia called from the other side of the room, "but given how much of that strawberry jam he likes to eat, I imagine he has a bit of a *sweet tooth.*"

She winked at the boy, who chortled in response to her attempt at humor. Sweet tooth, indeed. As if he were some young pup lapping up sugar all day.

He contemplated dipping a finger in the tempting jelly, just for a discreet little taste, but he was stalled when Lydia started speaking again.

"Benedict, may I introduce you to the Stafford Female Reform Society?"

The women all eyed him curiously. And wasn't that a thing? They'd just heard the same shocking confession he had—that Lydia had a connection to the famous radical author who'd caused a stir with his newspaper articles criticizing the corruption in the House of Lords—and yet he walked into the room, and they all gave their attention to him instead of the hugest news of the year.

Perhaps he should chalk it up to the expert work of his tailor. Everyone knew women were overwhelmed by a well-shaped shoulder in a perfectly fitted jacket. *Or something.*

"And may I present to you all," Lydia continued holding her hand out toward Benedict as if she were announcing him as the next singer at a musicale, "Benedict Southcott, Lord Lovell."

"A blooming lord," one of the women whispered.

"A blooming *viscount,*" he replied with a wink.

The woman twittered.

"Didn't you know that your own hostess is a lady?" he asked. It seemed strange they would be so impressed by his title when they were already staying in the earl's house.

"Miss—er, my lady…we didn't know—" the woman beside Lydia stammered.

"It's quite all right." Lydia laid her hand on hers. If Benedict remembered correctly from last night, this was the group's leader. "You called me Miss when we were first arrested together, a moment I shan't forget anytime soon,"—the group chuckled, doubtlessly as Lydia had intended—"and that was quite all right with me. I don't want us to stand on formality."

A pregnant woman seated halfway down the table folded her arms over her belly. "Forgive me, my lady, but I have to ask. How is it, that a fine noblewoman such as yourself is acquainted with the radical writer Democratium Liberum?"

Benedict saw this as a good opportunity to take a seat with his plate of food. "Yes, Lydia," he drawled, "how *do* you know Democratium Liberum?" His voice and posture were relaxed, yet he felt anything but.

Like everyone else who received the newspaper in London, he had been obsessed with the articles last year. He'd eagerly searched the newspaper each morning, hoping for a new piece. When they'd mysteriously stopped, he'd read the old articles over and over again. Democratium Liberum's arguments were compelling. As a member of Parliament, Benedict often wished he could sit down with the man and discuss how the House of Commons could be fixed.

Only nobody knew the man's real identity.

Except, it turned out, for Lydia. But she had never breathed a word.

She looked around the room, but locked eyes with just him when she replied, "I didn't say I *knew*…him. Merely that I have a connection to the author."

"What's this connection?" he asked, leaning forward. "A friend of a friend?"

"I'm afraid," she answered, raising one eyebrow, "that I cannot reveal my source."

"You cannot reveal your source?" Benedict parroted.

"I can't."

"Or you won't?"

"Can't *and* won't," she fired back.

"Well, that's rather selfish of you."

"It's rather selfish of you to ask!" she said through gritted teeth.

The others in the room swiveled their heads back and forth at Lydia and Benedict's quick retorts.

The leader of the group cleared her throat. "Well, this is excellent news. And I quite understand your wish to keep your connection private, especially with the new power given to Mr. Staines and the Office of Public Order. They grow more dangerous to our movement with each passing week. We experienced ourselves what the man does to peaceful reformers."

The others nodded.

"Perhaps we could meet up later this afternoon, my lady," the leader said. "That will give me and the other members of the society a bit of time to outline our wishes for the pamphlet we'd like you to pass along to your connection. Hopefully, Democratium Liberum will be amenable to helping us."

Lydia consented to the plan and rose from the table. Benedict shoved the last bit of breakfast in his mouth before surging to his feet.

"Oh, look at that," he exclaimed, after striding to catch up with her. "We finished at the same time and now we can chat. How fortuitous."

Lydia rolled her eyes. "We can talk Benedict…"

He thought of their talk yesterday, pressed close together in the dark confines of the linen closet. His skin tingled.

"…but" she continued, "it won't be in a closet this time."

"Of course not," he agreed. Best to not examine the pang of disappointment too closely.

Chapter Eight

IN THE SITTING room, Benedict sprawled on the sofa across from Lydia, who perched in a chair. It was imperative he discover her link to Democratium Liberum. He needed to know in order to keep Lydia safe, to keep her beloved Ladies Charitable Association safe, and—he realized belatedly—also to keep his sister's reputation safe. And if he played his cards right and could finagle a meeting with the man himself, perhaps he would learn what could be done to keep parliament safe from further corruption.

However, given the Sphinx-like expression on Lydia's face, he doubted she would give up her secrets easily.

Best to use top-notch interrogation methods. "So…"

Lydia merely raised an eyebrow in reply. Perhaps he needed to rethink his top-notch interrogation methods.

"You know Democratium Liberum?" He sprawled even more lazily upon the sofa. Perhaps she would think him only idly curious if he embraced the idle look.

"I already explained it. I don't know the man, but I do have a connection to him."

Benedict shifted back on the sofa even further. A few more inches and one might be able to describe him as lounging. "And what is your connection?"

Lydia shot him a skeptical look. "Why should I tell you?"

Benedict shrugged, no easy task when one was nine-tenths of the way to laying down. "Why shouldn't you?" he drawled.

Lydia held his gaze. The expression in her deep-blue eyes was an interesting mix of mischief, wariness, and curiosity. It seemed that although she was enjoying this little game of cat and mouse, she also wanted to know why *he* wanted to know.

He decided to lay his trump card on the table. "I'm concerned about Staines in the Office of Public Order. We know he's already looking at the LCA. It seems incautious to have this connection with a known political firebrand. If the man is worried about your charity group now, what will he do when he discovers you are housing an entire reform society under your roof *and* that you are using your social connections to add an infamous writer to their cause?"

Lydia frowned and worried her bottom lip with her teeth.

Her bottom lip was so full and pink. What would it feel like to nibble it with his own teeth? To lathe that plump mouth with his tongue? To inhale her sweet moans as he devoured her mouth with his own?

"Benedict?"

He was yanked out of his reverie. How embarrassing—the front of his breaches had grown tight in the last few moments. He pulled himself upright and seized a nearby pillow to hug to his lap.

"Are you unwell?" Her brow furrowed in concern.

"Just woolgathering." He cleared his throat. "So do you agree with me, that this connection to Democratium Liberum places you, your guests, and your organization in danger?"

"I'd hardly say *danger*." She drummed her fingers on the chair arm. "But I do see your point."

Benedict smiled in victory.

"I'll simply have to be extra cautious is all," Lydia said.

Benedict felt his smile vanish. The victory had been short-lived.

He huffed and squeezed the pillow tight. "You're taking all

kinds of risks, Lydia. I promise not to tell your brother, but I must admit to being quite worried. First you end up in Newgate, then you invite an entire pack of strangers into your home, and now it turns out you're chummy with Democratium Liberum? The risk is just too high."

She glared at him. "And I say it isn't. Progress can't happen without a bit of risk. And after all, weren't *you* a risk taker back in your wild days? It's not as if you earned your rakish reputation without getting into some trouble first."

Benedict forced a laugh, but even to his ears, it sounded hollow. "Ah yes, my rakish reputation. And what, pray tell, do you know about my past troubles?"

Lydia grimaced, and for a moment he thought—he hoped—that she would not answer, that she *had* no answer. But it seemed the fates were not granting boons on this particular day. At least, not to him.

"It's no secret that you were quite a—" Lydia paused, and her cheeks turned pink—"skirt chaser, when you first got out of school and assumed your title. I'm sure I've heard stories. References to...to a house party." She looked down. "As well as the usual things—gambling, drinking..."

Benedict's skin felt too tight, and he leapt to his feet. He shouldn't feel so disappointed. It wasn't like the things Lydia was saying weren't already associated with his name. But somehow, he'd always assumed that she knew him better than the nameless, faceless gossipers who lived to wag their tongues amongst the aristocracy.

"Yes, the usual things." If his tone was bitter, so be it. He paced around the sitting room, too full of uncomfortable energy to pretend he was just a lounging loaf anymore.

"Benedict, what are you saying?" Lydia asked.

As he paced, he examined the art on the wall, the fabric of the draperies, and counted the number of steps from one side of the room to the other. Anything to keep from looking at her. He couldn't bear to see the expression on her face right now. He could bear so many things, but not her scorn or derision and especially not her belief that he was only a pleasure-seeking rake with one very sordid house party in his past.

"It's nothing," he gritted out.

He felt her eyes on him. He ceased his pacing and stopped in front of a window to look outside. The morning sun was bright, but it was still too early in the year for it to contain any warmth.

Several moments of silence passed.

It was Lydia who finally broke the quiet. "I'm afraid that I cannot tell you about my connection to Democratium Liberum, and I am most sorry for it." He heard her shift in her seat behind him. "But there is something I can do for you, something that I owe you."

Benedict gave a little grunt in reply.

"There's a salon being held tonight at Lady Blaire's house. I wasn't planning to attend, but given our arrangement, perhaps we should go together."

Benedict watched as a bird flew by. He'd been to salons before. People who considered themselves great thinkers enjoyed showing off their intellect to one another. He never participated in their long-winded discussions. Instead, he amused himself by whispering imaginary retorts to whichever acquaintance was in attendance.

He was fun company. Everyone said so. No one considered him to be a great thinker though, and so he usually stuck to the edges.

Benedict sighed. "Why should we go to this salon together?"

"Our arrangement of course. Have you forgotten?"

Benedict turned away from the window and raised a brow in question.

"I promised to help rehabilitate your wild image." Lydia had turned in her seat to watch him, and she'd clasped her hands together as if she were some innocent girl eager to do a good deed for a sweet friend.

He saw the devilish gleam in her eyes, however, and he

braced himself.

"Tonight," she announced, "will be phase one in declawing the Lovell lion."

THE FOOTMAN SHUT the door to the carriage, and Lydia was once more ensconced in a dark and cozy space with Benedict...and Mrs. Abbott, who was once more snoozing in the corner of the carriage. Truly, it seemed that becoming a grandmother had quite worn the woman out.

But Lydia was lucky her old housekeeper was amenable to accompanying her again. It would not do for Lydia's reputation to emerge from a kidnapping unscathed only to be tarnished by something as simple as an evening out.

Benedict's long legs stretched across the carriage into her space. As they bumped along the road on their way to the salon, one of them frequently pressed against hers. His leg was warm and muscular, even through the fabric of their clothing.

Lydia was glad for the dimness of the carriage for it kept her blushing cheeks hidden from his view.

Benedict had been rather stiff ever since their conversation that morning. She wasn't quite sure of the cause. Perhaps something she'd said had upset him. Could it have been her comments on his rakish reputation? She considered the idea but then dismissed it. Benedict was so easy-going, the first to laugh at a joke. Why would someone like him get upset about his own tarnished past?

She broke the silence. "I haven't thanked you, you know."

"What do you mean?" His familiar voice, so low and deep in the darkness, made her shiver as if it were a caress.

"You've done so much for me. Escorting me to Westminster, getting me out of prison, and then bailing out the others as well. Not to mention staying over so that you could keep an eye on everything. It's more than most people would do."

"I wouldn't have left you in Newgate," he said. "I *couldn't* have."

"Because I'm Jack's sister?"

"No." He'd answered so quickly, it was as if the denial could not be contained. "No," he repeated in a quieter voice, "not because you're Jack's sister."

Something strange swirled in Lydia's stomach. "So, you would have done it for anyone?"

"Lydia." His voice was velvet in the darkness, brushing against her skin. "I used every last bit of my power and influence to pull a magistrate away from his son's wedding party so that he could order the warden to release you from Newgate. Then I spent a fortune on bribes to release the others. So no, I wouldn't have done it for just anyone."

"Oh," Lydia breathed. *Oh.*

He done all that, for her. She felt weightless and golden, as if she were full of champagne bubbles. He bribed and pressured and cajoled…for *her.*

What did it mean?

Lydia, who was so good with words that she'd actually been kidnapped because of the power of her writing, could think of nothing to say. They rode the rest of the way to the salon in silence, but it was a warm, tingly sort of silence. And even though Benedict was across the carriage from her, it felt as if he were holding her hand. All too soon, they arrived at Lady Blaire's home.

Shortly, Lydia and Benedict were following a footman toward the back of the house where the salon was to be held. Mrs. Abbott trailed behind, a little bag with her knitting over her arm.

"I'll just find a wee corner and keep my hands busy," she had assured them both.

Lydia could feel the heat of Benedict's body through the fine wool of his jacket. She'd rested her hand in the crook of his arm as he held it out to escort her. His delicious scent teased her, and she inhaled it like a balm as the sound of many voices filtered into the hall, mixed together to create an indecipherable swell of noise. She couldn't let him know how much she longed to stay here with him a moment longer. Indeed, she'd promised to help him repair his reputation; they were required to be seen.

Lydia said, "Lady Blaire is a bit eccentric, but I believe her to be a most excellent hostess. I have high hopes for this salon." She gave his arm a little squeeze and felt the enticing swell and hard muscle of his bicep.

"How do you know her?" Benedict asked, as they continued to follow after the footman.

Lydia shrugged. "I've probably known her since I was little. My parents used to throw salons and parties and gatherings for all sorts of people. Artists, philosophers, political radicals... My parents were...neglectful... and no one stopped me from roaming the giant salons in my home, night after night, even though I was a young child."

Benedict's eyebrows bunched together. "Jack's mentioned that a few times. He made the upbringing you two had sound rather...unconventional."

Lydia snorted. "That's one word for it."

As they approached the end of the hallway, he slowed his footsteps. "What word would you use?"

Lydia wasn't sure why, but his question asked in that gentle tone made her eyes prick. She cleared her throat. "Chaotic."

They could stall no more, thankfully, and they entered the salon. It looked as if Lady Blaire had opened up double doors to connect a series of rooms so that her guests might have comfortable space to form groups of conversation. Some stood about in informal circles, drinks in hand, while they debated. Others were seated in clusters of chairs and chaises. Everywhere she looked people were talking, nodding their heads as they listened, or frowning their disagreement as they waited for their turns to make their points. Mrs. Abbott waved before making her way to a comfy chair in the corner.

"What do you think?" she asked Benedict.

"I think we both need a drink before we wade into this." He quirked a brow at her. "Champagne? Lemonade?"

"Lemonade, please."

Lydia surveyed the room once Benedict had left in search of refreshments. It was rather strange to be back in the world of salons again. Memories from her childhood pressed against her, causing Lydia's breath to catch in her throat. She ducked behind a potted plant and breathed slowly. This was fine. There were no children here. No neglect.

As she caught her breath, a group of women paused on the other side of Lydia's hiding spot.

"Did you see that Lord Lovell is here tonight?" one of them asked. Lydia recognized her voice. The woman was a widow although still young.

"I hear he's quite…adventurous." The second woman spoke in nearly a purr.

"Doesn't mind dipping his wick into more than one pot is what I heard," another said with a throaty laugh.

"Ah, look, there's Lady Clark. Let's say hello."

And with a whisper of swooshing silk, the women were gone.

Lydia frowned. She'd heard references to some scandal in Benedict's past and knew he was considered a rake, but the little snippets of gossip she'd heard here and there didn't create a clear picture of what had happened.

And…truth be told, it was hard to reconcile the public perception of Benedict with what she saw in private.

She reminded herself that was the reason they were here. She *knew* it was her job to rehabilitate his reputation. She *knew* his past was blemished in some way.

Did she need to know the sordid details to continue with their agreement?

Lydia exhaled slowly.

No. No, she did not.

With a nod to herself, she moved around the potted plant and spied Benedict approaching with their drinks.

"Lemonade for lovely Lydia," he said, handing her the glass with a smile.

She nodded at his glass of champagne. "And bubbles for Benedict?"

"Brave Benedict. Bold Benedict."

She quirked an eyebrow. "*Babbling* Benedict?"

He shook his head, but before he could offer what would surely be a lively rejoinder, their hostess approached.

"Lydia, darling! I'm so glad you could make it." The ostrich feathers from Lady Blaire's turban curved like a question mark to her forehead and quivered as she spoke.

"I'm so thankful you thought of me, Lady Blaire. I hope you don't mind that I brought a guest with me tonight. Please allow me to introduce Benedict Southcott, Lord Lovell."

Benedict took their hostess's hand in his and leaned over it, bussing his lips against her knuckles. "A pleasure, my Lady."

Lady Blaire twittered, causing her feathers to do a merry dance. "You are most welcome my lord. Although… I am rather surprised to see you here. With Lydia."

Lydia could not help but be impressed with Lady Blaire's ability to bask in Benedict's mild flirtation while simultaneously chastising him with her tone and one sharply raised eyebrow.

And here was where Lydia would do her part.

"Oh, Lady Blaire," Lydia gushed, "Benedict has been such a steady presence for me and my brother as of late. In fact, Jack was saying just the other day how he has come to rely upon Benedict's calm and steady advice both for matters in the House of Lords and also for the running of his estate." Lydia blinked up at Benedict in adoration.

His jaw pulsed a few times, but then he replied in his usual drawl, "I am most lucky in my friendship with Lord Hartwick."

"It sounds," Lady Blaire said, a look of consideration on her face, "that Lord Hartwick is lucky in his friendship with *you*."

Another lady was passing by, and Lady Blaire summoned her

over with a wave of her hand. "Winnie, darling! Come say hello to Lady Lydia and Lord Lovell."

Winnifred Richards had been Lady Blaire's longtime companion, ever since the death of Lord Blaire many years ago. The lady was as austerely dressed as Lady Blaire was ornamented. The severe cut and straight lines of her gown, while different from the current fashion, suited her frame, and the two women standing side-by-side made quite a picture.

In fact, Lydia suspected that they not only stood side-by-side in the salon, but also walked through life together side-by-side as lovers. Some might be scandalized by such things, but Lydia believed that love was love, and it warmed her heart to know that eccentric Lady Blaire had found the companion of her heart with whom to spend her life.

"Welcome to the salon," greeted Winnifred, her voice rich and mellifluous. She gazed between Lydia and Benedict, and her eyes shone with curiosity behind her spectacles. "I do admit, Lady Lydia, I expected to see you here with your brother and his new bride, and not with…this gentleman." Her voice dripped with suspicion.

With Winnifred, she would have to take a different tactic.

"My companion accompanied us, so there's no need to fret." Lydia gestured to Mrs. Abbott happily knitting a hat for the baby in the corner. "Unfortunately, Jack and Pippa were unable to attend tonight, so my brother sent me in his stead. And with Jack unavailable to entertain Lord Lovell here, I thought it best to provide the poor, bored man with a bit of…*stimulation* here at the salon."

Beside her, Benedict made a choking sound, but Winnifred let out a hearty laugh.

Lydia grinned at her.

"Stimulation you say?" Winnifred asked with a mischievous smile. "We can provide intellectual stimulation by the buckets, but for any other type…" She trailed off with a shrug followed by an eyebrow waggle.

"Oh Winnifred!" exclaimed Lady Blaire. "You are too naughty by half. Beware, or you shall scandalize the young people."

Benedict shifted from foot to foot, his discomfort evident.

"I think the only person I scandalized is poor Lord Lovell." Winnifred gave him a teasing wink.

Lydia assessed her companion. He did appear most uncomfortable. Perhaps she should have prepared a bit more for this evening, but she had to admit that he had reacted exactly as she had hoped. By stiffening up at her naughty comment, he had demonstrated to Lady Blaire and Winnifred that he was a respectable gentleman and that Lydia's reputation was quite safe with him as her companion. By the end of the salon, word of this *on dit* should have spread throughout the guests, and everyone would go home knowing that Benedict was a proper fellow.

This was only the first phase in her admittedly unfinished plan to rehabilitate his reputation, but it seemed like a good start.

After a bit of small talk and reminiscing about Lydia's parents, their hostess and her companion excused themselves to see to the other guests.

"That went about as well as it could go," Lydia whispered before sipping her lemonade.

Benedict didn't say anything.

Lydia searched his face. Though he had resumed his usually affable smile, she could see the tension in him. There was a slight tightening in his eyes that she'd noticed from time to time, when he seemed to be hiding his true feelings behind the veneer of a happy-go-lucky fellow.

"Are you having second thoughts about this?" She asked. "I just thought, with your promise to your sister…"

Benedict drew in a long breath. "No, it's fine. I suppose I hadn't considered how this little project would force me to look at my public persona straight on." He shrugged as if it were of trifling importance, but Lydia knew better.

"Benedict, you don't have to do this." Had she made an error? She hadn't meant for this to hurt his feelings. But it made sense that society showing their skepticism at one's suitability to escort a lady to a salon would sting.

He shook his head. "It's not important. Come. Let's find a group to join. Perhaps," he said, his tone turning teasing, "I can impress you with my opinions on the meaning of humankind or analysis of some ancient piece of art."

Lydia bit her lip in consternation but trailed after him in search of a group to join.

It was going to be a long night.

Chapter Nine

A S IT TURNED out, Benedict did not need to opine on the nature of humankind in order to participate in a conversation at the salon. Instead, he listened to a series of delightfully puzzling tales from Lydia's childhood.

"…and then the tiny child tiptoed over to me, pulled on the hem of my coat, and demanded that I teach her ten words in German." Baron von Pfistermeister, a white-haired gentleman originally from Bavaria, smiled fondly at Lydia.

"I think that by the time you finally left that house party," Lydia replied, "we were all the way up to verb conjugations."

The baron spoke in his native tongue, and to Benedict's shock, Lydia replied in what sounded like flawless German.

He leaned over to whisper in her ear, "Who are you?"

She shifted beside him on the chaise lounge. "I told you before, my childhood was rather chaotic. I ended up meeting a lot of interesting people and learning a lot of interesting things."

He stared into her deep-blue eyes, stunned into silence. He had known that she was brilliant, but not that she'd started to learn German as a tiny child from a guest at her parents' house party. He didn't think there was anyone else like Lydia in all of England. No, that couldn't be right; in all of the *world*.

Another member of their group leaned forward to speak. Like the rest, she was much older than Benedict and Lydia, and had been full of stories from what she referred to as the "golden days" of endless house parties, salons, and gatherings at the Hartwick country estate. It seemed that most of the older generation here at the salon had at one time or another been good friends with Lydia and Jack's parents who'd offered open invitations to all they knew to come to their home in the countryside and keep them entertained with lively salons.

What wasn't mentioned was how the parents' quest for continual gaiety led to the neglect of their estate, and more importantly, their children.

"You were always right there in the thick of things, Lydia dear," Lady Fleming said from her perch on a brocade chair. "I remember your brother Jack preferred to keep to himself when your house was full, but you always wanted to be right in the midst of the conversations. Do you remember the time when you challenged a theologian to prove that God existed?"

Lydia laughed. "If I recall, he came at me with some Descartes, and I was unable to think of a good counterargument."

Lady Fleming shook her head. "You must have been no more than ten or so. What a clever little thing you were."

"And what a clever lady she remains," Benedict interjected. These stories were fascinating, but it felt as if the baron, Lady Fleming, and the others knew the Lydia they had encountered as a child but no longer knew her as a woman full-grown.

Mrs. Ashford, another in their group who had joined in the reminiscing, said, "I'm sure you are quite right, Lord Lovell. Why, it's as plain as the nose on one's face that Lady Lydia has a keen intellect. In fact, I would be quite interested to hear your thoughts, my dear, on this recent movement for voting reform."

"An important topic, wot?" thundered a gentleman with bushy gray eyebrows. "I've been reading in the newspaper that the farmers and laborers of England wish to have a say in government. What do you have to say to that?"

"Well," Lady Fleming interjected, "it only seems sensible given the current corruption in the House of Commons."

Lydia leaned forward, and Benedict felt excitement vibrating off of her. "I wholeheartedly agree, Lady Fleming. As long as the House of Commons positions are apportioned through corrupt measures, England will never have justice or fair elections."

"Hear, hear," cheered Lady Fleming.

The others joined in with comments of their own, but Benedict heard them as if they spoke at the end of a long tunnel. The back of his neck prickled. Some wisp of a thought passed through his mind, but he was unable to latch onto it to recall where he'd heard Lydia's words before.

As long as the House of Commons positions are apportioned through corrupt measures, England will never have justice or fair elections.

He *knew* those words.

Perhaps Lydia had said them to him before? But he was certain they had never talked about voting reform until their encounter with the Stafford Female Reform Society.

"… and what do you think, Lord Lovell?"

Benedict blinked and found the group looking at him expectantly.

Where had he heard those words before? He couldn't get the question out of his mind.

"Er, I'm afraid I was woolgathering," he admitted, still distracted.

"We wondered what you thought on the question of ladies getting the vote," Lady Fleming said.

Benedict replied even as he racked his brain trying to recall where he'd heard those words before. "Oh, I think everyone should be allowed to vote."

The sudden quiet pulled him out of his thoughts.

Everyone was staring at him. Lydia's eyes were wide, and her mouth formed a perfect circle of surprise.

"Is that true?" Lydia asked, her voice pitched low. There was a certain urgency to her expression, as if his answer was of vital importance to her.

"Give *everyone* the vote?" Mr. Eyebrows exclaimed. "That's

quite a statement from a member of the House of Lords."

Benedict shifted in his seat. *Damn.* He should have been following the conversation more and being distracted by Lydia's comment less. Was it imprudent for him to say such a thing? He was a viscount after all. He belonged to the aristocracy. He had received his title, his fortune, and his land through no work of his own. Through no merit. Through nothing that he had earned or done or fought for. He'd simply been born the first son of another viscount.

And although he enjoyed his life and was grateful every day for all the benefits his position entailed—such as the ability to remove over a score of people from Newgate in one day—he also realized that the system was most unfair.

Why should he have a say in the running of the country when most of the people who actually lived in the country did not? Was he any smarter? Any nobler? Any more English than his fellow Englishmen and women?

"I know it's a bit radical," he finally answered, "but I do believe that every English adult ought to have a say in the running of England's government."

He glanced at Lydia, but before he could take in her expression, the others in the group reacted. Eyebrows leaned over and clapped him on the back. The baron raised his glass in salute. And Lady Fleming smiled at him so widely that he could probably count all her teeth.

"Lady Lydia, let me congratulate you on your choice of escort for this evening's salon," said Mrs. Ashfield. "It's quite clear that Lord Lovell is a fine and sensible man. Salt of the earth. Not at all like I'd heard."

And there it was again, the spectre of his reputation rising up to haunt him once more.

But before the itchy feeling of shame crept upon him, Benedict felt pressure against his foot. Glancing down, he realized that Lydia had pressed her foot to his. She hadn't said a word. She wasn't even looking at him right now. And yet he felt her support and approval all the same, and it warmed his chest in a most peculiar way.

He was about to lean over to ask her if she was ready to head home when someone called his name. "Benny!"

He turned to find his sister bearing down upon him, her eyes alight in unholy delight. Her call had turned several heads turn in their direction. Benedict lowered his head and groaned.

The night had just grown much more complicated.

LYDIA MADE THEIR excuses to Lady Fleming, the baron, and the others before she and Benedict walked over to greet Emelia.

"Benny," Emelia exclaimed, "what on earth are *you* doing at a salon? You do know that this is where the smart people socialize, right?"

Benedict rolled his eyes at his sister. "I'm more than just a pretty face, imp."

Lydia smiled. Instead of feeling jealous at their casual sibling banter as she might have in the past, she simply enjoyed their teasing since her relationship with her own sibling had improved so much in the past year. Truly, the difference between staid, duty-focused Jack and kind, supportive Jack—in love—was quite stark.

Emelia poked him in the ribs. "If I knew you were coming, I would have attended with you instead of accompanying my friend, Alice, and her family. Actually," she narrowed her eyes at him, "I haven't seen you at the house at all today or yesterday."

Lydia bit the inside of her cheek. He hadn't mentioned to his family that he was going to stay somewhere else? Where did they think he'd gone? If he was trying to avoid scandal to increase Emelia's prospects this season, then staying as an overnight guest at her house was quite counterproductive.

Benedict gave one of his famous lazy smiles and drawled,

"Worried about me, imp?"

Emelia frowned. "Actually, I am."

Benedict's smile faded from his face. "Er…"

But he was saved from having to come up with a Banbury tale by the arrival of a gentleman holding two cups of lemonade.

"Miss Southcott, I'm afraid I lost you in the crowd." The gentleman handed Emelia a lemonade, and she beamed at him.

"I'm so sorry, Lord Throckmorton," she replied. "I did not intend to abandon you, but when I saw my brother across the room, I simply had torture him a bit."

Lord Throckmorton's eyes widened, but then he relaxed once Benedict smiled affectionately at his sister. Lydia would bet all her pin money that the lord was an only child.

"It's nothing but torture and teasing until you need your quarterly allowance, and then I'm your favorite person in the world," drawled Benedict, but a twinkle in his eye took away any sting from his words.

Emelia made the introductions. Lord Throckmorton was slightly built with dark hair and kind eyes behind a pair of spectacles. And he was quite obviously infatuated with Emelia.

"And how do you find the salon, my lord?" asked Lydia.

Throckmorton sipped his lemonade before replying. "Miss Southcott and I just had a most enlivening discussion about quills."

Benedict eyed Throckmorton's glass of lemonade. "Quills?"

Lydia bit back a laugh. He'd said the word as if he suspected it was code for some instrument of debauchery.

"Well, quills *and* ink," Throckmorton clarified with a self-deprecating smile. "Most of human progress throughout history is owed to people writing down events, ideas, and arguments. And so, our little salon group discussed not only the messages, but how they were recorded."

"Although I wasn't able to contribute much to the conversation, I did find it quite fascinating." Emelia's light brown eyes, the exact same shade as her brother's, sparkled as she spoke. "I had always assumed a quill was a quill, but did you know that there are different sorts for different purposes?"

Throckmorton gazed at Emelia with such genuine enthusiasm that Lydia wondered if Emelia would soon have a beau.

"It's refreshing to find someone who also has such enthusiasm about the importance of both the written word *and* how it's recorded." Lydia smiled at Throckmorton. "I myself am quite partial to quills that haven't been treated with aqua fortis."

"Ah, yes," Throckmorton replied, "I've found that the aqua fortis treatment used to color the quills also makes them brittle."

At that, Benedict made a choking noise. Lydia shot daggers at him until he rolled his eyes in acknowledgement of his poor behavior and settled his face into an expression of bland curiosity.

"You're so knowledgeable," Emelia cooed at Throckmorton, fluttering her fan.

Was she being facetious? Lydia examined how Emelia was leaning toward the man, her bright eyes glued to him. It seemed she was truly entranced by bookish Throckmorton and his quill talk. Lydia hid a smile. Emelia had hidden depths, and it seemed she enjoyed a man who cared for more than just brandy and horse races.

He stared at Emelia, seeming to have fallen into a momentary trance under her regard. At last, he replied. "P-perhaps we could visit Bond Street one day this week. My favorite stationer shop has a vast ink and quill selection."

"I would be honored." Emelia fluttered her fan and lowered her eyes modestly, but Lydia could see her smile of triumph behind the fan.

Ah, the lady *had* found herself a beau. Good for her.

Throckmorton seemed to recall it wasn't just him and Emelia in the conversation because he blinked as if to clear his eyes and turned his attention to Lydia. "Are you a quill connoisseur, Lady Lydia?"

"A *quill* connoisseur?" repeated Benedict, his eyebrows halfway up his forehead.

Lydia wondered if anyone would notice if she stomped on his foot. Couldn't he see that a young romance was blossoming before their very eyes?

"I favor the crow quill myself," said Lydia. Although goose quills were more common, crow quills allowed for smaller writing. "I fit more onto each page that way, and my writing tends to be quite longwinded."

"Do you write very many letters then?" asked Emelia.

"Oh, letters and…er…all sorts of things," Lydia prevaricated. "The truth is, I haven't spent as much time at it the last handful of months." She felt that familiar twitch in her fingers. It was as if all this talk of quills and writing and preserving ideas for history— and voting rights—had brought her old desire to write about politics front and center once more.

She *did* miss it. But with the reform ladies, perhaps she'd find a way back to it.

Beside her, Benedict inhaled sharply through his nose. Lydia looked at him, but he was staring off into the distance, a pensive frown on his face. She couldn't help but admire the sight. What a jaw line Benedict had, and such noble features. He could serve as the model for a sculptor who chiseled Roman centurions or Greek gods.

"You know," Throckmorton said, "I also dabble in a bit of calligraphy. Miss Southcott, your initials would look quite elegant in a calligraphy monogram, the E and the S swirling together."

"I suppose it would look better than Benny's initials." Emelia's grin was pure devilry.

It took a moment for her meaning to sink in. Benedict Southcott's initials would be a monogrammed BS.

Lydia hid her chuckle by coughing into her hand. Throckmorton blinked at Emelia, a mixture of delight and shock in his expression. To be fair, she had that effect on many people. Rather like her brother.

Perhaps hoping to salvage the conversation, Throckmorton turned his attention back to Lydia. "And what is your surname,

Lady Lydia? I'm certain your monogrammed initials would be quite fine when done in calligraphy as well."

"Dashwood," Lydia replied.

"Ah, DL." Throckmorton stared into space for a moment as if drawing the two letters in his mind. "The combination of the straight lines in the elegant curves would be most pleasing to the eye."

"DL." Benedict stared at her, his expression growing hard. "DL," he repeated.

"I think my brother is wishing *he* knew how to do calligraphy," Emelia teased. "Or at least, more than two letters of the alphabet." She winked at Lydia before turning her attention back to Throckmorton. "Shall we circulate the room, my lord? There are so many interesting people in attendance tonight, and we simply must meet them all."

Throckmorton blinked, perhaps overwhelmed by meeting *all* those in attendance, but he readily agreed, and the two bid their farewells.

"Did we bore you with our talk of quills and calligraphy, *Benny?*" Lydia teased once they were alone.

Benedict's grave expression didn't even flicker at the nickname. "I need to speak to you in private. Right now."

"All right." Lydia frowned. What had she missed? "I suppose I could ask Lady Blaire if there's a room—"

Benedict shook his head. "Now."

He took her hand, and without another word he led her out of the salon rooms and back down the hallway. After checking a few closed doors, he walked them into a dim, cozy room. A faint glow came from embers in the fireplace, showing two overstuffed chairs and a few bookshelves filled with well-worn novels.

Perhaps Lady Blaire and Winnifred liked to retire here in the evening, reading together in companionable silence or sharing favorite passages while they sipped a bit of cognac. What a cozy picture. Would Lydia ever have that with someone? What sort of person would be *her* person? She glanced at Benedict and looked quickly away.

He pulled the door mostly shut, that little inch of space keeping them, while not exactly above reproach, at least somewhat respectable.

What was going on?

"Benedict, what's this—"

"Don't," he interrupted, pulling away from the cracked door.

Lydia frowned. Benedict had never spoken to her that way before. In fact, she had never heard him speak to *anyone* that way before. Benedict was the fellow who liked to joke, to laugh, and to be self-deprecating. He wasn't stern and stony.

But *this* Benedict paced the room while she watched in perplexed silence. She'd seen him do this yesterday at her home as well. Perhaps that was how his mind processed, each step assisting his brain in churning through his thoughts.

"Lydia," he finally said, "how long have we known each other?"

Lydia shook her head. "I don't understand. Why…?"

A muscle in his cheek pulsed as he stopped to look at her before he continued his pacing.

She huffed. "I suppose…ten years or more?"

Benedict nodded. His jaw was like granite. She felt a moment of sympathy for his poor molars that were surely being ground to dust. "Benedict what—"

"No." He stopped again and held up his hand to stop her from speaking.

Lydia put her hands on her hips and glared. This was ridiculous. He had every right to be mad or grumpy or whatever was going on right now, but that did not give him the right to *silence* her. She was about to tell him such when he began to speak.

"*You* have a favorite quill."

She narrowed her eyes at this *non sequitur*. "And?"

"You used to have ink-stained fingers all the time." He gave her a knowing look. "At least until a handful of months ago. And then you stopped having *any* ink on your fingers."

She'd stopped writing after her kidnapping. But he didn't know that. He didn't know any of it. So...where was he going with this? A trickle of unease crept along Lydia's spine.

"This happened," he continued, "around the same time that Jack told me you had been ill. No one saw you for over a week."

Lydia swallowed. "I was... I had come down with a fever. It was contagious."

He shook his head. "I don't think that's true. You see," he said, his tone turning almost conversational, "the lack of ink on your fingers, your prolonged absence from society with this alleged illness, and the cessation of articles from Democratium Liberum all happened at the same time."

Lydia's mouth dropped open. It felt as if a giant chasm of ice had opened up in front of her and she balanced on the very precipice. "I don't...what..."

"What you said when we were discussing voting reform back in the salon." He stared hard at her. "It was so familiar, but I couldn't recall a single time you and I had ever engaged in such a conversation. But then it hit me—it was the same thing written in an old Democratium Liberum article. I know, because I've read every single one of them countless times."

"You...you did?" Why, in the midst of this startling conversation, did she latch onto this particular comment? Perhaps she wanted to refuse to allow herself to look a step or two ahead to what she feared was coming. Or perhaps the fact that Benedict studied her words, had pored over them to the point that he had committed them to memory, meant something to her. She couldn't articulate why, but it was true.

"I've read them scores of times," he growled. "Perhaps hundreds of times." He moved to stand an arm's length in front of her. "I think I just about have them all memorized. Those articles have helped me search my values and beliefs as I've questioned what our government should be. *Who* our government should be. But it seems that *you* have the words memorized as well."

Lydia swallowed.

He took a step closer. "Why would that be, I wonder?"

Her heartbeat thundered in her chest. The warm light of the embers from the fire bathed his face in a golden glow, showing his light-brown eyes, the color of sherry. The faint lines that radiated from the corners of those eyes, hinting at the frequency of his smiles, and laughter. And the lush fullness of his mouth that looked almost obscene on such a tall, strong man. All of it, all of *him*, was focused on her. And even though she feared what would come next, something in her ached to close the final distance between them. To press herself against him. To fill his arms and have them wrap around her and hold her close.

It seemed he had fallen under the same spell, for his gaze roamed across her face and settled on her lips. Lydia let her tongue dart out to nervously lick at her dry lips, and something darkened in the depths of his sherry eyes.

He took another step forward until his legs pressed into the fullness of her gown. It felt like an echo of the closeness of their legs in the carriage on their way here tonight.

"And," he murmured, still staring at her mouth, "your initials. LD."

She couldn't look away or blink. She couldn't even draw a full breath. He was about to say her secret. Out loud. And there would be no way to turn back once it was said.

"Lydia Dashwood. LD. Democratium Liberum. DL," he rasped.

Lydia *had* to silence him. There was only one way.

He continued. "It's y—"

She rose up on her tiptoes and grabbed Benedict by the back of the neck. And then, she pressed her mouth to his.

For an endless, excruciating moment neither of them moved. Her skin burned in mortification even as the dangerous glacier chasm of fear threatened to engulf her.

But then…but then, he kissed her back.

His lips moved against her, soft and sure, and Lydia melted. His arms tightened around her. Her soft breasts pressed into the hard planes of his chest. His delicious scent enveloped her. And deep inside, Lydia quivered.

Benedict moaned in his throat, and her heart beat so quickly, she feared it might explode. When his tongue traced the seam of her lips, she gasped in surprise. Without hesitation, he licked into her mouth.

And now it was Lydia who moaned, but she could not feel embarrassed. All she could feel was pleasure. Her mouth tingled from Benedict's searing kisses. Her skin hummed where his hands roamed—across her back, into her hair, along her jaw. Everywhere he touched blazed, and the demanding beat of wanting pulsed through her body.

He pulled away from her mouth, and she gasped her displeasure. But he was not leaving. He was only moving to a new, untouched part of her, trailing kisses along her cheek, down her neck, and across her collarbone, then up the other side to behind her ear. And then back to her mouth once more. His mouth was everywhere. *He* was everywhere.

In between kisses he spoke. "Lydia. My heart. How I have dreamed of this moment."

His words turned her legs into water. She sagged, but the strength in his arms was more than capable of holding her up.

"Benedict," she gasped when he found a particularly tender spot on her neck.

This was *Benedict* she was kissing. Her brother's best friend. He of the drawling voice and sprawling form, like a powerful lion reclining as he surveyed his domain.

And he was kissing *her*. Lydia Dashwood. Writer of radical political articles. Scandal waiting to happen. If she were discovered…

She pulled back, gasping for breath.

His hold loosened, but his eyes continued to burn as if he consumed her with his gaze alone. "Lydia," he rasped. "I want…"

She pulled back more, shaking her head.

His arms tightened around her for the briefest moment, and

then he blinked and seemed to come back into himself. Perhaps he, too, was recalling who they were to each other. And perhaps, what he had been about to say before she'd kissed him and how those words, once spoken, could never be undone.

She raised her fingers to her tingling lips.

This kiss could not be undone either.

He exhaled slowly before speaking. "We should—"

But Lydia cut him off. "I want to go home now." She tucked her trembling hands behind her back.

He stared at her, his chest rising and falling with his rapid breaths. Despite the hunger in his eyes, the way his hands flexed as if he wanted to haul her against him once more, she wasn't afraid or worried. He wouldn't do anything she didn't wish him to do. She was certain of it.

His neck moved in a swallow and then shutters fell over his eyes. Would he mention Democratium Liberum again, and finish his accusation?

Instead, he gave a curt nod.

Lydia's legs wobbled in relief, and she clung to the side of the nearest chair to steady herself. Benedict peeked into the hallway before exiting, and she took a steadying breath before following him out of the room.

Lydia was barely aware of collecting Mrs. Abbott, making their farewells to their hostess, or waiting for the carriage. The ride after they'd returned Mrs. Abbott to her daughter's house was silent aside for the clip clop of the horses' hooves on the street.

Their legs didn't touch once.

But when they'd reached her home, they both came to a standstill in the foyer. The butler bobbed his head before disappearing from sight. All the reform ladies and their children seemed to be abed already, for the house was quiet, and it felt still.

She licked her lips before raising her gaze to his. They needed to say *something*. Surely they couldn't pretend nothing had happened. "Benedict…"

He tried to don a lazy smile, but it kept sliding off his face like little Timmy down the banister.

"Tomorrow," he finally said, his voice like gravel. And then he climbed the stairs and disappeared from sight.

Chapter Ten

B ENEDICT ATTEMPTED TO roll over in his bed, but the sheets were so twisted about him that he could not move. He opened one bleary eye to find the early morning sunshine peeking through the curtains of his room here at Lydia's house.

He groaned as he tried to untangle himself.

Had he even gotten a single hour of sleep?

He'd been unable to turn his mind off after all that had happened at the salon last night. First had been confronting the legacy of his reputation in the little comments the others made. Then he'd publicly confessed his support for universal suffrage, not the wisest move, given his position in parliament. That had been followed by his sister making moon eyes at some intellectual.

Just those would have been enough to affect any man's rest.

But no.

That had all paled in comparison to what came next. He'd discovered that Lydia was Democratium Liberum. And then she'd kissed him.

She'd. Kissed. Him.

Benedict wiggled in his bed.

It had been glorious. He had long dreamed—fantasized even—about holding her in his arms and kissing her senseless. But to actually taste her lips? To feel her tremble in his arms? It had been so much more than he'd imagined.

He finally managed to roll over and pressed his stiff cock into the mattress with a groan.

His memory of it was crystal clear. Lydia's lips moving against his own. Her tongue, so slick and sweet. And the little sounds she had made in the back of her throat, signaling her pleasure.

But what actually shook him to his foundation was more than just the pleasure to be found in the physical.

With his attraction to Lydia, it had always been *all* of her. Her quick mind, her clever retorts, and the way she never backed down from a challenge. God, he was so completely gone for her.

And then Jack's warning sounded in his mind, as clear as if they were sitting at a table in White's at this very moment.

She's not for the likes of you.

"Shit." He smashed his face deeper into the pillow.

If Jack found out what he had done...

Well, truth be told, what *she* had done. He couldn't decide between a smile and a howl. Lydia had kissed *him*. He was only guilty of kissing her back. Even so, Jack had warned him that Lydia was off-limits. And Benedict knew she'd only kissed him to stop him speaking. But... that didn't mean she hadn't meant it. Her ardor, her passion, that had all been real.

As real as his feelings for her.

And as real as the mess he now found himself in.

With another groan—his last of the day, he promised himself—he flung off the covers and crawled out of bed.

While completing his morning ablutions, he recalled another wrinkle in last night's outing—his sister staring up with those moon eyes at Throckmorton.

When his mother and sister had ambushed him the other morning before his ride, it had been an easy thing to agree to mind his reputation. Emelia wanting to improve her chances at a good match that season was completely reasonable. But it was all theoretical at that point.

Now Emelia had her sights locked in on her quarry. Benedict knew that most of society probably viewed his sister as pretty, witty, and great fun to have at a party. But what she usually kept under wraps outside of their home was her wicked sense of humor, her penchant for mischief, and the spontaneity of her desires.

When Emelia wanted something, she went for it.

He remembered when she'd been a small girl and had become enthralled with Benedict's stallion. She had waged such a cunning and unrelenting campaign for a horse of her own that within a month, Benedict had gifted a fine and high-spirited mare to her. Their mother claimed she was scandalized since most girls Emelia's age and size only rode ponies, but Benedict had seen her indulgent smile when Emelia tore across the green on the horse. And their father—

Benedict inhaled sharply and tugged his cravat into a ruthlessly tight knot.

The expression on his sister's face when she'd looked at Throckmorton had been exactly the same as when she'd first clapped eyes on his stallion. His sister was entranced with the man, and although the scholarly fellow would not have been Benedict's first choice for her, who was he to decide where affection or love would lay?

After all, he was certain the contents of his own heart would shock every last person in all of England.

He scowled into his mirror as he attempted to tame his hair. It had not seemed prudent to bring his valet with him here. The fewer people who knew where he rested his head at night, the less chance there was for scandal.

Scandal.

Now that the theoretical had become the tangible in terms of Emelia's prospects this season, he needed to keep any whiff of gossip away from him and his family name. And there was the rub. Because here he was, sleeping in Lydia's house, under the same roof as a score of women who had all just been in prison two short days prior. He was literally rubbing elbows with enemies of the Crown.

And one of them was the most infamous radical political writer in all of London. If anyone were to discover who Democratium Liberum was and then discover that Benedict was not only her friend but had also paid a substantial bribe to spring her from Newgate, then his reputation would be irrevocably ruined.

Emelia would be ruined.

And he just couldn't do that to his sister. But…he couldn't abandon Lydia either.

At least with the house full of reformers, he and Lydia were well chaperoned. If push came to shove, they had at least a modicum of protection to her reputation.

Benedict sighed.

Before exiting the bedroom, he shoved his feet into his tight boots. Blasted Hoby. Why did the famed bootmaker create such snug footwear?

Benedict strode down the hallway. There was only one way forward for him now. He would have to confront Lydia again, and this time he wouldn't let anything—not even a kiss or any other sensual ploy that might be in her arsenal—stop him from voicing his suspicion and demanding an explanation.

As he headed downstairs, he sniffed, but there was no tempting scent of bacon in the air. It was still too early to find her in the breakfast room then. Perhaps she was still abed.

For just a moment, he let his imagination picture it. Lydia, with her cheeks flushed with sleep and her hair strewn across the pillow. Perhaps her full pink lips would be parted as she breathed, slowly and steadily. What would she wear to sleep in, a thick flannel gown buttoned up to her neck? Or perhaps just a thin chemise that would show her sweet curves and hint at all the secret places of her body?

He swore quietly and viciously.

He heard a gasp, and a scandalized footman averted his gaze

before scurrying off. Benedict closed his eyes in regret at his profanity for a moment before continuing on his mission. What must her servants think of him here? What must they think of this whole situation, with country women and their babes roaming the earl's home?

He returned his attention to the matter at hand. Lydia. If she wasn't in bed—and he would not let himself picture that again for fear of scandalizing more than just the poor, beleaguered footman with his reaction—then she was most likely in her office.

And given what he'd learned last night, or at least suspected, he had an inkling of what she did in there. Usually, offices were the domain of men who oversaw their estate with a staggering amount of paperwork. From Benedict's experience in his own family, it seemed that women enjoyed spending their days in the sitting room, doing things like needlepoint, or sipping tea with their friends.

Although come to think of it, he couldn't picture Lydia or any of the LCA ladies spending their days in such a sedentary fashion. They were doers, filled with an energy and drive that he didn't fully understand yet. And the fact that Lydia would actually have a room she called her "office" should have filled him with suspicion. Ladies had sitting rooms and drawing rooms, but he'd believed until only recently that just men had offices.

And yet, here he was, knocking on the closed door of the room Lydia called "her office". Truly, it made his heart sink. How could he have been so blind? He gave the portal three hard raps.

"Come," she called in return.

Benedict opened the door slowly, as if he were opening the last present on Christmas day and wanted to prolong the sweet suspense for as long as possible.

"Is it time for breakfast already?" she muttered, clearly preoccupied as she bent over her desk with her quill—from a crow and without the usual aqua fortis treatment, if he had to guess—in her hand.

"Not quite."

She jerked up in surprise.

They stared at one another. Her blue eyes were wide as she took him in, and a pink flush crept up her cheeks. He'd kissed those cheeks just last night. He'd kissed those lips that even now her teeth worried at while she continued to stare.

"Good morning," he finally said, stepping into the office before tilting his head at the door in a question.

She nodded her consent, and he pushed it closed.

Lydia set down her quill and ever so casually draped another piece of parchment on top of the paper on which she'd been writing. Her fingers were dark with ink. And there was something about her, some vibrancy or spark, that had been missing for many months.

Ever since her illness, he realized.

"You," he blurted out, "are Democratium Liberum."

She swallowed. Her eyes rounded and the pink drained from her cheeks.

The air between them crackled with tension. She sat at her desk, every line of her body rigid and tight. What would she say?

When it seemed to Benedict like the silence was about to strangle him, she gave a sharp nod.

Benedict's chest hollowed out. He'd been right. And in that moment, he wished more than anything that he'd been wrong.

He exhaled, long and slow, before asking, "Will you explain it to me?"

She studied him for a moment, before she asked, "Will you tell my brother if I don't?"

Benedict stepped closer and shook his head. "I hope you'll tell me because you *want* to tell me. Because you *trust* me."

Lydia's brow furrowed, and she looked down at her stained fingers. "Surprisingly, I do want to tell you. But I…I can't tell you the whole of it. Other people were involved, and I cannot share their secrets."

He gestured to the small settee positioned under a window in the cozy room. She rose from her desk, and her shoulders were no longer tight with tension. Instead, they had an almost defeated slope to them.

Once they were both settled in and angled toward each other with their knees a scant inch apart, she began to speak.

"As you heard last night, I had a rather untraditional upbringing. My parents loved to throw house parties for their friends. They seemed to collect artists, thinkers, and anyone they found interesting in the same sort of way that others collect trinkets." She glanced down for a moment before continuing. "They paid little attention to me, and so I found my own entertainment, and perhaps my education, by interacting with their guests."

Benedict nodded. "The people at the salon last night seemed to have many fond memories of you as a child."

Lydia gave a rueful smile. "I was rather precocious, I admit. I joined in the debates and demanded to be taught that which I did not know. And in this way, I developed an interest and knowledge of political theory. John Locke, Rousseau, Montesquieu…" She shook her head. "Most girls my age were practicing their watercolors with the governess, but I was debating natural law and theories of consent of the governed."

Benedict forced himself to remain still on the settee and ignore the instinct to take her hand as she spoke of her youth.

"And where was Jack in all of this?"

Lydia's eyes turned sad. "Our parents were…not responsible in any sort of traditional way. They forgot to pay the servants or to collect the rents from the tenants. Why deal with those mundane things when there were parties to host?" Her laughter held no mirth. "And so, Jack did it."

Benedict frowned. "He found someone to take over the running of the estate?"

She shook her head. "He did it himself."

Benedict's eyebrows shot up, but he didn't say anything for fear that she'd stop speaking.

"He was just a child, but he took the housekeeper along on that first day and went out to collect the rents. He paid the servants so they wouldn't all walk out. The rest of the money, he locked up so our parents wouldn't spend it all." She sighed. "As you can imagine, running an estate as a mere child didn't leave him much time for his little sister."

Benedict decided to hell with restraint and clasped Lydia's hand in his. "That sounds so, so difficult."

Had there ever existed such inadequate words? His own father had not been an affectionate or loving man, but he hadn't abandoned Benedict and Emelia, and leaving them to deal with the harsh realities of life while he went in search of his own pleasure.

She stared down at their clasped hands. "It was difficult, but I think between the two of us, my brother had the harder road."

Benedict trailed his thumb over the back of Lydia's hand. Her skin was soft as silk, but he knew if he turned it over, he would find ink stains on her fingers, evidence of the labor that she undertook with her quill.

"How did all of that lead you to writing political essays for the newspaper?" He hoped she wouldn't spook now that they were at the crux of it. Part of him felt guilty for pushing for answers, but then he thought of his sister and pressed on.

Lydia did not speak for several moments, and Benedict wondered if she would answer at all. Perhaps she was merely gathering her thoughts. She squeezed his hand and then continued her tale.

"You saw last night the kind of influences I had as a child. Lady Blaire, the Baron, and the others—they're all what some might call 'radical thinkers'. They believe in universal suffrage, and they were never shy about sharing their reasons for it. My friend Jane would say that they planted seeds in the fertile soil of my young mind. And then those seeds were watered and fertilized as I continued to ask questions and read. The more I learned about politics, especially all the corruption, the more I felt compelled to speak up."

She tilted her chin back and glared up at the ceiling. "I just get so *mad*." Her hand flexed in his.

Benedict frowned at the *non sequitur*. "You're mad about…the corruption in government?"

Lydia huffed. "Yes, of course the corruption. It's enraging how the wealthy manipulate the rules to seize power. But what I meant is that, now, what really makes me to want to punch every single man right in his smug mouth is how women's voices are silenced."

She pulled her hand out of his. Benedict decided not to take that action, or her desire to punch all men, personally. This was his time to listen. To listen and learn, as she had about politics when she was young.

"It goes beyond society not listening to women," she continued. "Society *actively* stops us from speaking. We're taught these insipid, mindless things, the so-called *feminine arts*, instead of actual knowledge of the world." She grimaced and shook her head. "Actually, that's an unfair comment. Many women honestly enjoy needlepoint and the like. But we have no *choice*. Girls aren't sent to Eton. We're not allowed at Oxford or Cambridge. In most instances, a woman can't own property and doesn't even have a right to her own children if her husband decides to take them away for some reason."

Lydia jumped up from her seat, clearly too agitated to sit still. "Did you know that if a man grows tired of his wife, he can simply have her forcibly placed in an asylum? He pays off a doctor to call her insane, and the woman has absolutely no recourse."

Lydia moved to a bookshelf. She began pulling out books, barely glancing at their titles, and then inserting them somewhere new. It occurred to Benedict that Lydia coped with her strong emotions by rage organizing.

"I didn't know about women being stuffed into asylums," Benedict said. "That is truly horrifying."

Lydia swirled to face him, a book in each hand. "And what about the rest of it? The other things I told you—women being silenced and under-educated? Having no rights to property or their own children?"

Her chest heaved as her breaths sawed in and out, and her eyes were twin blue flames. He had never seen Lydia this angry before.

And he had never thought about what it really meant to be a woman in England—or anywhere, honestly—until this moment. Her anger was real. And it was completely justified. As a man, he didn't have to worry about losing his hypothetical children. He would never be plagued with concern that no one would listen to him. It had never even crossed his mind that a relative could potentially take a dislike to him and thrust him into an asylum for the rest of his life.

How *truly* reprehensible.

"All these things," he said slowly, clasping his hands together, "when you spell them out like this, when you line them up one after another and shine a light on them... are completely shocking."

Lydia's mouth worked. Perhaps she had been gearing up for an argument. But how could any decent man be presented with all this evidence and not agree that it was reprehensible?

Benedict closed his eyes when an ugly realization hit him.

Hadn't he done just that? He was a decent man—at least, he hoped he was. Aside from forcing someone into an asylum, he'd already known all the other pieces of evidence she had presented. It was common knowledge, but had he ever spent time, real, soul-searching time, thinking about women's lack of voice or power? Had he even once considered formulating a plan on how he could create change? And he was in the House of Lords. He actually *could* make change. Wasn't he just as bad as the rest of his gender with his inaction?

"Lydia." He took a moment to swallow past the lump in his throat. "We've failed you. Men. All of us, including...including myself. We've accepted what is instead of questioning what could be. What *should* be. And that's...so very wrong. I'm sorry."

Her chin quivered, and he saw her swallow, then swallow

again.

"Thank you for hearing me." Her voice was shaky.

Benedict nodded.

They stayed like that for the long span of many heartbeats—her standing in front of the bookcase, two heavy tomes of learning hoisted in her hands. And him, seated on the comfortable settee, his hands at leisure. *How symbolic.*

She let out a long, loud breath and finally set the books back onto the shelf before rejoining him on the settee. "I'm so angry. All the time."

"Anger is a reasonable reaction to such oppression."

Her eyebrows drew together. "You're a lot more open-minded to all of this than I had imagined. It didn't even occur to me that you would…"

Benedict's mouth twisted. "It didn't occur to you that a rake like me, a thick-skulled and pampered aristocrat with a scandalous past, could comprehend the ways in which women have been rendered *less than?*"

The corner of Lydia's mouth quirked upward. "Well…yes."

Benedict leaned back, giving himself a moment to process all that she'd said. His eyes roamed around her study, taking in the bookshelves, packed with knowledge. The stacks and stacks of paper covered in what he guessed were likely political writings. And the half-used pots of ink, discarded quills; all of it, he suddenly noticed, were covered in quite a bit of dust.

"You haven't been in here for a while."

She started beside him. "What?"

"It's dusty in here. My guess is you don't allow anyone else to clean your study because you don't want the servants to know your secrets." He paused, thinking. "For some reason," he said slowly, "you haven't been in here yourself for a while."

What had stopped her writing?

She stared at him, her gaze assessing. She was weighing right at this moment whether or not to tell him more of her secrets.

Would she trust him? Benedict leaned forward. It felt like

everything hinged on this moment. Whether she opened up to him or not would determine their entire future together.

She leaned forward as well, and Benedict's heart thundered in his chest.

She opened her mouth. "Last year—"

The door flew open with a bang. "My lady," gasped a maid. "You're needed downstairs. Immediately."

LYDIA SPED DOWN the stairs, her hands ghosting along the top of the banister. Benedict was right on her heels.

She hadn't even asked the maid what had happened, but had merely gasped out, "Where?"

Was it news of Jack and Pippa? Had something befallen her brother and sister-in-law? Her stomach clenched at the possibilities. Or perhaps Jane and her new husband Dev? But surely they were safe on their honeymoon?

Or perhaps something had happened to the reform ladies or their children. Had Timmy finally taken this very banister with too much speed and cracked his skull on the marble floor below?

With that sobering thought, Lydia checked her own pace. It would not do to have two bloodied patients for a doctor to examine. She yanked open the door to the sitting room with sweaty palms but then stopped short. Benedict ran right into her.

"Oof," she grunted, staggering forward.

Benedict followed her in, and they stood side-by-side, staring at the visitor.

The man sat in Lydia's favorite chair. A tray with tea things had already been delivered to the room. He sipped out of one of Lydia's finest teacups, from the china set reserved for special guests, with one eyebrow cocked as if inquiring why they had interrupted his leisure. As if this was his sitting room. The gall of the man.

"Mr. Staines," Lydia gritted out. "To what do we owe the *pleasure?*"

Staines lowered the teacup and delicately dabbed at the corners of his mouth with a napkin before answering.

"Lady Lydia Dashwood," he greeted, his voice as cold as an icicle. "And Mr.... I'm sorry, but you did not give me your name last time we met. Friend of the family, wasn't it?"

The man's flat gray eyes assessed them, and Lydia pictured a wolf hunting its prey in the dead of winter. She shivered.

"It seems you've made yourself comfortable," Benedict replied instead, completely ignoring the request for his name.

Staines set the teacup down on the low table in front of him, turning the cup in the saucer until the handle was at an exact ninety degrees from the table's edge. "Ah, yes. The servants were quite accommodating." He paused. "Once I told them I was from the Office of Public Order."

His eyebrows lifted the barest amount, as if he had thrown down some sort of gauntlet. Lydia hid her fisted hands in her skirt. This man was the personification of all those things she had said to Benedict upstairs in her office—how women were silenced, kept ignorant, and often had no legal recourse to protect themselves. She thought about them, and they made her angry. *He* made her angry.

And her anger gave her strength.

Lydia caught Benedict's eye. His mouth was pinched as if he smelled something distasteful. Thank goodness he was here. She couldn't imagine facing this nasty, wretched man on her own. Not that she couldn't. She knew she was strong. She knew her worth and her power. But even a strong person needed support sometimes. And, strange though it may be, over the last few days Benedict had become *her* support.

She blinked at the realization. She *did* rely on Benedict, and she *did* trust him. Somehow, he'd slipped beneath her wariness of men since her kidnapping. And she was so glad that he had.

Lydia moved to the sofa and Benedict followed suit, perching at the other end. With shaking hands, she poured them both a cup of tea, because it was what a person did when visitors—invited or not—arrived in one's home. Though she doubted she would touch hers. She moved her cup to the side table before she said, archly, "Tell me, Mr. Staines, how may I help you today?"

Staines tapped a finger against his chin. "I had assumed your visit to my office the other day would be the end of our interaction. But then, I heard a most peculiar rumor." He let the words hang in the air for a moment.

Lydia's breath caught, and beside her on the sofa, Benedict stiffened.

"Oh?" She fought to keep her tone free of trepidation.

"It seems, my lady," he said, seeming to relish his words, "that you found yourself in a bit of trouble with the law after our little chat."

Damnation.

He knew about her arrest. Did that mean he also knew that the reform group was staying here with her?

"Ah, yes." She managed a stilted twitter. "Can you imagine my surprise when I left Westminster only to find myself swept up into a *protest*? And they hauled me in to prison with the rest of them. Outrageous! Thankfully, my dear family friend"—she gestured to Benedict—"was able to secure my release, and I did not have to spend the night in a jail cell."

Staines tapped his chin again. Was that a hint of a smile on the fiend's face? "Yes, my sources told me all of that. But they also told me..." The dreadful man leaned forward to pick up his teacup, take the veriest of sips, and then return it to the saucer, spending several long moments turning it to just the precise angle before he gave Lydia his attention once more.

Oh, she hated him, and yet, she couldn't help but admit that he was a master at this sort of thing. The silence stretched on for several agonizing moments. Lydia would not give him the satisfaction of asking.

The ormulu clock ticked loudly into the endless silence. She wouldn't ask. Absolutely not.

"Told you what?" she blurted before biting at her lips. *How vexatious.*

"My sources told me of the others who were released shortly after you. Those *reform women*." He said the words as if they tasted foul upon his tongue. "Although it is quite understandable why *you* would be released from Newgate, my lady, I'm sure you can understand my curiosity as to why the others were also set free. Unfortunately, it seems the warden misplaced the paperwork from that day, and so I find myself at loose ends and looking for answers." He cocked his head to the side with an almost lazy movement. "Looking for answers…from you."

Chapter Eleven

S TAINES TRULY HAD the most punchable face Benedict had ever
seen. The man's appearance would be vastly improved with a
crooked nose, a swollen eye, and a bit of blood in his teeth.

While he could not and would never fully know the anger
that Lydia and other women had to live with every day due to the
inequality in their society, he felt like this current hot coal
burning in his chest was perhaps a small piece of the conflagration
they must feel all the time. He looked at Lydia beside him on the
sofa. She met his gaze, and he saw in her lovely blue eyes a
mixture of fear and fury.

He cocked an eyebrow. *Shall I punch him?*

She shook her head. *No.*

Then the corner of her mouth twitched. *At least, not today.*

How incredible, to be able to hold an entire conversation
using only the smallest of facial movements. They'd known one
another for years, but the last few days had created a closeness
between them that hadn't been there before.

Lydia turned back to Staines. "And how might *I* help you in
this matter?"

Again, Staines went through the motions of sipping his tea
and taking his sweet time to return the cup to the correct spot on
the table. The way the man aligned it with such care suggested
that if it were a hair's breadth out of place, an incendiary device

would be triggered, and the entire house would come crashing down upon their ears.

Staines touched his forefinger to his chin. "There was some indication from the guards that the radicals left in your care."

The way he stared without blinking at Lydia reminded Benedict of a reptile.

"The guards said that?" Lydia frowned. "How odd. I thought their job was to monitor those *inside* Newgate, and not those who had been properly released from the premises."

Staines's eyes narrowed. "Did the radicals," he asked, biting each word, "leave in your care?"

Lydia leaned forward and pinched the delicate handle of her teacup. She raised it to her mouth, her arm like an elderly ballerina, slow and graceful, before taking the tiniest of sips. With great care and concentration, she returned the teacup to its saucer…and then flicked its handle, causing the teacup to wobble until it settled in a location on the saucer of its own choosing.

Benedict managed to avoid applauding, but it was a near thing.

"I believe I *do* recall the reformers of whom you are speaking." Lydia put a finger to her chin in an uncanny impersonation of Staines's strange habit.

She turned to face Benedict. "They asked for help in securing some hackneys, didn't they?"

"Well, let me think…" Benedict took a long minute to add cream and sugar to his teacup, stirring them in with care before tapping the spoon twice against the edge of the cup. Then he took a loud, slurping gulp and plunked the teacup down on the bare wood of the table, completely ignoring his saucer.

It was pure anarchy. Well, the English version of it, anyway.

He didn't let himself look up to gauge either Staines or Lydia's expression for fear he would laugh. How odd, to share in this amusing teatime game along with Lydia in the midst of all this tension.

Benedict made a show of scratching his head as if in deep

thought. "Why yes, I do seem to recall that those ladies had asked for help. Can't say that I blame them. If *I* had been peacefully protesting and then thrown into prison with my young children, I suppose *I* would be a bit discombobulated too."

Lydia nodded several times. "Yes, it's most upsetting to find oneself thrown into prison when one hasn't committed a crime. Have you ever found yourself behind bars, Mr. Staines?" She blinked her wide blue eyes innocently.

A deep red spread across Staines's face. "I've never been to prison," he bit out. "*I* follow the rules."

"Isn't that interesting," Lydia chirped, tilting her head. "I don't believe *I* broke any rules as I was leaving Westminster, and yet I *did* find myself behind bars. Either I must have hallucinated the whole thing, or perhaps there are some flaws in our justice system." And she blinked her eyes some more. "It's *so* hard to know."

Staines shot to his feet. "Now see here—"

Benedict stood with his usual, leisurely speed. "I do believe," he said, picking an imaginary bit of lint off of his coat sleeve, "that *you* need to see here."

"What—how dare you—" Staines sputtered.

"*What* I am," Benedict drawled, "is a viscount."

Staines's face turned redder still.

"And *how I dare*," Benedict continued, "is because I'm a member of the House of Lords."

Benedict glanced over at Lydia. "My dear Lady Lydia," he asked in a conversational tone, "do you happen to know what the House of Lords has control over?"

"No," cooed Lydia, resting her chin on her hand as if completely enthralled with the topic. "What *does* the House of Lords have control over?"

Benedict was enjoying this far too much. "Well, I am but a lowly member of our nation's Parliament, so it's hard to know for certain...but I do believe the Lord's has control over the *budget* for the Office of Public Order."

Benedict flicked his gaze to Staines. The man's face had gone quite white—rather a sight given its ruddy hue only moments before—and his eyes resembled those of a ragged rabid dog Benedict had seen once, right before it attacked a man and tried to rip his arm off with its froth-covered teeth.

"Any further questions for us, Staines?" Benedict asked, as he examined his fingernails.

Even still, as he kept his posture and median loose and lazy, Benedict watched the man out of the corner of his eye and was ready to pounce if he so much as twitched in Lydia's direction.

The ticking of the ormulu clock on the mantle rang through the silent sitting room.

At last, Staines seemed capable of unlocking his tension-seized joints. "I shall see myself out," he spat through gritted teeth.

Benedict watched him throw open the sitting room door, listened to his angry footsteps across the marble foyer, and heard the crash as the front door slammed.

"What a charming man," Benedict drawled. "We must simply invite him over for a dinner party sometime soon."

⇶⇜

LYDIA SLUMPED BACK onto the sofa and threw her hand over her eyes. What had they done?

"I fear," she said, "that I may have let my temper get the best of me."

"Oh?" Benedict's weight sunk back onto the sofa. "Was that perhaps when you taunted him with his own maddening tea routine? Or perhaps when you so obviously pretended not to know anything about the reformers?" He chuckled. "I must admit, I did enjoy giving that blighter a hard time with you."

Lydia smiled behind her hands, but still groaned, "What a mess."

And it *was* a mess but had been strangely invigorating too.

Having Benedict at her side and facing a challenge together had proven to be quite helpful. If she'd had to face Staines alone, who knows how the meeting would've gone.

Mrs. Smythe burst into the sitting room, her mobcap askew. "He's gone then?" she asked, out of breath.

"Yes," Lydia said, sitting forward. "Where are the reformers?"

The housekeeper wiped the back of her hand across her forehead. "The instant that Staines fellow arrived, one of the footmen notified me. I ran upstairs and gathered all the guests telling them to be nice and quiet. I took them up the servant stairs to the top floor."

The top floor was the servants' quarters. With an entire floor between that level and the one they were on now, it would've been unlikely that any noise would have filtered down to Staines.

"Well done," Benedict said, all traces of the usual droll voice he adopted with the housekeeper gone. "That was very fast thinking."

"Oh, it was nothing," Mrs. Smythe twittered. It seemed she wasn't immune to his charm even when he wasn't trying to use any.

Naughty man. He was probably planning a way to receive a lifetime supply of strawberry jam. Lydia fought back her smile and rose to her feet. "Shall we head upstairs?" she asked Benedict.

They followed Mrs. Smythe to where the reformers had gathered in several of the empty servants' quarters. There were only a few that were currently unoccupied since Mrs. Smythe had hired extra temporary servants to assist with the houseful of guests.

Agatha surged to her feet and rushed over as soon as she sighted them. Her face was lined with worry. "What's happened?"

Lydia took her hand. "Staines heard a rumor that we assisted you after your arrest and came to see what he could sniff out. But," she assured the reform group's leader, "He's gone now."

Murmurs arose from the other women in the room. More

were gathered in the hallway behind her and Benedict.

"Are we putting you in danger?" Grace asked, rubbing her hand over her pregnant belly.

"Although Staines is a government official with much power at his disposal," Benedict answered, "he doesn't want to tangle with a member of the House of Lords. I can promise you that we are in no danger."

Grace's shoulders sagged in relief.

"But what does this mean for us?" asked Harriet, little Timmy at her side.

Lydia looked at Benedict. They hadn't had time to discuss their options with Mrs. Smythe dashing in so soon after Staines had left. Although his expression was calm, she saw the hint of worry in his golden-brown eyes.

Lydia scanned the faces of the women. Everyone looked concerned. "As long as you stay here," she told them, "you're safe. And you are welcome to stay here as long as you wish."

"I fear we've pulled you too deeply into our troubles, love," Agatha said. Her voice, usually so strong and sure, now sounded thin.

Lydia shook her head. "In this instance, your troubles are my troubles too. Reform and suffrage have been important causes to me since I was child."

Agatha's eyebrows shot up. She clearly thought Lydia was telling a Banbury tale just to reassure her.

"It's true," Benedict said. The soft timbre of sincerity in his voice supported his words. "Lady Lydia was reading Montesquieu when she was practically still in her leading strings."

Lydia rolled her eyes. But when she glanced over at Benedict, she found herself staring at the mirth dancing in his eyes and the fine curve of his full lips. As it seemed to do every time she was around him, her stomach flipped over.

She'd kissed those lips. She'd seen the flare of desire in those eyes. Desire for *her*. Oh, merciful heavens. What a time to dive back into her memory of their kiss!

"Well, I'm not too sure about this Mont-squiggle fellow," Harriet said, pulling Lydia back into the conversation. "But if you support the cause and are unafraid of the risks, then I vote we stay and fight."

"Stay and fight! Stay and fight!" Timmy chanted, dancing a little jig that caused his mop of sandy hair to bounce about.

Lydia smiled at the boy. "You aren't afraid of going to prison again?" There was a real possibility that they might all see the inside of a Newgate cell once more if they continued down this path.

"I already been once," Timmy bragged. "It ain't so bad."

Harriet pressed her hands to her mouth. *Oh dear.* Had the thought of her child being in prison again upset her?

To Lydia's surprise, Timmy's mother began to snicker.

"How can Staines possibly frighten us?" she said with a grin. "Timmy has the right of it. We've already been to prison, and *it ain't so bad.*"

Timmy beamed up at his mom, showing off the adorable gaps in his teeth.

Lydia's chest tightened as she looked around the room. These women and their children were so brave. The reformers had been locked up, but they weren't deterred.

In the face of their courage, Lydia felt humbled. Her own fear after her kidnapping had been paralyzing in many ways. She'd stopped writing. She hadn't even contacted the editor of the newspaper where she had sent her articles, via a courier, to explain her absence. She'd simply ceased to send anything at all. And although her kidnapping had lasted for a full week instead of just the few hours she and the reformers had spent in Newgate, the sense of helplessness at being locked up was the same in both cases.

But what had Lydia done after her rescue by Jack and Pippa? She gave up Democratium Liberum without a second thought.

She'd simply stopped writing.

And she'd also stopped trusting. The man she had thought

could be her beau had merely been manipulating her, attempting to woo her so that he might lure her away and into his employer's grasp.

But she was seeing now that there was another response to a fearful experience: she could be brave. Like sweet little Timmy. And like Grace, Harriet, Agatha, and all the rest of the reformers.

Lydia took a deep breath, then asked them, "Have you talked about next steps?"

Although the reformers had remained safely ensconced inside her house since their arrival, she knew they had been meeting to plan their strategy. They hadn't come all the way from Stafford to merely vacation for a week in an aristocratic home. They wanted to fight for change.

"We've been talking," Agatha said, "and we'd like to go to places where the working-class folks congregate here in London. Perhaps the markets or public houses? We want to distribute pamphlets and see if we can bring others into our cause."

Lydia's fingers twitched.

"Have you heard from your source?" asked Grace. "The one who knows Democratium Liberum?"

Lydia felt Benedict's gaze on her, calm and steady, and she knew—now—that he would support her, no matter what she did.

She straightened her shoulders. "He's agreed to write for you. In fact, he's already sent over a draft for your pamphlet."

Excited murmurs came from the reformers.

Agatha nodded, looking impressed. "That was quite quick, love."

"Well," Lydia said briskly, "my contact shared how urgent this was."

Again she experienced a twinge of guilt for lying to these good people, but secrecy had become second nature to her since she'd joined the Ladies Covert Academy. Secrets were the only way to keep herself, the LCA, and even these reformers safe.

Her gaze flicked back to Benedict. He knew. Would he keep her secret? She waited for that familiar feeling of distrust to weigh down her stomach, but it didn't come.

Benedict was showing her who he was, and it was someone completely opposite of the men who'd planned her kidnapping.

"Well, my friends," Agatha began, scanning the room and hallway and taking in her group of determined reformers. Her gaze lingered on her pregnant daughter, on little Timmy, and on the rest of the children. Her jaw tightened with determination before she continued. "Since we're moving ahead with our plans, we're going to do this safely. We'll leave the children here, if that's all right with you?" She addressed the last to Lydia.

She nodded. She would speak to Mrs. Smythe about which of the maids would be a good fit as a temporary nanny.

"We will not wear white," Agatha continued. "We don't want to make it any easier for Staines or the authorities to spot us. And—" she looked her fellow reformers in their eyes—"we split up."

Murmurs of dissent came from the others.

Agatha raised her hand. "I know this is different from how we've operated before, but it will keep us safe. If there are several small groups of us, it will be easier for us to split up if any trouble comes. And if some of us are taken…" She trailed off.

The other reformers watched their leader, their faces grave. A few nodded. One woman wiped at her eyes. Another held her child close.

Lydia clutched her hands together. Benedict glanced at her, his mouth tight. They both knew what these women were saying.

If some of them were taken and thrown into Newgate for a longer stay, the others would at least be safe and care for the missing mothers' children. They didn't need to speak the words aloud. They all knew.

Lydia thought of her friends in the Ladies Covert Academy. Jane and Pippa. Meera and Lady Rowling and all the others. The connection between these reformers reminded her of the bonds between Ladies Covert Academy members. It was the same—the unspoken connection to one another, the silent vow to assist if another should be in need of aid. She remembered how she and Pippa had come to Jane's aid a few months earlier when Jane's now-husband Dev's distant relative had tried to steal his title. And how Jane had come along with Jack to rescue Lydia. She'd climbed up the side of a rain-slick building in the middle of a violent storm to rescue her and had fought off armed men with an ornamental sword she'd pulled off the wall.

These friends, they didn't think of the cost. They simply did what was right, what was needed to help a friend.

And it was the same with these women.

She turned to Benedict, wanting to share this realization with him. He was already watching her, his face, now so familiar to her, etched with understanding. Lydia contemplated slipping her hand into his, but… no. She didn't feel brave with her affections in front of others.

"When shall we go?" ask Harriet.

Lydia turned a questioning gaze to Agatha.

"As soon as possible," their leader said.

Lydia nodded. "I'll give you the draft from Democratium Liberum," she said. "After you've made any edits, I'll send it to a printer I know. She's quick and discreet, two things we need right now."

And then she looked at Benedict. He gave her a small nod of approval. They were in this together now.

"We'll go tomorrow," she said, addressing the women.

But her gaze never strayed from Benedict.

Chapter Twelve

BENEDICT STRODE THROUGH the familiar hallways of his home. "Emelia? Mother?"

"In here," his sister called from the back of the house.

He never knew where to find them. His mother had preferred to keep herself very busy ever since her husband had passed, and she usually had three or four projects underway at the same time. And depending on his sister's outlook each day, Emelia could either be found assisting her mother or avoiding her presence.

Guilt sat heavy on Benedict's shoulders.

He owed them an explanation for his absence during the last few days. It wasn't unheard of for him to not return home at night. When Parliament was in session and he was busy with debates and voting, he sometimes slept at his office in Westminster. But as he had been gone for more than a single night, he wanted to explain his absence.

It was the explaining part that was difficult. Hopefully, at any moment his subconscious would fabricate a perfectly plausible tale.

He could hardly admit to staying at Lydia's house without a chaperone. Twenty or so sensible women from the countryside were surely adequate for the job, but since he couldn't publicly speak about them, invoking their presence as agents of propriety was not an option.

Although it was of lesser importance, he'd also needed to return home to grab more clothes. He'd originally instructed his valet to throw in enough for just a few nights, but his stay at Lydia's house was looking to be more than that. And besides, Benedict had a rather dashing bottle green waistcoat he was itching to wear in front of Lydia.

Not that he wanted to impress her or anything.

Benedict pinched the bridge of her nose. Of *course*, he wanted to impress her. There was nothing more important to him of late than impressing Lady Lydia Dashwood.

"Are you coming, or have you gotten lost in your own home?" called Emelia.

Well, maybe. Nothing was more important than his family. With that admonishment, Benedict ambled into the small sitting room toward the back of the house. A much grander sitting room close to the front door was used to receive company but this room, in contrast, was entirely for the family's private use. The furniture was comfortable and too worn to be fashionable. Piles of books, baskets of yarn, and a stack of newspapers cluttered the room. Benedict thought of this place, one where he'd spent so many hours with Emelia and their mother, as a sanctuary of sorts.

"I was beginning to wonder if you had forgotten our address," Emelia said archly when Benedict entered the room.

Flopping beside her on the sofa, he grumbled, "I haven't been gone *that* long." He gently nudged her shoulder.

She nudged back. "No more bumping me about. You'll cause me to drop a stitch."

Benedict examined her knitting. "Another scarf?"

"I only know how to do rectangles," she moaned, waving the scarf in the air. "Anytime I ask mother to teach me more stitches, she insists I do embroidery instead." She shuddered. "I despise embroidery. It's basically a nerve-wracking game of *when will I next draw blood?*"

Benedict smiled. His sister was one of his favorite people in the world. He would do anything for her. Even, it seemed, address the old rumors of his bad reputation.

His smile faded.

Emelia moved her knitting to the side. "Where have you been the last few days?" she asked softly.

Benedict fidgeted, plucking at a feather he'd noticed sticking out of the cushion. "I've been staying at Jack's." It was all he could come up with, and it had the benefit of being true.

Sort of.

"But is there a reason you've stayed away?" asked Emelia, her forehead creasing.

Benedict shook his head. "I've taken on a bit of a…project. At Jack's place. It's been easier to stay there and give it all my focus. But I should be home soon." He arched an eyebrow and tried to inject a bit of humor into his tone. "What, are you that bored without me around to torture?"

Emelia sniffed. "Certainly not. I merely wished to ascertain whether or not you were dead in a ditch."

"Would you have allowed yourself one single, perfect tear if that had been the case?"

"Are you joking?" Emelia flung her hand to her chest dramatically. "I would have to go to the cemetery and stomp on your grave for forcing me to wear black crêpe for an entire year. It's a ghastly color with my complexion."

Benedict laughed. "Well, I shall avoid ditches, if only for the sake of your complexion."

They fell into a companionable silence, and Emelia took up her knitting again. Benedict watched her fingers' deft movements.

"Do you enjoy knitting?" he asked.

"Certainly. How else would we all keep our necks warm?"

He continued to watch her needles clicking back and forth. "And what of the other so-called feminine pursuits you and other young ladies are encouraged to take up? Do you enjoy them?"

Emelia glanced up from her knitting. "What a strange thing to ask."

"It's just that someone pointed out to me," he said, his face feeling hot, "that women aren't given the same opportunities as men. You are taught to paint watercolors and knit and even do that horrible game of guessing when you'll prick your finger. But…did you ever want to do something else?"

Emelia rested her knitting on her lap and eyed him speculatively. "Is this a trick question?"

Benedict held up his hands. "I genuinely want to know. The inequality between men and women has recently been pointed out to me by someone I respect, and… I'm looking at things with new eyes."

She pursed her lips, then blurted out, "Mathematics."

"Mathematics?" Benedict repeated, surprised.

"You know, that thing men do where they add and subtract numbers?" Emelia's mouth twisted up at the side. "At finishing school, I was top of my class in mathematics. I loved it. Solving difficult equations and studying mathematic principles…it was fascinating to me. But we were only allowed to take so many academic classes. We needed to leave time in our schedule for more important training in the so-called feminine arts. We had to study deportment, dancing, and pouring tea in the most elegant manner, on the off chance that the Prince Regent ever stopped by for a cup. I suppose," Emelia said, her voice turning bitter, "that mathematics was not considered useful in finding a husband. Or impressing princes."

"Oh, Em," he murmured. "I'm sorry I never thought to ask before. What a selfish bastard I've been."

"Language," Emelia scolded, but it lacked her familiar teasing lilt.

"It's not too late you know." He itched with the urge to do something immediately. To make this right. To fix it now. "I could arrange for a mathematics tutor before the end of the week."

Emelia blinked at him in surprise and examined his face for a moment. "You really would, wouldn't you?"

Benedict laid his right hand over his heart. "Whatever you ask, I will try to do."

He hoped it wasn't too late to make a difference for his sister. He couldn't change society—although perhaps he could see what might be done in Parliament—but he could change how his family worked and ensure that the women in this household knew that they had power and choices.

What would Lydia think? Over the last few days, it was her opinion and her viewpoint that mattered more than anyone else's. Before, he'd wondered what Jack might say, or even his mother, but now…it was just her.

"Whatever I ask, hm?" Emelia's eyes glinted with mischief. "And what if I asked you to escort me to Lady Marwood's ball tonight?"

Benedict leaned back and groaned. "You are an imp."

Emelia threw her ball of yarn at him. "*You're* an imp."

"What an impressive retort," Benedict drawled, tossing the yarn from one hand to another.

She snatched the ball of yarn back. "But will you take me? Mother's not able to go tonight, and someone will be there who I would like to see."

Benedict arched an eyebrow. "Might this 'someone' be Throckmorton? He of the quills and calligraphy? Don't tell me he's this season's catch."

Emelia's chin went up. "I don't care two figs about this season's catch. I know that Lord Throckmorton isn't the traditional tall, dark, and handsome sort of man, but I *like* him. He's sweet, kind, and earnest. There's something very attractive about a person who is unapologetic about their interests, unique though they may be."

Benedict hummed in reply. He'd not seen this side of his sister before. She was much more likely to tease a beau than defend him. Perhaps Emelia really had met her match.

"And what does our mother think about him?" he asked.

"The more interesting question," she replied, arching a delicate eyebrow, "is what does our mother think about you and Lady Lydia Dashwood?"

Benedict folded his arms over his chest and remained silent.

Emelia laughed and threw the ball of yarn at him once more. "What? Did you think you could attend the salon with your best friend's little sister, and I wouldn't say anything? Didn't you just identify me as an imp?"

Benedict rose from the sofa with a put-upon sigh. "Fine, I will escort you to this evening's ball. And I have no idea what our mother would think about me and Lydia, and neither of us will find out because in exchange for my escort tonight, you will agree not to say anything to her."

"You used to be fun," she grumbled.

"We'll pick you up at eight. Don't keep us waiting." Benedict strode toward the door.

"We?"

"*We*, imp. If you want Throckmorton, then I need to be seen as a respectable gentleman. That means Lydia is coming too."

⇾⟫⟩⟨⟪⇽

"LORD LOVELL, MISS Emelia Southcott, and Lady Lydia Dashwood."

Lydia noticed many heads turn when she, Benedict, and Emelia were announced at Lady Marwood's ball.

She hadn't planned on attending tonight, especially given the reformers' plans to distribute pamphlets the following day. But when Benedict had suggested attending with his sister, Lydia had realized that the ball was full of opportunities. And thankfully, Mrs. Abbott had agreed to play chaperone once more, although she'd eschewed the receiving line, saying she'd find a quiet corner to work on her knitting as was her wont.

Lydia could continue her promise to Benedict to reform his reputation in society. Lady Marwood was viewed by the ton as an upright and proper woman. Just by showing up, Benedict would be rendered less disreputable merely by association. Many of the powerful matrons of the ton would be in attendance tonight as well. With Emelia at his side, Benedict could be shown off in a very advantageous light to those who loved to gossip.

The other opportunity Lydia saw would prove a bit more elusive. She knew that several wives, sisters, and daughters of prominent members of the House of Lords would be in attendance. A ball was the perfect place to slip in a few casual questions to these women about their husband's or family member's view on a certain Staines and his Office of Public Order. Knowledge was power, and the more she and Benedict had, the safer their reformer friends would be.

"Shall we?" Benedict crooked both his arms, and Lydia slipped her hand through one side while Emelia did the same on the other. Together, they descended the staircase into the crush of attendees.

Emelia scanned the room. "I wonder if Lord Throckmorton is here?" she asked, her voice breezy even as she reached up to smooth her coiffure.

Lydia smiled. Emelia was lovely and viewed as quite a catch amongst the ton. With Benedict about so often, Lydia had heard many tales of his usually unflappable sister. Seeing her now so flustered over a gentleman was both surprising and refreshing.

"He must be," Benedict muttered. "Seems like every single aristocrat in all of England is here tonight."

Lydia patted his arm. "There, there, Viscount. I'm sure we could get you some smelling salts if you begin to feel faint."

Benedict narrowed his eyes at her, and Lydia's smile only widened.

"Aha!" Emelia crowed to her brother. "I knew I wasn't the only person in England who enjoyed torturing you. It's simply much too fun to keep to myself."

"Heaven help me," he mumbled, shaking his head. "I'm accompanied by *two* imps tonight."

Lydia caught Emelia's eye, and the two women laughed.

Whenever they'd mingled at social functions in the past, Lydia had found Emelia to be good company, but she hadn't spent so much time with just her and Benedict before. Based on how the evening was going so far, it seemed like a friendship was possible. With her house full of guests, Lydia hadn't been to the LCA in a handful of days. Given that Pippa and Jane were both out of town, she was missing her friends and the particular joy that came from laughing with another woman.

Her pulse sped up when she spotted one of the most powerful dowagers of the ton—and a consummate gossip—standing alone nearby.

"Before you go in search of Throckmorton," Lydia whispered to Emelia, "might you assist me in my little project for your brother?"

Emelia followed Lydia's line of sight, and her eyebrows shot up. "You don't start out small, do you?"

"Is anyone going to ask me what I think?" Benedict grumbled.

Lydia met his golden-brown eyes and tried to ignore the way her heart fluttered as she looked at his handsomeness straight on. Benedict in his formal wear was a sight to behold. Even the simple knot of his gleaming white cravat against his black jacket seemed to match the curves of his full lips against the straight lines of his teeth.

"I think I shan't inquire as to your opinion on the matter," she mused to him. "It will help build your character, experiencing what we ladies face on a regular basis."

Emelia stifled a snort behind her fan.

Benedict pouted at her, but his eyes twinkled. "I suppose you'd best give me my marching orders then."

"Go fetch three lemonades, and then meet us by that column." Lydia gestured to the area where Lady Culpepper was standing.

"Three?" he asked. "I don't drink the stuff."

"Don't worry your pretty little head about my plan," Lydia

teased.

Benedict rolled his eyes but headed off toward the refreshment table.

Lydia turned her attention to Emelia. "Does a bit of harmless fibbing offend your moral sensibilities?"

"As long as I am entertained," Emelia said, "feel free to say whatever you want about my brother. If you like, I could swear that fairies delivered him to our doorstep in a basket after I begged my parents for a pet."

Lydia raised an eyebrow. "But he's older than you."

"Like I said," Emily replied with a smirk, "as long as I'm entertained…"

Lydia eyed Lady Culpepper once more. A powdered wig of longitudinal proportions adorned the lady's head, and although her face was lined with age, there was a sharp alertness in her myopic stare.

The general outline of Lydia's plan took shape, but they needed to act quickly before the lady was approached by others.

"Follow my lead," she told Emelia before approaching the dowager with the widest smile she could manage affixed to her face. "Lady Culpepper!" Lydia greeted. "It's so lovely to see you here at the ball tonight."

Lady Culpepper raised her lorgnette to her eyes and peered at Lydia. "Good evening to you, Lady Lydia. It has been far too long I think."

Although cut from a very different cloth than the old friends of her parents that Lydia had spoken to at the salon, Lady Culpepper had been an occasional guest at her parents' many gatherings. Where better to find the juiciest gossip than to be present as scandalous events unfolded?

"And who have you brought with you this evening?" Lady Culpepper asked, fixing her attention on Emelia.

"Oh, this is my very dear friend, Miss Emelia Southcott. She is sister to Benedict Southcott, Viscount Lovell."

The lady's mouth tightened in distaste. "A bit of fuss about that one a handful of years ago, if I recall. A house party where things took a salacious turn..."

Lydia flicked her fan through the air as if waving away stale gossip. "Oh, that bit of nonsense? Happened years ago when he was fresh out of school. I can assure you, Lord Lovell is quite reformed. In fact, just the other week he helped Emelia and me deliver woolen booties that had been knitted by the Ladies Charitable Association to an orphanage just outside of town."

Lady Culpepper tilted her head to the side. "Oh?"

Her wig began to tip, and Lydia shifted to the side so that she might catch it if the need arose. She flared her eyes at Emelia.

Thankfully, Emelia picked up on the hint. "Er, yes, my brother is most charitable. He just *loves* charity. And helping people. And doing good deeds."

Oh dear.

She would've bet all her pin money that Emelia could fib like a champ. Thankfully, all her pin money had already been sent to the printer, along with the final draft of Democratium Liberum's piece for the pamphlet.

Emelia continued to speak, "—and then he told me how much he just loves orphans—"

Lydia coughed with great enthusiasm into her fist.

"My dear," Lady Culpepper said, thumping Lydia on the back, "are you unwell?"

Lydia continued to cough. It was rather difficult to get the balance just right between maintaining her delicate ladylike decorum while also coughing loud enough to disrupt the conversation. She flicked her gaze over Emelia's shoulder and nearly sighed in relief at the sight of Benedict approaching with three glasses balanced in his hands.

"Benny," exclaimed Emelia, "you're just in time with the lemonade." She took a glass from her brother and handed it to Lydia. "Here, it will help calm your coughing."

Benedict's brow tightened in concern. "Have you taken ill?"

Lydia sipped her lemonade, then cleared her throat delicately before smiling. "Ah, much better now. It was merely a small tickle in my throat."

Benedict gave her a skeptical look. Lydia merely blinked back, all innocence. He shook his head before turning his attention to the others in their little group. After handing a glass to his sister, he said to Lady Culpepper, "Do you wish for a lemonade, my lady?"

The Dowager inspected the glass of lemonade through her lorgnette before peering at Benedict. "Most kind of you, m'boy," she said, taking the glass.

"Lady Culpepper," Lydia said, "may I present Miss Emelia's brother, Lord Lovell?"

"Pleased to make your acquaintance, young man." Lady Culpepper reached up to adjust the angle of her wig with the hand holding the lorgnette.

Lydia watched in horrified fascination as the device caught on the stylized hair and pushed it to a precarious angle. Would Lady Culpepper's wig roll across the floor like some rascally lap dog?

But apparently the lady was used to such things for she merely jostled her head, untangling the lorgnette and righting her hair before continuing. "Am I to understand that you are reformed from your previous rakish ways?"

Benedict blinked at her.

Lydia stepped into the conversational fray. "I was just telling Lady Culpepper about all the good work you do assisting us at the Ladies Charitable Association. Those orphans were ever so grateful when you recently helped to deliver those little woolen socks to keep their feet warm through the cold winter months."

Benedict drew a deep breath—likely for patience at her flagrant lying—before turning his easy, charming smile to Lady Culpepper. "It was the very least I could do for those poor, sweet orphans. In fact, Lady Lydia was just telling me that she plans to pay off the orphanage's coal bill for the month."

Lydia blinked. *The cad.*

"How could I not," she cooed, "after you had promised to

pay for a physician to make weekly house calls for an entire year?"

Benedict's eyes narrowed. "Ah, but I was inspired by *you*, my dear Lady Lydia. After all," he drawled, "*you* are the one who volunteered to hire them a schoolteacher."

"Lord Lovell," she said through gritted teeth, "you are *too* kind."

Emelia was watching the back-and-forth with barely disguised delight. And Lady Culpepper seemed to have forgotten all about her lorgnette, her bright eyes wide as she took in their exchange.

"It seems you *are* reformed, m'boy." Lady Culpepper toasted him with her lemonade glass. "You've inspired me to make a donation of my own. Will a hundred pounds for the orphanage be acceptable?"

Benedict took a gentle hold of her hand that gripped the lorgnette. With a gallant bow, he swept a kiss along the back of her knuckles. "You are all that is generous and kind in this world, Lady Culpepper."

And to Lydia's consternation, the Dowager twittered like a schoolgirl. Or like Mrs. Smythe, the housekeeper. Or just like any other of the countless ladies whom Benedict had charmed over the years. The man's lazy smile at full power was a hazard to womankind everywhere.

"May I escort you to your chair, my lady?" Benedict asked Lady Culpepper, offering his arm.

After handing him her lemonade for safekeeping, the Dowager took his arm and directed him across the room where several of her friends had gathered, their heads bent together as they doubtlessly shared the latest *on dits*.

Lydia and Emelia stood side-by-side, watching in silence as Benedict bent low to whisper something in Lady Culpepper's ear, causing her to cackle.

"If you're free later this evening," Emelia muttered, "perhaps you could do me a small favor."

"Certainly," Lydia replied. "What is it?"

"Well, it seems you have a special talent," Emelia said dryly, "for making others see a shiny guinea where before there'd been a tarnished pence. I'm rather hoping Lord Throckmorton will choose to put this particular coin in his pocket."

Chapter Thirteen

B ENEDICT CIRCUMNAVIGATED THE ballroom, making his way back to Lydia. His sister was at the far end of the room, seeming to have made good on her plan to hunt down Throck-morton. Whether she could implement the second part of her plan—convincing him to fall in love with her—remained to be seen.

Before Lady Culpepper had released him, she had introduced him to the other doyens of the ton. Despite the other women's skeptical looks, Lady Culpepper had extolled his virtues. Benedict had never felt so deucedly awkward in his life. All he had really done was fetch a glass of lemonade. He hadn't even known that the third glass was intended for her.

Although thanks to Lydia's machinations, it seemed that the powerful matriarchs of the aristocracy now regarded him as a kindhearted do-gooder. He supposed he'd take that over being seen as a rakish wastrel any day, but being lauded for charity he hadn't actually done didn't sit well with him.

It looked like some random orphanage on the outskirts of London was about to receive quite a hefty donation.

He sighed and turned his attention to the woman who was his destination.

Hadn't she always been his destination?

It occurred to him that tonight—and, to be honest, every

time of night or day that he saw her—Lydia was absolutely stunning. Before, there hadn't been time for him to truly appreciate her when they'd been rushing to collect his sister. But now, he could look his fill.

She wore an emerald-green gown, and the smooth satin embraced the sweet curves of her breasts before falling gracefully to the floor. Benedict longed to stare, but he wouldn't allow himself to gawk. Because he was a gentleman. And also, because Lydia would likely gouge his eyes out if she caught him gaping at her like some ill-mannered lout.

Her blond hair was pulled up into a delicate arrangement of twists and braids atop her head. Curling tendrils trailed along her neck. What would it be like, to pull out all the pins from her coiffure and watch her silken hair tumble down to her bare shoulders?

He swallowed at the image. Then Benedict exhaled and paused, taking a moment to fix his attention on the dance floor. He needed to cool his ardor before he approached, else she would see the straining at the front of his trousers. He needed to get his body under control immediately. He thought of boiled potatoes without salt. The smell of the stables on a hot summer day. Lady Culpepper's wig.

Ah, that had done the trick.

He closed the distance between him and Lydia.

"I do believe," she drawled, in a manner that could only be mocking his own usual way of speaking, "that you owe me a rather fat purse."

"Is that so?" Benedict drawled back. He stood just a few inches closer to her than was proper, forcing her to tilt her head back to meet his gaze.

"I'll have to do a bit of investigating to determine the cost of a teacher's annual salary as well as the price of a coal shipment, but I shall be sure to send you the bill posthaste." Lydia crossed her arms as if she were greatly put out by all of this, but he'd seen that glint in her eye before.

She found him amusing.

And that made him very happy.

Benedict mimicked her stance, folding his arms across his chest. "I look forward to your bill. Please do keep your eyes out for your correspondence as I shall be sure to send *you* a bill for a year of physician's visits. And," he added, "it seems I am in need of knitting lessons as I have promised to deliver quite a few woolen socks."

Lydia's mouth quivered. "I believe there are many people who would pay quite a sum to see the mighty Benedict South-cott, Viscount Lovell knitting little woolen booties."

He grinned at her. She smiled back. Benedict's chest felt warm and light.

Lydia glanced away, and her expression changed as she took note of something across the room. "It seems our little exercise has worked."

Benedict followed the line of her gaze around the ballroom. Many women similar in age to his own mother were eyeing him above their fluttering fans. Their expressions looked ra-ther…appraising. A few were pointing at him as they whispered to their daughters.

"What's happening?" he muttered out of the side of his mouth, afraid to take his eyes off the calculating matrons.

Lydia grinned. "Word has spread quickly."

Just then, Emelia waltzed by. Her dance partner, Throckmor-ton, twirled her about the room with ease. His head was cocked to the side as he listened with rapt attention to whatever clever things his sister was undoubtedly saying. When Throckmorton's back was to them, Emelia shot Benedict a wink over his shoulder.

Such an imp.

As the couple moved to the opposite side of the room, Bene-dict recalled what Lydia had just said. "Wait. What? Word has spread?"

"Word of your newfound respectability," Lydia explained, her voice sounding tight. "Emelia must've heard the gossip. Now she knows that the path is clear for Throckmorton to court her."

Benedict jerked his gaze away from his sister, and all the middle-aged women and their daughters who were staring at him to peer down at Lydia. "That's certainly good news."

"Yes." Lydia smiled, but there was no warmth in her eyes.

Benedict frowned. "Shouldn't they all be staring at Emelia instead of me?"

Lydia shook her head, the motion jerky. "You didn't just make Emelia a catch on the marriage market with your suddenly refurbished reputation."

Benedict's heart skipped a beat as he realized what Lydia was saying.

She hammered the last nail into his coffin. "Now," she told him, "you're a catch too."

⟫⟩⟩⟩✕⟨⟨⟨⟪

LYDIA SMILED AND then smiled some more. She smiled so vigorously that her cheeks hurt, and her jaw ached.

What would it take for her to drop her *façade* of happiness? A server delivering a glass of curdled milk for her to drink? A dancer stumbling into her and tearing the seam of her lovely green gown? No and no. Someone would have to smite her dead here in this very ballroom in order for her to drop her fake cheer.

"… so very pleased to make your acquaintance," said a petite lady with red hair, the latest of the many young ladies who'd come by in the last half-hour to pay court to London's newest eligible bachelor.

"Perhaps you would do me the honor of a dance later?" Benedict asked, his lazy smile set to the maximum charm level.

The girl examined her dance card, and her expression drooped. "I fear I have no more open dance spots left, my lord. But perhaps we might dance at the next ball?" Her eyes lit up with hope.

Lydia smiled wider. Was she showing too many teeth? It felt like she was baring them like an enraged wild animal at this point.

"I look forward to it." Benedict bowed over the young lady's hand.

With a few long glances over her shoulder, she was led away by her mother.

"My goodness." Benedict snagged a glass of champagne off the tray of a passing server and gulped back a swallow. "It's rather draining to be the belle of the ball."

"I still have those smelling salts available," Lydia said through clenched teeth. And a smile, of course.

That was the only expression allowed now. She was completely unbothered by anything that was happening. And, she was absolutely certain that this strange tightness in her chest was most definitely not jealousy. Definitely not. Why on earth would she be jealous of all the lovely, sweet, accomplished young women whose mothers had brought by to meet Benedict? All the unmarried misses with whom he gently flirted with, flashing that famous smile and twinkling those golden-brown eyes, and bowing low over their delicate hands.

None of those women had ink stains on their fingers.

Lydia tightened her hand behind her back.

"Ah, the smelling salts." Benedict inspected her. A sly glint came to his eyes and he smiled—much more naturally than she certainly was.

"Perhaps," he said, all innocence, "you need to save them for yourself?"

Lydia bared her teeth at him, but the cad merely laughed.

A statuesque woman with smile lines at the corners of her eyes approached, a similarly tall young lady in tow.

"Your Grace." Benedict bowed to the woman, and introductions were made.

The Duchess of Wolfingham and her daughter, Lady Mary, both had dark hair and striking gray eyes. And despite Lydia's decidedly jealous emotions of the last half-hour, she couldn't help but like the two women, who seemed warm and genuine.

"Is the Duke with you here tonight?" asked Benedict.

The Duchess shook her head. "Unfortunately, there was a bit of business for him to attend to at Westminster this evening."

Benedict nodded in understanding. "Wolfingham is very dedicated to his duties in the Lords. It doesn't surprise me to hear he's burning the midnight oil with Parliamentary work."

The Duchess sighed. "I'm quite proud of his dedication, but I fear it's difficult at times with so many little ones still at home. They miss their papa dearly when he is gone."

Benedict addressed the duchess's daughter. "How many younger siblings do you have, Lady Mary?"

The young woman began to rattle off names and ages while Benedict listened attentively. Lydia glanced at the duchess. Her husband was an influential member of the Lords, and he was up to *a bit of business* at Westminster at this very moment.

Perhaps this was the perfect opportunity for Lydia to pursue her second goal of the evening.

"It must be something quite important," Lydia said to the Duchess, "to pull him away from a lively ball with his beautiful wife."

The Duchess smiled and touched her wedding band. "He hated to disappoint me. He knows I adore him twirling me around the ballroom during a waltz, but he received an urgent note just as we were about to leave. He left immediately, which means the poor man is traipsing about the halls of Westminster in his dancing shoes."

Lydia fluttered her fan and said lightly, "Perhaps if more of our leaders in the Lords and Commons were fond of dancing, they would pass laws that would ensure them contended dance partners."

"Just so."

They both laughed, but then the Duchess of Wolfingham lowered her voice and asked, "Do you perhaps refer to legislation that would aid women?"

Lydia took a moment to adjust her fan. She needed to tread carefully here, or else she would lose this opportunity. "I've read a few articles in the newspaper lately that have me curious about the matter," she said, glancing at her companion. "It's most interesting. Some say that laws favoring women and children would benefit *all* families of England."

The Duchess sipped her champagne, her eyes watchful over the curve of her glass. "I have read similar articles myself," she said carefully.

Lydia's mind whirled. *How best to play this?* She glanced out at the couples spinning by on the dance floor and stepped farther away from Benedict and Lady Mary, as if she simply wished for a different view of the dancers. "I did see something in the paper the other day about a new governmental office. I believe it was called the Office of Public Order?"

The Duchess had followed suit, stepping over and creating a bit of distance from Benedict and her daughter. Lydia tilted her head for a quick listen. Were they still discussing Lady Mary's plethora of siblings?

The Duchess spoke again, her voice low. "I know of the Office of Public Order and its head, a man named Staines. My husband has...many thoughts on this topic."

The two women stood side-by-side, both looking out at the dance floor. However, Lydia doubted either of them paid attention to the intricate moves of those swaying to the music. She knew *she* didn't. She spoke. "This office..."

"Yes?" the Duchess murmured.

Lydia took a steadying breath. *It was now or never.*

"Well...I heard a very concerning rumor recently."

"A rumor?" The Duchess glanced over at her, but kept her voice casual.

"It seems," Lydia said, speaking at barely above a whisper, "that Staines ordered the arrest of a score of innocent women who were peacefully gathered outside Westminster to support reform."

The Duchess swiveled to face Lydia. "Staines had *women* arrested?"

Lydia nodded. "And," she said, hoping she was right about her audience's sympathies, "the women's young children as well. All of them, thrown into Newgate."

The Duchess inhaled sharply through her nose. "Children? Thrown into Newgate?" Her face hardened. "This is reprehensible."

Lydia's mouth pulled tight. "It's a stain upon our nation's conscience that more people do not share your viewpoint."

The Duchess raised her champagne glass to her mouth but did not drink, as if she was trying to protect anyone from watching her words. "This is not idle ballroom conversation, Lady Lydia. You now know where my sympathies lie. Speak plainly."

Lydia faced the duchess. Should she trust her?

They had only met that evening, but the woman seemed to be both sensible and sympathetic. And her husband was a very influential member of the House of Lords. If the duke of Wolfingham was the sort of politician who was called in at the last minute to handle *a bit of business*, then he likely had the authority and reach to contain Staines and his Office of Public Order.

Lydia's jaw tightened.

It was *worth the risk.*

She leaned close to the duchess, holding her fan up to hide her words from any who might be watching. "I have personal knowledge that Staines is continuing to investigate the women in the reform group, despite their peaceful protesting and lack of any crimes. I fear what he may do, given his apparent hatred of reformers and the lack of oversight of his office." She raised her eyebrows. "If a powerful member of the Lords were to question Staines's overreach and spending in the Office of Public Order, perhaps it would clip the man's wings and keep women and their children safe from his tactics."

The duchess exhaled slowly. "I cannot make any promises," she whispered, "but I will speak to my husband about this. Innocent children thrown into Newgate is not something he will take lightly, either."

Lydia pressed her hand against her belly, trying to calm the quaking there. "Thank you, Your Grace."

The other woman nodded before turning toward her daughter. "Mary," she called in a cheery voice, "I do believe I see your cousin across the ballroom. We simply must greet her."

The duchess and her daughter said their farewells, and then she and Benedict watched them depart in silence.

Benedict sipped his champagne, then said, "Dare I ask what you were up to?"

Lydia wrinkled her nose. His light woodsy scent was most distracting, now that he was standing quite close once again. It reminded her of their embraces…and their kiss. Why couldn't the man smell of stale sweat, or smoke, or greasy bacon? Anything would be better than this appealing, intoxicating scent that seemed intentionally designed to plague her.

"Lydia?"

She glanced at him. "What makes you think I was up to anything?"

Benedict fixed his sherry-colored eyes upon her. "I spent the last five, endless minutes asking a series of increasingly inane questions about Lady Mary's fifty-two siblings so that you might continue your clandestine *tete-a-tete* with the Duchess. I would think my pain and suffering from hearing each sibling's favorite dessert grants me compensation in the form of knowing what you're up to." Benedict's expression remained one of lazy congeniality, but there was a tightness in his eyes. He wasn't happy being kept in the dark.

Lydia held his gaze. Of course, she would tell him. They were in this together, two peas in an increasingly intimate pod. But…riling him up a bit first was its own kind of pleasure and one she would not deny herself.

"What," she murmured, leaning close to his ear, "will you give me if I tell you?" She peered up at him through her eyelashes. Was this how flirting was done? It was delicious.

Benedict's gaze shot down to her mouth, and his neck moved as he swallowed.

"Don't you know?" he asked, voice husky. "Anything you want from me, I will give to you gladly."

Lydia's face heated under the intensity of his expression. She remembered kissing him, the masterful way his lips had claimed her own. The heat of his hands as they'd stroked along her back.

She wanted that again. And she wanted more.

"Lord Lovell," came a voice, breaking their reverie.

Benedict stepped away and offered another charming smile— this one a bit strained around the edges, Lydia was pleased to note—to another matron of the ton with a daughter in tow.

"Oh my!" Lydia exclaimed, flicking open the unused dance card hanging from her wrist. "I do believe this is our dance, Lord Lovell."

The mother's face dropped.

"Our dance. Of course." Benedict's eyes laughed at her before he turned to address the woman and her daughter. "Perhaps we could speak again later?"

Before they could answer, he took Lydia's hand, leading her onto the dance floor where he twirled her around, gracefully moving them into the steps of the waltz. "You," he murmured close to her ear, "are rather naughty."

His hand pressed, warm and oddly intimate, at her waist. "I have learned from the master." She couldn't speak without sounding breathless.

Benedict's thumb caressed the back of her hand, resting in his. "I think you were up to mischief long before I came along. After all, you managed to keep secret the identity of Democ—"

"*Shh!*" Lydia glanced around to see if anyone was listening. All the dancers nearby seemed caught up in their partners or counting their own steps, fortunately.

But then, Benedict checked their position and twirled them off of the dance floor and through nearby double doors. Lydia gasped as their dance momentum carried them across the darkened balcony. Benedict led them into the far corner, where they were sheltered from view by an array of potted plants.

Although the winter air through the open doors had felt refreshing inside amongst the crush, out here it was quite chilly. Lydia shivered and cupped her hands over her bare arms.

"Here." Benedict shrugged out of his jacket before draping it over her shoulders.

Lydia slid her arms through the sleeves and pulled the jacket tightly around her. His warmth still clung to the fine fabric, and she was enveloped in his scent. "Thank you," she breathed.

He merely watched her.

She licked her lips as she tried to gather her scattered thoughts. His gaze darted down to her mouth, and he inhaled sharply.

"You didn't like me paying attention to those other women," he said, stepping closer.

Lydia gripped his coat and her hands flexed. "No," she confessed.

His lips curved up, and he stepped closer still. "You've been thinking of our kiss all night."

Lydia clamped her mouth shut.

"Haven't you?" he murmured, running a finger down the lapel of his jacket until they met her hand. His touch grazed the swell of her breast, and Lydia shivered, but not from the cold this time.

"Lydia," he said, the name both a warning and an entreaty.

She couldn't stay silent any longer. But she had no voice to reply. Lydia nodded, and his eyes flared in response.

Benedict leaned toward her. "Shall we do it again?" He pressed his cheek against the side of her head to whisper in her ear. "Shall we kiss one another out here under the stars?"

Lydia, who'd spent so much of her life playing with ideas,

turning over thoughts, and concentrating on which words to select in her writing, was suddenly mindless. No thoughts. No cautions or curiosities running through her brain.

Just sensation. Feeling. Wanting.

And so, she rose up on her tiptoes and pressed her mouth to his in a searing kiss.

$$\sim\!\!\infty\!\!\sim$$

Chapter Fourteen

I'M KISSING LYDIA. *Again.*

He wrapped his arms around her and held her gently in his embrace. But his Lydia was no delicate flower. She reached her hands around his neck, dug her fingers into his hair at the nape, and tugged him closer still.

"More," she whispered against his mouth.

Benedict's blood flowed through his veins like lava raging down a volcano. His lips moved against hers in devouring kiss after kiss. She nipped his lower lip, and he tangled his tongue against hers, the gentle thrust and retreat of the movement making him dizzy.

But she was not some experienced woman. Benedict wasn't certain, but it seemed as if their kiss at the salon had been her first kiss. He needed to take things slowly. He didn't want to scare her with the intensity of his passion. He would simply kiss her, keeping his hands on her back like a gentleman.

And then... she grabbed his bottom.

Benedict gasped in surprise as her hands roved across his posterior.

"Is this all right?" she gasped, even as she continued to squeeze and explore his backside.

"Y-yes." He had not expected her to take the lead, but he liked it. She could boss him around all day, every day, and he would beg for more.

But perhaps turnabout was fair play.

Even as they continued to kiss, the sweetness of her warm mouth like honey against his own, he trailed his hands down her back to her waist…and then down to her pert, round behind.

"Is *this* all right?" he asked.

"Yes," she gasped.

He stroked her soft curves. Her bottom was deliciously round, perfect for a gentle squeeze. Everything about her—her startling, intelligent eyes, the smooth softness of her skin, and all her brilliance, her cleverness, and her genius with words and arguments in politics was mesmerizing. Lydia was beautiful.

And, Lydia was everything to him.

"Touch me more," she demanded.

Benedict smiled as he trailed kisses across her cheek and down her smooth neck. "I am touching you," he murmured into her skin.

"More," she insisted.

Benedict trailed a hand up her back, across her shoulder, and around to her chest, touching just inside his jacket. He stroked the smooth skin above her *décolletage*.

"Here?" he asked.

Lydia moaned softly. "Lower," she directed.

Benedict felt like laughing with joy. She was unapologetically Lydia, so completely herself, even in this. And he loved it.

He loved *her*.

He'd been in love with Lydia Dashwood for very long time. And now she was in his arms and directing him to touch her sweet breasts. If this was a dream, he never wanted to wake up.

"As you wish," he whispered against her ear, and she shivered in response.

He nibbled on her earlobe and trailed kisses behind her ear and along her neck while his fingers continued their exploration.

"Benedict," she breathed as he continued to stroke the soft swells of her breasts above the edge of her gown.

She was so warm. So responsive. And oh, so soft. He could spend hours touching her just like this. He could do this for days, for weeks, for a lifetime…

It occurred to him that *that* was what he wanted with her. A lifetime of loving. Of touches and kisses and sharing thoughts. Teasing and getting into and out of scrapes together. He wanted it all. With her.

"Lydia, my love," he murmured, and then he rubbed his thumb across the peak of her breast.

She gasped and trembled.

"More?" he asked, between kisses.

She nodded her head and then claimed his lips in another, searing kiss.

He cupped her breast fully in his hand. The soft weight fit perfectly and the tender point of her nipple poked against his palm. What he wouldn't give to tug down the neckline of her gown and gaze upon her loveliness in the moonlight. But for now, touching was enough. Feeling her, holding her, and worshiping her with his mouth and hands. With the heat they created. It was more than enough. It was more than he had dreamed.

Lydia's hands roamed over his chest, and through the layers of his shirt and waistcoat, her touch seared his skin. He pressed his hips more tightly against her, easing the stiff ache in his cock by pressing against her softness.

Lydia gasped.

Had he gone too far? Benedict eased his hips away, but she made sounds of protest and rubbed against him.

"God, Lydia," he panted. "How I want you."

Everything was heat and touch and sensation. Everything was her. Her scent, like a garden in the spring. Her warmth. Her softness, a softness that contained so much strength.

"Benedict," she whispered, pulling back to stare into his eyes. Her cheeks were rosy with her flush, and her lips were swollen from their kisses. She looked like a goddess, like she contained within her all the power of the earth and sky.

"I want you." She bit her lip, her eyes searching his. "I've never... I've never felt like this before."

Benedict pressed his forehead to hers. "Me neither."

She cupped his cheek with her hand. "Truly?" she whispered.

He nodded, and they remained like that for an endless moment, their breath mingling, their heat cocooning them from the chill of the night air, and some intangible connection was made tangible as they leaned into one another.

Should he tell her what was in his heart? He knew she was uncertain of him. He didn't want to spook her. And yet..."Lydia," he murmured, pulling back to gaze into her deep-blue eyes. "Lydia, I l—"

"Ahem."

Benedict froze. Lydia inhaled sharply and pulled back. They turned to look at the person who had interrupted them.

"Benny." His sister stood there, her arms crossed over her chest, and her foot tapping in impatience. "I can't believe it."

"Emelia," he groaned, rubbing his hand over his face as he stepped back, putting more distance between him and Lydia. "What are you doing out here?"

"What am *I* doing out here?" Emelia hissed, pointing at him and then Lydia. "How about *what are* you *doing out here*? And without Mrs. Abbott anywhere in sight?" She shook her head. "Never mind. Don't answer that. I already saw too much."

"Emelia," he growled in warning.

His sister waved her hands through the air as if she could swat away his warning or what she'd seen. And if she'd only come out within the last minute, she'd seen them resting their foreheads together and whispering sweet nothings to one another. Well, not sweet *nothings*. For him, the words he'd said, the words he'd been about to say, had been *everything*.

"I didn't say much when our mother cornered you before your ride the other morning," Emelia said, her nostrils flaring. "But she was right. You *are* ruining my chances this season.

You're careless and reckless with your reputation, with our *family's* reputation. And with Lydia's as well. What were you thinking, kissing at a ball full of hundreds of aristocrats who love nothing more than to gossip? And I had finally met someone—"

Her words choked to a halt.

Benedict burned with regret. With shame.

And with anger.

"Emelia, I never did—"

"I don't want to hear it," she hissed. "There's nothing you can say that can excuse this. The only thing now is to make it right. Keep your hands to yourself from now on. Keep Lydia and our family's reputations out of the scandal sheets. And maybe, if I'm lucky, Lord Throckmorton won't learn of your indiscretion."

"Emelia," Lydia began, but his sister cut her off, swiping her hand through the air as if she were cutting the very fabric of the evening in two.

"I want to go home," his sister bit out. "I'll see you in the carriage in five minutes." And with that, Emelia stormed away, leaving a frozen silence in her wake.

Benedict stared out at the empty balcony.

She was right.

Not about the whole of it, but he *had* been careless. Emelia had asked him to accompany her to the ball specifically so that she might see Throckmorton, for whom she had formed a *tendre*. And how did he honor her wishes to right the family's reputation? By practically seducing his best friend's little sister on a balcony separated from a throng of people by only a few anemic, frozen plants.

She's not for the likes of you. He'd forgotten. Or allowed himself to forget. He turned to Lydia, an apology on his lips.

"If you say sorry to me," she warned, a finger outstretched, "I swear, Benedict, I will throw you over the balustrade and leave you to writhe in pain on whatever sad, twisted tree you impale yourself upon."

Benedict took a step back.

Lydia was fierce in her anger, her chest heaving, her cheeks red, and her eyes flashing.

She was upset with him right now, and he couldn't blame her. He hadn't protested when his sister had insinuated that kissing Lydia was tantamount to the complete destruction of their family's honor. As if he'd committed murder. Or arson. Or served cheap wine at a ball.

"Lydia, my sister is wrong," he said, voice low. "Although it could cause a scandal if others had seen us, I'm not ashamed to have kissed you."

She pulled his jacket tighter around her. "Perhaps you should be. Your sister seemed to think quite poorly of my behavior just now."

Benedict raised a hand to touch her, to reassure her, but she turned her head away, giving him her profile.

"We can't do this again," she whispered.

He closed his eyes. The idea of not kissing Lydia again was like contemplating a lifetime of breakfasts without strawberry jam—unfathomable.

And yet...his sister was his family. How could he ignore her plea to not tarnish his reputation any further? He'd been so close tonight. He'd begun to rehabilitate his image with the ton. His sister had danced with Throckmorton, looking so very happy. And Benedict had held the woman he loved in his arms.

But somehow it had all vanished in the space of a few minutes.

Benedict closed his eyes and pinched the bridge of his nose. "We won't do that again," he agreed.

Silence.

What was she thinking? What would she say? He rubbed his face and looked up.

Lydia was gone. His jacket hung lopsided over the balustrade as if she had flung it down. He gathered it up, holding it close to his face so he might inhale her scent, might feel a bit of her lingering warmth.

And if he happened to press the fabric to his eyes to absorb a little moisture, no one was there to see.

LYDIA THREW BACK her covers with a groan. She'd been attempting to sleep for at least two hours since she'd returned. Thankfully, a woman she knew from the LCA had been waiting for her carriage when Lydia had stormed out of the ball. She had kindly offered to give her a ride home, sparing her a carriage ride with Benedict and Emelia.

Sparing her an *excruciating* ride with Benedict and Emelia. Truly, she would have simply expired from the emotions churning inside her if she'd been forced to ride home with them.

And surely Benedict had seen the kindly Mrs. Abbott home to her daughter and new grandchild. Truly, she owed her old housekeeper a very generous gift to thank her for the way she'd been treated on her recent outings with Lydia. Abandoned snoozing in a carriage and then briefly forgotten once Lydia had been arrested. Abandoned in a ballroom with naught but her knitting to keep her company. Well, Lydia wouldn't abandon her again. She made a mental note to send a princely sum to Mrs. Abbott as soon as she was able.

And now, sleep eluded her. How was a woman supposed to find rest and comfort in her bed after being kissed the way Lydia had been kissed by Benedict? After pushing her breast into his teasing hand? After feeling her heartbeat pulse in all the intimate places of her body?

After being accused of potentially causing a scandal wicked enough to ruin someone's life?

And that didn't even take into account the damage she could have done to her own reputation. She'd been fortunate in emerging from the kidnapping with her good name intact. Was she a fool to put it on the line again?

Lydia shoved her feet into her slippers and yanked her wrapper over her night rail. She was tired and grumpy and aroused all at the same time. It was a terrible combination. The only cure was a very dull book.

She padded silently through the house, a candle held aloft, until she reached the library. Her brother kept some excellent tomes on crop rotation that she was sure would do the trick.

She eased the door open. A shadowy figure moved inside.

"Oh!" Lydia's hand clutched at her chest.

"Oh, love, I'm so sorry I frightened you." On the sofa, Agatha uncurled her legs from beneath her and set a piece of parchment aside on a nearby table. "I didn't think anyone would be up."

Lydia exhaled, trying to calm her rioting pulse. "I didn't either." She moved into the library, using her own candle to light a few more before flopping onto the other end of the sofa. "Couldn't sleep?"

Agatha's mouth pulled up on one side. "I'm too nervous about tomorrow."

The older woman's hair was plaited into a fat braid that hung over her shoulder. The flickering candle caught glints of silver amongst the strands. Her nightgown was thick, serviceable flannel, and her feet were bare.

Lydia reached over the side of the sofa and pulled a lap blanket out of a basket. "Here," she said, tossing it onto Agatha's legs. "I love snuggling up with a book here in the evenings, so Jack keeps the room well stocked with cozy blankets and such."

Agatha spread the blanket over herself, tucking her feet underneath the warmth. "Your brother sounds like a good person."

Lydia smiled. "He is." She missed him. It was strange being here without him and Pippa. The reformers had kept Lydia occupied for the last few days, but she suddenly wished for nothing more than a solid hug from her solid brother.

"And how was the ball?" Agatha asked.

Lydia grimaced. "Oh, you know…those things are all the same."

"Actually," Agatha replied, "I don't."

A blush crept up Lydia's cheeks. How presumptuous of her, to assume everyone had a lifetime of identical balls behind them. What a life of privilege she led. "I'm sorry. I didn't mean—"

Agatha shook her head. "Think nothing of it, love. I have never attended a ball, but we do enjoy the occasional country dance back home in Stafford. Ah, I used to glide about the dance floor like I was made of feathers, my feet barely brushing the ground." She smiled, her mind clearly revisiting fond memories.

Lydia snuggled into her corner of the sofa, finding the most comfortable spot to rest her head. "Is that where you met your husband?"

Agatha reached up to pull a necklace out from under her nightgown. She rubbed the metal pendant hanging from the chain. "My Clifton wasn't one for dancing." Her eyes turned soft. "But he was kind, and gentle, and the hardest worker I knew."

Lydia's breath caught. Agatha spoke of her husband in the past tense.

"It's been five years now," Agatha said, as if sensing Lydia's thoughts. "Died in our bed after a fever. It was the worst day of my life."

They sat in silence for a moment. Lydia considered and discarded several possible expressions of sympathy, but they all felt too small, too inconsequential, for the weight of Agatha's grief. It may have been tempered by the passing of time, but Lydia could feel it still, in the way the woman touched her necklace, in the wet gleam in her eyes, and in the way her voice had cracked when she spoke of his death.

"Tell me more about him," Lydia finally said, hoping she wasn't overstepping.

Agatha straightened and a soft smile spread across her face. "Oh, my Clifton was a remarkable man. He worked from sunup to sundown every day on our farm. He still had energy to dote on our Grace. And then at night, he'd hold me close and say how I was the best thing that had ever happened to him..." Agatha blinked rapidly.

Lydia felt her own eyes grow damp. Although Agatha's husband was gone, it was clear their love wasn't. After a bit of quiet, Lydia asked, "Was it love at first sight?"

Agatha's smile was tinged with nostalgia. "Oh no, definitely not love at first sight. He lived on the farm next door to me, so I grew up always knowing him. He was a scamp back then, a right rascal."

Lydia started. A rascal Agatha had known for years? She tried to banish Benedict from her mind, but it was impossible.

"One time when I was fourteen or so," Agatha continued, toying with her necklace, "I was playing down at the creek. He'd been fishing downstream a bit and came up to me. That boy put the dead fish he'd caught right in my face and said the fish was going to kiss me. Well, I took one look at that dead, scaly thing and screamed like a banshee. And then," Agatha said, her expression turning smug, "I shoved Clifton into the creek."

Lydia chuckled. "You've been a fighter your whole life."

Agatha sighed and smoothed out the blanket. "You're not wrong. Oh, I suppose I was a rascal too, back when I was young." She huffed a little laugh, then grew quiet. "There were a lot of years in between our wild youth and his passing that were peaceful though. Once Clifton and I settled down and had our Grace…" She touched her pendant on the necklace again. "Those were wonderful years. Years of loving and laughter…and a bit of strife too. No one is perfect, and my Clifton liked to leave his dirty socks on the floor."

Lydia wrapped her arms around her knees and pulled them tightly to her chest.

Would she ever have that? Someone to settle down with, someone to share peaceful years of love and laughter? Someone whose dirty socks would one day make her smile with bittersweet memories?

She thought of Benedict holding her on the balcony, of how he'd looked into her eyes like she was all he'd ever wanted in the world. If she could just—

Lydia shook her head.

He'd made it clear what he thought of her, what he thought of something between them, when he'd agreed with his sister that she was a scandal waiting to happen. Truly, if he had apologized for kissing her in that moment, she would have pulled her hair, gnashed her teeth, and howled angry tears up at the uncaring moon.

She sighed. If only there had been a nice, chilly creek for her to push him into.

She was done with the fantasy of what could be between her and Benedict. She would not allow herself to wonder anymore. It was over.

Agatha picked up the sheet of paper she'd first set aside, pulling Lydia back from her musings. She recognized the writing. It was her article for the pamphlet that she'd given to the reformers before they'd sent off the final draft to the printing shop.

"And now," Lydia asked softly, "is it time to fight again?"

Agatha held the sheet close to one of the flickering candles. "Democratium Liberum says it is. He says that our place in this country is worth fighting for."

Lydia knew the words. She knew them by heart.

It is not the aristocrats and wealthy who make up England. It is this country's farmers, mothers, grocers, miners, dock workers, shop girls, and all the rest who toil day after day to provide for themselves and for their families. Who struggle to pay the high price of grain under the Corn Laws. Who have no voice in Parliament since only land owners are given the vote. And yet, these people are England. And they will speak up loud and long, they will fight with all their courage, until those in power heed their cry for representation and reform.

Agatha stared at the words on the parchment, as if seeing each sentence inked on the page would make them more real. "I fight for myself," Agatha said, tracing the lines on the paper. "I fight for my Grace. And I fight for the little one in her belly. If the common people of this land have no voice in the running of England, what will our country become?"

Lydia bit the inside of her cheek. Agatha had the right of it. What would become of them if they didn't change, and if the rules didn't expand the definition of whose voice mattered?

Agatha and the other reformers believed in this idea. So many did. Lydia hadn't come up with this argument. But…they were her words on the pamphlets they'd distribute tomorrow. They were her words that the reformers would rally behind. They were using *her* voice as part of their battle cry.

Lydia might never have a grand love in her life. What had happened tonight with Emelia and Benedict had reminded her that trusting in a man was folly. She had been so closed off since the kidnapping, and Benedict had brought something dormant inside of her back to life. But what had happened at the ball had nipped it in the bud just as quickly.

But this battle against these unjust laws was something that she *could* be a part of. Where she could make a difference. Where what she said and did and thought would matter. Where the voices of women were valued.

"Tomorrow," Lydia said, her voice shaky, "whatever happens, I'm with you."

Chapter Fifteen

LYDIA STIFLED A yawn, surprised she was still so sleepy given all the hustle and bustle of the reformers gathering in her foyer.

The pamphlets had arrived earlier that morning. Young Timmy was delivering stacks to each woman from the box the printer had sent them in. Agatha was organizing the reformers into groups of three, and the housekeeper, Mrs. Smythe—who Lydia was relieved to find was up for a bit of good trouble and secret keeping—had suggested locations around town where working-class Londoners would be congregated and convenient for the reformers to approach.

Lydia was to be with Agatha's pregnant daughter Grace and Harriet. Timmy was quite disappointed when told he would not be able to join his mother, but Harriet had calmly explained that if she were to be put in jail again, she would need Timmy to come and rescue her.

"But I don't know how to break you out of jail!" Timmy had fretted.

Lydia had knelt down to his level and asked him a very important question. "Do you know what it means to pick a lock?"

Timmy shook his head, eyes wide.

Lydia glanced up at Harriet, who gave her a nod of approval. Lydia continued, "It's a way to open a locked door without a key.

And," she paused for dramatic effect, "I know how."

Timmy's eyes gleamed.

"If you like," Lydia said, keeping her voice casual, "I could show you what I know when we get back. That way, if you ever do need to rescue your mother from prison, you'll know how to unlock the door."

Timmy bounced on the balls of his feet with excitement. "Now I'll always be able to get into mama and father's bedroom."

Lydia stood up and gave Harriet a quizzical look.

The woman blushed before leaning close to whisper, "We're not the sort of people who lock doors in our home, but on occasion when my Harry wants a bit of privacy—for the two of us at night, if you catch my meaning—and we're reasonably certain Timmy is asleep, well…"

Lydia's face grew as hot as Harriet's looked. She cleared her throat before replying, "Perhaps I'll merely give Timmy a demonstration so he's not able to…go where he shouldn't." She recalled something Harriet had mentioned and asked, "Your husband's name is Harry?"

Harriet shook her head in amusement. "What a pair we are, Harriet and Harry. When I was pregnant, some in the village suggested we name our child Harvey, but thankfully, better sense prevailed."

"It's not too late," Lydia teased. "Perhaps someday you'll have a daughter, and you can name her Harmony."

Harriet laughed, but then Agatha clapped her hands to get the group's attention.

"I know we've gone over the plan, and we are prioritizing our safety," their leader said, standing on the top step of the wide staircase. "But I just received a letter this morning from one of the leaders at the Blackburn Female Reform Society."

Murmurs came from the group. The Blackburn Reformers had been the first all-women organization to form in the reform movement. This group, created in their hometown of Stafford, had been modeled after it. In fact, the movement had spread to many towns across England, and all the groups were loosely affiliated.

"There is to be a rally," Agatha announced.

Lydia's fingers flexed around her stack of pamphlets.

"It will be in four days, at the town square of Nottingham-shire, which is one day's travel outside of London." Agatha scanned the group, her jaw set at a determined angle. "If you don't feel comfortable, don't bring it up when you're passing out pamphlets. But…if you do feel safe, spread the word about the rally. I feel that this shall be remembered in history one day as an important turning point in our reform movement. Today, we are making a difference in the lives of the working people of England. In the lives of mothers and children. In the lives of our own families. And we will succeed."

Lydia looked at Grace and Harriet. They each had a glow of excitement and possibility about them. If the world was different, Agatha Shepherd would be a famed orator in parliament. Instead, she was a farmer's wife from a small town in the northwest of the English countryside. But perhaps even with the limitations society placed on women, she would still change the course of history as she'd told her fellow reformers.

It occurred to her that they would be leaving here in a few days to head to Nottinghamshire. The house would be so quiet and lonely, and some essential energy or vibrancy gone once all the reformers left.

Lydia stared down at the pamphlets in her hand. Could she make a difference as well? Could more than her words spur reform? When the Stafford Female Reform Society headed to the rally, Lydia would go with them.

After a final round of instructions, copious hugs for the chil-dren, and a repeat of directions for the maids who were to serve as temporary nannies for the day, the women left the foyer in small groups, following Lydia's directions to a nearby hackney stand.

Soon it was Lydia, Harriet, and Grace's turn to leave.

Agatha gripped her hand tightly. "Thank you, love," she whispered. "We wouldn't be able to do any of this without you."

Lydia merely nodded because she feared she could not speak around the lump in her throat. And then she and her partners were off, walking the few blocks to the hackney stand and giving directions to a driver for a nearby market.

As the carriage rumbled across the uneven cobblestones, Lydia pressed her hand to her stomach. Although she had been involved in the fight for reform long before these women had entered her life, she'd always done it from relative safety behind her desk. Well, *safe* except for that one glaring exception where she was kidnapped. Regardless, it was easy to write words when she didn't have to say them directly to another person. What would it be like today, actually speaking to people who weren't wealthy land-owning men and who, therefore, had no voice in the country's governance?

"It will be all right," Grace said from across the hackney, apparently reading her mind. "You've already been through the worst of it with our trip to Newgate. Today will be like a walk in the park."

Lydia gave her what she knew was a tight smile and drew a deep breath to try to calm herself. She was a part of this team, and she couldn't let her nerves get in the way.

The hackney rolled to a stop. The women clambered out, and Lydia paid the fare. As the hackney clapped away, she took in the scene.

They were at a market set up in an open square. The buildings making up the perimeter housed a pub, a candle shop, a shoe store, and many other businesses. Inside the square were set up stalls selling fruits, vegetables, fish, and handheld meat pies for those who needed a meal on the go.

"Quite a bit different than Bond Street, I imagine," Grace said as she looked around, her hand resting on her belly.

Lydia watched people rushing by with baskets of food under their arms, their clothes tidy but serviceable, their shoes worn at the toes. Their worries were so different, so much more essential, than those of aristocrats who lazily strolled between luxury shops. Not that aristocrats had no worries. She knew firsthand how worrisome life could be, even as the sister of an earl. After all, she'd been kidnapped and nearly killed. But...she never once had to wonder if she could afford to feed her family because of parliament's restrictive Corn Laws.

Lydia replied, "The people here know the value of a pence far better than the lords and ladies overpaying for their snuff and kid gloves at Bond Street."

"Shall we start over there?" Harriet pointed to a produce stand where a handful of women were selecting vegetables.

They approached, and Grace pretended to browse the vegetables. Lydia stood at her side, uncertain if she should speak.

"Good morning," Grace said, smiling at the other women after picking up a bunch of carrots. "Any suggestions on how to cook these? My husband is ever so sick of me just boiling them."

A couple of the women merely nodded before finishing up their purchases and moving along with their day, but the others stayed, suggesting their favorite carrot recipes.

After a minute, Harriet drew a few pamphlets out of her basket. "If you've been having trouble paying for carrots or other food for the table lately, you might be interested in this article about reform in Parliament."

One of the women wrinkled her nose and left, but the others stretched out their hands to take a pamphlet. Grace used this as an opportunity to mention the rally in Nottinghamshire.

"My sister lives there," exclaimed one of the women. "I might send her a letter about the rally." She took a few extra pamphlets to give to her neighbors.

After another minute of discussion, the women bid them good day.

"That went so well," Lydia said. Excitement fizzed through her blood. "You were both naturals in talking to those women."

Harriet laughed. "Those women *are* us. Working folk, trying to stretch each shilling as far as it will go. It's like being in my own market at home, talking to my neighbors."

Lydia nodded, her cheeks feeling hot with embarrassment. This cause mattered to her, but in some ways, it *wasn't* her cause. She would benefit from women's suffrage, but so much of the reform movement was aimed at helping farmers and workers, not genteel ladies who had no calluses on their hands.

She looked down at her shoes. The toes peeked out from beneath the hem of the plainest gown she owned, the fine leather gleaming. She had over a dozen shoes at home—shoes for dancing, for riding, for walking outside, or for staying home.

"How many pairs of shoes do you own?" she heard herself ask. Lydia slammed her mouth shut, horrified. Had she really just blurted that out loud?

Harriet huffed out a laugh, likely guessing at the train of Lydia's thoughts. "I've got one pair for every day and one pair for Sundays to wear to church. Shall I ask how many you've got?"

Lydia shook her head. She didn't want to confess it aloud to these women who had quickly become friends. She didn't want to sully this place where regular people worried about the price of bread with her talk of fine satin dancing shoes.

Lydia exhaled slowly. What was she even doing here? Shame washed over her, pressing her shoulders and head down, making her feel like the biggest kind of fraud.

Grace laid a hand on her arm. "Reform isn't about where we come from. It's about where we want to go."

She met Grace's gaze. Was that true? How could she be so kind to her, when Lydia was living such an easy, privileged life?

"We live such different lives, you and us," Grace continued, "but you don't look down on us for the circumstances of our birth. That was clear from that very first day in Newgate. And we don't look down on you either. Or perhaps I should say," she clarified, quirking an eyebrow, "we don't look *up* at you."

Lydia quirked the side of her mouth to show her appreciation for the humor. But she didn't feel ready to smile yet.

"You're *here*," Grace continued. "You're doing the work. And that's what matters."

She was here. She was doing the work. That's what mattered.

Lydia placed her hand over Grace's and squeezed, grateful. These were tricky waters to navigate, but her reformer friends did so with kindness and grace. Her new friend was especially well named.

"Enough of these tender emotions," said Harriet, throwing in a wink to gentle her words. "We've got pamphlets to distribute and a rally to promote."

An hour later, they had passed out all the pamphlets in their baskets. Even so, many women had not wanted to listen or take a pamphlet. Perhaps their day was already too full to spare the time, or perhaps they did not agree with the reformers' message. But many more women had stayed to listen. And if they stayed, they took a pamphlet—or more—with promises to share them with neighbors and friends as well as spread the word about the rally in Nottinghamshire.

"This has gone so well," Lydia said, glancing around. "But since we're out of pamphlets, perhaps it's time to head home now." Truly, a small part of her had feared that a band of soldiers from the Office of Public Order would show up and clap them in irons. But there had been no sign of trouble. Grace and Harriet agreed, and as they made their way through the square toward a hackney at the far end, they debated whether or not the other groups had done as well as them.

Lydia stopped abruptly when a figure stepped into their path. He was a bulldog of a man, brawny, with small, mean eyes and a nose flattened from too many fights.

"Now look what we got 'ere," he sneered, his breath reeking of alcohol.

Lydia's skin prickled, and she stepped to the side, hoping she and her companions could hurry around the man. But then he was flanked by two others, not nearly as massive as him, but mean-looking just the same.

"Heard ye've been stirring up trouble," grunted one of the bulldog's companions. His eyes were glassy, and judging by the way all three men swayed, Lydia guessed all of them were well into their cups.

"We heard tell," the bulldog said, stepping forward so that he loomed over them, "tha' ye've been passing around papers…" He hiccupped. "Tha' say women are as good as men."

The other minion stepped closer, cracking his knuckles. "They're not," he slurred. "Women are just…women."

"Gentlemen," Lydia said, holding out her hands as if the meager show of resistance would force them to stop.

Please let them stop.

"Listen to this one," chortled the first minion. "She finks we're gen'lemen."

"Call me *guv*," demanded his companion, smirking. "Say it in that fine voice a' yours."

"Should we call for help?" Harriet whispered.

Several people in the market had stopped to watch, but no one appeared inclined to interfere. Lydia couldn't blame them. She wouldn't want to tangle with three hulking drunk men with cruelty in their eyes, either.

"Or run?" Grace asked, even as she cradled her stomach. She wasn't so far along in her pregnancy that she waddled when she walked, but it was doubtful she could make much of a dash either.

As neither suggestion seemed to have very good odds of success, Lydia made a different suggestion. "I'll keep them talking, and you two head for the hackney stand," she whispered over her shoulder. "Ask the driver to pull up right alongside me, and I'll hop in. Tell him I'll pay triple his usual fare."

"What're ye buzzing about?" asked the bulldog, seizing hold of the edge of Lydia's basket and tugging.

She stumbled forward, taken by surprise.

Grace gasped and Harriet lifted her own empty basket up as if she were preparing to bludgeon the giant of a man with a bit of dried wicker.

"Go," Lydia hissed to them as she righted herself. "I'll be fine."

Grace tugged Harriet away toward the hackneys across the square even as Harriet brandished her basket like a weapon in her wake.

"Go on, call me *guv*," crooned the bulldog in a gravelly voice. "Else I'll make ye."

"Fine." Lydia stepped back and squared off her shoulders. "Guv, I would appreciate it if you and your companions would allow me to pass."

One of the minions hooted in laughter.

The other grumbled, "She didn't call me *guv*."

He stepped closer, so that she was bracketed in on the side. Lydia backed up more. She did not want to be surrounded.

"I fink before we lets ye go, ye have to swear to no more a' this revolution rubbish." The bulldog gestured around the square, as if the entire neighborhood had colluded with the reformers by accepting pamphlets.

"I swear I shan't be involved in any rubbish," Lydia vowed.

The bulldog scratched his head as if trying to find the loophole in her promise overly taxed his brain.

"And," he huffed out, taking another step closer, "you 'ave to give me a kiss."

Lydia stepped back and tried to peer over the man's massive shoulders to see if the hackney was approaching. None were in sight. Her arms tensed as she prepared to copy Harriet's technique with the basket.

"I'm afraid, guv," she said, "that I shall have to decline your generous offer."

"Wot's tha'?" One of the minions stepped closer, coming at her from the other side. They were almost surrounding her now. "Did she just tell him no?"

"Fings get ugly when girls tell me no," Bulldog growled, snapping his head to first one side and then the other. The vertebrae of his spine made popping sounds.

Lydia stepped back again, but she came up against one of the stalls. A potato rolled to the ground at her feet. She looked behind her, but the stall keeper was backing away from both his table full of potatoes and any potential trouble, his eyes downcast.

She was alone.

And in that moment, she wished more than anything that Benedict had come with her today. That he didn't agree with his sister that she was a scandal. That he still wished to be involved in this push for reform with her. And most of all, that he was here to keep her safe.

Because no matter what she encountered, she knew if Benedict was at her side, no harm would come to her.

One of the minions sneered. "Why don't ye jus' give him a kiss?"

"Because," Lydia grunted, winding up her basket. "I don't"—she swung it around—"want to."

The bulldog grunted as the basket slammed into his face. Lydia felt a moment's elation, but he merely shook off the blow and ripped the basket out of her hand before chucking it over his shoulder. "That wasn't wise, girl."

Lydia's heartbeat pounded in her ears. *Damnation.* She was going to be murdered by three drunk goons in front of a heaping table full of potatoes. This was not how she intended to go.

"Lydia!" she heard, followed by the clatter of hooves on cobblestones, the rumbling sound of wheels, and the squeaking of the hackney that came hurtling through the square with Harriet hanging out the window. The driver was scowling, and he pulled the horses right up to the ruffians, causing the men to dodge for their lives. One of horses nipped at a minion as he lunged past. The man yelped, rubbing at his arm.

"Leave the lady alone!" the driver hollered at the men.

The horses neighed, the bitten man continued to yell, and Harriet and Grace were shouting as well. The table of potatoes must have been hit by one of the scrambling louts because it collapsed, and potatoes tumbled to the ground and rolled underfoot like a pack of puppies. One of the ruffians tripped over the rolling spuds and windmilled his arms for balance before finally plummeting to the ground with a shout.

It was pure pandemonium.

Harriet, hanging out the hackney window, swung her basket and clocked the nearest brute over his head. He turned with a bellow, and Lydia used the distraction to dash around the horses and to the other side of the hackney.

"Hurry," Grace urged, holding the door open. Then her eyes widened at something over Lydia's shoulder.

Lydia glanced back, but the bulldog was already on her, his mean little eyes narrowed into furious slits.

"You bitch," he hollered, swinging a beefy arm.

Lydia ducked, but the punch clipped her shoulder, and she fell to the ground. Pain shot through her arm.

Please don't let it be broken.

"If you fink," the bulldog grunted, struggling to regain his balance on unsteady feet, "you can come up 'ere wif your papers and 'oity-toity airs, telling our girls wot to fink, well then…"

He made another clumsy swing, but Lydia was being lifted off the ground and pulled out of reach. Harriet grunted as she heaved Lydia into the hackney. Grace pulled the door shut, and the carriage lurched forward. The angry bellows of the three men gradually faded as the driver hurried the hackney out of the square.

Lydia lay on the dirty floor of the hackney, gasping for breath.

"Are you hurt?" Grace ran her hands lightly over Lydia, seeming to check for injuries.

"That was the scariest bloody thing that's ever happened to me," Harriet wheezed. "And I've been to prison!"

Lydia snorted a laugh from where she was huddled.

"At least if she's laughing, we know she's not dead." Grace sat back in the seat with a sigh.

"Let's get you up." Harriet pulled at Lydia until she was sitting, and then helped guide her up beside her. "Are you all right?"

Lydia cradled her arm. "I hurt something when I fell," she said with a strangled laugh, gesturing to her left arm.

"You didn't fall," Grace bit out. "You were *punched*."

Lydia snickered.

"Why are you being so mean?" Harriet asked Grace.

Grace huffed. "I'm sorry. I guess I get grumpy when I'm terrified that my friends and I will be murdered. And apparently, fear gives *her* the giggles." She pointed at Lydia.

"I-I'm absolutely terrified." Lydia laughed and began to shake.

"I think she's in shock." Harriet wrapped an arm around Lydia.

Lydia leaned into her warmth. Her whole body felt frozen and trembly. "Take me home," Lydia gasped into her shoulder. "Please. I just want to go home." And she continued to laugh even as she sobbed, tears rolling down her cheeks.

Chapter Sixteen

BENEDICT SHIFTED ON the formal sitting room's dainty chair, the spindly legs creaking. Such furniture was not built with his proportions in mind, but when he had moved toward the sofa, his mother had hissed for him to take a chair instead.

Apparently, the sofa was reserved for Emelia and her suitor.

"Tell me about your hobbies, Miss Southcott," Throckmorton said from his undoubtably comfortable seat on the sofa next to Benedict's sister. His shorter height and lean frame would have been perfect for the delicate chair.

Benedict tried not to glare at the man.

"Hobbies?" parroted Emelia, as if a question about her had taken her by surprise.

What sort of insufferable, self-important popinjays had courted her in the past that any interest in her as a person was seen as unusual? Benedict ground his teeth together. He would be a better brother. He would pay more attention to Emelia and his mother, and less to the desires of his own heart.

He pictured Lydia as he'd seen her the night before out on the balcony. Her face gone white at Emelia's accusations. Her beautiful, kiss-swollen lips pinched tight with hurt. With the hurt *he* had caused, by allowing his sister to speak so poorly of what they shared.

He loved his sister.

And she had been right in her worry over the family's reputation, but Benedict deeply regretted allowing her to speak such words that had cut Lydia to the quick.

"… knitting, watercolors, and of course, needlepoint." Emelia managed to hide her grimace at the mention of the finger pricking game by sipping her tea.

"That all sounds very…lovely," Throckmorton said, eyes casting about as if looking for a better word.

Disgust sat heavy in Benedict's stomach. His sister couldn't even speak openly to a man she was considering spending her life with about her true passion. The way their society stifled women was so obvious, so clear, once a person's eyes were open to seeing it.

"Tell him about mathematics."

Lydia's head swiveled to face Benedict, her eyes wide in shock.

From her own uncomfortable chair, his mother glared. "Benedict!"

Benedict squeezed the delicate arm of his chair until he heard the wood creak. "Oh, for heaven sakes, mother, Emelia despises needlepoint. She keeps stabbing herself and bleeding over the threads." He gestured at his sister. "Tell him, Emelia. Tell him what really interests you."

Emelia's gaze ricocheted between her mother—practically vibrating in her seat, such was her displeasure—and Throckmorton. The lord gazed at Emelia with open curiosity but, Benedict was glad to see, no judgment.

"I… I…" Emelia's hand fluttered around the strand of pearls around her neck.

She looked at Benedict, and he saw the yearning there in her eyes. She wanted to be her authentic self, here in her own home, surrounded by family, and seated next to the man she had set her heart on. And yet…she was afraid.

Benedict held her stare, giving her a nod of encouragement. He hoped she would see all the support and love in his expression that he couldn't voice at the moment. He'd tell her too, later, when it was just the two of them.

Emelia cleared her throat and turned to face Throckmorton. "What I most enjoy," she told him, her voice growing firm, "is mathematics."

Benedict's mother released a soft moan.

Throckmorton's eyes lit up. "Mathematics is a passion of mine as well. Have you studied the new formula dealing with…"

While the two lovebirds discussed the joys of addition and subtraction, Benedict took his mother's limp hand, leading her to the window seat at the far side of the room. They sat together, his back against one casement and hers against the other, their knees touching in the middle as they both looked outside where the sun was shining.

"Why did you do that?" his mother asked, her voice shaky.

He studied her.

Margaret Southcott, Lady Lovell, was a lovely woman, her expressive brown eyes framed by fine lines of laughter. She was over a foot shorter than him, and Benedict recalled when he'd finally surpassed his mother in height. He'd still been a boy, and it had seemed so odd that he should be bigger than his parent, who was an adult full grown with all the authority and power that entailed.

"Emelia does not like to needlepoint," he finally replied.

"Lord Throckmorton doesn't need to know that," she whispered back, as if Emelia's feelings toward needlepoint were a scandalous secret that could make or break the couple's courtship. "She should pretend."

Benedict sighed.

He was so tired of the idea of *should*. Emelia should like needlepoint, simply because she was a lady. Emelia shouldn't like mathematics, because it might drive a suitor away. Benedict shouldn't kiss Lydia, because it might cause gossip at a ball. And he definitely shouldn't love her, because *she was not for the likes of him*.

He stared across the room at his sister, who was speaking animatedly to Throckmorton, a genuine smile on her face.

"Mother, if Throckmorton were to propose, shouldn't he know the real Emelia? Shouldn't he know what she genuinely likes and dislikes? And if they share a love for mathematics, isn't that something that will connect them even more?"

His mother glanced over at the couple as well, and her expression shifted into something softer. Something nearly forlorn flashed across her face.

She looked down at her hands, clasped together on her lap. "You don't know what it's like," she whispered, "being a lady. Always being judged. Living at the whims of others, the whims of men."

Benedict shut his eyes. In all his anger at a society that stifled his sister and Lydia and all the other women in their situation, he had not once considered that the same society had also stifled his mother. What had she borne in her fifty years on this earth?

"Where you…were you unhappy? With Father?"

She looked up, her eyes glassy with unshed tears. "I was so very fond of your father. In the beginning, it felt like love. But later…he stopped paying attention to me. And I realized that he never really knew the real me. Who I was on the inside. My private self, I suppose, as opposed to what ladies are supposed to show the world."

She blinked rapidly as if trying to stop any tears from escaping.

"Your sister is so vibrant, so full of energy and enthusiasm. I just worry…" She cast a glance over her shoulder once more to where Emelia and Throckmorton were laughing together on the sofa.

She turned back to Benedict. "Well, perhaps I don't have to worry. Perhaps she *can* show her private self to someone she cares about. Perhaps that person would love her for who she is on the inside, just as she would love them. Who's to say such a thing could never be?"

Benedict took his mother's hand. "I'm sorry," he said, keeping his voice gentle, "for all the things you had to endure. That Father never looked for who you were inside. He was—"

His mother squeezed his hand, and Benedict left the rest unspoken.

"Thank you," she said. "For helping your sister. Both now," she gestured over her shoulder, "and over the last few days. She told me what you and Lady Lydia did, cleaning up your reputation at the salon and ball. It will give Emelia a chance at happiness. And I'm so very grateful."

Benedict couldn't speak past the lump in his throat. The cost he'd paid had been so very high.

A servant entered the room. "A message for Lord Lovell," he announced before carrying a letter to Benedict on a silver tray. Benedict frowned at the unfamiliar handwriting.

"I'd best check on the tea," his mother murmured before leaving him alone on the window seat.

Benedict broke the plain seal on the simple paper.

Lord Lovell, I thought you would be wanting to know that Lady Lydia has been injured after her outing with her new friends. I've sent for the doctor, but I would appreciate if you could come over. Sincerely, Mrs. Smythe

Benedict's heartbeat pounded in his ears, and he had no recollection of rising to his feet but, he realized, he was standing. However, it didn't matter. What did matter was getting to Lydia as soon as possible.

"Benny?" his sister asked, her voice concerned, as he stormed to the door. "Is aught amiss?"

"I have to check on a friend," he called over his shoulder. He didn't wait for a reply.

BENEDICT PUSHED PAST the startled butler at the door to Lydia's home. "Lydia!" he bellowed, storming across the foyer.

"You received my note." Mrs. Smythe trotted in, her hands clasped together.

"Where is she?" Benedict asked the housekeeper as he headed up the main staircase.

"In her bedroom," Mrs. Smythe called up to him. "Take a right at the corridor and then it's the second room on the left."

Benedict had no recollection of his mad dash out of his house, the wait for his horse to be saddled, or the ride across Mayfair. But the pinched look of worry on Mrs. Smythe's face just now had permeated the fog of fear that had enveloped him the moment he'd read her message. Even more disturbing was the way little Timmy sat forlornly on the bottom stair in the foyer, idly swapping a ball from one hand to the other.

And Benedict could feel his own emotions in this moment, as if his heart had left his chest. As if his heart beat twice as fast in his fear for Lydia.

Please let her be all right.

He burst through the door of her bedroom but pulled up short at the sight before him.

The room was filled with women. All wore the same look of concern. One was getting a bedwarmer ready with coals from the fireplace. Another was pouring steaming water from a kettle into an ewer. Others were gathered around the bed, murmuring over the figure Benedict knew was huddled there.

Lydia.

He gently pushed his way through, hearing a few murmured comments about what had happened.

She looked so small, lying under heaps of blankets in the massive bed. Her teeth were chattering, and her face was white. And even beneath all the covers, he could see her form trembling. For some reason, she was freezing.

"Put the bed warmer in, now," he commanded.

The woman working with the coals jumped to attention.

"No warm water," he said to the woman at the ewer. "Water will merely diffuse her own heat." The lady nodded her understanding, stepping away from the steaming bowl of water.

The best way for Lydia to be warm would be to share body heat with someone who was hot. And right now, Benedict's fear had him blazing like a bonfire.

"Everyone out," he commanded, his voice soft but firm. "Have Mrs. Smythe send the doctor up as soon as he arrives. Otherwise, we're not to be disturbed."

Agatha approached him from the other side of the bed. She laid her hand upon his arm. "You'll warm her up?" she whispered.

Benedict nodded impatiently. The sooner they all left, the sooner he could help Lydia.

"We should've thought to do that ourselves. Thank you." She squeezed his arm, and then herded the rest of the women out of the room, pulling the door shut behind her with a soft click.

Lydia's eyes remained closed, but he had the sense that she was awake.

"I'm here," he murmured, working at the buttons of his clothing. "I'm going to lay with you, darling, and warm you up."

She made a little hum of assent.

It seemed as if his clothes had suddenly tripled in thickness, as if the buttons had grown larger than the buttonholes and his boots had shrunk, not wanting to release his feet.

Benedict growled in impatience, tugging, and yanking and swearing until he was dressed only in his smalls. He stared at the bed for a moment, thinking. "Are you injured?" He didn't wish to bump against any part of her that might be hurt.

"My left arm," she whispered.

Benedict bit back another curse. He had hoped that her only injury would be the chill that wracked her body.

Please, let the doctor arrive soon.

He crossed to the right side of her bed and slid beneath the covers, scooting over slowly and taking care not to jostle her. He sucked in a breath when he reached her. Her skin was frigid. He eased himself to her side, slipping one arm under her head and wrapping the other around her waist. He tangled his legs with hers.

"So hot," she murmured. Her eyelids fluttered, little light-brown and gold fans against her pale cheeks. And then she opened her eyes at him, blue and bright with tears. Her lower lip trembled before she caught it in her teeth.

"It's all right now," he whispered. "I'm here. The doctor is coming, and Mrs. Smythe and all the reformers are here to help too."

"I feel so stupid," she admitted, continuing to hold his gaze. "When the man struck me, I fell and hurt my arm, but I didn't injure anything else. I don't know why I became so cold and shaky."

Benedict's thoughts skittered to a halt, and it took a moment for him to be able to speak. "A man *struck* you?" He heard a growl, and then realized it came from himself.

She made a little squeak of protest, and he loosened his grip around her.

"I'm sorry," he murmured, kissing her temple.

She sighed and snuggled in closer to him.

"Who was it?"

Lydia stilled. "Who was who?"

Benedict kept his tone conversational. "The man who struck you. I just want to have a little chat with him."

Lydia rolled her eyes, and Benedict had never been so glad to have her do that. She could roll her eyes at him however much she wished, as long as she was all right.

"Benedict," she said, tone exasperated.

"Lydia," he mimicked.

She huffed. "I don't know his name. He was some drunken imbecile who didn't like what we were doing. I think the ideas that women should be part of the reform movement, or even be able to vote, upset the sensitive balance of his soul."

Benedict's lips quirked. "The sensitive balance of his soul?"

Lydia's attempt at distraction had worked to an extent. His initial fury at someone striking her had dissipated a bit. Perhaps he could not extract retribution upon the coward who drank too much and decided to beat on women, but Benedict could ensure that she was never in such a position again.

She stretched, and the curve of her hip rubbed against him. Benedict buried his nose in her silky hair, inhaling the fresh scent. He allowed his fingers the small freedom to move a scant inch over her waist. He could feel the warmth of her skin through the thin layer of her chemise.

Good. She was beginning to lose her chill. He eased his hips back, not wanting to embarrass either of them with the evidence of his arousal. Lydia grumbled in protest and scooted closer.

"Don't move away," she said. "You're helping to vanquish the cold."

Benedict sighed but acquiesced. Once again, they were laying close together. If she noticed his erection pressing into her hip, she didn't say anything. He closed his eyes. He would imprint this moment on his heart, on his very soul. Lydia in his arms, so soft and sweet. The two of them nestled in bed together, like lovers.

If only they were in truth.

"The others say that I went into shock," Lydia murmured. "I suppose I'm not as tough as they are." There was a strange edge to her voice.

Benedict smoothed her hair back from her face. "No one insults my friend like that."

She blinked up at him.

"You," he explained. "You're my friend, and I don't like hearing you speak ill of yourself. You're the toughest person I know."

It was true. Lydia was smart and fierce and bold. And she'd gotten away with authoring the Democratium Liberum articles, with no one in London the wiser as to the writer's identity.

"But the instant something went wrong, this happened to me." She pointed her chin down to indicate her body under the mound of blankets.

Benedict was relieved to see she'd stopped trembling.

"Are you sure that's true?" Benedict asked running a finger along the soft curve of her cheek. "The *instant* something went wrong?"

"Well…" Lydia wrinkled her nose. "Perhaps not the instant."

"I heard what the reformers were discussing when I walked into your room. It sounded like it was your quick thinking that saved Harriet and Grace."

"I just sent them to get the hackney."

Benedict raised an eyebrow at her. "And stayed behind with the drunk, violent man yourself?"

Benedict's entire body felt clammy at the thought of what had happened, of what *could* have happened to her. To his Lydia.

She bit her lip, then nodded.

Benedict swallowed against the lump in his throat. "Lydia, you mustn't put yourself in danger like that. Something terrible could have happened—"

"Something terrible *did* happen," she corrected. "But it all worked out in the end."

He shook his head. "Promise me next time you'll bring along footmen. Armed guards. An entire battalion." He inhaled. "Or me."

She searched his eyes for a moment. "I…I wasn't sure you'd want to come. With the risk of scandal—"

"No," he interrupted. "That's not what really matters, not in the end." His heart thundered. "What matters is…" He trailed off, uncertain what to say. Uncertain of his thoughts, his feelings, in this moment.

But it seemed Lydia didn't need certainty from him. She pressed her mouth to his and silenced all his doubts with a kiss.

Chapter Seventeen

LYDIA HAD FINALLY defrosted. The terrible tremors that had wracked her body earlier were gone, and it no longer felt as if she'd been bobbing in the frigid ocean for hours and hours.

But perhaps the greatest reason why the cold was disappearing was the way that Benedict set her senses on fire.

The whole time he'd been warming her up while they talked, he'd also been slowly bringing her body to life. Touching her hair. Stroking her waist. Rubbing his muscular legs, dusted with hair, against hers. And staring at her with fire in his eyes.

She knew it was unwise to turn to him, but that was a problem for future Lydia. Present Lydia wanted to feel his lips against hers once more.

He kept the kiss gentle, but Lydia felt the flex of his fingers against her waist, as if he struggled to not devour her. And that's what it had felt like at the ball the night before. He had *devoured* her. He had consumed her with his kisses, with his touch, and with his gentle words.

And with the look in his eyes.

She'd been too frightened in the moment to accept what she saw there, but perhaps the incident in the market had made her brave.

The look in his eyes had felt a lot like love.

And so now, she kissed him with all that was in her own

heart. She was too shaken to examine it closely, but it was strong, and powerful, and real. She told him, with each stroke of her tongue, each kiss with her lips, and each breathy sigh how she felt for him.

"Lydia," he whispered, trailing kisses from her mouth to her neck.

"Touch me," she commanded, her breasts aching for his caresses.

He hesitated, so she grabbed his hand and slid it up from her waist to just under her breast. He paused there, fingers flexing against her rib cage, and then with a growl, he moved his hand.

Lydia moaned at the sensation of his hand moving over her breasts. Her nipples were tight and tingly, and she felt her body's pulse between her legs.

"Benedict," she gasped.

He kissed his way down her neck, down her collarbone, until his mouth was at her chemise's edge. "Can I?"

"Yes," she breathed.

And then he tugged her chemise, and his mouth was on her bare breast. She gasped, arching to press herself against his delicious mouth even more. The lathe of his tongue, hot and slick across her nipple, sparked pleasure through her, and Lydia pressed her thighs together, trying to ease the ache at her core.

"So sweet," he murmured against her skin. "So beautiful."

Lydia wanted him to do this forever. And she also ached for more. She rolled toward him, wanting to press herself more firmly against him, but the motion jostled her arm.

She gasped in pain.

Benedict pulled back immediately, his mouth pinched with concern. "Did I hurt you?"

She swallowed. "My arm." She carefully rolled herself onto her back. "It wasn't you. I just tried to move it and..."

Benedict pulled back further until half a foot separated them. He exhaled, rubbing his hand down his face. "I'm sorry." He was quiet for a moment, then added, "I should have been more careful."

Lydia looked away. It sounded like he was referring to more than just her arm.

"Do you feel warm enough?" he asked.

Lydia nodded, staring up at the ceiling. He was doing it again—apologizing for intimacy between them. Pulling away. Why did she get her hopes up?

"I… I'll get dressed then."

And Lydia listened to the rustle of his clothing before he left once more.

THE NEXT MORNING, Lydia thanked her lady's maid, sitting back in the chair at her vanity once she had left. She gave her left arm an experimental twist. It was still quite sore, but the wrap and icing the doctor had prescribed yesterday had done much to help. Thankfully, he had diagnosed her injury as just a sprain and nothing serious.

And it had been shock, he'd told her, which had sent her into her state of chills and shaking. "It's common," he had said, "for women to find themselves in such a state. They have such delicate nerves, you see."

Lydia gritted her teeth, and once the man was gone, instructed Mrs. Smythe to not call upon his services again.

Delicate nerves.

As if what happened yesterday wasn't proof that *men* were the ones with delicate nerves. The way that the bulldog and his two oafish companions had gone into a rage simply because Lydia, Grace, and Harriet had been distributing pamphlets was a perfect example.

She felt around in the back drawer of her vanity until her fingers felt a familiar packet. She slid it into her pocket before making her way downstairs to the breakfast room. Agatha, Grace, Harriet, and Timmy were seated around the table, lingering over their meal.

"Good morning," she greeted.

Apparently the others had already finished their breakfasts. The group as a whole was made up of early risers, she noticed.

"How are you feeling, love?" Agatha asked, her eyebrows drawn together with worry.

"Lucky," Lydia admitted, holding up her left arm with the wrap for them to see. "Thank you for helping take such good care of me yesterday. I'm so glad everyone else was unscathed."

"Those *brutes* wouldn't have been unscathed if I'd had a few more minutes with them and my basket," Harriet muttered.

"What's that, Mama?" Timmy asked.

Harriet blanched. Apparently, she hadn't shared the full story with her son.

"Timmy, I have something for you to play with," Lydia said, hoping to distract him from his questions.

The lad hopped out of his chair and dashed around the table. His sandy hair stood up at odd angles, he had a smear of jam beside his mouth, and his blue eyes were wide with curiosity. He was, Lydia decided, the most adorable child in all of England.

"Yesterday, I promised to show you how to pick a lock, but with my arm being sore, I'm afraid I can't do that today."

Timmy's shoulders drooped, but he said, "That's all right. We can do it another day."

"Well," Lydia said, reaching into her pocket, "I thought a good substitute would be playing with the lock picks and seeing if you could sort out how they work."

Timmy reached out to the little bundle in Lydia's hand, but then he glanced at his mother.

"It's all right," she assured him. "Just be sure you don't open any doors you shouldn't, and don't get yourself trapped in some far-off room."

After nodding to his mother, Timmy took the kit. "Thank you!" he exclaimed, bouncing on his feet. "I'm going to be an expert. I'll be able to rescue people all the time now."

And then he dashed out of the room.

"Be sure to wash your hands," Harriet called after him, but there was no response. She sighed. "That boy is somehow always sticky. I don't know how he manages it."

Agatha chuckled. "You were that way too," she said to Grace.

"I was not a sticky child," Grace objected, but smiled at her mother, nonetheless.

Lydia's stomach growled. She excused herself and headed to the buffet but realized it would be a challenge to put food on her plate and carry it at the same time.

Harriet noticed her dilemma and jumped up to help. "Let me." She dished a few things onto Lydia's plate, and both of them returned to the table.

"You need me to cut anything for you?" Harriet asked, eyes twinkling. "As a mother, I'm rather an expert on cutting up other people's food."

Grace patted her rounded stomach. "I suppose I'll need to get some training in that myself."

Lydia chuckled and slid her plate toward the woman. Once she was contentedly munching on tiny squares of cut bacon, Lydia listened while the others chatted about the baby.

After a few minutes, Agatha cleared her throat, and Lydia looked up.

"Lydia, love," the reform leader said, "yesterday took such a frightening turn. I think it would be best if your role in all this was over."

They couldn't mean it. Lydia dropped her fork. "What? No."

Agatha exchanged glances with Harriet and Grace.

"We've been talking," Agatha said. "And we all agree that we've asked too much of you. You've done so much already, getting us out of Newgate with Lord Lovell and then inviting us to stay here. You've even gotten Democratium Liberum to write for us, and you set up the pamphlet printing. It's more than we ever imagined when we came to town. You don't need to be part of this anymore. If something were to happen to you—"

Lydia raised her chin. "If something happens to *me*?" She shook her head. "As if my life is more important or valuable than yours? That's the opposite of everything we've been saying. That's the opposite of the entire reform movement. If we believe that everyone is equal, then I shouldn't be more deserving of safety than the rest of you."

"I hear what you're saying," Grace said, her hands clasped together on the table, "but the truth is that *society* values your safety more than ours. If one of us were hurt, it would be a tragedy of course, yet it would not make the newspaper headlines. But if an aristocratic lady was harmed doing reform work, well…" She spread her hands wide. "People would read about it on the front page and believe that it's dangerous to fight for reform. That would bring the wrong kind of attention to our cause."

Lydia looked down at her plate, trying to rein in her emotions. She didn't want her actions to bring harm to their cause. She was practical enough to understand the logic of their point.

And yet…she was a part of this group now. She felt connected to their work in a meaningful way, and this had come into her life when she was feeling adrift after the kidnapping and ceasing her reform articles for the paper.

Was there perhaps a way for her to be involved that wouldn't place the movement in jeopardy?

She stared at the little mound of scrambled eggs on her plate while her mind searched for an answer. It looked like the cook had sprinkled a bit of fresh herbs into the eggs this morning. She could smell the fragrant scent, and it reminded her of her friend Jane's botany laboratory at the LCA.

Her head jerked up. Jane's laboratory. Jane's herbs. Jane's *special* herb.

She faced Agatha. "I know how we can keep everyone safe."

Agatha frowned. "What?"

Lydia clasped her hands together, then winced when her left arm protested the movement. "I belong to a group…a secret group. It's similar to yours, in fact."

"You're in a reform society as well?" Harriet asked.

Lydia looked at the three women sitting at the table with her. If she were going to reveal this means of self-defense, she would have to tell them how it came to be. Could she trust them with the secret of the Ladies Covert Academy?

Agatha's forehead was knitted with concern. Harriet glanced worriedly between Lydia and Lydia's plate, as if she were fighting the temptation to cut her bacon into little pieces for her. And Grace's hand rested atop her belly, her mouth pinched with worry.

In such a short span of time, these women had become very dear to her. And she *did* trust them. She'd trusted them with her life yesterday at the market. And she would trust them now with her secret. "It's not a reform group that I belong to," she began, fiddling with her fork, "but I suppose in our own way, we're reforming our own lives. It's called the Ladies Charitable Association. It's an organization here in London that does charity work. Knitting booties for orphans, sewing bandages for soldiers, and such."

She drew a deep breath. This was the point of no return. If she told them, she could not take it back.

"And although we *do* engage in charity, the group's true purpose is to allow women to study, train, and practice in fields that society does not allow them. The charity group is a cover for our real purpose."

Agatha's head was cocked to the side as she listened. Grace was leaning forward, her body still. And Harriet's eyes were wide with excitement.

"One of this group's members is my friend as well," Lydia continued. "She's a talented botanist and came upon a plant that has interesting properties. When dried and ground up into powder, it works as a means of self-defense. Anyone who has this powder blown into their face will have stinging eyes, coughing, and burning lungs. My friend bottles the powder into little vials and has given it to all the women in our group so that they can go out in the world knowing they have the means to defend themselves, if the need should arise. Knowing they aren't helpless."

Agatha leaned back in her chair, studying Lydia for a moment. "Your friend would share these vials of powder with us?"

Lydia replied, "She's on her honeymoon right now, so I'm unable to ask her. But we're very close and run the group together along with another woman, so it won't be a problem."

"This is astonishing," murmured Grace. "A secret society of women who don't have to fear being overpowered by men."

"If we can protect ourselves, think of what we could do." Harriet smacked her hand down onto the table, causing the silverware to rattle on the plates.

"Thank you for trusting us with your secret." Agatha held Lydia's gaze. "What is the name of your group?"

"It's the Ladies Covert Academy. I can take you there today, to see about getting the vials." Lydia's chest expanded with pride. It was so rare that she was able to speak about the incredible organization to which she belonged. To do so with her new friends felt like its own sweet victory. She'd told them her secret, and they would keep it safe.

A throat cleared behind her. It held a masculine timbre and the back of Lydia's neck prickled with awareness. She turned to see who stood in the doorway to the breakfast room, even though she already knew who she'd see. Her heart began to pound.

"My mother always taught me it was rude to eavesdrop." Benedict leaned against the doorframe, arms crossed, in a lazy pose that did not fool Lydia for one second. "But in this instance, it seemed it was worth the bad manners."

Chapter Eighteen

BENEDICT MAINTAINED HIS unaffected pose even when Lydia jumped from her seat, causing her chair to crash back onto the floor.

"B-Benedict," she stuttered, all the color drained from her face.

Benedict recalled how she had looked the day before in her bed—pale, trembling, and cold as an icicle. He did not wish to cause her distress. However, at the moment, *he* was in too much distress to offer her comfort.

He continued his idle lean against the doorframe, unfolding his arms to inspect his fingernails as if their state were of great importance to him.

"Have you...been there long?" she asked.

The other women at the table sat watchful and quiet. He had no doubt they would leap to Lydia's defense if they thought she needed it. However, she had nothing to fear from him. He would not harm one hair on her head, but the tangle of emotions wrapping him up right now was nearly unbearable.

She had kept *so* many secrets from him.

Had Jack and Pippa as well? For some reason, the thought of their potential betrayal didn't sting the way Lydia's did.

Benedict stretched his mouth in a wide smile. He imagined he was showing all his teeth like some sort of crocodile. Lydia flinched.

Good.

She knew the difference between his fake and real smile. His fake and real joy. *His fake and real trustworthiness.*

No.

Not that apparently.

"How long have I been standing here?" he repeated, now giving his attention to the fingernails on his other hand. A wastrel like him couldn't let his grooming lapse, now could he? He unclenched his teeth before answering. "Well, I came along around the time you shared the secret of the Ladies Charitable Association. Or shall I say, the Ladies *Covert* Academy?" He raised an eyebrow.

Lydia swallowed.

"I heard you share the secret that the charity is mostly a ruse. I heard you share the secret that Jane is a weapons botanist. I must say, that one was quite surprising, although now that I recall the herb she slipped into that woman's tea to get her to confess to trying to steal Dev's title, well, it makes a bit more sense."

"Jane doesn't want to hurt anyone with her discovery," Lydia said, her mouth pinched in anger. "She stumbled upon that by accident and realized it could be used for self-defense."

"No need to get upset." Benedict raised his hands and offered his crocodile smile once more. "No one is upset here. Not you. Not me." He paused and gave her a look. "Unless...there's a *reason* for me to be upset?"

Lydia held his gaze for a moment, her expression defiant, before she looked away in silence.

Not that he expected her to say anything. She had made it quite clear who was trustworthy in her mind. And these women whom she'd known less than a week were told her secrets, but he, who had shared intimacy and closeness with her—well, *he* had believed they'd shared closeness—had not been privy to her secrets.

And that stung more than any past betrayal he'd ever experienced. Unfortunately, he was rather an expert on that topic. He pushed thoughts of his father away. Now was not the time to dredge up old hurts.

"I also overheard," he continued, keeping his tone conversational, "that you're planning to arm the reformers with this weaponized herb. And take them to retrieve it from the Ladies Covert Academy, if I'm not mistaken?"

He let his glance brush over Harriet, Grace, and Agatha. The women's expressions gave nothing away and he had to admit he was impressed with their steadfast and silent support for their friend.

"It's not necessary for us to visit the LCA." Lydia straightened her spine and looked him dead in the eye. "We had just hoped for a bit of protection since we didn't have any yesterday."

Bloody hell.

Benedict absorbed the body blow of her words. They needed protection because *he* had not been with them. He had chosen his sister and her demands to protect her reputation over Lydia and the reformers' cause.

Now they wished for a bit of protection.

Very well.

He pulled away from the doorway and dusted his hands off. "A trip to the Ladies Covert Academy sounds like a smashing idea. Shall we be off?"

If he was a petty person, he would have been gratified by the way Lydia blanched at him. However, he found no satisfaction in her discomfort.

No, what he was feeling was gutted. Lydia didn't trust him, and it was crushing his heart. But he'd be damned if he left her unprotected again.

"My Lord," began Agatha from the far end of the table.

But whatever she had intended to say withered in the face of Benedict's hard stare. He attempted to communicate that he was upset but not a danger. And he wanted to protect them since he hadn't been present to do so the day before.

Either Agatha could read minds or she was well versed in the art of eyeball conversations because she gave Benedict a small nod before turning her attention to Lydia.

"Love, I do believe Lord Lovell wishes to accompany us to your secret academy. Given what happened yesterday as well as the threat that Staines presents, I think it would be a good idea to have him with us."

"Mother!" Grace protested.

Agatha held up her hand. "I know that I've taught you that women are just as capable as men," she told her daughter, although her words were likely for the rest of them as well. "But there are times when it is a benefit to have a big, strapping fellow along. Let us not look a gift horse in the mouth."

She turned to Lydia. "We shall fetch our cloaks and meet you in the foyer in ten minutes."

Agatha gave a look to Harriet and Grace, and they followed her out of the room. As Harriet passed by Benedict, her eyes were shining brightly, perhaps with excitement. Meanwhile, the look Grace shot him clearly signaled she wished she could wallop him over the head with a very sturdy frying pan.

Once they were alone in the dining room, Lydia folded her arms across her chest. "Did you go home yesterday, after you…visited me?"

Benedict was gratified to see a blush across her cheeks. "I did not."

She frowned. "So, you stayed here again?"

"I did."

Had he ever spoken so formally in his life? He was practically imitating her brother Jack, who Benedict often teased for his focus on duty and all the dry conversation that went along with it.

"But I thought your sister…" She trailed off.

Benedict stepped closer to her. The distance stretching between them wasn't enough, even as it was much too far.

He replied, "I couldn't have left the house last night, not after what happened to you. Not for any reason."

Lydia inhaled. "I see."

Their gazes tangled. Benedict allowed his shields to drop, wanting her to see what he felt in this moment. His worry for her. His caring. And also, this deep, gouging hurt that she had not trusted him.

Lydia inhaled sharply before dropping her gaze. "I… I have to fetch my cloak." She fled the room.

And Benedict was left alone with a buffet full of breakfast delights. But not even the prospect of his beloved strawberry jam could take away the ache in his chest.

⟫⟫⟫⟨⟨⟨⟨

LYDIA MARCHED GRIMLY along the sidewalk, Benedict at her side and the other three women trailing behind like reluctant ducklings.

It was a fifteen-minute walk from her house to the headquarters of the LCA. The Academy was also the home of her friend Jane and her new husband Devin Stokes, the Marquess of Rowling.

Together, Lydia, Jane, and Pippa ran the Academy. With both Jane and Pippa out of town, Lydia should have been paying frequent visits to the LCA, checking in with the ladies, ensuring all the bills for instructors and supplies were paid, and always, *always*, monitoring that their secret remained hidden from society.

Unfortunately, she had failed in all her tasks. Not only had she neglected to check in at the LCA because of her involvement with the reformers, but she'd also been quite negligent with the secret. And the number one rule at the LCA was—don't talk about the LCA.

At least with anyone outside their circle.

Lydia's brother Jack had learned of the LCA after Lydia's

kidnapping. He had thought she was there doing charity work, but when she failed to return home at the end of the day, he had stormed inside, demanding that the organization's founder, now retired, assist him in hunting down his sister. She had refused to become involved, fearful that the LCA's secret would get out and destroy the entire endeavor if the organization participated in a hunt for a missing woman.

Desperate, Jack had blackmailed Pippa into helping him after he spied her fencing lesson from the back garden. Luckily for everyone, Jack had proven as trustworthy as they came, and he and Pippa had fallen in love on their journey to rescue Lydia.

Dev, Jane's husband, had known about the Ladies Covert Academy from the very beginning. He was the founder's stepson, and the marquessate's true heir. Because of complications in proving his legitimacy and mysterious threats on his life, he had posed as a servant in the household while he worked behind the scenes to claim his title. When a suspicious burglary had closed the LCA, he and Jane had teamed up. He would help her solve the mystery of the burglary so that the LCA might safely reopen, and in exchange she would help him prove his claim to the title and uncover who threatened his life. And as he and Jane had worked together, they too had fallen in love.

Like Jack, Dev had also been completely trustworthy.

So more than just the LCA's members knew its true purpose, but never had such a breach of secrecy happened as what Lydia had allowed today. In one single conversation, she had let four people know the LCA's secret. Perhaps since she'd only meant to tell three, Benedict didn't really count?

She glanced over as he trudged beside her down the sidewalk of Mayfair. A muscle in his cheek pulsed.

She'd hurt him. Badly.

Would she change any of it, if she could? Lydia wasn't certain of the answer. He didn't deserve to know her secrets, but they had grown so close this past week. They'd been a team in so many ways, helping the reformers and fighting against Staines.

She understood why he would feel hurt that she hadn't shared everything with him.

"I'm sorry," she said softly.

Benedict grunted in acknowledgement.

"It involved more than just me," she added. "I told you that when you discovered that I was Democratium Liberum. Those secrets weren't mine to share."

He adjusted the leather gloves over his hands. It was a cold morning, and their breath fogged in the frigid air.

"Who else knows?" he asked, speaking for the first time since they'd left her home.

Lydia glanced over her shoulder, but the other three had fallen back a bit. Perhaps they sensed that Lydia and Benedict needed privacy for this conversation.

"Lady Rowling founded the organization."

His eyes widened. "Dev's stepmother?"

Lydia nodded. "Her family forced her to marry a much older man when she was just seventeen, to save the family's station when they lost their fortune. She hated not having a choice in her life, in what her life was going to be. Once she was a widow and had control of the unentailed money her husband had made in India, she decided to use it to give other women the opportunity that she hadn't had to choose the course of their life."

Benedict grunted.

"So Dev knows, and Jack discovered it last year when I was kidna—" Lydia clamped her mouth shut. *Oh no.*

Benedict came to an abrupt halt, whirling to face her. His eyes were thunderous. "When you were *kidnapped?* Was that what you are going to say?"

Lydia balled her hands into fists. Glancing back, she saw that the others had stopped as well, giving her and Benedict a bit of space. Agatha was keeping a close watch though. The woman's maternal instincts were a balm to Lydia's soul since her own mother hadn't seemed to have any.

She looked back at Benedict, who held himself so taut that he practically vibrated. He'd learned so much today that she might as well tell him the whole truth. Lydia took a deep breath.

"I've been a member of the LCA since its inception. I did my political research there and wrote all my Democratium Liberum articles there as well. I didn't want Jack to know." She quirked a brow at him. "Can you imagine what his reaction would've been?"

Benedict gave her a stern look. He would not be swayed out of his temper by a bit of shared Jack teasing.

"Last year, a gentleman began to court me," she continued. "An attorney by the name of Aubrey Andrews. He flattered me and made me feel special, and I…I believed it was real."

Lydia looked down at the sidewalk. The old familiar shame burned in her stomach. She had thought she was so clever, being a member of the LCA and writing a successful column in the newspaper that everyone talked about. But she'd been given a bit of flattery and a few charming smiles by the first man to court her, and she'd abandoned good sense and reason faster than a child abandoned old toys on Christmas morning.

She didn't know which was worse—not trusting others after the kidnapping, or not trusting her own judgment.

"You *are* special," Benedict said fiercely. "Don't let that pestilence of a human being cast even one doubt in your mind on that front. You are remarkable and clever and brave. You are beautiful and kind and loving. *That* is what's real." His eyes blazed as he spoke. Something cracked and damaged inside of Lydia knitted together with his words. Especially with the certitude with which he spoke them. And with the way he was looking at her, here and now.

Despite all the tension between them—at their kisses, his sister, his reputation, and the secrets—he *did* believe she was special. And that made her believe it too.

"Thank you," she breathed, wishing she could lean her head against his firm, steady chest. But they were in public and had an audience, so she hoped he saw all that she was feeling in her expression.

She continued her story. "That 'pestilence', as you called him, lured me into a secret carriage ride that turned into a kidnapping. I thought it was all so romantic, until we were careening up the Great North Road and he refused to let me out of the carriage. It turned out he had been hired by Lord Somerset to bring me north by any means necessary."

Benedict had started at the familiar name. "Somerset was removed from the House of Commons last year and then vanished. No one knew why."

Lydia huffed. "Perhaps he'll send word from Australia one day."

Benedict barked a laugh. "Australia? Jack must've ensured that it was handled quietly."

Lydia nodded. "Somerset had been in the pocket of a coal investor, a man wealthier than Croesus, who was manipulating the broken system that elected members to the Commons. He would bribe members for votes, votes that would benefit him and his cronies. I'd known that the system was corrupt, but I hadn't known the manipulation that was occurring on such a massive scale until they kidnapped me."

His mouth parted. "They took you because you're Democratium Liberum."

Lydia quirked her eyebrows in assent. "Somehow, Aubrey Andrews had uncovered that I was the author of the articles. Perhaps he bribed someone at the newspaper. It doesn't matter now. What does matter is that he handed me over to Somerset, who was in cahoots with the coal investor who master-minded the whole thing. They locked me in a room and forced me to write articles retracting everything I'd said. And if I didn't cooperate..." She shrugged.

Benedict's eyes darkened, and he clenched his hands so tightly, Lydia feared he might hurt himself.

"But they didn't hurt me," she said grabbing one of his hands and brushing the backs of his fingers with her own until his fist relaxed. "I'm here now. I got out."

He exhaled slowly, and his other hand loosened as well. He frowned in thought. "When you were so sick last year…"

She nodded. "That was the story Jack came up with to protect my reputation while he searched for me. They kept me alive because they needed me to write new articles that went against everything I'd written before about corruption in Parliament. If the Democratium Liberum articles were suddenly untrustworthy, then no one would give credence to anything I'd written in the past."

Jack tenderly cupped her hand between both of his, as if to keep her warm against the harsh cold of the world around them. "How did Jack find you?"

"He teamed up with Pippa, who is quite observant and together they found enough clues to get them close. I'd also hidden a secret code in the articles they forced me to write, which Pippa discovered. Together, Jack and Pippa rescued me."

With her free hand, she tugged her cloak tighter about her. Goose bumps had broken out across her arms, and she feared her teeth would soon begin to chatter. Who knew what Benedict would do if he noticed she was chilled? Perhaps he would strip down again and snuggle up against her, right here on the sidewalk.

She recalled the warmth of his hands roaming her body under the covers in her bed the day before. His bare legs tangled with her own. And his mouth, hot on her breasts.

"I wish I knew what you were thinking right now," he murmured, looking at her cheeks.

Lydia knew she was blushing. The memory of what they'd done in her bed together caused everything inside her to heat. Her goosebumps had disappeared. She stepped close to him and whispered, "I'll give you one guess." Benedict's gaze dropped to her mouth. She leaned a few inches closer, but his hand tightened on hers, reminding her where they were, and who was around.

She stepped back.

He glanced at Grace, Harriet, and Agatha, then tucked Lydia's arm through his. They resumed walking.

"We have so much to discuss," Benedict murmured as they crossed the street.

Lydia peered up at him. "And here I was thinking we'd just *had* a discussion."

"That," Benedict said, "wasn't a discussion. *That* was a confession."

Lydia pondered his words.

Had it been a confession?

The thought that she owed anyone her secrets didn't sit well with her. But keeping all those things from Benedict—the Benedict she'd come to see so much more clearly this past week—didn't sit well with her either.

"What would you like to discuss then?" Lydia said.

They were almost to the LCA which was just around the corner ahead, so if he wanted to bring up anything sensitive or private, there wasn't much time left.

Benedict ran a gloved hand across his hair. He glanced at her and then looked forward again. If she didn't know better, she'd think he was nervous.

"There's something I want to tell you," Benedict said at last. "It's about you and me."

They turned the corner, and Lydia felt buoyed at the sight of the LCA ahead. But her attention was drawn to several figures standing across the way in the square.

"Lydia," Benedict was saying, his voice low and intense, "there's no easy way for me to tell you this…"

The back of Lydia's neck prickled. She scanned the group of men and gasped.

Benedict was still speaking. "…but for years now, I have been in l—"

"Get down," Lydia hissed, seizing Benedict's arm, and dragging him down behind a cluster of low bushes along the edge of the square.

"What's going on?" Benedict's voice was tinged with some-thing like disappointment, but Lydia had no time to ponder why.

She looked back and waved for Agatha, Grace, and Harriet to similarly hide themselves.

He touched her arm to get her attention. "Lydia?"

"Those men up ahead," she whispered gesturing to the peo-ple in the square. "They're watching the house." She worried her bottom lip with her teeth, biting down hard enough for it to hurt. "And I recognize them."

Benedict went on high alert, poking his head above the bush and surveying the square. "Who are they?"

Lydia pulled him back down so he couldn't be seen, and then sunk down even lower behind the bush before answering grimly, "They work with Staines in the Office of Public Order."

Chapter Nineteen

BENEDICT PACED BACK and forth on the sidewalk around the corner from the square, his hands linked behind his back. He, Lydia, and the others had beat a hasty retreat so they were out of sight of the men. Now, they were discussing next steps.

"They have come to your house," Agatha said to Lydia, her brow furrowed with worry, "and now they have guards posted here at your secret academy as well?" She shook her head. "This has gotten far too dangerous. We have to stop."

Grace spoke, her hand absentmindedly rubbing her belly. "I agree with my mother. We have to put our safety first. We didn't do that yesterday and look what happened to you, Lydia." She gestured to Lydia and the wrap on her arm, visible between the edge of her cloak and her gloves.

Lydia's eyes narrowed, and she nibbled on her lip. Although that lip nibble was rather distracting, Benedict stayed on high alert. That was Lydia's *I'm thinking* expression. And in this instance, whatever she was up to could only lead to trouble.

Benedict moved closer to Lydia. "Agatha's right," he said, urgently. "The risk is too great now. We should return to your home at once."

She peered over his shoulder. Benedict glanced back, but all he could see over the roof of the house near them was the upper stories of the buildings across the way, a few interspersed with tall, stately trees.

"What if I told you," Lydia said, watching the others intently, "that I could get us into the LCA without anyone seeing us enter?"

Harriet leaned in. "What's the plan then?" Her skin was flushed in apparent excitement.

No wonder Timmy loved to fly down the banister. He was just like his mother, a thrill seeker.

"We'll go around the back—" Lydia began.

"But what if they have guards in the back garden?" he asked.

Lydia shot him a chiding look. "Let me finish. This is a good plan."

Benedict took a few steps away, and then returned. Lydia watched him, her eyebrows raised.

He had been so hurt earlier when he'd discovered that she didn't trust him. He didn't want her to feel that same way, that he didn't trust her or her ideas.

But he wanted her to be safe as well.

Benedict closed his eyes and breathed. Should he take the reins on this, or let her lead? He pictured Lydia's face, so bright with determination and intelligence. She was far too clever to put her friends into known danger. He would trust her.

He opened his eyes. He gave her a nod, and Lydia's eyes lit up in gratitude. They held one another's gaze for a moment. The connection between them remained stronger than before, even. He could feel it like string pulled taut between them, vibrating with energy. Humming with potential.

God, how he wanted her. *All of her.*

Lydia looked away then to address the others. "A few months back, when my friend Jane, who leads the LCA with me, and her now-husband Dev were doing a bit of sleuthing, they became acquainted with the servants in the house next door. Apparently, one of the scullery maids likes to keep an eye on the comings and goings behind all the houses. Jane thought it could prove helpful for us all to meet these servants. The lord and lady of the house are often away, which leaves the housekeeper in charge. It seemed prudent to maintain good relations with the neighbors, given that we're often, er, up to something at the LCA." Lydia gave a small shrug as if it were of little consequence.

Benedict avoided growling, but just barely. Although he could no longer be surprised at the idea of Lydia getting *up to something* given all the mischief she'd accomplished in the last handful of days, he still worried for her safety.

Harriet rubbed her hands together in glee. "So, is there a secret tunnel dug between the two homes that we'll traverse? Can I hold the torch?"

Agatha rolled her eyes heavenward.

"No secret tunnel, although we'll have to keep that option in mind for next time." Lydia's lips twitched. "We'll actually go in the opposite direction."

"The *opposite* direction?" Benedict asked. Were they going to take a hot air balloon to the roof of the LCA?

"There's a tree between the LCA and the neighboring house. Each building has a window aligned with some sturdy branches. We'll go into the neighbor's back garden, knock at the servants' entrance, and sweet talk our way into the correct room."

"Climb across a tree?" he asked. "But what about your arm?"

Lydia rotated her injured limb slowly. "It's not so bad anymore. I promise." She looked at him, her gaze steady.

Lydia was her own person. He wouldn't insult her by claiming to know her physical limitations better than she did herself.

"You've done this before?" Benedict asked. Perhaps climbing across wouldn't be so bad, especially if many people had done it safely in the past.

"No," Lydia said cheerfully, "but I've been thinking about it for a long time. It turns out, being kidnapped and locked in an upper story room for over a week leads a person to always be on the lookout for good escape routes."

"Kidnapped?" Agatha and Harriet said at the same time, although they had very different expressions on their faces. Harriet actually looked intrigued at the prospect. The thought occurred to Benedict that she must love reading adventure novels.

Lydia waved her hand through the air. "That's a story for a different day."

"I hate to burst anyone's bubble," Grace said, "but I fear I'm too close to bursting, myself, to be shimmying out across tree branches."

Everyone stared at her rounded belly.

Lydia got that thinking look on her face again. "That actually makes the plan work even better," she announced after a moment. "We need someone to act as lookout in the neighbor's back garden. If anything were to go amiss, you could pretend that you're going into labor and draw away attention while we make our escape."

"No one would believe she's about to go into labor," Agatha argued. "She still has months to go."

"You know that, and I know that, but the people we're trying to evade are *men*. Most likely, they know nothing about women and pregnancy. Though they may *think* they do."

Benedict started, but the truth was—she was absolutely right on both counts.

Lydia's eyes gleamed. "Using men's stupidity against them is one of life's greatest pleasures." Her eyes flickered briefly over to Benedict. "I mean no offense."

Benedict held up his hands and said mildly, "None taken." Lydia was so bold and brave and fierce. He pitied all the other men who would dash themselves upon the rough shores of her wit and strong beliefs.

"So, if I'm understanding you correctly, love," Agatha said, her expression stern, "we are to sneak to the neighboring house's back entry, pin all our hopes on a group of lackadaisical servants, climb a tree from one building to another, fetch this secret powder from your mysterious group who does not know we are arriving, and hope the bad men in the square don't notice us?"

Lydia's eyes twinkled. "That about sums it up."

Benedict couldn't decide between grinding his teeth together or laughing, so he settled for a good eye roll. This plan was growing more preposterous by the minute. And yet…it *did* sound like it could work. It had to—they had no other choice. Or plan.

Harriet clapped her hands together in excitement. "Oh, what an adventure this shall be."

Grace and her mother exchanged a glance. If the two women agreed to Lydia's proposal, Benedict would go along with it. But if they expressed reservations, he could side with them and outvote Lydia and Harriet. Assuming they were operating on democratic principles. These were suffragists, after all, and if anyone was going to hold to democratic principles, it should be suffragists.

Keeping Lydia safe had become a full-time endeavor.

"All right, I'll do it," Grace said, straightening her shoulders. "I'll be your lookout, and if need be, your distraction."

"And you? Are you up for climbing across the tree?" Lydia asked Agatha.

The older woman raised an imperious eyebrow. "I was climbing trees when you were still in leading strings, missy. I'll be fine."

What a formidable group of women were assembled here. Benedict almost felt sorry for the guards in the Office of Public Order.

Lydia led them the long way around the block into the mews behind the row of grand houses. They snuck in to the back garden of the house neighboring the LCA, careful to move quietly in case anyone was stationed in the back garden of the Academy.

"Do you have any money with you?" Lydia whispered as they approached the servants' entrance in the back.

Benedict fished a few coins out of his pocket and handed them to her. "I thought the servants were sympathetic to your group."

"It never hurts to sweeten the pot." Lydia tapped on the door.

A scullery maid answered. She surveyed the group, and her

eyes lit up when she spotted Benedict. She examined him boldly, with an interested expression. He couldn't help but shift from foot to foot and wondered if this is how women felt when a man ran assessing eyes over them. It was uncomfortable to say the least.

"Look what the cat drug in," she purred.

"Oh, stop that, Franny," Lydia scolded.

"Cor, I can't help meself," she said, fluttering her eyelashes. "You ladies from next door always bring the handsomest chaps 'round."

Benedict fought the urge to hide.

Lydia held up one of Benedict's coins. "We're hoping you can help us out with a small favor."

The scullery maid's hand flashed out, and the coin disappeared with remarkable speed. "What sorta favor?" Franny asked, her hand on her hip.

"We'd like to head upstairs and utilize the room beside the tree to get across to our place next door."

Franny cocked her hip against the doorframe. "Locked yourselves out, 'ave you? Such a shame, what with all those servants what works next door, and not one of 'em can let you in."

Lydia sighed and held up another coin. It, too, disappeared like its predecessor.

"And she stays back here," Lydia added, gesturing to Grace.

"No skin off my back—" Franny sniffed—"iffen she wants to stand out in the cold." She concluded her pronouncement by holding out her hand.

Lydia huffed and gave her another coin. Franny flashed them a cheeky grin before holding the door wide open. "Follow me and keep yer hands to yourself."

Agatha hugged her daughter goodbye, and then they entered the house, trailing behind Franny through the kitchen. Several servants eyed them curiously before shrugging and returning to their work.

"Keep our hands to ourselves?" Benedict whispered to Lydia.

"Does she think we're going to steal the silverware?"

"Why, do you need a new set?" Lydia teased.

Benedict shot her a look that he was sure spoke volumes.

"I don't care what she thinks, as long as we can get into the LCA without being spotted," Lydia said.

They went up the servants' stairs, down a hallway, and into what looked like a guest bedroom. The curtains were open, and sure enough, sturdy tree branches butted right up against the window.

"It's perfect," Lydia said, rushing to the window and peering out at the tree. "We're far enough back along the buildings that they shouldn't see us from the square."

Franny's gaze sharpened. "You know 'bout the men what's been 'anging round the square the last few days?"

Lydia glanced back at Benedict and widened her eyes.

Time to do a bit of rescuing.

"They're looking for me, I'm embarrassed to confess," Benedict said smoothly. "I fear I lost quite heavily at a gaming hell the other night, and I haven't scratched up enough blunt to pay off my vowels yet."

Franny shook her head, muttering something under her breath about spoiled rich toffs. "Don't be thinking you can pinch anything from 'ere on your way out," she warned. "Just come on back through the kitchen when you're done."

She stomped off, and Agatha shut the door behind her.

"Well, that was easy." Benedict smiled at Lydia.

"Yes," Lydia said dryly, "you are very good liar. Congratulations."

Harriet snickered, and Benedict shot her a wink.

Agatha pulled open the window, and she and Lydia stuck their heads out, inspecting the tree.

"The branches do look quite sturdy," Agatha said. "But how will we get in the other window?"

"I know the lady who works in that room. She is usually there working on her mathematics this time of day."

"Mathematics?" Benedict asked. Could Emelia join the ladies of the Academy? She would have comrades with whom to work on her equations. Suddenly, he began to reassess the worth of the LCA. Yes, it may put Lydia in the midst of suspect activities, but if it could provide the desires of Emelia's heart—or, rather, her brain—then he was in full support of it.

"Certainly," Lydia said distractedly, as she continued to assess the tree. "We had to secure her a new tutor recently as she had advanced so far in her studies that she had surpassed her old one. If she were allowed to attend Oxford or Cambridge, she would likely change the world of mathematics as we know it."

Benedict frowned. While he found he could support the work of the LCA, Emelia didn't need to belong to some secret academy in order to study mathematics. After all, he could easily get her a tutor. And keep her safe at home—unlike Lydia, who was currently opening the window to get at the tree.

But…what about all the ladies who didn't have brothers or parents willing to be unconventional? He glanced at Agatha and Harriet. And what about those who could never afford a private tutor? What of their dreams, their talents, and the contributions they might make to society?

His chest tightened as he realized yet again how little of the injustice against women in society he'd seen. It had always been there, but he hadn't been paying attention.

Well, he was paying attention now. He could so clearly see how unfair the system was. And this change in him was all because of Lydia.

He wondered if he should offer to climb the tree first, since he was the man and… But, no. He needed to change his thinking. And besides, intrepid Lydia already had one leg stretched over the windowsill.

"I'll go first," she said. "Once I signal that it's all right to cross, each of you can follow, one at a time. Benedict, why don't you come last. Be sure to leave this window open a bit for our return."

Her expression said that he was the one she trusted to take care of any problems. He nodded. She was right. Whatever *she* needed, he would do.

Benedict, Agatha, and Harriet watched in silence as Lydia slowly lowered herself to the tree. It swayed a bit under her weight, but there were no ominous creaks or snaps. Holding onto a branch with her good arm at head height for balance, she walked along the thick limb, foot over foot, until she reached the trunk.

As she eased herself around the curve of the trunk, her dress snagged on a branch. Lydia gingerly reached back with her injured arm to untangle her garment, and her weight shifted to the side. She leaned a little more and then wobbled.

Benedict's breath froze in his lungs. *Hell and damnation.* He was too far away to help her. But then, Lydia adjusted her grip on the branch above and righted herself. With slow movements, she tugged her gown off the offending branch and straightened. She looked over her shoulder then, and gave him a nod. She was all right.

Benedict exhaled in relief.

Beside him, Agatha sagged against the window frame while Harriet unclenched her hands. They'd all been tensed up, as if their straining muscles could assist Lydia in keeping her balance out there on the precarious perch.

She crept farther away from them now, climbing onto a bough that reached out to the LCA's window. Closer and closer she moved, until she was able to lean against the window ledge. She tapped on the glass and waited.

Was no one in there? Would this whole thing be for naught?

Lydia tapped again, and a moment later the window slid open. A woman with dark hair poked her head out, looking from Lydia to Benedict and the others. Lydia said something to her in a voice too low to carry, and the woman flashed a smile before opening the window all the way and assisting Lydia through.

Benedict felt his shoulders sag as the last of his tension

drained away. He was ready to drop to his knees. She'd made it even with her sore arm. He knew he couldn't have stopped her even if he'd wanted to, but damnation, that had been tense.

He sighed and then glanced over at the others, doing a double take.

"What?" Harriet asked, voice defensive as she tied her skirts up around her waist. "You saw what almost happened to her. Our gowns are a danger out there on the tree. Besides, I doubt a lad like you hasn't seen a pair of drawers before."

Agatha huffed but copied Harriet; before long both women's long skirts were secured around their waists, their drawers and stockings the only things covering their lower halves.

"I'll go next," Harriet announced, moving sprightly onto the window ledge.

She made her way across without mishap, and Benedict had to admit that securing their gowns had been the right decision.

"Are you sure you're up for it?" he asked Agatha. "You could always stay here and be on lookout as well."

"I live on a farm, son," she said, laughter in her eyes. "If I can hop the fence to the cow pasture and walk the wall around the garden, I think I am up for a little bit of tree climbing."

And then she was out the window, albeit a bit more stiffly than Harriet. Benedict watched with trepidation until she made it across into the other building. Now it was his turn.

He swung his legs over the windowsill and rested his feet on the sturdy branch below, easing his weight out of the window and holding onto the branch above. But unlike with the lighter weight of the women, now the branch gave an ominous creak. Benedict cursed under his breath. Trying to balance speed with safety, he quickly made his way to the trunk and breathed a sigh of relief. The branch was much thicker there, and he felt more secure than he had at the ends.

Lydia kept watch through the window. She smiled in encouragement, and something in his chest shifted. Her cheeks were pink from either the cold air or the excitement. Tendrils of her hair had come undone from her coiffure and framed her face in beguiling blond tendrils. And her eyes glowed brightly, perhaps with adventure.

Benedict was glad to be here in this adventure with her. To share this moment, to be united in her plan...it felt important and connecting. He continued to work his way around the tree trunk and stepped onto the new branch. Again, he made his way with both speed and care. He was almost there.

But when he was about five feet away from the open window, the branch beneath him gave an ominous crackle and he could feel a vibration through the soles of his boots. He looked down.

"Hurry," Lydia urged.

Benedict edged out farther on the branch, and it creaked even louder this time. No. He wouldn't give up. He was so close now. Just a little bit more, and he would be inside the LCA with Lydia and the others. He took another step, trying to put more of his weight on the branch he was hanging onto with his hands. But then, the limb beneath him groaned again before snapping away from the trunk of the tree.

LYDIA SHRIEKED AS the branch beneath Benedict gave way with a loud crack.

He dangled from the limb onto which he'd been hanging, but now it drooped under his weight, creaking ominously.

Lydia looked down. It was a long drop, and although it might not kill a person, it would certainly break some bones. Her heart sat in her throat, pounding hard enough to make her whole body shake. "Benedict," she whispered.

His eyes met and locked with hers. She was shocked to find he didn't look frightened. Instead, determination blazed in his golden-brown eyes. He tightened his jaw, and then began to move along the branch, hand over hand. Thank goodness he wore leather gloves or the bark from the tree would surely scrape up his skin. Thank goodness he had those muscular biceps and that strong chest. She doubted she would have the strength to hang and move as he was; her own muscles ached just from the thought of doing what he was doing. Or maybe that was because they were tight as she imagined herself dangling out there with him, helping him to safety.

"Almost there," she murmured in encouragement.

Harriet, Grace, and Agatha were also crowded around the open window, and she could feel the tension radiating off them like heat from a fireplace. Behind them, Alice waited, wondering why her office at the LCA had been invaded. They all remained quiet. Perhaps they felt like Lydia did—that any sudden movement or loud sound might frighten the fickle branch from its secure hold to the tree trunk.

He was almost to the window now, the branch sagging lower under his weight.

Lydia held her breath.

The branch creaked and Benedict swung his legs to get his body swinging. Lydia could see what he was trying to do and stepped back from the window.

"Move back," she instructed the others.

He was swinging toward the house. Right as he reached the top of the arc, the branch broke. The momentum carried Benedict toward the window. With a loud grunt, he slammed against the side of the house. His hands hooked around the window frame.

"Benedict," Lydia cried. She rushed to grab hold of his arm with her uninjured one.

"Hang on to me," he gasped. Benedict looked up at her, his golden-brown eyes burning with determination. "Don't let me go."

"No," Lydia whispered. "I won't."

With the assistance of the other women and an additional,

spectacular show of arm strength from Benedict—*and* a rather long string of curses—they got him inside the room.

He lay on the floor, his chest rising and falling as he continued gasping for breath. "A walk," he gulped, "in the park."

Lydia knelt on the floor beside him. "Are you hurt?"

He closed his eyes for a moment, and then shook his head. "I'll probably have some lovely bruises tomorrow, but I'm all right."

Lydia took his hand in hers. "That was terrifying."

"I'll say," exclaimed Harriet from behind them. "I haven't seen anything as brave and exciting as that since they dug those lads out of the mine a few years ago."

Grace looked up at the ceiling and shook her head.

Agatha took Harriet by the arm and led her way to the other side of the room where Alice watched on. The three women made introductions.

"I fear Harriet may try to top your feat," Lydia murmured, brushing his hair back from his forehead.

Benedict smiled, his lips curving in a slow, warm movement. Something hot and tingly unspooled low in Lydia's belly at the sight. Sometimes she forgot how handsome he was. His cheeks were ruddy from exertion, and his hair mussed from the wind and his adventure in the tree. In fact, there was a twig threaded through his locks. She plucked it out, then ran a finger along his cravat, which was rumpled in a most delightful way. It made her think of undressing, and other things a proper young lady probably should not be considering. Like the feeling of their near naked limbs as they'd tangled under her covers…

His smile turned wolfish. "I wish I knew what you were thinking."

Lydia swatted his shoulder, and he grasped it with his hand, giving a mock groan of pain. "Oh, how you wound me Lady Lydia," he moaned. "You struck such a blow!"

At that moment, the door to the room flew open with a bang, and two figures paused in the doorway, taking in the scene before them. A man brandished a silver candlestick. A woman clutched a thick quill as if it were a dagger and she was ready to plunge the pointed writing end through her foe's heart.

The one with the candlestick stepped forward, holding his makeshift weapon up in the air. "Get out at once, or I shall alert the authorities!"

"Parth." Lydia scrambled to her feet.

Recognition crossed his face, and he lowered the candlestick. Behind him, Meera heaved a sigh of relief and dropped her quill.

"Lady Lydia," Meera said, slipping past her partner into the room. "You gave us such a fright!"

Parth and Meera were long-time members of the household. They had traveled from India with Lady Rowling and Dev, Jane's husband, and helped establish the LCA. Meera had served as Lady Rowling's secretary, and continued in that role now that Lydia, Jane, and Pippa had taken over leadership of the Academy. She was dressed in a beautiful blue sari, and her dark hair hung down her back. Parth was Dev's best friend and had been elevated from servant to steward once Dev had claimed his title. Together, the two of them kept the Ladies Covert Academy running smoothly on a day-to-day basis. Lydia trusted them implicitly.

"I'm so sorry we startled you," Lydia explained, "but there are men watching the house, men we do not wish to encounter, so we had to be creative with our entrance."

"I'll say," Alice, mathematician extraordinaire and occupant of the room, drawled.

Lydia shot her an apologetic glance while Benedict got to his feet with minimal cursing.

"Are you hurt?" Meera asked, moving to his side.

"Nothing a little brandy won't cure." Benedict dusted himself off and offered her a smile.

"Do you know those men?" Parth asked. "They've been out in the square for several days now. They haven't approached the house, but it's clear they're watching."

"It has the members rather spooked, truth be told." Meera

gave Lydia a look.

Secrecy was the most important element for the survival of the Ladies Covert Academy. All its members had been impressed with the necessity to keep a low profile when entering and leaving the house, and to always have a story prepared for what sort of charity work they'd been doing with their time there. It made perfect sense that a group of official-looking men suddenly keeping watch would have everyone on edge.

"They are with the Office of Public Order." Lydia wanted to kick yourself for not thinking to notify Parth and Meera, as well as the other members of the LCA, about Staines's letter and a potential investigation. "I'm so sorry I didn't warn you. The head of the office is investigating what he views as radical reform groups, and somehow the Ladies Charitable Association caught his attention."

"But he doesn't know what we do." Parth said. He moved his gaze to Agatha and Harriet. "Do *they* know what we do?" he whispered.

"Yes," Agatha whispered back. "Lady Lydia took us in her confidence."

Meera and Parth both turned to stare at Lydia, their expressions incredulous.

"They're trustworthy." Lydia held her hands up. "I swear."

"Once you spend an afternoon in Newgate together, you're bonded for life," Harriet offered up as an explanation.

Meera's eyebrows shot up almost to her forehead. "Newgate?"

Lydia waved her concern away. "It's a long story, and I promise to tell it to you someday soon. But today, we're here for a different purpose."

"Has anything happened to Dev and Jane? Or your brother and Pippa?" Parth's hand flexed around the candlestick.

"No, no, it's nothing like that," Lydia hastened to assure him.

Parth had accompanied them on their adventure to claim Dev's title a handful of months ago, and the whole group had become fast friends. Not to mention that he and Dev had grown up together back in India.

"Do you need our assistance?" asked Meera.

"We hope you can share your secret weapon with us," Harriet piped up.

Meera looked at the woman and then cut her gaze back to Lydia.

Lydia bit back a smile. "Jane's powder," she clarified. "We're hoping to take as many vials as she has stored with us."

"Lady Lydia," Parth exclaimed, his eyes wide. "Are you going to war?"

"No," Agatha said dryly, "we're going to a reform rally."

Chapter Twenty

BENEDICT TRAILED BEHIND Lydia as she gave them an abbreviated tour of the Ladies Covert Academy.

"I won't show you everything," she said as they walked down the hallway. "I don't want to interrupt anyone's privacy. But I can show you where Pippa, Jane and I all work."

Benedict wondered if this was how explorers felt upon reaching a new shore. He'd only learned of the existence of the Academy this morning, and although he was seeing it with his own eyes, it still didn't quite feel real.

He could only guess some of the women's endeavors behind closed doors. From one room came a resonant sound of tapping, and he pictured someone with a hammer and chisel carving away at a marble sculpture. From another room, it sounded as if a woman were trying out different lines in a play. Was she actually writing her own script behind that door? How astounding. And from another echoed the metallic sound of metal on metal. Benedict had dabbled in fencing enough to recognize the sound of one epee striking another epee.

Lydia knocked on that door and after a short pause, a voice bid them enter.

"Señor Martin," Lydia greeted, smiling at a man and two women inside.

The room was sparse and open, with protective gear and

various swords hanging from hooks and racks along the walls. Mirrors lined one wall, assumedly so the people fencing could study their own form and technique.

"Good day," greeted a striking man with a Spanish accent. He was wiry and lean with a hint of mischief in his eyes.

"This is Señor Martin, Pippa's fencing instructor," Lydia explained.

"And ours as well," piped up one of the two women who both held swords.

Lydia grinned. "Fencing has become quite popular at the LCA, and thankfully Señor Martin was able to accommodate requests for more lessons." She plucked a saber off the wall and demonstrated a lunge and perry. Benedict rocked back on his heels. Lydia only grew exponentially more dangerous the longer he knew her.

It was exhilarating.

"So any of the members of your Academy can train in fencing?" Harriet asked, her eyes gleaming.

"They can train or study or work at whatever they want here," Lydia answered.

"Astonishing," Agatha whispered, looking around. She turned her attention back to Lydia, a speculative gleam in her eyes. "You can work at whatever you want? Fencing, math, or perhaps even…writing?"

Lydia stiffened and shot a quick glance at Benedict. Had the wily reformer leader figured out that Lydia was Democratium Liberum? He could only shrug back. It was up to her to decide how to proceed.

Thankfully, Harriet pulled Agatha's attention away with a question. "Do you think we can start something like this in Stafford?"

Agatha tapped a finger against her chin. "I'm not sure how much money it would take to run a place like this, but it's something we could look into. I imagine there would be a lot of interest from the ladies in our reform group."

"I would be happy to share any information with you that might prove helpful," Lydia offered.

Benedict shook his head. The way these women organized themselves, offered to assist one another, and gladly helped carry each other's burdens was just so impressive. Even more, it was incredible.

Lydia hung the sword back on the wall and bid Señor Martin and the two sword fighters goodbye before leading the group down the hall and opening another door. Benedict knew at once to whom this room belonged. The clutter of books, the ink splotches on the desk, and the scattered sheets of paper proclaimed this to be Lydia's domain.

"And here is where I work." Lydia looked around at the room, a mixture of pride and sadness in her expression.

How hard it must've been for her to give that column up. Benedict wished they were alone so that he might comfort her. When those men had kidnapped her, they had taken away more than just her freedom.

Harriet and Agatha explored the room. Harriet trailed her fingers over the language books on the bookshelves, while Agatha picked up a quill from the desk.

"What kind of work did you do here?" Harriet asked, picking up a sheet of paper and scanning the text. "This…looks familiar." She glanced up at Lydia, her expression quizzical.

Benedict watched Lydia open and close her mouth a few times. She'd shared the secrets of the LCA with these women, but it seemed revealing her own work at the Academy was a struggle.

"I think I know," Agatha murmured, pointing at Lydia with the quill. "You write articles."

"Articles?" Harriet asked, cocking her head to the side.

Agatha nodded firmly. "Articles that changed the way many people view politics and our role in England's government."

Harriet's eyes slowly widened as she took in Agatha's meaning.

Benedict stepped closer to Lydia in case she needed help, but

Lydia, his fierce, brave Lydia drew a deep breath and then smiled.

"I'm Democratium Liberum."

Harriet shrieked. Agatha smiled in apparent satisfaction.

"You?" Harriet asked, seizing Lydia's good hand. "I can scarcely believe it. But it *does* make sense, now that I'm thinking on it. Wait until the others hear the news. Oh, this is extraordinary." She spun around. "I'm standing in the room where you wrote the Democratium Liberum articles. Right here at this very desk." She let go of Lydia and reached out to touch the wooden surface with reverence.

"Perhaps," Agatha said, "with this very quill." She ran her finger over the feathered end.

Lydia examined the writing implement. "Most likely not *that* quill. I write so much that I go through them rather quickly, but..." She rummaged through a drawer in the desk for a moment, emerging with a pair of battered, blunt quills in her hand. "I'm certain I wrote some of the articles with these."

She handed a quill first to Harriet, who clutched it to her chest and squealed, and the other to Agatha. The woman reached out both hands as if accepting a scepter from her monarch. She exhaled slowly once Lydia had placed it across her palms.

Benedict briefly considered requesting a quill for himself, but he didn't need a memento of Lydia. She was right here beside him.

"Thank you," Agatha said, her eyes glistening with tears.

"For you," Lydia said, "anything." Her lips curled up on one side. "After all, we're prison comrades. Isn't there some code of honor amongst criminals?"

Harriet and Agatha laughed in response, but Benedict did not. The thought of Lydia, *his* Lydia, thrown into the disgusting bowels of that prison still filled him with anger. He wished there was an easy way for him to put an end to Staines and the Office of Public Order. Although they had the Crown's approval, it was clear from everything Benedict had observed that they were a menace to the people of England.

"I'll show you Jane's botany lab next," Lydia said, moving out of her office. "That's where we'll find her vials for self-defense."

She led them to a room at the end of the hallway, and once she let them in, it was clear why her friend Jane had been given a corner room. Light filled the lab from two walls of windows. Many varieties of plants sprouted from pots of various sizes. Shelves and racks along the wall contained dried specimens and labeled jars as well as botany books and what looked to be lab notes. This was a serious operation, run by a serious scientist.

Benedict was very impressed.

Meera popped her head in. "Have you found the vials?"

"I haven't started looking yet." Lydia did a spin to look around the room. "Who's been watering while Jane has been on her honeymoon?"

"Dev made Parth swear a solemn vow that he would check on her plants every single day while they're on their trip." Meera crossed the room to a cabinet, opened the doors, and pulled out a large box. Benedict hurried over to assist, and she directed him to place it on a large wooden worktable.

"Here's everything she has dried and bottled so far," Meera said, peering into the box. "She's already distributed ten times this amount to women that we know across the city." She pulled out a handful vials, handing one to each of them.

Benedict held his up to the light. It was a bit smaller than his thumb, made of glass and stopped with a cork. Inside were dark, dried flakes. They looked so innocuous, like an herb one might find floating in a stew. But he'd witnessed firsthand the effect when digested. Jane had put some into a tea that she served to Dev's distant relative who'd been trying to steal his title and who'd also admitted to murdering Dev's father. The woman had choked and gasped, her face turning red as she struggled for breath. Jane had said the woman would die if she did not confess her crimes and receive the antidote in return.

It turned out, there was no antidote because the herb was not fatal, merely extremely irritating. Someone who'd been doused needed to drink a lot of water and wash their face if it had been blown on them. At the time, Benedict hadn't thought to question why Jane had this herb. Looking back, he could scarcely believe his *naivete*.

It *had* always seemed to him like there was something more going on with the Ladies Charitable Association, but he'd been so wrapped up in his own life that he hadn't given it much thought. Now that he knew about Ladies Covert Academy, it all made much more sense.

"So what do we do with these?" Harriet asked, rolling hers back and forth in her palm.

"Jane has found it to be most effective when blown at an attacker," Meera explained. "She recommends keeping it tucked in one's pocket, reticule, or *décolletage*."

She paused and glanced over Benedict, as if realizing that she should not refer to the general area of women's bosoms in mixed company.

"It's quite all right," he reassured her. "I *have* heard tale of this mysterious *décolletage* before."

Lydia jabbed him in the ribs with her elbow, but he could see the corners of her mouth twitching.

"So," Meera continued, apparently deciding it would be best to ignore Benedict's existence completely, "if you need to protect yourself, you unstop the vial, pour the contents into your hand, and then blow it into your attacker's face. You do need to be rather close for this to work. It can also be ingested, but that takes more proximity and time. Once you're done, you should wash your hand off as soon as possible, or at least wipe it off on your gown."

Agatha examined the vial. "I can hardly imagine," she murmured, "how women's lives would be different if every single one of us had this at our disposal. Imagine, never having to fear for your safety again..."

The others grew silent, and again Benedict felt a squeezing sensation in his chest. He had been so blind to the plight of women before. He'd simply accepted a status quo that said his sister and mother, Lydia, and all the other ladies he'd ever met shouldn't go out in public alone. Should fear strangers. Should accept that the world was a dangerous place. And that didn't even take into account women like Harriet and Agatha, women who weren't aristocrats and didn't have the protection—or perhaps he should say the *restrictions*—of genteel society to look after their safety.

How ugly the world was. Could something as simple as a little vial of dried herb balance the scales?

"How many can we take?" Lydia asked.

Benedict peered into the box. It looked like there were several hundred vials there. How had Jane managed to bottle the irritating herb without suffering its effects? But, the Academy members seemed capable of anything. He looked forward to asking her all about it once she returned from her honeymoon.

Meera stared down at them and seemed to be thinking. "If you take half, will that be enough for your needs? I don't want to leave the LCA and Jane without any."

Lydia nodded. "That will be plenty. Thank you so much."

Meera found a burlap bag, and they transferred half of the vials into it before tying the top securely.

"If you are being watched, we should disguise this in some way," Meera suggested.

Lydia glanced around the room, and her expression brightened. "Jane used to take baskets of fresh herbs to the neighbors. We'll make it look like that."

Benedict pulled an unused basket down from the top of one of the shelves while Agatha snipped some known and edible plants from their pots. Harriet tucked the bag into the bottom of the basket and then arranged the herbs carefully on top.

Meera examined it critically from several angles. "I think that will do the trick."

Benedict looked around him. Agatha adjusted the herbs in the basket, her brow furrowed in concentration. Harriet carried the box of remaining vials back to the cabinet, humming while she worked. Meera cleaned off the clippers they'd used for the fresh herbs.

And Lydia was watching him. She glanced around and then back, arching an eyebrow as if to say *what do you think of all this*? Benedict held her gaze. Her eyes were their usual, brilliant, sapphire-blue, and he would have happily stared into them for hours. But he knew she was curious about his reaction to this special, secret place of hers. So he, too, looked around and then back at her before raising his eyebrows and nodding to show how impressed he was.

A slow smile curved across her face. Her soft pink lips looked so rosy against the white flash of her teeth. God, how he wanted to kiss her again. And more than that, he just wanted to be with her.

Would they ever get that chance?

Agatha interrupted his musings. "How will we get out?" she said, handing the basket to Lydia. "With the tree branch broken, we can't return the way we came."

"We haven't seen them patrolling the back garden, but that doesn't mean that way is clear." Meera tapped her finger against her lips. "But…I might have an idea."

Meera excused herself, and Lydia led them downstairs and into the kitchen.

"My lady!" Young Archie left his job scrubbing potatoes and ran up to her. "I haven't seen you in days and days."

Lydia ruffled his bright-red hair. "Is it me you miss, or my coins?"

Archie, the son of one of the kitchen servants, had been her runner, delivering her Democratium Liberum articles to the newspaper each week. Unfortunately, that was how the kidnappers had figured out that she was the author. Next time she needed someone to slip in and out of a place unseen, she would pick a person with duller hair.

"Mostly you," the lad said before adding cheekily, "but also the coins."

Lydia laughed and fished the last coin Benedict had given her out of her pocket. "No mischief now," she warned before handing it to him.

"If I'd known you'd be filling the pockets of all the servants in the square," Benedict murmured, leaning close, "I would've brought more blunt with me."

Lydia inhaled. Along with the delicious scents of the kitchen—baking bread and something savory simmering in a pot—she could smell Benedict. Her nose filled with the fragrance of soap and linen, and something that was uniquely him. If she could battle this *Eau de Benedict* and sell it on Bond Street, she would have a fortune.

"I don't think you'll miss a few coins," she murmured, sneaking another sniff of him.

He watched her, his mouth curving up as if he knew what she was about. "I have more coins than I could ever spend," he confessed. "The last few days, I've been wondering how I can put them to good use."

"Do you mean giving money to charity?"

He nodded. Lydia's gaze traced his face. The cheerful curve of his full lips. The kindness in his eyes. How could she have ever believed him to be an idle rake?

Agatha approached and pointed to the clock in the kitchen. "It's time."

"Hopefully none of this will be necessary," Lydia said, adjusting the basket over her arm.

Harriet strode to the back door and gripped the handle. "If it is, we're more than up to the challenge." And she grinned.

Truly, how had Lydia not noticed Harriet's love of a thrill right from the start? She was surprised the reformer hadn't begun digging her way out of Newgate with some spoon she'd stolen from one of the guards the moment they'd been placed in that jail cell.

"Let's go," Benedict said, his voice relaxed and easy.

But Lydia noticed the tense set of his shoulders. He didn't like this any more than she did. Potentially walking into a trap was not how she envisioned their exit from the LCA. At the end of the day though, not every factor could be calculated, especially not the strength of tree branches.

Lydia nodded and Harriet pulled the door open. The four of them strolled out, keeping their gait casual and steady.

"Such a lovely day for a walk," Lydia said, surreptitiously peering around the garden as they headed toward the mews.

"Thank you for inviting us to take a stroll with you, my lady," Harriet called out as she craned her neck in her search for officers.

Perhaps not all of them were cut out for clandestine operations.

They were almost to the back gate. Perhaps this subterfuge hadn't been necessary at all. That meant there had been no need to climb across the tree in the first place. Lydia shook her head at herself. Well, it had been fun, in its own strange way. Perhaps Harriet was on to something with her adventure seeking.

"Halt!"

Three men burst through the gate into the back garden. "Stop in the name of the Office of Public Order," one of them shouted. In spite of preparing for this possibility, it still took Lydia by surprise. She stepped backward, clutching the basket to her chest.

But Benedict was undaunted. "How shocking," he drawled, stepping forward so that he was between her and the reform workers, and the guards. "What possible reason could guards from the Office of Public Order have for invading the garden of a marquess in the middle of Mayfair on this fine day?"

"We have orders from our commanding officer to surveille the property, my lord." The guard spoke respectfully enough, but there was a hardness to his expression that set Lydia on edge.

"And who might that be?" Benedict asked, examining his fingernails.

Lydia was on to him now. He'd done that same move to her just that morning in the breakfast room. But she could see now that it was a ploy to put your adversary on their back heels, to make them think that you are completely unaffected by them.

And Lydia finally had to admit the truth herself. She had *always* been affected by Benedict. Even in years past when she would just roll her eyes at his teasing, there had always been something about him that made her heart beat just a little faster or her stomach flutter.

The fourth figure entered the back garden. "I am the commanding officer."

At the familiar sight of the man's cold gray eyes and ruthlessly short, dark hair, Lydia felt a chill travel up her spine. *Staines.* Not only had he sent his men to surveille the LCA, but he had come himself. How had he known they would be here? How closely had he been watching them?

She shivered.

"My men reported not seeing you or your companions enter the premises, Lady Lydia," Staines said, voice mild.

She gave a dramatic gasp and pressed her hand to her chest. "What a shocking dereliction of duty on the part of your officers, sir. Perhaps they passed the time playing games of chance instead of keeping watch as you have instructed them." She tutted. "Any manner of dire things may have occurred as a result of their inattention. Just think—women could be delivering baskets of herbs to their neighbors!" She held up the basket.

Staines's mouth tightened and he took a step forward, but Benedict stepped to the side to be in between him and Lydia, and the man checked himself.

"And what have you been doing here, Lady Lydia?" Staines asked, a thread of metal in his voice.

"Oh," she said as if his question had taken her by surprise. "Why, I was simply meeting with my fellow members of the

Ladies Charitable Association to sew blankets for a local orphanage. We all must do what we can to help those in need. Don't you agree?"

A muscle in Staines's jaw pulsed. He didn't answer, but instead turned his attention to Harriet and Agatha. "And who might you be?"

Lydia's hands tightened around the basket. He hadn't been present at their arrest in Westminster, had he? If he recognized them as members of the Stafford Female Reform Society, he'd toss them into Newgate without a second thought.

"Perhaps you've seen me at the orphanage?" Agatha allowed a hint of annoyance to slip into her tone, as if she wished to chastise him for his breach of propriety but chose not to bother, as it was a hopeless case. "I head there once a week with my fellow LCA members to deliver the blankets we sew and the booties we knit for the wee children. Perhaps you do charity work there as well and saw me one day?"

One of the officers behind Staines snickered, but quickly turned the sound into a cough when his commanding officer turned to glare at him.

Staines narrowed his eyes at Agatha. "I received reports yesterday of several groups of radical women forcing their vile literature on unsuspecting Londoners. In one instance, three innocent men were assaulted by an accomplice of the radicals, who attempted to murder them with his horses."

Agatha stared back impassively at the man.

"Is that so?" Lydia hoped her tone didn't betray the pounding of her heart.

"Yes," Staines barked at her. "That particular group of radicals was made up of three women. One was blond and another was pregnant." Staines gave a knowing stare to Lydia's blond hair, then turned to inspect Agatha and Grace's middles.

The two women gasped as if scandalized by his open perusal. He huffed when he realized neither of them were visibly pregnant. Thank goodness they had made Grace stay behind and hidden behind the garden wall.

Staines turned his icy gaze back to Lydia. His mouth had grown even tighter as his anger mounted. "And the basket? Those don't look like blankets."

"Ah, no," Lydia said. Her instinct was to lay a protective hand over the top of the basket, but she managed to keep herself still. "We collected some fresh herbs from our indoor garden to make a nourishing soup for the orphans as well. Do you like soup, Mr. Staines?"

"That is neither here nor there," Staines said through gritted teeth, "as you well know, my lady. Now, show me what's in the baskets."

And he stepped forward. His officers moved into formation behind him. One of them rested his hand on the butt of a pistol.

Lydia took a step back, her heart pounding in her chest. *Would this work?* If not, she'd better find a spoon for herself in the next few moments because she would need to dig herself out of Newgate.

Staines was nearly upon her now.

She stepped back again. *Damnation.* The plan wasn't working.

Behind her, the back door slammed open, and a swell of noise emerged.

Staines jolted to a halt, and he looked over her shoulder at what she knew would be a swarm of LCA members talking loudly amongst themselves as they fanned out and around the garden.

"What is the meaning of this?" Staines shouted.

But soon he and his men as well as Lydia, Benedict, Agatha, and Harriet were engulfed by a score of women. Many held large baskets that would impede the officer's movements, and some took their sweet time opening parasols at waist height to block their view.

Lydia stepped back farther, digging into the basket.

"Hand it to me," Benedict whispered.

Lydia pulled out the bag of vials from under the herbs.

"Here."

And while the chattering swarm of women caused enough commotion to distract everyone in the back garden, Benedict slipped over to the side wall and reached over. Lydia dragged her gaze away, not wanting to draw Staines's attention to Benedict.

"Enough!" roared Staines. His face was red and mottled. He batted a parasol away and pushed at several baskets as he marched to Lydia. He ripped her basket out of her hands before rummaging inside.

Holding up a fistful of rosemary and thyme, he screamed, "What is this?" Spittle flew from his mouth.

"My good man," Benedict drawled, "I do believe you've just spoiled the ingredients for the poor orphan children's soup."

He'd made it back to Lydia's side so quickly that she hoped Staines wouldn't even realize he'd moved during the women's charge. Despite his lackadaisical tone, he'd placed himself right at Lydia's side, and his hands were balled into fists. Lydia had no doubt he'd pummel Staines if the dreadful man tried to hurt her.

Staines flung the herbs to the ground. "I know you're up to something," he hissed, leaning into Lydia's face.

"Yes," Lydia said, staring back unblinking. "We're up to soup making."

His mouth twisted in fury and his face shook. For a moment Lydia feared his rage would overtake him. It was men like Staines who led women to carry those vials for self-defense.

And they said women were the emotional ones.

He took a step back. "This. Isn't. Over."

Staines snapped his fingers, and his officers followed him out the back gate. Lydia watched until they were out of sight, then dropped the basket with lifeless fingers.

"Bloody hell," she whispered.

Benedict was at her side, wrapping his arms around her. "You did so well," he murmured against her ear. "You were so brave and clever."

Lydia closed her eyes and let herself rest against his firm, warm chest. Even though they had an audience, she would stay here just a moment longer, just long enough to absorb a bit of his strength and confidence.

"We did it," Harriet crowed.

With a sigh, Lydia pulled back, and Benedict let his arms slide away. Meera approached, a smug smile on her face.

"Thank you," Lydia said, pulling the woman in close for a hug.

Meera remained stiff in her arms for a moment—they had never exchanged such signs of affection in the past—and then relaxed, returning Lydia's squeeze.

"It took me a few more minutes than I'd anticipated to get them all gathered together," Meera said. "I'm sorry."

"You were right on time," Lydia said, stepping back. "You were perfect. Thank you, everyone. Thank you so much."

The twenty or so ladies of the LCA milled about, chatting excitedly. It wasn't every day they got to thwart an evil government official in his tracks.

"Are they gone?" came a voice from the neighbor's garden.

Grace! She, Agatha, and Benedict bid the others farewell before hurrying into the neighboring back garden where Grace stood, holding the bag full of vials.

Her mother rushed over to embrace her. "Are you all right?"

"I'm fine," Grace reassured her before turning to address the others as well. "I'm just glad I was standing so close to the wall that separates the two gardens. I was trying to hear what was happening over there, and all of a sudden a hand reached over with this bag."

"You saved the day," Benedict said.

"Well, I did have a backup plan in place," Grace said.

"Oh?" Lydia asked. Had she been about to pretend to go into labor?

Grace reached into her bodice and pulled out four vials. "I'm almost disappointed I didn't get a chance to use these on those horrid men."

Chapter Twenty-One

BENEDICT WALKED INTO the breakfast room, and while there was plenty of food, there were no reformers seated around the table. Since they'd gone to the LCA, the women had been waking up earlier and earlier over the last couple of mornings. Today, not even Timmy, a self-proclaimed sleepyhead, had lingered over his breakfast to keep Benedict company. So after rushing through some eggs and strawberry jam on toast—and bacon, of course—Benedict went in search of the reformers.

And Lydia.

Although why he bothered to pretend he *wasn't* looking for her, he didn't know. He had resigned himself to always knowing where she was whenever he walked into a room. It was as if all his senses were attuned to her, as if she were a magnet and he was a compass needle, always pointing straight to his true north. His Lydia.

First, he went to the ballroom. Agatha had set up a command center there, taking tables from various rooms throughout the house so that she, Grace, and Harriet—as well as any other reformer members who were interested—could read over the handful of articles that Democratium Liberum had penned for them.

That *Lydia* had penned for them.

Benedict strolled to the table where Agatha had several pieces

244

of paper strewn out in front of her. Her hands were stained with ink, and she was making edits to one of the articles. He inspected her writing tool. "Would you like me to find you a new quill? That one looks quite dull and worn."

Agatha shook her head. "This is the quill that Lydia gave me, the one she used to write some of her Democratium Liberum articles for the newspaper. And it's the only quill I want to use right now."

"Fair enough," Benedict said, offering a smile.

"Oy, Benedict," Harriet called from her makeshift desk. "Which of these conclusions do you think is more rousing?"

He strolled over to her. "Rousing?"

"You know, *rousing* to the masses. Speaking to the heart of people. Getting a crowd to be excited about your ideas. *Rousing.*"

Benedict offered her a lazy smile. "And here I thought you were trying to sweet-talk me."

She chortled, and then showed him the two endings she was considering. After Benedict gave her his suggestion, he bid the reformers farewell and made his way to the front sitting room.

There, under the watchful eye of one of the maids-turned-nannies, Timmy and the other children organized pamphlets into stacks. Timmy saw him at the doorway and gestured him over with excited hand waving.

"See what I've been working on?" the lad asked Benedict. He held up a bundle of pamphlets with a bit of twine tied around it and finished with an uneven bow.

"I did a 'speriment to see how many pamphlets would fit in one lady's pocket. It turns out, twenty-five will fit. So me and the other children are putting all the pamphlets into bundles of twenty-five. Isn't that clever?" Timmy grinned up at him, the gaps in his smile where he had lost teeth giving him the look of a lively imp.

"Very clever," Benedict praised.

He stayed for half an hour, helping the children count to twenty-five—a challenge for some of the younger children—and even showing a few how to make a proper bow with the twine.

"Thank you for letting me help," Benedict told Timmy after the lad tied a neat, even bow. "I'm off to see who else might need my assistance."

"Are you hoping it will be Lady Lydia?" Timmy blinked at him, all innocence.

Benedict laughed. "Perhaps." With a wink at the child, he headed on his way.

As he walked toward the rear of the house, several women hurried past, holding white clothing. All the reformers had gotten their protesting gowns washed, and now it was time for a bit of starch and ironing in preparation for tomorrow's rally.

The entire house felt alive, buzzing with an unfettered energy. When he was here, he felt more alive as well. He was part of something bigger than himself. Even though he was neither a member of the LCA nor of the reform group, they had embraced him as one of their own. And aside from the young sons in the group, he was the only man helping with their preparations.

Finally, Benedict walked into the back garden where Lydia was instructing a group of reformers on how to use the self-defense vials.

"Since our pockets will be full of pamphlets, you should tuck the vials into your stays." She demonstrated by reaching her hand down her *décolletage*.

Benedict's mouth went dry.

He'd been fantasizing about what he and Lydia had done together on the day he warmed her up in her bed. The last several nights, he'd even considered tiptoeing to her bedroom and knocking on the door to see if she would let him in. They could talk, kiss, touch, or whatever she felt like. But deep in his heart, he yearned to hold her in his arms once more, to kiss her sweet breasts and feel her heart beat rapidly in her chest because of his touch. Because of her desire for him. Her feelings for him.

And if they did spend the night together, wouldn't they have to get married?

Married to Lydia. Before he could delve deeper into the thought, the sound of a throat clearing pulled him out of his reverie.

Benedict realized with a start that Lydia and the reformers were all regarding him with curiosity.

Apparently, they'd caught him staring at Lydia. His cheeks warmed.

"Ah, I've come see if I can assist you in any way," he offered.

"In *any* way?" Lydia asked him mildly.

"Certainly."

She gave him a wicked smile. "It turns out that we do have a need of your assistance, Lord Lovell. Your timing is impeccable."

Oh hell. What had he signed himself up for? As he approached the group, several of them whispered to one another and then snickered.

"You stand here," Lydia directed him, and then turned her attention back to the other ladies. "All right, you finally have a chance to practice blowing the herb onto a real-life test subject."

Benedict's mouth dropped. "What?"

She gave him a chiding shake of her head, but her eyes danced with laughter. "Don't you want to be of service to the reform cause, Lord Lovell?"

Benedict ground his teeth together. Of course, he wished to be of service, but the idea of having that wretched powder blown into his face repeatedly, leaving him a wheezing, weeping, incapacitated mess, was not appealing.

In Lydia's eyes, there gleamed a challenge. She thought he wouldn't do it.

Very well then. He *would.* Benedict straightened his shoulders and took a deep breath. "I'm ready."

"Now, when you blow this herb into an assailant's face," Lydia instructed the women, "make sure they are downwind from you if possible. You'll want to wash your hand off as soon as you can, or at the very least wipe it off on the hem of your clothing."

One of the women spoke. "But isn't this—"

Lydia interrupted her. "Who wants to go first?"

Grace raised her hand before sashaying to the front. "It's nothing personal, my lord," she cooed.

The other woman laughed.

Benedict fisted his hands and took a deep breath of air—perhaps his last without pain for some time. "I'm ready."

Grace pulled the stopper out of the vial, poured the contents in her hand, and blew it right into Benedict's face.

He braced himself for burning pain. He waited. And waited. Nothing happened. He smacked his lips and tasted...stew seasonings?

"What?" Benedict wiped the dried herb off his face.

Lydia was grinning. "Did you think we would actually use it on you?"

"I don't understand." This wasn't a self-defense herb?

Grace approached, a clean cloth in her outstretched hand. "We needed to practice blowing the herb into an attacker's face, but we didn't want to actually hurt anybody. We borrowed some old cooking herbs from the kitchen and placed them in clean vials."

Benedict accepted the cloth and wiped his face. "So this is just some old sage and thyme and whatnot?"

Lydia took the cloth from him, shaking it out before dabbing near his eyes. "I wouldn't hurt you," she murmured. "Not intentionally."

Benedict held still as she peered at his face, dabbing away bits of dried herb that stuck to his skin. She was standing so close, he could feel her warmth and smell her clean, floral scent. Her eyes, laughing only moments before, were now serious. Her chest rose and fell as she continued her ministrations. Benedict closed his eyes. He would absorb this moment, like plants absorb the sunshine.

"There," she whispered before stepping back.

Benedict blinked his eyes open and their gazes caught and

held. He longed to set aside all the complications between them. To just grab her in his arms and hold her tight. To love her out in the open instead of in the quiet stillness of his own heart.

And yet…

She is not for the likes of you.

But with the scandal of his past hanging over his head, would Jack even permit him to court her? To ask for her hand? To link her name to his for all time? Benedict clenched his teeth for a moment before pushing the hard questions aside. Instead, he turned his most dazzling smile to the reformers.

"Who is next?" He drawled. "I am open and available for seasoning for the next hour."

After all the reformers had taken repeated turns blowing the herbs onto Benedict, Lydia praised their work and sent them back into the house.

Benedict wiped his face a final time. He truly smelled like some delicious stew or roasted chicken, and he was certain a good long soak was the only way to remove the small bits of herbs from his body. He shuddered to think what his valet would say if he saw the state of Benedict's clothing.

"That went quite well," Lydia said, a bounce in her step as they followed behind the reformers toward the house. "Thank you for volunteering to be our practice villain."

"I only hope there is not a need for any of them to use it." He realized he'd become quite fond of the reformers since their arrival into his life that day in the courtyard of Westminster. The idea of them ever being threatened by someone bigger or stronger or who just wished them harm was a sobering one.

Lydia was silent.

Benedict slowed to a halt. "You anticipate trouble at the rally?"

She nibbled on her lips. "We received more information from the other reform societies, and it seems the rally organizers are well prepared with every element planned and accounted for. But…"

Benedict watched her thinking. Lydia's mind at work was always an awesome sight to behold. "But you fear things might take a turn?" he asked.

After a hesitation, she nodded. "The way Staines behaved when he was at the LCA..." She shuddered. "I just cannot let go of this idea that he and his guards from the Office of Public Order are going to show up at the rally, intending to do as much harm to the reform movement and the reformers themselves as possible."

Benedict took her hand. The very idea of her walking into danger terrified him. But he knew Lydia far too well now to even consider asking her not to go. She was her own person with her own ideas, and he would not try to sway her. Plus, he knew she wouldn't take any unnecessary risks. Being bold was not the same thing as being reckless.

"You've taught me so much," he told her, stroking her hand. Her skin was so soft, yet her hands held such power. She could write incredible words that had the ability to change the mind of an entire nation.

And perhaps do something else powerful as well.

"I want to teach you something now," he said.

Lydia quirked an eyebrow. "How to give hand massages?"

Benedict dropped her hand he'd been rubbing and huffed in mock outrage. "This is a much more essential skill, I promise you." He held up his own hand and curled it into a fist. "I'm going to teach you how to punch."

Lydia pursed her lips and stared at him in consideration. "You think I might need to punch someone at the rally?"

"Hopefully, you'll never need to use this. But," he said, "what if you had the chance to punch Staines right in the face? Wouldn't that feel nice?"

Lydia smirked. "I believe in peaceful protest, but if I needed to defend myself...then yes, a punch right to his face would be most satisfying."

Ah, his sweet, intelligent, bloodthirsty Lydia. How he adored her.

"First, make sure you keep your thumb on the outside and braced along your other fingers." He held up his own fist in demonstration.

Lydia copied him.

"Good. Now, you'll stand like this." He modeled the correct stance, standing at an angle to one's opponent with fists up and weight on the back foot.

When she wasn't standing quite right, Benedict moved behind her, placing his hands on her hips to rotate her body a bit. She inhaled sharply at his touch. He yearned to linger, but this was important, and he needed to focus. *She* needed to focus.

Focus.

He pulled back and cleared his throat. "Ah, yes. That's it. Next, you'll throw your back hand, rotating your hips and shoulders while you transfer weight onto your front foot. That will give your punch force."

Lydia raised a skeptical eyebrow. "Throw, rotate, and transfer all at the same time? Benedict, I'm a writer, not Gentleman Jack. How am I supposed to do this?"

"It's complicated, but not impossible," he replied, "much like keeping your identity as an infamous political firebrand a secret, some might say."

She laughed. "Point taken. All right, show me again."

For half an hour, they practiced, Lydia becoming more and more comfortable with the mechanics and movements to throw a cross punch.

"Thank you," she said once they'd finished, wiping at her brow. "That was actually fun. I think I'll feel safer knowing another way to defend myself. Not that I'll need to use it."

Benedict took hold of her fist and smoothed her fingers open. This hand, this *woman*, meant so much to him. There was no way he could let her walk into potential danger without him.

He stroked along her palm. "I've decided to accompany you to the rally."

Lydia's eyes widened. "But you can't!"

He stroked his thumb across her fingers, smudged with ink stains. "Whyever not?"

"Your sister," Lydia said, as if it were the most obvious answer in the world. Perhaps to her, it was.

But it was neither obvious nor simple to Benedict. He had gone over this again and again as he tossed and turned in his bed at night, alternating between desirous thoughts toward Lydia, concern for Lydia's safety, and speculation about what the future might hold for him and Lydia.

So basically, his thoughts were entirely about Lydia, all the time.

And yet, his duty and obligation to his family also tugged at him. It was no small thing to set his sister's request aside. He did not want to create scandal. Or at least, no more than he already had.

No more than he'd been accused of, at least.

"I will take care of things with my sister," Benedict said.

"But that night on the balcony, Emelia said—"

"All will be well, Lydia. Please, trust me."

Lydia got that thinking look on her face once more, and Benedict wondered at the thoughts racing through her magnificent mind. She finally nodded.

He squeezed her hand before saying goodbye.

He needed to head home and speak to Emelia. And hope that all really *would* be well.

BENEDICT FOUND EMELIA playing the pianoforte in the music room. Quite badly.

She played what he might have recognized as a popular love ballad though it was hard to be sure. Still, it made him think that all was well in her campaign to win over Throckmorton's heart.

Unfortunately for all people with ears, Emelia possessed neither natural musical talent nor the discipline to practice. At all.

And yet, she persisted. So for that, he gave her credit.

"Benny!" she cried when she spotted him across the room, dropping her fingers down onto the pianoforte keys with a dissonant crash. "Guess who took a barouche ride through the park today with a certain compelling gentleman whose name rhymes with 'Grockmorton'?"

She beamed, and Benedict struggled between twin desires to celebrate her happiness with her and reluctance to cause her smile to dim by bringing up a difficult subject. He leaned against the pianoforte. "All is going well on that front, then, I gather?"

She clasped her hands together. "Quite well. Oh, Benny, I do believe I have found my soulmate."

Benedict raised his eyebrows. *Soulmate?* He was tempted to call it all a lot of poppycock, but then he thought of Lydia and the ease, comfort, and peace he felt in her presence while at the same time his very skin seemed to vibrate with an effervescent joy. *Soulmates.*

He decided to keep his mouth shut about that, and instead he veered toward the subject he needed to discuss. "I'm very glad for you," he replied. "Even imps deserve happiness."

She laughed. His sister was always ebullient, but this joy seemed to come from a deeper place. It was not merely surface.

Throckmorton was not exactly what society would deem a catch. However, as Benedict turned the idea over in his mind, he realized the man was a very good listener, an excellent conversationalist, and unabashedly enjoyed the same things that brought his sister joy. Now that Benedict was seeing the world more clearly since his time with Lydia and the reformers, perhaps someone like Throckmorton *was* a catch, and all the others were simply well-dressed, square-jawed popinjays of good fortune and small minds.

Benedict turned his attention back to his sister. "There is something I wish to speak to you about, Em."

She glanced down at the piano keys. "To be honest, I thought you'd come by to have this conversation days ago."

Benedict cocked his head. "What?"

Emelia tapped out a melancholy chord on the pianoforte. "About the other night on the balcony—"

Benedict interrupted. "I never meant—"

She pounded her finger down on a single key, the angry note cutting him off. "Please don't interrupt me, Benny. It will only make this harder." She raised an eyebrow at him. "Plus, it's rude."

Benedict exhaled slowly. "You are right. My apologies."

She offered him an imperious nod before turning her gaze back to the pianoforte keys. "I was quite taken aback that night of the ball, seeing you out on the balcony with Lady Lydia. Based on your past behavior, I've always suspected you held a *tendre* for her, but for some reason I never thought you would actually do anything about it."

"You and me both," he muttered under his breath.

"What's that?" she asked, but based on the wicked gleam in her eye, he knew she had heard him.

He simply rolled his eyes at her.

"Well," Emelia continued, "what I'm trying to say is, seeing you and her getting so cozy on the balcony was disconcerting for me in the moment. And... I behaved badly." She looked up at him. "I said hurtful things to both you and to Lady Lydia. And I'm very sorry." She pressed her hands together over her chest. "I love you, Benny, and I want you to be happy."

Benedict swallowed, and then swallowed again trying to clear the lump in his throat.

"Oh blast," Emelia said, rising from the piano bench. "Have I made things worse?"

Benedict shook his head. "It's just that I..."

Emelia moved close and laid one of her hands on his arm. "What is it? But only tell me if you want to, not because you feel you should."

He gave a watery laugh and was embarrassed to feel a bit of

moisture on his cheeks.

"Oh, Benny," Emelia cried, throwing her arms around him in a tight hug. "It's all right. Just because you're a big lug of a boy doesn't mean you aren't allowed to cry."

Benedict wrapped his arms around his sister and leaned his cheek on top of her head. "You're my favorite imp, you know."

"If you are wiping your tears into my hair, I'll do something so vile that you'll never call me your favorite again," she warned.

Benedict pulled back and wiped his eyes. "What made you change your mind? About me and Lydia, and the threat of my reputation?"

Emelia sighed and sank back down to the piano bench. "I suppose I just realized that I wanted Throckmorton to like me for *me*, not because of my perceived suitability in the eyes of an uncaring society." She shrugged. "Plus, to be honest, the more I thought about those old rumors about you, the less they seemed likely to be true."

Benedict's breath seized in his lungs. "Emelia," he croaked.

She watched him intently. "I don't know why you wouldn't tell anyone that the rumors weren't true." She sniffed. "Especially not your adorable, clever, little sister, but I suppose that's your business."

Now it was Benedict's turn to stare at the pianoforte keys. Black and white, black and white, the keys marched along in such a straight and orderly line. Nothing was blurry. Nothing was uncertain. Everything was either-or. Right or wrong.

But life wasn't like that. So often, a person just had to do what they thought was best in the moment. No one could see into the future and know the consequences.

He certainly hadn't. And couldn't.

He exhaled. "Lydia has befriended the members of the Stafford Female Reform Society. They were all thrown into Newgate together when the reformers were peacefully protesting at Westminster."

Emelia's mouth fell open.

"The reformers have been staying at Lydia's home, and I've stayed there as well, to make sure everyone was safe. I know that's quite scandalous, but I would do it again."

Emelia was watching him, her eyes wide. Perhaps it was unfair to dump all of this on her at once, but he wanted her to know *what* she was accepting if she accepted him, *all* of him, the way she wished for her beau to accept all of her. How odd, that it was his sister's romance that sparked him to see himself as someone worthy of love, just for himself without needing to change or be something or someone different.

"Tomorrow, there is to be a giant rally for reform in Nottinghamshire," he continued. If he was going to tell her, he'd best tell her the whole story. "Lydia and the members of the reform group will go. And I… I will go with them."

He held her gaze and saw a swirl of emotions in her eyes.

"I…I hope to have your blessing in this."

"You hope to have my blessing," Emelia said slowly, as if thinking through each word, "but you're going to go regardless?"

Benedict hesitated for a moment. This was the tipping point. He could not split himself in two.

"I'm going to go," he affirmed, his voice rough. "Regardless of how it affects my reputation in the eyes of society. I'm sorry. I know you want more of me."

Emelia leaned back on the bench and crossed her arms over her chest. The silence stretched between them, and he found himself in the bizarre circumstance of wishing for more of her wretched piano playing.

She dropped her gaze to her hands and gave a decisive nod. "Well, I suppose that's that then."

Benedict froze. Did that mean that she didn't accept his decision? That she was done with him if he put another's wishes over her own? He had to admit, he had come here hoping for acceptance on her part. Perhaps, even, for her support.

But she was her own person, and she got to decide what was best for herself.

"I… I understand." He turned away but kept a hand on the top of the pianoforte. He wasn't sure his legs would support his weight otherwise.

"Should we head to your dressing room?"

His stopped. "Dressing room?" His voice sounded thin. Was she going to build an effigy of him out of his finest clothing and then set it aflame in the back garden?

"I don't trust that valet of yours to pack properly for your trip. Especially if you are trying to please a certain lady's eye." She stood up from the piano bench and moved to grasp his arm. "How many days will you be gone? Do you think you'll need a valise or a trunk? I've heard that the women suffragists wear white to these things. Are you supposed to wear white too? Because truly, Benny, I don't think that color would suit you."

And as they crossed the music room together, Benedict threw back his head and laughed in sheer relief. He was going to the rally with the sister's blessing.

Everything was going to be perfect.

Chapter Twenty-Two

LYDIA STEPPED OUT of the carriage, glad they'd stopped at her family's nearby estate. They'd paused to freshen up and eat after long hours on the road from London, before traveling the last few miles to Nottinghamshire.

"I'm sorry, my lady, but this is as far as I can take you," the carriage driver called down from his perch. "The streets are too crowded." And it was true; the outskirts of Nottinghamshire were crowded with carriages, carts, and horses as thousands of people streamed into the town for the rally.

Lydia took it all in while Benedict, Grace, and Agatha climbed out of the carriage behind her and the other carriages—borrowed from Benedict and several of her LCA friends—pulled up with the other reformers inside.

Families chatted amiably as they streamed by, many with picnic baskets in their hands. People were dressed in what looked like their Sunday best, with many of the women in white. Children were in the crowd as well, some laughing with excitement while others held their parents' hands, looking a bit overwhelmed by the number of people heading to the town's square.

Harriet clambered out of another carriage, Timmy right beside her. Her cheeks were rosy.

"Be a good lad and help me with the banner," she said to

Benedict.

"Being a good lad *is* my top goal in life," he replied, glancing at Lydia with eyes that danced with laughter.

She felt like giggling herself. He likely hadn't been called a lad since he'd passed six feet in height. At the age of five or so. What a mountain he was.

And…she was simply happy. The excitement of the other reformers and the crowd was palpable and infectious. Everyone here was expressing their desire for change—change in who could vote and change to the laws passed by a parliament that seemed to have little care for the well-being of England's working families.

Benedict worked to attach the banner—hand-sewn by one of the reformers who had a very neat stitch—to the top of a wooden pole. Timmy assisted, telling Benedict how he was doing it wrong. Under the child's confident—and at times, contradictory instruction—at last it was attached.

Harriet raised the pole, and their banner fluttered in the breeze. *Stafford Female Reform Society* was stitched across the top in blue letters against a white background, and below that were two embroidered hands, clasped together.

Agatha had explained that all the female reform societies would bring their own banner as a sign of both unity for their cause of women's suffrage and also as a show of strength with just how many groups had formed in the past year.

"It's beautiful," Lydia said. She hadn't expected the sight of it to stir her, and yet she found herself fighting back tears.

Benedict leaned in close. "So are you."

She blinked a few times to clear her eyes, and then gave him a tremulous smile. "Intelligence is far more important than beauty."

"Well, it's just too bad then." He shook his head in mock sorrow. "You've been cursed with both."

She poked him in the ribs, and he gave her a playful, mock frown in response.

"Gather around," Agatha commanded, and the reformers pulled together in a tight group on the side of the road. Carriages and wagons were turning around, and people continued to stream past, but here in their little huddle, the group had a moment of calm before entering the rally.

Lydia felt Benedict's presence behind her, and she realized he'd positioned himself to be between her and the crowd. She leaned on her heels, not enough that anyone would notice, but just the right amount so that she felt his reassuring strength gently pressing against her back.

"I'm so proud of each of you," Agatha said, her gaze landing on each member of the group. "We've been gone from home far longer than any of us expected, but I do not regret our time together. For far too long, those in power have ignored the voices of people like us. Women. Workers. Farmers."

The reformers nodded.

"But today, they will be able to ignore us no longer," Agatha continued, her chin tilted up, determined.

A few of the ladies cheered, and several of the children jumped up and down or clapped, although they likely didn't know the cause of the celebration.

"We don't expect any trouble but remember your training and stick together." Agatha met Lydia's gaze, and she gave the older woman a nod. They all had spent countless hours practicing in the back garden. They were ready.

Agatha continued. "The carriages will meet us on the out-skirts of town at sundown, and we will return to Lady Lydia's family's estate to spend the night. After that, we'll make our way home to Stafford on the mail coaches."

"Actually," Lydia interjected, "I've arranged for the carriages we rode in today to take you all home tomorrow."

Murmurs of excitement came from the reformers. Several of them patted Lydia's arms or shoulders. She smiled at them, so glad that she could do this small thing to help make their travels easier.

"On the count of three," Agatha said, "votes for women!"

When the group shouted, "Votes for women!" Harriet shook the banner, and Timmy whooped. Then the reformers merged into the crowd making its way into Notthinghamshire's square. Thousands and thousands of people had come to the rally. Lydia couldn't recall ever seeing this many people at once before.

Benedict took her hand. She glanced up at him, surprised.

"No one will notice," he murmured, leaning in close.

And it was true. With this many people, no one would even see their joined hands, let alone think anything of it. Here, they weren't a lord and lady with reputations to preserve. They were just two reformers amongst many. They'd both worn their plainest clothes, and with Lydia in white, they looked like any other couple.

A couple.

Lydia examined the thought, looking at it from all sides and angles and perspectives. Did she *want* to be part of a couple with Benedict? Her logical brain said no. Women lost so much freedom when they bound themselves to a man in the state of matrimony. But her heart said something different. As did her body, if she were being honest with herself.

She had no more time to consider this as their group gathered in an open space in the square and gathered together.

"I'll find you after the speeches," Agatha said. She took the banner from Harriet and, with Timmy shouting goodbye, made her way through the throng toward the platform at the front of the square.

Along with those giving speeches at the rally, leaders of the various female reform societies were to be seated on the platform, each holding their group's banner. It was a great honor, Agatha had explained.

But Lydia couldn't help but feel trepidation as Agatha, who although sprightly as a younger woman would soon be a grandmother, was swallowed up by the crowd.

Lydia moved closer to Benedict and surveyed the square.

Buildings ran along all four sides, hemming in those who'd gathered, with streets stretching to the rest of the town from each corner. The mood of the crowd was genial. Young children rode on their father's shoulders or perched on their mother's hips. Some were visibly pregnant, others were old with white in their hair, and others were young women, just starting out their lives as adults. People greeted one another, made introductions, and, of course, traded pamphlets.

"We should start passing these out," Harriet said, pulling a bundle out of her pocket. "Stay with your team."

Lydia reluctantly pulled her hand away from Benedict's clasp and pulled out her own stack of pamphlets. "I'm teamed with Harriet and Grace," she told him.

"Then so am I," he answered simply.

Lydia's shoulders relaxed a degree. Even though the crowd was peaceful and the weather mild, she couldn't shake her anxiety. There was a knot in her stomach that would not go away. But having Benedict accompany her group alleviated some of her worries.

"Shall we head toward that part of the square?" Grace asked, pointing to the side farthest from the platform where it would be easier to navigate the crowd. Lydia, Harriet, and Benedict agreed with her suggestion, and Benedict—as the tallest and widest member of the team—led their way amongst the sea of people.

"Are you interested in a pamphlet about reform and voting?" Lydia asked a family.

They accepted her pamphlet and immediately began to scan the contents. Lydia knew she should move on to the next cluster of people, but in that moment she could not make her feet move one step.

When she had written as Democratium Liberum, she hadn't seen the effects of her words firsthand. She knew from gossip at social events that people spoke of the articles, but she had never seen someone read her article, read her words, from the newspaper.

But here, this young mother with dark hair and a little girl clinging to her skirt was reading over Lydia's words, along with her husband who had his arm tucked around her waist. Both their heads were bent over the pamphlet, and the woman pointed something out to her husband, perhaps a point of interest or something that caught her eye.

Lydia had known the power of words for most of her life. But to see the power of *her* words was something else altogether.

"They are completely engrossed in your writing," Benedict murmured into her ear.

Lydia shivered at the sensation.

"Just as engrossed as I was," he continued, "even though I had no idea they'd been penned by you when I'd read Democratium Liberum in the newspaper. You have a gift, Lydia. And you are using it to make the world a better place."

She looked up at him. "Do you think it will? Make the world a better place?" His answer mattered so terribly much.

The golden-brown of his eyes gleamed with sincerity. "I do."

Lydia swallowed and nodded. It was all she was capable of in that moment. And since they were in a crowd of people where husbands were free to put their arms around their wives' waists, Lydia leaned into Benedict and pressed her cheek against his chest. His arms closed around her. His hand rubbed a gentle circle across her back. And no one noticed. No one cared. They were just normal people here in this place. Two people who cared for one another.

"Do you have any pamphlets left?"

Lydia jerked back at the sound of Grace's voice. "Um, I still have some here." She fumbled in her pocket and pulled out her stack of pamphlets.

Grace took them and pinched their thickness. Lydia flushed in embarrassment. She'd only given one away, so her stack was still quite thick. And Grace had most likely seen her moment of intimacy with Benedict.

"I've been talking to a group of miners and their wives over in the corner there, and they're quite interested in our work," Grace said. "How about I take these to them and leave you two to your...*chat*?" She gave Lydia a saucy wink before leaving.

Benedict chuckled. "Not much gets past Agatha *or* her daughter."

"Imagine all the things that Parliament would accomplish if those two were allowed to run for a seat."

Benedict's face sobered. "I hope to see it in my lifetime."

Change often happened at a glacial pace. But at some point, the change did occur. Slowly, slowly, and then all at once. Perhaps that was how it would be for women's suffrage and reform.

Shouts and whistles drew her attention to a large public house in the middle of the row of buildings along the backside of the square. Big windows in the front had been thrown open, and inside she viewed a group of soldiers and officers watching the square.

Lydia gasped.

Those were men from the Office of Public Order. They held tankards of ale in their hands, and based on their flushed cheeks and glassy eyes, those were not the first drink for most of them.

Benedict was eyeing them as well. "That can't be good," he murmured.

Lydia shook her head. If the officers were here, then Staines was here as well. She knew it, with an instant certainty. The back of her neck prickled. Was he watching her even now? She looked around, and her breath caught. There he was, on the edge of the square, sitting up high on a horse. Had he spotted her or the others?

It didn't seem like it. All the same, she wanted to get away from there.

"Let's collect Harriet and Grace and head back," she said.

Benedict agreed, and soon they were back at their original spot in the square. Most of the reformers had returned with empty pockets and exciting stories about those who had been eager to receive their pamphlets or discuss reform.

A cheer erupted from the crowd as a carriage slowly made its way from one of the streets to the platform.

"That's most likely Henry Hunt," Grace said, watching the carriage with wide eyes. "He's to be the first speaker."

Henry "Orator" Hunt was a famous political speaker, known for his rousing speeches aimed at the working classes. He promoted universal suffrage as well as the immediate repeal of the Corn Laws and was very popular among reform groups all across England.

The carriage reached the platform, and a man emerged. A great roar went up from the crowd and Lydia tensed. Benedict put his arm around her waist, but despite their enthusiastic noise, there was no pushing or shoving. The crowd remained calm and safe. After a few moments, his arm relaxed around her.

She caught his eye and smiled. Together, they joined the chanting.

"Unity and strength! Unity and strength!"

Lydia let herself rest against him, the heat of his arm warming her skin through the cotton of her gown. They were here together, and in this moment, she truly felt like part of something bigger than herself. She and Benedict both were not only helping the reformers, but they had *become* reformers. Their cause was now hers and Benedict's as well.

Henry Hunt began to speak, and the crowd grew quiet to hear his words.

Lydia allowed herself to dream, for just a moment, that this would be the moment everything would change. Universal suffrage would happen. Women would have the vote. All the wretched corruption in Parliament would be eradicated. At last, the government of this nation would implement laws that actually helped its citizens, instead of continuing harmful policies like the Corn Laws that left the tables of families—like those standing around her—empty.

Shouts came from the very back of the square. Were some of

the reformers unaware that the speech had started? Lydia and Benedict turned to see what was going on.

Benedict's arm tightened around her waist. "Oh, bloody hell," he whispered.

Lydia's skin broke out in goosebumps and her heart stuttered in her chest. There at the very back of the crowd of tens of thousands of protesters, a large group of mounted soldiers stood. She was afraid that these were the same men who had been drinking heavily in the pub. Staines appeared to be yelling orders at them. As an entity, they drew their swords and pointed them up to the sky. Fear engulfed Lydia. They were about to descend upon the peaceful crowd, and there was nowhere to run.

✥

Chapter Twenty-Three

B ENEDICT'S BLOOD TURNED to ice.

"Disperse!" cried the soldiers on horseback. "Disperse at once!"

Around them, people began to shout and cry out. Things were about to turn ugly, and possibly even deadly. Thousands of people were on all sides of them. The square was lined with buildings, and of the four streets leading out of the square, the back two were blocked by the soldiers.

Benedict searched frantically for a way out of the square but could see none. His heart pounded in his chest. He had to get this group to safety, immediately. He had to get *Lydia* to safety. If he didn't...

He shuddered.

The crowd was moving as one toward the front two corners of the square where both roads led to the rest of the town. There were tens of thousands of people here. There was no way they would all fit through those narrow passages, at least not quickly. What were the soldiers thinking, demanding the crowd disperse but then blocking half of the ways out?

This was pure madness.

"Benedict." Lydia clutched his hand. "What do we do?"

Ahead of them, Harriet gathered Timmy onto her back so that she might carry him through the surging crowd. Benedict tried to stay with them and the rest of the reformers from their group, but the push and pull of the crowd was too great.

"Lady Lydia!" shouted Harriet, her eyes wild when she looked back.

"Find the meeting spot," Lydia shouted to her. "If you can get to the carriages, they'll take you back to the estate."

With all the screaming and crying, Benedict doubted Harriet even heard Lydia's instructions. But Harriet was clever and resourceful. The whole group was. They would know where to find safety.

The screams at the back of the square intensified. Benedict glanced back and he cursed at the sight of soldiers riding their horses through the crowd, mowing people down left and right. They swung their swords with no regard for who they might hit. Benedict thought of all of the families gathered here today. Children. Pregnant women. Elderly people. Families with picnic baskets and in their Sunday best, gathered here in peace.

His stomach roiled, and he feared he would be sick.

Lydia wrapped her arms around his waist. "Benedict," she gasped. "Benedict, please, we need to get out of here."

Her words and the press of her warm arms steadied him. He stared into her face, like a starving man sighting a hot meal. Lydia. She would give him strength. And courage.

She was pale and drawn, but her blue eyes blazed with determination. He would get her out of there. He would get them *both* out of there, and then they would find the others and they would be all right.

He took her hand in his. "Don't let go."

She nodded and squeezed his hand.

They *would* be all right.

He repeated it over and over as they moved with the crowd. The squeeze of bodies was oppressive, and the shrieks and screams of terror hammered his ears. Slowly and surely, he moved them to the left. They were still caught up in the crowd as it surged toward the street exits, but with each movement forward, he also moved them to the side. His goal was the shop fronts along the border of the square, where hopefully a door would be unlocked, and they could make their way out of this deathtrap.

"Benedict," Lydia cried, tears streaming. "If this is the end—"

"No!" he shouted. "I'll get you out of here Lydia. I swear it."

Louder screams came from behind, and he turned to see a soldier on horseback gaining ground. Blood dripped from the man's sword, and his face was twisted by either fear or hatred. Probably both. What a dangerous combination.

"I want you to know," Lydia choked out, her mouth close to his ear, "that I love you. I love you, Benedict."

The whole world went perfectly still and quiet. Everything was clear and sharp. The mass of people were merely obstacles, the soldier merely a far-off worry. It was as if there was nothing between the two of them and their safe exit out of this hellish place. He held her hand tightly as he surged toward a tobacco shop. If the door was locked, he would break it down. He would rip the whole side of the building open to clear a path to safety for them. To clear a path for Lydia.

Lydia who loved him.

With a roar, he pushed through the final stretch. He pulled on the door and cried out in relief when it swung open. They stepped into the shop, and more people followed them, pushing him and Lydia deeper into the store. Those behind them were likely just as scared as he felt. Parents clutching children. Babies crying. A man with blood gushing down his face. A woman wailing. Is this what war was like? The destruction of humanity before one's very eyes? If so, Benedict would choose peace every time.

"Let's find a back exit," Lydia shouted over the din.

More and more people funneled into the shop, and Benedict hurried past the display cases and behind the counter, then through a back storage room. And there, looking more beautiful than the crown jewels, was a door leading out of the store and away from the square.

He turned the doorknob and they burst out onto a narrow lane. People ran by, with their faces twisted in terror. A soldier on horseback thundered along, with a sword raised in his hand. Benedict realized that he and Lydia were out of the square, but they were not out of the woods.

"Over there." Lydia pointed to a bakery across the way where the door hung crooked, as if it had been wrenched open. "If we keep cutting through shops, we can get far enough away to be safe."

More and more people streamed out of the tobacco shop behind them, and soon this street would likely be overflowing with frightened people from the rally as well. He took Lydia's hand, and they ran across the street, dodging and weaving as they made their way toward the open door of the bakery.

From the bakery, they cut across an alley and then through a broken window into a shoe shop. From there, they cut across another street, through one shop and then another until they came to a stone inn, sitting sturdy on its block with a massive wooden door.

The door opened a few inches, and a woman poked her head out. "Come," she said softly. "You'll be safe in here with us."

Benedict looked at Lydia, and she nodded. They dashed to the door and then were inside the inn. The heavy door slammed shut behind them, and the woman lowered a board into two brackets, securing the entrance.

"Never thought we'd need to use this." She patted the wooden beam. "But I'm thankful today that my father installed it all those years ago."

Benedict tried to draw steady breaths, but his heart continued to race, and it felt like there wasn't enough air in the room. He sucked in breath after breath, yet his heart still pounded as if he were drowning.

"Benedict." Lydia shook his arm.

But he couldn't even look at her. If he didn't get enough air soon, he would die. He would die and leave her here alone in this terrifying situation.

Voices called out instructions about bringing him to sit by the fire, to fetch some water, to make way, but none of the words made sense. All Benedict could really hear was the rushing of his blood through his body and his tortured breath. He found himself in a wooden chair beside a fireplace with Lydia kneeling in front of him.

She clasped his frigid hands. "Benedict, we're safe now," she said, her voice gentle. "Breathe with me. Breathe in. Breathe out."

He tried to copy her breathing. The warmth of her hands slowly brought sensation back to his fingers. After a minute of breathing together, she offered him a cup of cool water. The world was slowing down, and he was in his right senses once more.

"I'm sorry," he rasped. She had needed him, and he'd fallen apart.

"Don't you dare," she said fiercely, shaking his hands. "You're the one who got us out of that square. You're the one who led us through all the shops to this place. Because of you, we're both alive, Benedict. Because of you, we're safe, so don't you dare apologize for feeling overcome."

He drew in a slow, shaky breath and parsed through her words.

Maybe she was right. He *had* been overcome, but they were safe. Maybe he didn't have to be perfect. Perhaps he didn't have to control his feelings at every moment of the day. Together, they'd found safety. And right now, that was all that mattered. He nodded to Lydia, and she squeezed his hands.

After a long exhalation, he looked around the inn. This room—the dining room—was dim, and Benedict realized that heavy shutters had been pulled shut over the windows. With the door barricaded, the inn was safer than any other place where they may have landed. Truly, he and Lydia, along with the thirty or so people who milled about, were beyond fortunate.

One woman cradled her arm, her mouth tight with pain. A man with gray hair was pressing a cloth to a gash on the side of his face. A few people were crying, and a baby wailed while the mother crooned softly to calm her child. All these people have been given sanctuary by the kindly innkeeper.

The woman approached and patted his shoulder. "Feeling better, lad?" She was middle-aged with creases along the sides of her mouth that hinted at frequent smiles and laughter. She searched for his face. "We all took quite a fright today. People react in different ways. I learned that when my boys came back from the war in France. Some people cry. Some get angry. Some bottle it up, and it comes out later when they least expect it. And there are some what need to let their mind have a wee rest, and then they return to the situation with a clearer head. 'Tis nothing to be ashamed of."

Something hot and tight eased in Benedict's chest at her words.

"Thank you," Benedict told her. "You saved us." He gestured around the room. "You saved all of us."

The woman gazed toward the street and sighed. "A group of them soldiers started their morning here in my place, and they was all heavy in their cups. When they announced they were heading to the square to put a stop to any talk of revolution, I knew there would be trouble. So I boarded up the inn and waited, and sure enough, a few hours later, all hell broke loose. I watched out the door, and if I saw anyone with a child or a woman wearing white, I'd bring them into my place for safekeeping."

"Thank you," Lydia whispered.

Others echoed the sentiment, and many approached the innkeeper to shake her hand or offer her a hug. And even though the room remained the same size it had been before, it felt like they'd all grown cozier somehow and that the fire burned a little brighter.

A man who had been peering out between a gap in the shutters spoke up. "Soldiers are still out there hunting down people. I don't think it will be safe for us to leave anytime soon."

The innkeeper sighed. "I think you'd best stay here tonight. I'm Dot and I own this inn. Pay for the room if you can, but if you haven't the coin, you're still welcome. Some of you will have to share a chamber, but I'm sure you'll agree that's better than being out there." She jerked her thumb toward the road.

Benedict jerked to attention in his seat.

Some of you will have to share.

Even in the soft light cast by the fireplace, he could see a blush creep up Lydia's cheeks. His own face grew hot as he pictured the two of them in one room, with one bed.

He turned his gaze to the floor. It was likely best that she not see his expression at that moment.

"Prue?" Dot the innkeeper called.

"Aye?" A woman with a thin face and a sullen expression shuffled forward from the shadows.

"Why don't you get our visitors settled in rooms, and I'll get a pot of stew going."

Prue's mouth pinched tight, but after a pause, she nodded in agreement.

"If you all come down in about two hours," Dot announced, "I'll have a hearty meal waiting for you. It won't be grand, but it'll be warm and satisfying, I can promise you that."

"Would you like help in the kitchen?" Lydia asked Dot.

The innkeeper patted her arm. "Thanks for the offer, but I'd rather do it myself so it turns out the way I like it. You get to be my age and you get stuck in your ways, even when it comes to stew." She winked.

"All right, you lot," Prue groused. "Stand beside your people, and I'll sort out who gets what room."

People shuffled about, and Prue began to circulate, directing people to their chambers.

Lydia moved closer so her skirt brushed against Benedict's leg. "I suppose…" Lydia trailed off and nibbled on her lip for a moment. "I suppose we'd best share a room."

Benedict's mouth went dry.

"I–I mean," she stammered, "since there might not be enough rooms otherwise."

Benedict tried to swallow, but his mouth had turned into a desert. He fumbled for the cup of water.

"And that way," Lydia said, examining the ceiling as if it were a Renaissance painting, "you can keep me safe, and I can keep you safe."

For the first time in his adult life, cheerful, easy-going Benedict could think of not a single word to say.

Lydia flicked her gaze down to him for a moment before turning her attention back to the ceiling. "I mean, if that's all right with you?"

Prue approached and curled her lip at them before asking, "You two together in a room?"

When they did not immediately reply, she folded her hands over her chest and glared. "Well?"

Benedict rose to his feet, took Lydia's hand in his, and nodded.

He and Lydia would spend the night together.

Chapter Twenty-Four

L YDIA PACED THE length of her room at the inn. Well…her and Benedict's room.

That they shared. *Together.*

Her stomach was pleasantly full after a bowl of warm, hearty stew in the dining room with the others who'd found refuge here. Later, the grumpy servant Prue had brought up an ewer of warm water, and Benedict had excused himself, allowing Lydia to wash up.

And now she was waiting for his return.

Outside, there were still distant shouts, but they came less frequently now. Regardless, Lydia was extremely grateful that they had shelter here. To be out in the cold, hiding from the marauding, violent soldiers…

She shivered.

What were Agatha, Grace, Harriet, Timmy, and the others doing right now? Had they found a safe place to hide? Or perhaps even made it to the carriages so they could flee to Jack's nearby country estate? Or…had something else happened?

Lydia wrapped her arms around her, chilled despite the cozy fire dancing in the grate.

It was the strangest sensation, to look death straight in the eye and believe that the end was nigh, and then a few hours later, obsess over just one bed and nighttime kisses with the man one fancied.

The man one *loved*.

Lydia covered her face with her hands and groaned. She'd told him she loved him. Like a big, stupid idiot. She'd confessed her love to Benedict as Death had approached on a frenzied horse with a bloody saber.

The humiliation scorched her until she was certain her entire body was blushing. Well, at least she was no longer chilled.

A knock sounded at the door. "It's me," came Benedict's voice. Lydia unlocked the door, and he entered, his hands in his pockets and his gaze everywhere except on her. After a pause, he said, gazing down at his feet, "It's quieted down outside."

Lydia cleared her throat. "Hopefully we can safely leave in the morning."

"Yes."

The fire crackled. Neither of them spoke.

It was agony.

Lydia blurted out, "I didn't mean to tell you—" at the same time Benedict said, "About what happened earlier—"

They each broke off.

"You go first," Benedict said gruffly.

"No, you. I insist."

He narrowed his eyes at her, and Lydia raised a brow in silent challenge. He huffed before flopping into one of the wooden chairs at the room's small table. "I suppose we need to clear the air, since…" He gestured at the bed.

Lydia nodded. Yes. Clear the air. The bed. Right.

He rubbed his mouth. "About what you said earlier in the square—"

"We don't need to talk about that," Lydia interrupted, once again burning from the flames of embarrassment. "Truly."

Benedict held her gaze and said softly, "But we do."

He held out his hand, and Lydia walked to him automatically, without thinking about it until she reached him. He gave her a gentle tug, and she tumbled into his lap.

"There," he said gruffly, positioning her on one leg and wrapping an arm around her waist to gather her in close. "That's better, isn't it?"

Lydia buried her face in his neck. She would just hide here. If she couldn't see him, then he couldn't see her. *Right?*

He jostled his leg and she finally answered with a nod.

"So, what I wanted to say," he told her, running his hand up and down her back, "is that I heard you in the square when you told me you loved me."

Lydia gulped.

He waited, but she didn't speak. She couldn't speak. She was balancing on the edge of a freshly trimmed quill tip, and the slightest of movements would send her toppling in one direction or the other, unable to see what awaited her below.

"I heard you," he whispered into her hair, and she shivered at the tingle that spread across her scalp and down her neck. "And I want you to know that I love you too."

Lydia jerked her head up in shock. It collided with Benedict's chin, and his head snapped back as he yelped.

"Oh! Oh no," she cried, cupping his cheek with her hand. "I'm so sorry. Are you all right?"

He rubbed his jaw and gave her a baleful look, but his eyes were twinkling. "I suppose I deserved that, springing such a declaration on you."

"Oh no," she murmured, tenderly running her fingers along his injured jawline. "You didn't deserve that at all."

"Then," he asked, his eyes glittering, "what *do* I deserve?"

Lydia licked her lips, and his eyes flared. "You deserve this." And she leaned forward and kissed him.

He hummed in satisfaction and deepened their contact. His lips possessed hers, claiming her in a scorching kiss that left no mystery as to how he felt about her.

As to how he loved her.

"Do you really?" she whispered, pulling back a hair's breadth. "Love me?"

He nodded, and his lips bumped gently against her mouth with the movement. She stole a kiss each time they passed.

"I do," he rumbled. "I have." He leaned in for another searing kiss. "For a very long time."

"Oh," Lydia gasped, but then he was kissing her again, and sensation overtook thought.

She was on fire, her skin seared wherever his roaming hands passed. Her back, her hips, the curve of her bottom, the swell of her breast. He touched all of her. Reverently. Passionately. Possessively.

"I want you," he murmured against her neck. "I want to take you to bed and do wicked things with you. But," he pulled back and gave her his gaze, "if you want, you can have the bed and I'll sleep on the floor. It's up to you. And you can change your mind at any time."

Lydia swallowed around the lump in her throat. This man. His passion and humor and tenderness and concern humbled her.

"Take me to bed…" she whispered.

His eyes turned from amber-gold to dark copper.

"…and do wicked things to me."

⤜⟫⟪⤛

BENEDICT ROSE FROM the chair, Lydia cradled in his arms.

His heart raced. Fierce joy raced through his veins along with the life-sustaining blood that pumped through them. Lydia loved him, and he loved her. And now they would go to bed and do wicked things to one another. If this was a dream, he was going to be so upset when he awoke.

"How I have longed for you," he murmured, nuzzling against her ear.

He felt her shiver against him, and then she turned her head, and they were kissing once more. Her lips were sweet and soft, and he moaned in the back of his throat at the taste of her. Her hot, slick mouth made him think of other hot, slick things, and his hands trembled even as they held her.

"To bed?" he asked. He held his breath as he waited for her reply. If she said no, he feared he would expire on the spot, but he would set her down and leave her be. She alone was in charge of herself. She alone decided what she did, and with whom.

"To bed." Her voice had turned sultry.

Benedict carried her across the chamber. Tightening one arm around her, he used the other to pull back the blankets. The sheets looked crisp and clean, and a light, lavender scent came up from the fabric as he adjusted the top sheet. He would pay the innkeeper—Dot—handsomely for this room before they left tomorrow.

And then he set her down on upon the bed as if she were fragile, as if she were precious. Because that's what she was to him, his most precious Lydia. But as he stared into the sapphire-blue of her eyes, he was reminded that she was not fragile. Lydia possessed a strength that humbled him. Her bravery, her boldness, and her determination to fight against wrongs in the world all made her so very powerful.

"Benedict," she murmured, reaching an arm out to him.

He shook his head. "First things first."

He reached for her feet and untied her shoes, pulling them off each in their turn. Then he began walking his hands in a trail up her calf, caressing her even as he tugged down her stocking which disappeared up into the voluminous folds of her dress.

"Is this all right?" he asked, forcing his hands to stop their ascent of her shapely legs.

"Yes," she said, her eyes glittering as she watched him through her eyelashes.

Benedict trailed his hand further up her leg, the fabric of her stocking doing little to disguise the warmth of her skin or the softness of her flesh. His hand disappeared under her skirt, the sight more erotic than any nudity he'd ever witnessed.

Lydia watched his hand moving at her thigh beneath the

fabric of her skirt. Her eyes were half-lidded, and she looked like a cat stretching itself out for a satisfying scratch.

His fingers toyed with the edge of her stocking, caressing the bare skin above. She was so soft, her skin like satin.

Lydia made a breathy sound and shifted on the bed.

"Shall I take it off?" Benedict whispered.

Lydia nodded, and he slowly plucked at the tie before rolling her stockings down the creamy expanse of her thigh, her knee, her calf, and her feet.

"You are so beautiful," he murmured, stroking along one of her legs.

"It's just my shin." She held her mouth still, but her eyes danced with mirth.

"It's my *favorite* shin."

"That's hardly fair." Lydia pouted. "You haven't seen my other shin yet."

Benedict felt a wicked grin stretch across his mouth. "I shall rectify that immediately." He repeated the process on the other side. "I fear I cannot decide," he said stroking along the fronts of both of her bare legs. "Each shin is so majestic in its own way."

"I never thought," Lydia said with a giggle, "that these *wicked things* you mentioned would include such an exhaustive examination of my shins. Especially when there are so many interesting parts of me"—she waggled her eyebrows—"that you have not yet uncovered."

Benedict laughed.

How magical this moment was, knowing what was to come for the two of them, and yet experiencing this shared joy between them. Laughing. Smiling. Being silly. He hadn't thought of sex as a time for laughter before, but he'd missed out.

More likely, he'd missed the right partner.

"I love you," he said, allowing himself to smile his true smile. Not the lazy, mocking one or the overly charming one, but the natural smile he used when he was truly happy.

"I love you too," she whispered, and then she held her arms

out to him. "Come," she demanded. "Come to bed with me."

Benedict quickly shucked his boots, socks, jacket, and waist-coat. He unwound his cravat and then tugged his shirt over his head.

Lydia's eyes widened, and she came up to her knees in the bed. "Oh my," she breathed and then she reached for his bare torso.

Benedict hissed in pleasure as her hands began their exploration. Across his stomach. Up his rib cage. Over his pectorals. Around his shoulders. Everywhere she touched, his skin sang. The front of his breaches grew even tighter than they'd already been, and her hands froze in place when she noticed. "Is that..." A fierce blush traveled across her cheeks.

Benedict covered one of her hands with his own, holding it in place right above his heart. "That is my cock, grown hard with my desire for you."

She stared down at him, and Benedict felt his own face heat. "Do you know how this works, when a man and a woman come together in this way?"

Lydia's hand flexed against his chest. "Yes. I know how it works. Jane and Pippa have been most forthcoming."

Benedict swallowed. "That's good. That you know. About..." *Bloody hell.* How had things become so awkward all of a sudden? "We don't have to—"

Lydia shook her head. "No, I want to. I'm just...nervous."

Benedict stroked his thumb against the back of her hand. His bold, brave Lydia was nervous. And truth be told, so was he. This felt different than when he'd been with women in the past. Those times had been pleasurable and often there was a sort of degree of caring. But none of that had been love.

"Perhaps we can lay here together," he suggested, "and just talk and kiss a little and see what feels right."

Lydia nodded before shuffling around on her knees so that her back was to him. "I would be more comfortable lounging in just my chemise," she murmured over her shoulder. "Will you undo my dress?"

Benedict ran his finger down the row of little buttons along her back. "Yes," he said, his voice grown husky. "Lounging in a chemise sounds much more comfortable."

He undid the row of white buttons, one after another, until the fabric of her gown gaped, and Lydia's smooth skin was revealed beneath. He pressed a kiss to the base of her neck, and she shivered.

"Your hair too," he whispered. "Would you be more comfortable if it was down?"

Lydia nodded, and he began to take the pins out, one at a time, until her soft blond tresses cascaded down her back. It was just as he'd imagined. Had fantasized. He stroked the gleaming waterfall of her hair. "So soft," he said.

Lydia shimmied out of her gown, and then removed her stays. Now she wore just her chemise. Benedict gulped before turning his attention to arranging the pillows and adjusting the blankets. He feared if he allowed himself to look his fill of her, covered only by the gossamer fabric of her chemise, he would say or do something stupid. Like propose.

His hands stilled on the pillow.

Propose.

Yes. He would, but not just yet. Not now, on this evening of passion when she might doubt the sincerity of his words.

Benedict exhaled before reclining back against the pillows and opening his arms for her. Lydia lay down within the crook of his arm, her head nestled on his shoulder and his hand curved around her waist. "Is this all right?" he asked.

Lydia sighed and snuggled in even closer. "It's perfect."

He ran his fingertips up and down her bare arm and when she shivered, he hooked the sheet with his foot and pulled it up over them. The fire had died down, and the room was cocooned in the warm glow of its embers.

"I'm so worried about the others," she said, rubbing her leg against his. "If anything has happened to any of them…"

Benedict tightened his arms around her. "I'm worried too," he admitted. "But as soon as it's safe to leave, we'll find them."

"Those soldiers…" She burrowed her face into his chest.

Running his hand over her hair, Benedict whispered, "That was the scariest experience of my life." He traced a gentle curl. "I wasn't sure we would make it."

"We have to do something." She leaned up on one arm, her face suddenly fierce. "We can't let Staines and that horrible Office of Public Order get away with attacking peaceful people. What happened today was a massacre. That's the only word for it. And we have to let Parliament know. Let the Prince Regent know. Let *everyone* know what happened here today."

Benedict's chest expanded at her fiery words. Lydia's message on paper was incredible. But Lydia's message in real life? Breathtaking.

"Yes," he whispered, reaching up to cup her cheek. "We'll take Staines down. That man and his officers shouldn't be allowed to have power over an ant, let alone human lives."

Lydia's eyes blazed, and she leaned down and claimed his lips.

Benedict clung to her, lost in the moment, lost in her, and lost in their passion. She moaned and clutched at his hair.

"Please," she gasped. "I want you."

Benedict rolled so that she was under him. "Lydia," he panted, tugging at the delicate bow at the neckline of her chemise.

He pulled and she wriggled until they'd lowered it to her waist.

"God, you're beautiful," he whispered before devouring her breasts.

She gasped and arched up against him, her fingers twisted in his hair. The little jolts of pain along his scalp somehow added to his pleasure, and he moaned.

"Please," she gasped. "More."

Benedict pulled back, although every part of him that had been touching her howled in protest. "Are you sure?"

She narrowed her eyes at him. "If I have to beg you to bed

me one more time, I'm going to kick you in the shins."

Benedict kept himself still as a statue, his arms stiff as he hovered over her. But then he couldn't help it, and he was grinning at her like a fool. A fool in love. "Your wish is my command," he said, and then he sat back on his heels to remove her chemise and drawers until she was naked. Beautifully, gloriously naked. He tossed her clothing over his shoulder.

But she nibbled at her bottom lip. Was she self-conscious?

"You are everything," he told her honestly, simply, hoping she understood what he meant. She was lovely and fierce and smart and funny, and he wanted to love her for the rest of their lives. And right now, he wanted to worship her with his mouth.

Benedict lay down between her legs and trailed kisses along her inner thighs.

"But surely you're not meant to be down there?" she asked, lifting her head up to peer down at him.

He nuzzled her center, and she gasped, throwing her head back. "Or perhaps…you should keep at it…down there."

Benedict chuckled and continued his exploration of her warm, slick center. He gently parted her folds and ran his tongue up to her bud of nerves.

"Benedict," she screeched, arching her hips up to press herself more firmly against his mouth.

He paused the flickering of his tongue. "All right, my love?"

She answered by grabbing his hair and directing his face back to its previous location. He smiled against her slickness. His Lydia. His love. Even as he swirled his tongue around her most sensitive spot, he traced her with his finger. Slowly, he pressed into her. She inhaled and tensed, and he froze.

"Keep going," she murmured. "It just took me by surprise."

"Anytime you want me to stop, just tell me and I will."

She hummed in agreement, and her body relaxed into his touch.

Again, Benedict lapped at her bud, slowly entering her with a finger. He crooked his finger and felt along the inside of her passage, and she moaned, tightening around him.

"Oh, Benedict. God," she gasped. "That feels so good."

He moved his tongue faster, licking and pressing even as his finger gently pumped into her and massaged that spot inside her. He was on fire with her taste. His skin was all nerves. He pressed his aching cock against the bed as he continued to see to her pleasure. He didn't even care what happened next. He just wanted to give this to her. To feel her come beneath his tongue, around his finger. To hear the sound she made as she found her release.

"Benedict," she moaned, her hips thrusting gently against him. "God! Oh, Benedict!" And she shuddered and gasped, her hands tightening in his hair. She was so sweet, so responsive, so fiery, and passionate.

He stayed with her, wringing out the last shivers of pleasure from her body. Then he pressed kisses along her thigh as she lay sprawled and replete.

"That was..." She panted. "Benedict..."

"I know," he murmured, climbing up her body. "I know, my love."

He lay beside her, and she cradled his head against her breasts, stroking his hair back from his forehead.

"I want to do that every single day," she proclaimed. "Maybe twice on special occasions."

Benedict cupped her breast. "We shall do it as often as you wish."

They lay together like that for a moment, and then a sly gleam came into her eyes. "Will you show me the rest?"

He propped himself up on one elbow and gave her a wicked smile. "Gladly."

Chapter Twenty-Five

LYDIA HAD NEVER felt more alive. Her body was buzzing. Her skin hummed. And between her legs…Suffice it to say, Pippa and Jane had left out a few important details. Which meant that it was time for her to learn the rest on her own. With Benedict.

"I couldn't help but notice," she purred, stretching out her body in a delicious way, "that you are not nearly naked enough."

"Is that so?" Benedict's eyes gleamed.

He trailed a fingertip down the slope of her breast until he reached her nipple. He circled her sensitive tip once, twice, and then gave a little squeeze.

Lydia gasped. Lightning streaked from her breast across her body, and she felt her pulse throbbing between her legs.

"Did you like that?" he asked, the smug smile on his face indicating that he already knew the answer.

But two could play at that game. Lydia lay her hand upon his chest and stroked along the firm muscle of his pectorals and down the flat plane of his stomach. But she didn't stop when she reached the edge of his trousers. Benedict's eyes flared as she cupped him through the fabric.

"Lydia," he whispered.

"I want to see you." She squeezed lightly and then toyed with the buttons at the front of his trousers.

He nodded, and Lydia's heart flipped in her chest. Slowly,

slowly she slid each button out of its hole. She lowered the falls on his pants and then loosened his smalls.

And there he was, his cock jutting proudly upward. Lydia stared. Men and women were so differently made. There was a kind of elegance, a potent power to the shape of him. The size of him. Everything about him felt so big and strong. Lydia reached out and traced a finger along his length. Benedict groaned and she jerked her hand away.

"No," he murmured. "It feels good."

With renewed confidence, Lydia reached out again. She traced her finger along him once more, following the vein that led down to the dark-golden hair at his base. Then she went back up, keeping her touch light, not sure what would feel good to him.

Perhaps it was as simple as asking. "What feels good to you?" she whispered.

"Any way you touch me will feel good to me." He ran a hand down her hair and along her back. "Here's one thing you can do, if you would like a suggestion."

He wrapped his hand around hers, circling her fingers around his shaft and moving her grip up and then down.

"Like this?" Lydia's heart rate picked up when he groaned. Giving him pleasure brought her pleasure.

"God," he panted. "Lydia."

She leaned down and kissed him, and their tongues tangled in a wild dance. She pressed her breasts against his chest, and again the lightning zapped through her. She squeezed her thighs together to ease the ache at her apex.

He stilled her hand. "I won't last if you keep touching me."

Lydia's heart raced. "What should I do?"

"You seem to enjoy taking charge," he said, a hint of his lazy drawl in his voice. "How would you like to be on top?"

Lydia's center pulsed as she tried to picture it. Merciful heavens. Her. On top of him. Yes. She wanted that *very* much. She gave an enthusiastic nod, and Benedict grinned before shimmying the rest of the way out of his clothes. He lay back on the bed and guided her leg so she straddled him, hovering over his lower abdomen.

"Put your hands on my chest," he ordered.

Lydia raised an eyebrow. "Just who's in charge here?"

"My apologies. My lady." He gave her a wicked smile.

Lydia thought she might combust from the heat of it. She leaned forward a bit, resting her hands on his chest, but then stilled, uncertain how to proceed.

Benedict licked his thumb, his eyes hot, and then pressed his slick thumb to that sensitive place between her legs. Lydia moaned, rocking against the pressure. Her movement caused her to brush against his cock. He gasped and flexed his hips in response, bringing his hardness against her heat.

Lydia arched her back and slowly rotated her hips, rubbing her core against him. Benedict's mouth opened on a quiet gasp, and his eyes remained locked on hers. A fire blazed in his sherry depths, and she could feel her own heat rising once more.

"When you're ready, you can lower yourself onto me." His hands flexed on her hips.

Lydia bent down for another searing kiss, and he rubbed her in just the right spot with his thumb. Her body ached for more. She rose up, hands on his chest again, and then slowly, slowly, aligned herself with his length.

"Lydia," he whispered, and the love she heard in his voice gave her courage. She lowered herself, slowly, slowly, and his cock slipped inside her. She gasped at the sensation, the fullness. The stinging.

"It hurts," she whispered.

His brow furrowed. "I'm sorry, my love." He pulled up on her hips, trying to ease her away. "We don't have to."

But Lydia refused to be moved. She tightened her thighs around his hips. "Touch me again with your thumb. Hard, and then soft."

Benedict licked his thumb again and complied, pressing in just the right spot. Press and release. Side to side. Again and again, until Lydia was mindless with pleasure, rocking against him. And slowly, slowly, she took him inside her. She gasped at the pinch of pain, but then it was gone. She felt full of him.

Benedict groaned, his fingers fluttering on her hips. "You feel so good. You feel like heaven," he rasped out. And then he pressed with his thumb again and Lydia threw her head back. "Yes," she gasped, gently rocking against him. "More, Benedict. More."

And he complied with her wishes as he always did, touching her just how she wanted to be touched while surging up into her again and again. He cupped her breast with his other hand, tweaking her nipple. That sharp bit of pleasure-pain pushed her over the edge, and she shouted out, rocking and surging and trembling and burning as she was overcome.

Benedict flipped them and pulled out of her, pressing his length against her abdomen. "Lydia," he groaned, rocking against her, and then his wet heat pulsed onto her skin.

Lydia gasped for breath. Her body tingled, and she could hardly feel her fingertips. Every part of her buzzed. Every part of her yearned for him, for his nearness and his strength and his gentleness and his love.

"Benedict," she said, her voice choked.

"I'm here, my love," he whispered against her temple. "I'm here with you."

After a minute of sweet kisses and stroking her hair away from her temple, he rose and cleaned them both off with a cloth. And then he crawled back into bed, pulled her close, and together they snuggled into one another before falling into deep, dreamless sleep.

BENEDICT YAWNED AND stretched, feeling rested and content in a way that was unfamiliar.

Speaking of unfamiliar…This was not his pillow, nor his sheets. A light scent of lavender drifted up from the bedding, and Benedict's eyes snapped open. Everything from yesterday—and last night—came back to him in a rush, and sure enough, Lydia lay beside him, her golden hair spread out on the pillow.

Benedict rubbed at an ache in the center of his chest.

It hadn't been a dream.

All of it had been real. Lydia declaring her love, him telling her how he felt, and their night of passion. She stirred beside him, and stretched, and the bedding slipped to reveal one beautiful, bare breast.

"Good morning." Benedict's voice first thing in the morning was gravel.

Lydia's eyelids fluttered and opened. And then they opened some more as she stared at him, her face turning a delightful shade of pink. "Good morning," she squeaked, before pulling the sheet up over her head.

Benedict bit back a smile. He adored fierce, strong Lydia, but sweet, shy Lydia was quite adorable too.

"What are you doing under there?" he asked. But he didn't tug at the sheet or duck his head under the blankets to be with her. If she needed a bit of space, he would give that to her.

"Um…"

"Just taking a minute?"

The sheet bobbed as Lydia nodded. Benedict kissed what he hoped was the top of her head through the sheet, and then slid out of bed. They should get going soon, but he could give her a few minutes to adjust to all that had happened between them. After all, he'd had years to adjust to his heart yearning for her. She'd had barely a dozen days.

Benedict quietly saw to his morning ablutions before sliding into yesterday's clothes. Then he went to the window and looked out at the street below. No one was out, and it was strangely quiet. All the usual morning hustle and bustle one would expect to see in a town of this size—people heading to the market, servants running errands, and people heading to work—was absent. It seemed as if the whole town had decided it was unsafe to leave their homes.

Bloody Staines and the bloody Office of Public Order. Benedict pictured those armed soldiers on horseback bearing down on innocent people. It had been horrifying. Terrifying. Shocking beyond measure. How many had been injured? How many had died? He pictured Harriet with little Timmy on her back, pushing with the crowd to find safety.

Please, please let them be all right. Let them all be safe and well. He closed his eyes and pressed his heated face against the cool glass of the window. Then he heard a rustle of fabric, and soft footsteps. Lydia leaned against his back and wrapped a bare arm around his middle. Just her touch brought him comfort. He lifted his head from the window and laid his arm over hers.

"I'm sorry I hid," she mumbled against his back. "I'm not much of a morning person. Plus, I've never woken up in bed with a man before."

Benedict stroked along her arm where it wrapped around his middle. "It's understandable. I've never woken up in bed with you before either. I must say, I was a bit discombobulated when I first woke up."

Lydia tried to slip her arm away. Had she misunderstood him?

Benedict turned around and took her in his arms. She had wrapped the sheet around her like a cloak and held the front together with her other arm. Her hair was mussed. and she had creases on her cheek from where she lay on the pillow.

She was so, so beautiful.

And she was studiously examining his cravat.

"What I meant to say," he murmured, "was that I was discombobulated at first, but once I saw you beside me, everything felt right."

She pulled back a few inches and studied him, her thinking

face on. He didn't try to hide his expression or adopt his customary lazy smile. He just looked back at her, feeling all the love in his heart. A slow, dazzling smile spread across her face, and she laid her hand on his chest. "It does feel right, being with you."

Benedict's chest expanded. Everything was going to work out between them. He just knew it. He lowered his head to kiss her. But a loud banging stopped him. He pulled back, and they both turned to look at the wall that separated them from the room next door. More banging sounded.

Benedict clenched his teeth and his jaw tightened. The quiet streets outside and the little cocoon of their love inside had created a false sense of complacency. They were still in the midst of this trouble.

"Get dressed quickly," he said to Lydia, rushing across the room. "I'll see what's going on."

He could hear her moving around the room as he reached the door. Turning the handle, Benedict braced himself to rush into the hall and face whatever challenge might be there.

But the door didn't open.

He swore and rattled the handle again.

"What is it?" Lydia asked, rushing over in her chemise.

Benedict turned to face her, his face hard. "We've been locked in."

Lydia's eyes widened in shock. "What?" She pulled at the door handle as if needing to see for herself.

"What could be the reason for this?" Benedict murmured, striding over to the window and looking down at the street far below. Could they tie the bedding together and climb down somehow? That didn't feel like a very safe option. He turned and found Lydia crawling on her hands and knees, peering under the bed.

"What are you doing?" Benedict asked. Had an article of her clothing gone missing? They'd been a bit frantic in their undressing last night. His blood heated as he recalled undoing the buttons of her dress, how she'd wiggled out of the gown and her stays once he'd set her on the bed…

He shook his head. They were trapped. This was not the time for such thoughts.

Lydia hopped up and began ripping the pillows and blankets off the bed. "I had something tucked into my bodice yesterday, and I can't find it now."

"Is it the powder?" Benedict asked. Benedict patted his pockets. "I have several vials here if you lost yours."

Lydia didn't answer and continued riffling through the blankets.

Benedict moved to her side. "Let's slow down and shake out each linen one at a time, all right?" Even though he didn't know what they were searching for, he helped her go through all the bedding.

When they had double checked the sheets and blankets and still found nothing, Lydia growled in frustration. Her face was flushed and her eyes glittered. A frustrated, angry Lydia was indeed a sight to behold.

"Perhaps whatever we're searching for is mixed in with the rest of your clothes?" Benedict suggested.

Lydia nodded before turning to the pile of garments laying in a heap beside her shoes. She picked up her stays, gown, and stockings and shook them out over the bed.

Whatever was she looking for?

Two soft plops sounded, and Lydia made a little noise of relief. Benedict peered down at the mattress, recognizing a familiar vial of Jane's herb. But what was this other item?

He picked up the bit of leather, rolled up and tied into a bundle. "Lydia, what is this?"

Lydia put her hand out and wiggled her fingers at him. "That," she said with a triumphant smile, "is my lock picking set."

Chapter Twenty-Six

L YDIA FINISHED DRESSING, and then brought a pillow over to the door. Dropping it to the floor, she knelt down on it and examined the lock.

"You are a very talented woman," he murmured, watching her lean to unroll the leather on the floor next to her and take out her tools. Lydia began. She closed eyes to help her concentrate. The two metal tools gently prodded inside the lock, and she listened to what was going on inside the mechanism, out of sight. She had practiced this so many times in the weeks and months after her kidnapping. Being locked in that room at some terrible lord's country estate for a full week had convinced her that she never wanted to be at the mercy of a locked door ever again.

The levers inside the mechanism clicked. Lydia stilled and pulled out her tools. Reaching over, Benedict turned the handle. Lydia held her breath as he pulled.

The door opened.

She sat back on her heels with a gusty sigh of relief.

Benedict reached out a hand. "Shall we see what's going on?"

She took his hand and squeezed it in gratitude as he pulled her to her feet. Although she'd rather they were not in this mess, there was no one she'd rather be locked in a bedroom with at an inn after a rally gone wrong than Benedict. They hurried to the room next door, and perhaps the occupants heard their footsteps because the banging started up again.

"Help," a voice called. "We're locked in."

Lydia exchanged a glance with Benedict. There was no key in the lock, but she could open it from the outside.

"Why don't you head downstairs and see what's going on, and I'll work on this door," she suggested.

He nodded and turned to leave, but after a few steps he turned back and wrapped his arms around her. He dropped a searing kiss on her lips, then pressed his forehead to hers. They remained that way for a few seconds, breathing together. Perhaps this would be their only moment of calm in the storm that likely lay ahead.

He pulled back. "Be safe," he said gruffly.

"You, too."

He disappeared down the stairs, and Lydia turned her attention back to the door. "I'm going to pick the lock," she called to the people inside. "It shouldn't take me too long." Since she'd already sorted out the workings of the mechanism on their own door, it took her less than a minute to get this one opened. A man, a woman dressed in white, and a child stood inside the room, their hands linked.

"Do you know what's going on?" the woman asked, letting go of her husband and child to clench her hands together.

Lydia shook her head. "We were locked in too."

"This doesn't feel right," the man muttered, and his child, a boy close to Timmy's age, stepped closer to him and leaned his head against his father's side for comfort.

"I'm going to check on the other rooms," Lydia said. "You might want to head downstairs but do so with care. We don't know what to expect."

As Lydia headed to the next room, she heard the family creep to the stairs.

It was the same up and down the entire hallway—locked doors, some with people banging or calling for help and others quiet, the residents still asleep. Lydia had picked about half the locks, sending the people downstairs with the same warning she had given the other family, when footsteps thundered up the steps.

Lydia rose to her feet and hid her lock-picking tools in the folds of her skirt. Were these soldiers rushing up to arrest them? Was it Staines?

Her knees wobbled. But Benedict appeared at the top of the staircase, and Lydia leaned back against the wall in relief. Behind him trailed Dot, the innkeeper, holding a ring of keys in her hand.

"Are you all right?" she asked them.

Benedict rushed to her side and planted a kiss on her forehead. "I found Dot tied up in the kitchen. Turns out her servant Prue has a brother in the Office of Public Order."

Lydia's hand tightened around her tools.

"Wretched girl," spat Dot. "Never should've hired her. She was a lazy, whining worker from the get-go. I told her as much when she was tying me up." Dot rubbed the side of her head.

Lydia quickly put the evidence together. "She snuck up on you and whacked you in the head, didn't she? Then she took your keys and locked us all in before rushing off to tell the Office of Public Order about an inn full of reformers from the rally."

Dot nodded, her mouth pinched tight. "I thought I was saving you lot, bringing you in to my place when it was so dangerous outside. But it turns out, I've placed you in danger from the soldiers yet again. I'm so sorry, dearie."

Lydia took the woman's hand. "You saved us." She gave Dot's hand a squeeze. "Prue's decisions are her own."

Dot nodded, then untied her apron and slipped it off her head. "Put this on," she instructed Lydia. "You won't stand out as much if you're not entirely dressed in white."

Lydia put on the apron. It was faded green cotton, but clean and pressed. She hadn't even considered that she would be an obvious target for the soldiers if found in her white suffrage dress.

"Thank you so very much," Lydia said.

"Thank your man too," Dot replied. "He paid the bill for

everyone who stayed last night." Then she gave Benedict a saucy little wink.

Lydia shook her head. Was there no one in all of England who wasn't susceptible to his charms?

Dot jangled her key ring. "I'll open the rest of the rooms. You two better get on out of here. That turncoat Prue left about an hour ago, so she could be back with soldiers any minute."

"Thank you," Lydia called to the woman's retreating back.

"Good luck to you both," Dot said over her shoulder. "Unity and strength!"

Lydia smiled to hear the kind innkeeper repeat the reformers' slogan.

"We need to go," Benedict murmured. His shoulders were tense, and he kept peering down the staircase.

Lydia followed him down the stairs. It appeared that everyone she'd released from their rooms had already left as the main dining area was empty.

Benedict opened the sturdy front door, the giant barricade bar propped against the wall beside it. He popped his head out and looked up and down the street.

"No one's there," he whispered.

Lydia moved closer, and he opened the door wide enough for them to both slip out. No soldiers were in sight, and from this narrow lane, they crept to another, avoiding the main streets where soldiers were more likely to congregate.

They paused for a moment in a recessed doorway. "Should we look for the others?" Benedict asked.

Lydia bit her lip, thinking, then shook her head. "We don't know if anyone was taken. They might all be back at Jack's estate."

Benedict pulled her close and she leaned into his embrace. Somehow in the course of one short day, she had become completely dependent upon his touch for comfort.

"Let's make our way to the meeting point then," he said against her temple. He inhaled, nuzzling her there for a moment, and Lydia's heart skipped a beat.

She leaned up and kissed him. "If no one's there to meet us, it's only a few miles to the estate."

By either stealth or luck, they were able to slip out of town without encountering any soldiers or officers from the Office of Public Order. And when they reached the edge of a copse of trees where they had originally planned for the carriages to pick them up after the rally, they found a surprise waiting for them.

"Pippa!" Lydia ran to her friend, who was leaning against a roughhewn wagon as if waiting for them.

"Oh, thank goodness you're all right," Pippa said, pulling her into a tight hug.

"I don't understand. What are you doing here?" Although Lydia was relieved to see Pippa, she was supposed to be up north with Jack.

"The situation up north wasn't as dire as we'd been told, so we were able to head back early. We stopped at the estate late last night, since it was too far to London to push on, and shortly after we arrived, a friend of yours showed up."

A friend.

Only one had made it back. Lydia reached out behind her, and as she'd desired, Benedict took her hand, bringing instant comfort. He moved to stand beside her.

"Who was it?" Lydia asked.

Pippa gave a wry smile. "She insisted that you called her Agatha, but I'm calling her Mrs. Shepherd, as she's rather formidable."

"And only she made it back?" Benedict asked.

Pippa nodded. "She says the others were taken by the soldiers and placed in a makeshift jail. Come, let's head home, and she can fill you in on the rest."

Lydia and Benedict climbed into the back of the farm wagon. It smelled of turnips and cabbage, but it would get them back safely and likely without arousing suspicion like a fine carriage might. Pippa was very experienced at covert operations.

And now, so was Lydia.

✦

Chapter Twenty-Seven

Benedict clambered out of the wagon, feeling as if his teeth still rattled in his skull from the bumpy road and unsprung transportation.

"Sorry for the rough ride," Pippa said, handing the reins to a servant. "Jack suggested I throw some hay in the back to make it softer, but I didn't want to waste any time."

Benedict helped Lydia down from the back of the wagon. "Where is Jack?" he asked. There was an important question he had to ask his friend. Plus, it was odd that Jack hadn't been with Pippa to wait for them. He was famously overprotective of his sister.

Pippa grimaced. "He went into town to look for you, himself."

Lydia clutched Benedict's arm. "It's dangerous in town. The soldiers were trampling and chopping at people without care."

Pippa wound her arm around her friend's waist and turned them toward the house. "Jack can handle himself. He took a pistol, a sword, and several vials of powder. He might be the most dangerous person in Nottinghamshire right now."

Benedict was glad to see Lydia's shoulders relax. Actually, they were drooping. And so were his own. He felt exhausted, wrung out in a way he never had before. It seemed that prolonged fear for one's life could really drain a person's energy. He would be sure that he and Lydia got a hot meal, a steaming bath, and a comfy bed as soon as possible.

But first, they had to speak with Agatha.

His stomach clenched with renewed worry for their friends.

Pippa led them into the country manor and through to a cheery sitting room with warm midmorning light streaming through the large windows. Agatha jumped up from her seat when she saw them.

Lydia let go of Benedict's hand and ran across the room to embrace her. He followed close on her heels.

"I'm so relieved," Agatha said as tears dripped down her cheeks. "I've been so, so worried. To know that you made it out gives me hope."

"Are you all right?" Benedict asked.

Though Agatha wore a fresh outfit, and her hair was neatly combed, there were deep purple shadows under her eyes. She waved away his question. "I'm probably the best off of anyone," she said, sinking back onto the sofa. "Don't you worry about me. It's the others we must think of."

Lydia sat beside her and took her hand. Benedict found a chair, and Pippa leaned against the wall, keeping an eye out the front window.

"What happened to you and the others yesterday?" Lydia asked. "Was anyone…" Her neck moved as she swallowed.

Benedict's stomach clenched as they waited for Agatha's answer.

"When I saw them last, our group was unharmed," she replied. "But there were so many others…"

They all sat in silence for a moment, the horror of what they'd witnessed the day before hanging in the air between the three of them, unspoken.

"I spoke to several people who were escaping the town while I was waiting for you," Pippa said softly. "Twenty people are confirmed dead so far, and hundreds more were injured."

Lydia's face grew white, and the urge to sweep her into his

arms, into his lap, made Benedict wish there was room beside her on the sofa.

"Was our group arrested?" Lydia asked, her voice pained.

Agatha closed her eyes and nodded. A tear trickled out of the corner of one of her eyes. "We had all been gathered up by the soldiers. They said we were under arrest for trying to overthrow the government." Her mouth pinched. "I was at the back of the group. And I guess the soldiers weren't watching me closely, assuming an old lady like me wouldn't be spry. Fools. And then sweet Timmy…" She pressed a hand to her trembling mouth.

Damnation. What had happened to Timmy? Benedict squeezed the arms of his chair until his knuckles creaked.

"Well, you know what a mischief maker Timmy is," Agatha finally continued. "He started hollering at the soldiers, saying that they couldn't arrest him and that he was going to…"

Agatha's mouth twitched, and Benedict feared she would begin weeping, but instead a bark of laughter escaped her. "He said that he was going to *pee* on them if they didn't let him go."

Benedict's mouth fell open. He couldn't find words. Any words. But then, *Good on you, Timmy,* crossed his mind.

Lydia, of course, wordsmith that she was, was able to speak. "Pee on them?" she asked, her eyebrows halfway up her forehead.

Agatha shook her head in wonder. "And I'll be darned if his ploy didn't work. All the soldiers stepped away from him, and Timmy gave me a little look over his shoulder before he started to undo his trousers. Well, you'd think he was about to pour boiling lava over those men, the way they shouted and hopped away. And since I was so much farther back than everyone else, it was an easy thing for me to slip into the shadows. And to leave them." Her voice quavered and she looked away.

"Clever boy," Pippa said with admiration.

"I left them," Agatha choked out. "The whole group. And my daughter. My Grace, and her wee babe." She began to weep.

Lydia wrapped her arm around the woman. "Shh," she crooned. "You've helped them by escaping. Now we have more people for our rescue team."

Lydia looked up at Benedict, and he saw that same blaze of determination in her eyes that had been there last night. If he were ever taken away by force, he wanted Lydia to helm his rescue. No one would fight harder for her friends. For the ones she loved.

Benedict moved then to kneel in front of Agatha. He touched her arm. "We'll find them," he said, his voice rough.

She looked up, her face wet and her eyes red.

"We'll find them and bring them back. I promise." As he said the words, something shifted inside of him. He realized he hadn't thought once about what this might do to his reputation. How this might reflect on his family, or on his sister's prospects. But, he realized, those things didn't matter if a person wasn't doing what was right.

And he wanted to be a person who did what was right. He *needed* to be that person. Both to be the man that Lydia deserved, and to be the man that he wanted to be.

Agatha sniffled and wiped her tears. "All right," she whispered. "I'll hold you to that."

He nodded, then glanced at Lydia. Her face was stern, and her eyes bright with resolve.

"Well," Pippa said from across the room, "if you're going to go off on some wild scheme to rescue innocent people from the bad guys, I suppose you should count me in. It's one of my favorite hobbies, after knitting, of course."

Lydia snorted, and Benedict guessed there was some sort of joke there.

"Did someone say wild scheme?" someone asked from the doorway.

Benedict turned to look.

"Jane!" shouted Lydia, hopping to her feet. "Dev!" She ran to her friend and her friend's new husband, pulling them both into a tight embrace.

Benedict rose to his feet and extended a hand to Agatha. "Do you feel up to meeting some new people?" he murmured.

"If they are up for a wild scheme," she replied, "then I'll meet anybody."

He escorted Agatha over, and introductions were made. Shortly, they were all seated, and a tea service had been brought in. He and Lydia both dove into the food. That bowl of stew at the inn had been a long time ago.

Jane, creator of the self-defense vials, had strawberry blond hair and an innocent expression that Benedict knew firsthand hid a wicked sense of humor. Her husband, Dev, was tan from years in India, with dark hair and blue eyes. When Benedict had first met him, he'd been posing as a servant in his own stepmother's house where the LCA was housed. Fortunately, they had been successful in a wild scheme of their own and had proven he was his father's true heir. In a very short time, he had elevated from servant to marquess, but he still retained a core of humble kindness. Benedict felt fortunate to call him a friend.

"How are you here?" Lydia asked between mouthfuls of pastry.

"We arrived home from our honeymoon yesterday, and Meera filled us in on the rally you planned to attend and how you expected trouble. And," she added, a glint in her eye, "she told me how you stole half of my stash."

Lydia merely shrugged. "Needs must."

"Well, I brought the other half along, just in case." Jane gestured behind her, perhaps referring to her luggage elsewhere in the house.

"So what's the plan?" Pippa asked, leaning forward in her seat. "There are five of us—"

"Six," Agatha interrupted. "I'll soon be a grandmother, but I bet I could toss a donkey farther than you."

Benedict coughed, choking on a bite of cheese and bread. "Have you found it necessary to toss many donkeys?" he finally managed to wheeze out.

Agatha sipped her tea, then replied, "A lady never tells."

Benedict felt something loosen in his tense muscles and he chuckled at her sly wink. Maybe it was the camaraderie of this group or knowing that he and Lydia didn't have to solve this on their own, but now he was beginning to actually feel hopeful that they could make it out of this mess.

"We have swords," Pippa said. "A *lot* of swords."

"And a lot of vials." Jane reached down the front of her dress and produced one in her hand.

"Darling," Dev murmured to his wife. "I thought we discussed getting you some pockets."

"Pish," Jane said, waving away his concern. "It's fine. I'm friends with everyone here." She shot a conspiratorial grin at Agatha.

Agatha reached down her own bodice and pulled out a vial herself. "Apparently, we are *bosom* buddies."

The ladies laughed. Benedict caught Dev's eye, and the man shook his head, but his eyes danced with laughter. Once the laughter died down, they continue to discuss their options.

"If only we knew what building they were being held in," Lydia said, tapping her finger on the sofa beside her.

Agatha set her teacup down. "Actually, I might know. The guards were discussing the large public house in the square as they were rounding us up."

Lydia met Benedict's eyes with her own. "That's where they watched the crowd from, at the start of the rally. And where they were drinking." She shook her head in disgust.

Her eyes grew unfocused, and she tapped her finger against her chin while her teeth nibbled at her bottom lip. There it was again, her thinking face. The others continued to talk softly and drink their tea, but Lydia was in a world of her own. How incredible, to be situated in one's own mind so firmly that outside people or noise failed to interrupt someone's concentration. Because he was watching her, Benedict saw the moment it all clicked into place. Her face softened, and a sly smile emerged.

Lydia leaned forward and announced to the group, "I have a

plan…"

⤜⤜⤜ ⋙⋘ ⤛⤛⤛

LYDIA SET HER quill down and shook out her aching hand. After a bath, another few cups of tea and a warm meal, and a brief nap, she had set about writing the most important article of her life.

She was hopeful that the old newspaper that had printed her Democratium Liberum articles in the past would accept another submission from the infamous political firebrand. But instead of talking about corruption in the voting for the House of Commons, this article spoke about the Nottinghamshire Massacre.

That's what she had decided to call it. There was truly no other word that more accurately described the soldier's actions then *massacre*.

And so she poured out all her words onto the paper. Descriptions of the reformers and their work for a better life for common people. A report on who had been present at the rally, especially the women and their children, and the families out with their picnic baskets. How the crowd had been peaceful and calm until the soldiers, drunk and undisciplined, had trampled the crowd with their swords drawn. She wrote of Staines and the Office of Public Order. How lack of oversight allowed this group to arrest people who had committed no crime. How this group was a hundred times the threat of any reformer to England and its people.

She had her first draft and then a second one, a copy. She liked to keep a record of her work, even though the piece would likely appear in print. She thought it was the finest thing she'd written. And there was only one person she wanted to share it with right now.

She left her chambers in a comfortable day dress. Thankfully, her wardrobe here had a few dresses for whenever she and Jack, and now Pippa, would come to visit the country estate.

When a servant had taken away her white dress earlier, dreadfully dirty and smelling of a root cellar, as well as the borrowed apron for laundering, Lydia had given her instructions on returning the apron to Dot, along with a sizeable purse. She and Benedict owed the woman their lives.

She knocked on the door to the guestroom that Benedict always stayed in when he visited them here. She heard footsteps, and then he was at the door. His feet were bare, and his hair was damp. She stared at the sliver of bare chest visible through his loosened shirt.

"It seems you have forgotten your cravat," she said dryly.

He leaned against the doorframe and smirked. "It seems you have forgotten which bedchamber belongs to you." He raised one wicked eyebrow. "Unless you wish to share again…"

Lydia rolled her eyes and pushed her way into the room, even as she felt a blush creeping up her cheeks. "I've written an article for the paper, as Democratium Liberum. I wanted you to read it before I sent it to the newspaper in London."

Benedict shut the door behind them and strode to a wide armchair in front of the fireplace. He patted his leg. "Come sit with me while I read it."

Lydia snuggled into his lap while he read her scribbled writing. Lydia wrote quickly, which meant it was rarely neat. She pressed her ear to his chest and listened to his heartbeat while he read. After a few minutes he lowered the papers, setting his arm along the armrest.

"What do you think?" she asked, suddenly feeling nervous. Whenever she had delivered her articles to the newspaper editor in the past, he had usually printed them with minimal changes. And she had never received any feedback from him. Asking someone in person what they thought of her writing was a new experience.

"It's brilliant," he said simply. "You perfectly capture the optimism of the reform movement, and the contrast between the reformers and participants and then the brutality of the soldiers is absolutely searing."

His words were positive, but something about his tone was off.

Lydia pulled back to look at his face more closely. "What aren't you telling me?"

Benedict ran his hand over his face. "Don't send this to the newspaper."

Lydia stiffened and pulled back further. "Why not? You said it was brilliant."

"The newspaper isn't the right place for this. I have a better audience in mind, an audience that could create actual change after having this read to them directly."

Lydia searched his face. He stared back at her, solemn. A suspicion came to her. "You think this should be read to Parliament. To the House of Lords."

Benedict hesitated for a moment, and then nodded.

"*You* want to read it." She jumped to her feet and stepped away from him.

"Lydia, you have to trust me," he said, reaching a hand out to her.

Lydia turned away from him and stared into the fire.

You have to trust me.

That's exactly what Aubrey Andrews had said when he'd kidnapped her. When the romantic carriage ride he'd promised had instead taken them along a dark country road where she had insisted he stop, insisted he let her out, insisted that he tell her what was going on.

You have to trust me.

For a long time after the kidnapping, she didn't trust anyone except for those in her inner circle. It hadn't felt safe. Then Benedict had somehow made his way into her circle, into her heart.

And he asked her to trust him.

She wanted to, but she knew what would happen. If he read her article, the members of the House of Lords wouldn't take it seriously because of his past behavior. She knew all of that was behind him now, but the world still viewed him as a rake. A wastrel. A lazy, grinning ne'er-do-well.

"Lydia?" he said softly behind her.

Lydia ached to turn around. To return to the warm comfort of his arms. To let him take the article and read it to parliament himself.

To trust him.

But she couldn't. Harriet, Timmy, Grace, and the others…their very lives depended on this, as well as the lives of countless others who had been arrested by the soldiers at the rally. And who knows how many in the future would be harmed if Staines and the Office of Public Order weren't stopped now.

And so Lydia shook her head and said into the fire, "I'm sorry, Benedict, but I cannot let you do that. I can't let you read it to Parliament. With your reputation, with everyone thinking you're a good-for-nothing rake, it would undo all our work. It would make my words meaningless."

Behind her, Benedict said nothing.

Despite the warmth from the fireplace, Lydia shivered. The room was suddenly chilly.

"I see," he said at last. His voice was completely devoid of any warmth.

She heard him stand and move about the room. She longed to turn to him, to wrap her arms around him, but she knew that if she looked into his face, the face she loved beyond measure, that she would not be able to hold firm to this decision. So even as she heard him put on his boots and coat and open the door and walk away, she resolutely stood beside the fireplace, staring into the flames.

Chapter Twenty-Eight

BENEDICT STOMPED DOWN the stairs and into the manor's foyer. His heart raced and his stomach roiled.

"Can you have a horse ready for me?" he asked a footman, trying to keep his voice calm.

The servant nodded and headed out the front door to the small stable that Jack kept here. Benedict had come along many times, for bits of hunting or fishing, and even the occasional Christmas celebration. The servants knew he was honorable and not a horse thief. But apparently not everyone under this roof had the same high opinion of him.

Lydia's words from a minute ago echoed in his mind. *A good-for-nothing rake.*

He wanted to shout. He wanted to smash his fist against the wall. He wanted to tear his hair out. And mostly, he wanted to cry.

He pressed his fingers into his eyes and drew steadying breaths. He would not break down here. He couldn't. He heard the door open, and he glanced up, expecting to see the servant.

But instead, it was Jack.

He blinked at his friend. Jack, who usually looked neat as a pin and perhaps a trifle constipated with his constant thoughts of duty, was beyond unkempt. He had a scrape high on his cheekbone, a rip in the seam of his jacket, and was liberally streaked with dirt.

"Are you all right?" Benedict asked, stepping closer to him.

Jack grasped his shoulder, his eyes a bit wild. "Is Lydia here with you? Is she unhurt?"

Benedict exhaled. "She's upstairs. She's fine. We're *both* fine."

Jack exhaled in relief. If he'd heard the sarcasm in his voice, he didn't let on.

"Nottinghamshire is a mess." Jack shook his head. "Hundreds of people are locked up. They had to make a makeshift infirmary inside a bakery." He ran his hand over his face. "And a…a morgue inside a fabric shop."

At that, they were both silent. In his mind, Benedict could see the soldier on the horse again, blood dripping from his sword, his face twisted with hatred and fear as he drew closer and closer. He shuddered.

But he couldn't think of that now. He needed to leave. Immediately.

"Lydia has come up with a plan to rescue people," Benedict said. "You should talk to her about it." He moved to step around Jack, toward the door.

Jack grabbed his arm. "You and I have a few things to talk about," he growled.

Benedict shook his hand off. "Later," he said, the word clipped. "I'm not good company right now."

Jack grabbed him again, his grip more forceful this time. "I know what you've done, Benedict," he said through gritted teeth. "Hadn't I told you that my sister was not for the likes of you?"

There it was again. That phrase. That reputation. Would he never be rid of it? Benedict saw nothing but red, and he shoved Jack away. "What does that even mean?" he roared. "*The likes of me?* We've been friends since Eton. *Best* friends. And you think me *unworthy?*"

Jack's hands flexed into fists at his side. "The rumors about you—"

"I'm so fucking sick of those rumors!" Benedict yelled. "What did you hear? That I was caught at some house party, fucking a married lady and her maid at the same time? That's what everyone thinks, isn't it? That's what everyone thinks I am." Benedict's voice broke, and he looked away.

"Yes." Jack's voice was tight. "That's what I heard. And so I tell you to stay away from Lydia, but then I hear you've been staying in my house? Spending the *night*? Staying in the *same* room at an inn with her? She's my sister, Benedict!"

Benedict swiped at his eyes with the back of his hands. "And I'm your friend. You never once asked me. You never even asked me if the rumor was true."

Jack sucked in a breath. "What are you saying?"

Benedict clenched his teeth. He had carried this secret for so long. And he hadn't realized until this moment what an ugly path of destruction it had created. The stain it had put upon his heart, his family, and now his love.

"It wasn't me," he whispered. His chest felt too tight, as if he couldn't draw a full breath. "I was there at that house party, but so was my father."

Jack made a choking sound.

Benedict couldn't bring himself to look at him. "Everyone said we looked so much alike. The lady's husband barged in and caught a quick glimpse before someone pulled him away. And when my father told him that it had been me in that bed with the wife and the wife's maid, the man believed it. *Everyone* believed it." He shook his head. "Everyone."

That's what hurt worse than the initial betrayal by his own father. That his own family and his closest friends had also accepted the falsehood without question. And that even after all they'd shared, Lydia had believed it. Or at least, had given it enough credit to assume anything he did or said would be worthless. Tainted.

Benedict wiped his cheeks. He hated crying. And to do so now, in front of Jack, with all his supposed sins laid out, exposed and bare… He could hardly stand it.

"Why didn't you say anything?" Jack asked.

Benedict continued to avoid looking at his friend. *At his ex-friend.*

"When I heard what everyone was talking about the next morning at the house party, I was in shock." Benedict's voice felt dull. Flat. But he had to finish the sordid tale. "I went to my father, and he told me…he told me what he had done. He said I had to help him now, I had to keep this from my mother. That it would destroy her to hear what her husband had done. And so, I didn't say anything."

"Benedict—" Jack began.

Benedict shook his head with a sharp movement. "Don't. Don't you dare. I knew that other people could believe such a thing of me. But I didn't think you did, not really. And I didn't think Lydia—"

He pressed his lips together tightly, refusing to give voice to the rest. To his pain.

When he had control over himself once more, he said, "I have to go."

Jack stood still and silent, as Benedict walked to the door and left.

LYDIA CLUTCHED THE banister at the top of the stairs, frozen by what she had just overheard.

Benedict was innocent of the old rumors about him. Not only was he innocent, but he had accepted the blame that belonged to his own father. He'd carried that heavy burden for years.

And he'd never said a word. He'd never defended himself. Even when she had thrown the repercussions of the false rumor in his face a bit ago.

Lydia closed her eyes and drew a shaky breath. She had hurt him beyond measure. She hadn't trusted in him, even though she knew the shape of his heart. Had she destroyed their love with her callousness, with her inability to trust?

She had to fix this. She had to fix this *now*.

She forced herself to unfreeze. Clinging to the banister, Lydia made her way down the stairs on legs that shook.

Jack's eyes widened when he spotted her. "Did you hear that?" he asked.

Lydia nodded. She didn't trust her voice right now. Jack moved to embrace her, but Lydia shook her head and tottered to the door. She flung it open and scurried down the stone steps. But before she could run to the stable, Benedict emerged on horseback. He took off at a gallop.

"Benedict!" she screamed, cupping her hands around her mouth.

But he didn't stop or even look back. He just continued to ride away. Away from her and the terrible pain she'd inflicted by betraying him, by assuming the worst of the man she professed to love.

She stood there, unmoving, long after he disappeared from sight. She felt numb. Frozen. What could she do?

"Lydia," Jack murmured from her side.

She turned to her brother, her face crumpling. He opened his arms to gather her close. Lydia hid her face against his jacket and wept.

"Shh," Jack murmured. "It will be all right. It will."

"No, it won't," Lydia wailed, clutching at his jacket.

Jack's arms tightened around her, and she had never been so grateful that she and her brother had finally become close after he'd rescued her from the kidnappers. For so many years, there had been a wall between them. A wall of duty on his end, and a wall of secrets on hers. But all that had changed last year, and she was so glad to have her brother with her now, offering comfort as she faced the possible destruction of Benedict's love for her because of her careless words.

"He loves you, you know," he said.

"Not anymore." She sniffled against his jacket.

Jack pulled away and held onto her shoulders as he peered into her face. "That man has loved you for years."

Lydia blinked up at him. "For...for years?"

Jack nodded, and his brown eyes were so terribly kind and sympathetic that Lydia almost began weeping again.

"He's always been different with you," Jack said. "I could tell that he had feelings for you, ever since you made your debut. But I warned him off."

Benedict had hinted that his feelings for her were long-standing, but he'd never expressed it explicitly. To hear that Jack knew, that he and Benedict had even discussed it, was a shock.

"You warned him off," Lydia repeated.

Jack's mouth tightened in regret. "How much of our conversation did you hear?"

"I heard everything."

"Then you know why I warned him to stay away from you." Jack's fingers flexed on her shoulders. "But I should've asked him about the rumors. I shouldn't have assumed. I've been such a fool."

"That's true for both of us." Lydia's body ached with her regret and her pain. "I love him too, you know. I told him yesterday when I thought we were going to die in the square. But I shouldn't have waited until fear prompted me to share my feelings. I should have told him out of love, out of joy. And now I've hurt him so badly."

Jack studied her face. "Something happened between you two before I arrived."

Lydia nodded. "He asked me not to send my article about what happened—the massacre—to the newspaper. He said he had a better idea for how to present it, and I assumed that he wanted to read it to the House of Lords. And then I..." Lydia tried to swallow past the lump in her throat. "And then I insulted him in the worst possible way. I said that because everyone believes the rumors about him, that no one would pay any mind to anything he said." She drew a shaky breath. "I basically said…he was worthless. That others' false opinions stripped him of any value." Her voice warbled. "How can he forgive me, when I've been so awful?" Lydia buried her face in her hands and wept.

Chapter Twenty-Nine

MANY TEARS AND hours later, Lydia crept through the dark, quiet town of Nottinghamshire. It was time for her wild scheme.

She, Jack, and Pippa skirted the town square which was empty of people yet full of wretched memories from the day before. A massacre had taken place here. This square, this town, and these people would never be the same again.

Jack led the way. Apparently when he'd been looking for her earlier that day, he had seen where the soldiers were taking all the reformers they had rounded up. Just like Agatha had thought, Staines had decided to use the large public house in the square as a temporary jail. Thankfully, Jack had scouted out the back and was familiar with the layout.

Farther behind the three of them, Dev, Jane, and Agatha moved silently through the shadows. They were to go to the front of the public house. If Lydia's plan went according to plan, the six of them would take out the guards at both the front and the back simultaneously.

Even with the intricacies of the plan and worry for her friends at the forefront of her mind, Lydia kept glancing over at the square. It was shadowed and dark, but she could still make out overturned picnic baskets, abandoned pamphlets, and even a trampled lady's reform society banner. And she knew if she checked in the light of day, there would be blood stains on the ground.

Had it only been yesterday that Benedict had taken her hand in his, and they had walked through the crowd together like a happy couple? She recalled how he'd stayed right at her side once the soldiers began their attack. People had been so easily separated in the surge and rush of the crowd, and yet he had stayed with her, keeping her safe.

And when the soldier had drawn closer and closer to them with his bloody sword drawn, in that moment, Lydia *had* to tell him what was in her heart. Just yesterday, just on the other side of the square, she had told Benedict that she loved him.

And then…she'd ruined it.

She hadn't believed in him, in the person she truly knew him to be, and she had laid waste to the tender love that had only just blossomed between them.

And he'd left.

Lydia rubbed at the ache in her chest.

"Are you all right?" Pippa whispered. Even in the darkness of night, Lydia could see the concern on her friend's face.

Lydia just nodded and kept moving. This was not the time to wallow over her broken heart. This was the time for bold action. She had to save her friends.

Jack signaled to Dev in the other group, and the two teams split in different directions. Jack scouted ahead and peered around the edge of the alley behind the public house. He nodded to Pippa who tucked her small epee sheath deeper into the folds of her skirt. Lydia patted her bodice, feeling the comforting vials of dried herb tucked there.

It was time.

Jack put his arms around his sister and his wife, and they all three rounded the corner, staggering and doing a very poor job of keeping their supposedly drunken talk at a whisper.

"Wot a lucky chap I am, finding two lovely birds to take to me home," Jack slurred in a decent imitation of the local working-class accent.

Pippa giggled. Lydia was supposed to laugh as well, she couldn't work up even manufactured mirth and settled for leaning her head against her brother's shoulder.

"Halt."

Two soldiers stepped out of the doorway at the back of the public house. Both of them had pistols at their sides, but they hadn't reached for them yet. Good. Their ruse was working so far.

"State your business," commanded one of the soldiers.

His companion bumped him with his elbow and snorted. "I think this gent's business goes without saying."

Lydia, Jack, and Pippa continued to approach, still staggering and leaning on each other like drunken fools.

"Oo, lookee what we've got 'ere," Pippa cooed. "Two 'and-some soldiers." Once again, Lydia had to admire Pippa's expertise in espionage.

The first soldier scowled at them, but his companion grinned and strutted forward.

"Hello, luv," he said, looking first Pippa, and then Lydia, up and down. "Come say hello to me and my pal."

"Jones," the first soldier said in a warning tone.

But the second soldier, Jones, waved him off. "Things have been quiet here," he murmured to his fellow guard. "We deserve a bit of fun."

Lydia wanted to punch these men in the face. Things had been *quiet* here? It seemed they had conveniently forgotten the horrific massacre just yesterday. A massacre they and their fellow soldiers had caused.

Along with Staines.

But instead of punching them, she sidled up to the first soldier. "Cor, what strong arms ye have," she slurred, making a show of feeling his muscles.

Pippa approached Jones and leaned against him. "Oh, you're much 'andsomer than that fellow." She jerked her thumb over her shoulder toward Jack.

Her husband snorted but went along with it. "Oy, you're supposed to come with me, luv."

Jones puffed up his chest. "Sounds like they want to be with us now. Why don't you shove off, mate."

"Cor," Lydia purred, trailing her hands all over the first guard. "You're so brave." He smirked at her and snaked an arm around her waist. While he was distracted by attempting to peer down her bodice, she eased his pistol out of the holster and hid it in the folds of her skirt.

"Hey!" exclaimed Jones.

Pippa had just stepped away from him and was unsheathing her epee. Lydia lunged back from her soldier and pointed his own pistol at his chest.

"Don't say a word," she hissed at him.

"What's going on?" Jones demanded, apparently slower on the uptake than his companion, who had already raised his hands in the air.

Jack grabbed the pistol Pippa had taken from Jones and tucked it in his pocket.

"You'll stay quiet if you want to keep your tongues," Pippa told the two soldiers coldly, "And your insides. And other things." Her epee whistled as she made slashing motions at their mid-sections, and below.

Lydia was grateful for the umpteenth time that Pippa was not her enemy. Her friend could be downright terrifying at times.

Jack pulled lengths of cord and cloth out of his other pocket. While Lydia and Pippa kept their weapons trained on the soldiers, he went quickly to work tying them up.

"You won't get away with this," Lydia's soldier spat.

"Hush, you." Jack shoved a cloth into his mouth before tying another length around his head to hold it in place.

"Actually, *you* won't get away with this," Lydia hissed. "The whole country will know what you did here yesterday, how you slaughtered innocent people. Families. Women. Children!"

The soldier attempted to respond, but it was just muffled noise.

Jack forced them to the ground, bound their feet, and tied the two men together back-to-back. "I don't think they'll be giving us any trouble," he murmured before he straightened and placed a quick kiss on his wife's cheek. "Have I mentioned lately how incredible you are? We need to do this more often."

Pippa smiled at him. "Oh, you. Focus." Then she turned to Lydia. "Ready to go inside?"

Lydia tightened her grip around the pistol. "Let's go."

This time Pippa led the way, her epee drawn but pointed toward the floor. If they needed to take someone out, her weapon would be quieter than either a pistol firing or the sputtering wheezes of someone who'd been doused in the herb.

They crept down a dim hallway. Pippa pushed a swinging door open a few inches and peered through before she gave the all clear to Jack and Lydia and continued on.

The main dining room of the public house was well-lit with a crackling fire and glowing candles. Lydia grinned at the well-illuminated sight of Agatha, tying a gag around a bound soldier.

Jane stood over another bound man who appeared to be unconscious and put her fingers to her lips before gesturing overhead. So there were more guards upstairs. That was where the reformers would be, as well.

Pippa pointed toward the stairs, her eyebrows raised. Lydia nodded, and the group carefully and quietly made their way to the staircase.

Again, Pippa went first, her epee in hand.

Jack was right behind her, holding a pistol. Lydia fished her vial out of her bodice and loosened the cork at the top. She knew that behind her, Dev, Jane, and Agatha were similarly prepared to fight and defend themselves.

As they neared the top of the stairs, they could hear low voices. The guards must be talking to one another, a lucky stroke for the rescue team since the soldiers hadn't heard any of their noises as they taken out the guards on the main floor.

They were almost to the top of the stairs and would be visible to anyone along the hallway that stretched out perpendicular to the staircase. Pippa glanced back at the group. Lydia drew a calming breath and tried to relax her tight grip around the vial. She nodded that she was ready and saw the others do the same.

This was it.

With that, Pippa burst up the stairs and pivoted to the right, epee outstretched. Jack ran to the left. Lydia was right behind her brother and saw a soldier taking a swing at him. But Jack mowed him over, and the two men fell to the ground with a grunt.

"Get the rope," Jack barked, grappling with the man's arms as he struggled to keep him pinned.

Heart racing, Lydia reached into her brother's pocket and pulled out a length of rope. While the soldier cursed and kicked, Jack rolled him over and Lydia quickly tied his hands and legs behind his back.

They turned to see how the others fared. Jane was wiping her hand off with the bottom of her skirt while a soldier lay on the ground, coughing and wheezing.

Agatha was tying the man's hands behind him. "Is it hard to breathe, dearie?" she asked him.

The soldier nodded and looked up at her pleadingly.

Agatha's eyes narrowed. "It was hard to breathe in that *stampede* you lot caused yesterday, charging with your swords at innocent people." She shoved his shoulder, and he tipped over onto the ground.

She rose to her feet and dusted her hands off, her expression determined. "Let's find them," she urged the others.

Dev finished tying up another guard while Pippa held him at sword point.

"Check the pockets for keys," Lydia called, bending over to pat down the soldier on the floor near her. There weren't any keys in his pockets though.

The others turned up empty-handed as well.

"I'll head back downstairs and see if any of the guards down there were carrying the keys," Dev said.

Lydia reached into her bodice again and pulled out her lock picking kit. She started at the door furthest to the left in the hallway.

"Do you have your second set on you?" Jane asked, approaching. "I'm not as fast as you, but I could open some as well."

Lydia shook her head while she felt inside the lock with her tools. "Unfortunately, I loaned my other set to a curious boy and never got it back."

Jane harrumphed then fumbled around in her coiffure. "They're much clumsier, but I'll try with some hairpins." She moved to the other end of the hallway and knelt down in front of the lock.

Lydia chewed on her lip as she concentrated. There was a click and she allowed herself a small smile. Her brother motioned her to move back, then he opened the door.

The room was filled with people. Women in white, young children, and families clinging to one another. Some of them bruised or cut. Everyone scared.

A large man stood closest to the door, his hands in fists. "We've done nothing wrong," he spat. "Curse you and your vile brethren."

Jack put his pistol in his pocket and held up empty hands. "We know you're innocent. We've come to release you."

The large man's face crumpled, and he rubbed at his sleeve which was stained a rusty red color. His blood, or the blood of someone he knew? Lydia clutched her lock picks until they pricked her skin. What these people had been through... It was beyond horrifying.

Jack gestured for them to exit the room. "Stay quiet and follow me. I'll take you to the back door, and if you stay in the shadows, you should be able to make your way to safety."

Lydia watched them filter past. Had they been given water or food? A private place to relieve themselves? Medical treatment?

It was shocking that their government was doing this to its own citizens—innocent people, peacefully gathered. Lydia wanted to scream.

A woman with a toddler in her arms paused in the doorway and touched Lydia's sleeve. "Thank you," she whispered. The woman's hair was matted with dried blood, and the toddler's eyes were glassy with exhaustion.

Lydia could only nod and blink back her tears.

Enough. She'd cried enough today. Now was the time for action. She needed to open more locks.

Lydia moved to the next door, the low sounds of people murmuring and their footsteps on the stairs barely registering as she concentrated on the next lock.

She had opened three more doors, and Agatha, Pippa, or Jack escorted the frightened rally attendees downstairs and out into the night where they would hopefully make their way to safety.

Dev returned. "None of them had a key," he said grimly.

Lydia stilled, her mind racing before she returned her concentration to the lock. "That means someone else has it. And they're not likely to be too far away."

Dev swore. "We don't have much time then."

Lydia tried to steady her hands. She'd never get this lock opened if she was shaking in fear. She drew a calming breath, adjusted her picks, wiggled a little more, and...*there*—the satisfying sound of the lock clicking open.

"I'll take them down," Dev murmured, and he explained what was happening to the frightened people inside the room before leading them down the stairs.

Lydia glanced down the hall to see Jane's progress on the doors. She was surprised to see that between the two of them working on the locks, they only had one left to open.

She still hadn't seen any of her reformer friends. If they weren't in this next room...

She shook her head. Now was not the time to think about the makeshift morgue her brother had mentioned, and who she might find here.

No.

Instead, she pictured Grace, her face serene as she touched her rounded belly. She pictured Harriet laughing with Timmy, his gap-toothed smile shining bright. They would be in the next room. They *had* to be.

Lydia hurried to the final door and knelt down. She took a deep breath and inserted the lock picks. Time passed as she lost herself in the intricacies of shifting the locking mechanism with only touch and sound as her guide.

She almost had it unlocked when the sound of a pistol cocking broke her attention.

She froze.

"I suspected I would find you here," a cold voice said.

Lydia turned her head.

Looming over her, an icy smile stretched across his face even as his eyes blazed in hatred, stood Staines with a pistol aimed directly at her heart.

Chapter Thirty

"GET UP," STAINES barked gesturing with his pistol for Lydia to rise.

She closed her hands around her lock picks, hoping he had overlooked what she'd been doing at the door, but he reached out and ripped them out of her hand.

"Interfering woman," he sneered. "When are you going to learn your place?"

Lydia looked past him. Office of Public Order guards had her friends surrounded. One of them held Pippa's epee. Another was patting Jack down and made a triumphant sound as he removed the pistol from his pocket.

Lydia's blood ran cold.

She cut her gaze back to Staines. His frigid gray eyes, his pompous sneer, and his arrogant looming all needed to be cut down to size. If Benedict were here, he would have some pithy retort that was certain to rile Staines up and throw him off his game.

Benedict.

Her chest felt hollow without him. She stepped away from the door. He might not be here, but perhaps she could channel his methods.

"When am *I* going to learn my place?" she repeated. "I think the *better* question is when are *you* going to learn my place?"

Lydia said it with a lazy drawl and leaned back on the wall opposite the final locked door. "Which is, by the way," she added, pretending to examine her fingernails, "at a voting station."

Staines sputtered for a moment, but then he clenched his teeth and seemed to get his temper back under control. He moved a few steps, circling her, so that now his back was to the locked door.

"Oh, I know where your place is, Lady Lydia," he replied, his voice like the Thames in the winter. "It's a cell in Newgate."

She forced herself to remain in her relaxed pose, even as all her muscles tensed.

"How interesting," she drawled. "And here I thought, as the mastermind behind the Nottinghamshire Massacre, *you* would end up behind bars."

Staines's face tightened. His hand holding the pistol trembled in fury, and Lydia was glad the barrel was pointed at the ground. She looked pointedly from his shaking hand and back to his face before raising a lazy eyebrow.

His mouth worked as if he could barely contain the invectives he desperately wanted to hurl at her, but he somehow forced his face into impassive lines. He drew one slow breath and then another.

"I know what you're doing," he murmured so that only she could hear. "And it won't work."

And as if to prove his point, he too leaned back, copying her pose of relaxed indolence. His back was against the last, unlocked door. He even folded his arms over his chest, his grip loose on the pistol.

Lydia heard a soft, familiar sound.

Bloody hell. Could it be?

Her heart raced, but she maintained her position, adjusting her feet so that she leaned back even closer against the wall.

"It won't?" she asked, her voice gently goading. "Are you *sure*?"

She held her breath and listened closely.

And there it was.

The sound everything hinged upon.

Staines's lips pressed into such a tight line that they vanished from his face. But he too adjusted his stance, moving his feet forward so that he was even more reclined against the door in an indolent pose mirroring hers.

"You have all these witnesses assembled, some of them doubtlessly peers of the realm," he whispered. "You hope to provoke me into losing my temper." He narrowed his eyes. "You hope I'll do something uncivilized so that your lapdog, Lord Lovell, may report me to Parliament."

Lydia ached at the sound of Benedict's name, but her rage burned hotter than her sorrow. "You already did something uncivilized, when you ordered your drunken soldiers to attack a peaceful crowd yesterday."

She flicked her eyes over to the others. Pippa gave an imperceptible nod. Jane twisted something in her hand. Agatha, Dev, and Jack all adjusted their stances.

They were ready.

"Mr. Staines," she said, each word sharp as a blade. "There is blood on your hands. And you will pay."

He tightened his muscles as if about to pull away from the door.

"Now," she shouted.

The door behind him flung open. Staines stumbled before crashing backward into the room and onto the hard wooden floor. Harriet leaned over his prostrate form and blew the contents of a vial directly into his face.

"I did it!" Timmy shouted. He pumped his hands in the air, one of them clutching Lydia's second set of lock picks.

Lydia took only a second to give him a relieved smile before whirling around to help the others. She ran toward a soldier whose back was to her and dropped her shoulder at the last moment, bowling him over.

"My thanks," Dev said with a quick smile before he reclaimed his pistol from the fallen man.

Another soldier was fumbling with his pistol in his holster, but Jane moved in front of him and blew the painful herbs right into his face.

Lydia hurried to where Pippa was grappling with one of the soldiers for her epee. Lydia smashed her foot into the back of his knee, and he crumpled. Pippa grabbed her epee away from him and then bashed him over the head with the hilt.

"Nicely done," Lydia complemented her friend.

Pippa winked before pivoting. *"En garde,"* she shouted to a soldier before striking his pistol out of his hand with her blade.

All along the hallway, chaos reigned.

The soldiers were trained fighters, putting them at an advantage over the rescuers. However, Pippa's friends had weapons they weren't prepared for. Several of the reformers had joined the fray, assumedly leaving Staines for the rest of their group to deal with.

Lydia received an elbow to the stomach as she prepared a vial. She dropped to her knees, gasping for breath.

"Lydia!" Had she hit her head? It seemed she was in such a state that she was now hallucinating Benedict's voice.

Warm hands wrapped around her shoulders, and then, he was there, kneeling beside her. *Benedict.*

She stared at him in wonder.

"Are you hurt?" he asked, his voice tight, as he ran his hands over her as if checking for injuries.

Lydia shook her head. He'd come back. He was here.

Nothing could hurt her now.

Loud footsteps pounded up the stairs, and a voice shouted, "Halt! You're under arrest."

Lydia froze.

Soldier after soldier, dressed in royal uniforms, swarmed up the stairs, spreading out along the hallway with pistols drawn.

"You're just in time," a familiar voice wheezed.

Lydia glanced back to find Staines in the hallway, his hands bound behind his back and several reformers holding on to him. His eyes were red and streaming from his dousing with the herb, but he still managed to shoot Lydia a triumphant smile.

"It looks," he choked out, "like I was right about Newgate."

Lydia glanced at Benedict. His eyes were warm, and he gently helped her to her feet.

"You came back," she whispered to Benedict.

"I'll always come back for you," he murmured, pressing his forehead against hers. "Always."

"Seize her!" Staines screamed, his face red and a vein throbbing at his temple as he struggled against the women holding him.

The leader of the new royal troops nodded to his soldiers. "Take them away," he commanded.

Staines threw his head back and laughed maniacally. "You lost! You lost, you stupid bitch, and now you'll pay!"

The royal soldiers seized their quarry.

Lydia's mouth dropped open as they grabbed the Office of Public Order guards and began to march them downstairs.

"What?" screamed Staines. "You're taking the wrong people! *They're* the criminals, not us."

"That's not what the Prince Regent has heard," said the leader of the royal soldiers, seizing Staines by the arm.

Staines thrashed and screamed, the sound unholy. Before more of the royal soldiers could get to their leader to assist in restraining him, Staines wrenched free, his bloodied hands twisted loose from his bonds.

He lunged at Lydia, hands outstretched and reaching for her neck. His eyes were crazed.

Lydia's heartbeat slowed down. She inhaled a steady breath through her nose and pivoted on one foot. And then she wound her arm back, just like Benedict had shown her, and let her fist fly. There was a satisfying crunching sound as she connected with his nose. Staines's head snapped back, and he crumpled to the ground.

"Yes!" Timmy hollered.

Lydia cradled her throbbing fist in her other hand. Benedict wrapped his arms around her.

"Bloody hell," he whispered into her hair. "Never a dull moment when you're around."

Lydia snort laughed into his chest. He was here and warm and holding her and she'd just punched out Staines. The world looked a lot brighter.

The commander of the royal soldiers cleared his throat. Lydia pulled back a few inches and gave him her attention.

"You and your friends did well here tonight, my lady," he said, his voice respectful. Then he looked down at Staines and his lip curled in disgust. "Get him out of here," he said to his soldiers.

The men dragged Staines's unconscious form along the hallway and then down the stairs. No one seemed overly concerned about his inert legs banging on each step as they carted him down.

"Will any charges be brought against the peaceful people who were arrested at yesterday's rally?" Lydia asked the leader.

He shook his head. "Once the Prince Regent read Democratium Liberum's article about what happened here, he ordered that all the wrongfully imprisoned be immediately released, and promised that the crown would pay restitution to the families of those who at the rally sustained an injury or..." He swallowed. "...or were killed." His voice had grown softer.

"Democratium Liberum's article?" Lydia breathed. "The—the—*Prince Regent* read it?"

The leader of the royal soldiers merely bowed and followed his men down the stairs.

Lydia turned to Benedict. "I don't understand."

He pressed a kiss to the crown of her head, then wrapped an arm around her waist so he could speak to everyone in the hallway. To all their friends.

Jack. Pippa, who held on to her sword with one hand and her husband with the other. Jane. Dev, who was dabbing at the delicate spaces between his wife's fingers with his handkerchief. Agatha, fussing over her daughter Grace, was patiently explaining to her mother that both she and the babe were fine. Harriet, who smiled indulgently, as Timmy ran up and down the hallway, whooping.

And all the other reformers, hugging one another, recounting their moments of glory restraining Staines and fighting soldiers, or introducing themselves to Lydia's friends.

"I think you have much to report to us, my friend," Jack said.

Benedict stared at him, and his hand flexed around Lydia's waist. She held her breath as the two men had some silent communication with their eyes.

"I do, *my friend*," Benedict finally replied.

The whole group seemed to relax, even those who didn't know about the men's fight that morning.

"Please, tell us how you arrived with royal soldiers in tow," Dev said.

Benedict glanced down at Lydia, and in his sherry eyes she saw it all—his apology, his love, and the pledge of his heart.

She nodded. Whatever he had to share, she was ready to listen and to let the others hear as well.

"I left the estate in a rush earlier today," Benedict said. "I'd been a complete idiot and walked away from this amazing woman after we'd had a misunderstanding."

"No," Lydia interjected. "It was all my fault." She wrapped her arms around him and squeezed tightly. "And I'm so, so sorry."

He smiled and dropped a kiss on her forehead. "Me too."

She stared up at him, her smile tremulous. He'd called her an amazing woman. And he'd come back. Her heart was overflowing.

She leaned toward him, tilting up her mouth for a kiss.

But someone cleared their throat. They both pulled back, and Benedict's cheekbones grew ruddy.

"And what happened next?" Agatha demanded, her hands on

`her hips.

"When I left, I grabbed Lydia's article and shoved it in my pocket without thinking," Benedict continued. "I rode to town and had a good think along the way. I'd been so hurt, but the more I sat with it, I could see why people believed such a terrible rumor about me. I *acted* like it was true. I was protecting my mother, I think, without even realizing it. For a few years, I even acted like some jaded rake who would seduce a married woman *and* her maid at the same time."

Harriet clapped her hands over Timmy's ears. "Language," she warned.

"Sorry," Benedict said, his lips twitching.

Lydia bit back a smile.

"I didn't allow you to trust in me because I didn't trust in myself enough to explain the truth." He shook his head. "I don't know if I'm ready to correct the story, since I'm not sure I could do that to my mother. But, at least, you all know the truth."

"I, for one, would like to hear more of this scandalous tale," Dev whispered to Jane. He had still been in India when the event occurred, so it made sense he hadn't heard the rumor.

His wife shushed him, but she was smiling.

"But what happened next?" Grace asked, rubbing her belly.

Benedict glanced at Lydia. She nodded. Whatever he had to say, she was comfortable with him saying it here.

She trusted all these people.

She *trusted*.

It was good to feel that way again.

"I went straight to the Duke of Wolfingham's house when I arrived in town."

Lydia glanced up in surprise. She had tried to get the duke's wife as an ally at the ball all those nights ago. Her husband was the preeminent leader of the House of Lords, and his influence with parliament, as well as with the Prince Regent himself, was vast.

Benedict nodded, clearly sensing the direction of his thoughts.

"When you spoke to her that night, I had an inkling that they might be able to help if we got into trouble."

She squeezed him tightly.

"Then what?" Timmy called out. "This story isn't very exciting."

The adults all chuckled.

"Sorry," Benedict replied. "I'll try to get to the exciting parts soon." He gave the lad a wink. "I gave the Duke Lydia's essay. That was who I wanted you to pass it along to in the first place. I thought it would be more powerful if the members of the Lords heard it from him, since he's so respected, instead of the risk of it being simply overlooked or ignored in the newspaper."

"Oh, Benedict," Lydia said. Her heart ached again, remembering how she'd accused him of wanting to read it himself, of how no one would listen to him. "I'm so sorry."

He shook his head. "You weren't wrong. I don't have the respect of the others in parliament." He raised one eyebrow. "Yet."

She smiled at him. "Yet," she affirmed. Her Benedict could change how he was perceived without hurting his mother, she was certain of it.

"Wolfingham took me directly to the palace, and..." Benedict looked down at the floor for a moment, then lifted his golden-brown eyes to hers. They sparkled as he smiled. "I met with the Prince Regent."

"Lud!" exclaimed Harriet.

"You talked to the Prince?" Timmy whispered, eyes wide. "That *is* exciting."

"Indeed," Benedict agreed, eyes twinkling. "But mostly, he read Lydia's article. It was her words, not mine, that swayed him to take action."

Lydia's breath left her body. *Her words.* Being read by the Prince Regent. Her words swaying him to help the reformers.

It was any writer's dream, to affect those who read their work, but to have such an impact...she could barely wrap her head around it.

"He immediately arranged for the royal soldiers to hurry back here with me. He issued the arrest warrant for Staines and shut down the Office of Public Order."

Lydia gasped. "The whole thing?"

"The whole thing."

It was astonishing.

"And you heard the officer explain that the Prince Regent declared that no charges will be pressed against any who attended the rally peacefully, and those who suffered a loss will be paid restitution. And…he's going to ask Parliament to reexamine the Corn Laws."

Gasps went up from the people in the hallway. If Parliament abolished the Corn Laws, it would drastically help the majority of people in England by making bread and all grains affordable again.

This was major change.

Major reform.

Because of her words. And because of the brave actions of those gathered here today, as well as the thousands of other reformers who had attended the rally.

And…because of Timmy.

"I think we've forgotten an important part of the story," Lydia said, peering down at the boy.

Timmy grinned up at her. "Do you mean how I unlocked the door?"

Lydia knelt down in front of him. "How did you do it?"

"I kept the picks you gave me, and I practiced all around your house, just like you said," he replied. "And I was lucky that I had them in my pocket when we came to the rally, because we all got locked in here. My *second* arrest." He beamed with pride.

Lydia glanced up at Harriet, and the woman raised her eyes heavenward. "What will my Harry say?"

The others laughed, and Grace nudged her with her arm. "You have that man wrapped so tightly around your finger that you could have *left* Timmy in prison and your husband would forgive you."

"Let's not give the lad any ideas," Agatha warned.

"He was working on that lock almost the entire time we were in there," Harriet explained. "But it was just too hard for him. We all took a stab at it, but no one had the knack."

"But then," Timmy chimed in, "I heard what was going on in the hallway, and I heard Lady Lydia pick the lock most of the way, so then I just tried a little more and I got that lock to click open."

Lydia took Timmy's hands. "I could hear you working on the lock when I was talking to Staines. And when I heard the quiet little click, I knew you'd done it."

Timmy beamed, displaying the adorable gaps in his teeth. "I was a hero."

"You certainly were," Lydia said, pulling him in for a hug.

"We could hear everything in the hallway," Harriet explained, "and we knew from the closeness of his voice that Staines was standing right against the door, so when you shouted *now*, we knew to fling that door open."

"It was perfect." Lydia rose to her feet. "I would go on a wild scheme with you lot any day."

With that, Timmy gave a whoop and began running up and down the hall again. His mother chased him laughing, and the other reformers went downstairs in search of food and water.

Lydia turned to Benedict.

"There's a question I would like to ask you," he murmured, pulling her close.

"Is it for my cook's jam recipe?" she teased.

He dropped a quick kiss on her mouth. "That's actually a rather good idea. Do you think she's still awake?"

Lydia poked him in the ribs, and he grinned.

"What I want to ask, my darling, brilliant, lovely Lydia, is if you would do me the honor of taking my hand in marriage?"

"Benedict," she breathed, tears pricking her eyes.

"Aren't you supposed to ask me for permission first?" her brother grumbled from down the hallway.

"Nope," Benedict replied, never taking his eyes off Lydia. "She's in charge of herself. Only *she* gets to decide."

Oh, how she loved this irresistible rake of a man. He was her perfect match in every way. "Yes." Lydia reached around his neck and pulled him down for a passionate kiss. "I'll marry you, Benedict. I love you."

"I love you, too."

And despite the protestations from Jack, they continued to kiss for many long minutes. They had a lot of love in their hearts, after all, and not even an audience would deter them.

THE END

Historical Notes

Sadly, the Nottinghamshire Massacre in this story is based on the true events of the Peterloo Massacre of 1819. In St. Peter's Field, a peaceful protest rally where women, children, and families had gathered, turned deadly when military leaders sent in troops, likely intoxicated, to clear the field. The name Peterloo references the bloody battle of Waterloo.

The crowd of an estimated 60,000 people was penned in on three sides by soldiers on horseback with swords, and many peaceful attendees were cut down or trampled. It's estimated that over 600 people were injured and 18 killed. Among the dead were women and a child. The orator Henry Hunt was imprisoned for two years for speaking at the event, journalists who were present were arrested, and one historian has called Peterloo "the bloodiest political event of the 19th century in English soil."

The Blackburn Female Reform Society was real, and the first of many female reform societies composed of working-class women who demanded change from government for the betterment of their families. They fought for voting rights since no women and only 11% of men could vote at the time, as well as an end to the Corn Laws.

Many of the leaders of those societies were up on the platform at Peterloo, holding banners that represented their groups. The work of the female reform societies in the Regency period paved the way for later suffrage groups who bravely fought for women to have equality in England's government. All women over the age of 21 could finally vote starting in the election of 1929, over 100 years after Peterloo.

Nevertheless, she persisted.

ACKNOWLEDGEMENTS

Writing The Ladies Covert Academy series has been such a treat, and I adored spending all this time with the bold, brave ladies of the LCA who dared to follow their passions in a world that didn't always offer much space for women. Pippa the fencer, Jane the botanist, and Lydia the political essayist were such wonderful heroines to create and find heroes worthy of them. I thank all of you wonderful readers who went on their adventures with me. I hope you enjoyed tagging along for a duel in the park at dawn, poisoning (mildly!) the bad guys, and rescuing reformers with both lock picks and political essays.

I am so grateful to my family who support me in my writing with hugs, plot suggestions (I still need to have someone mistakenly crack a raw egg on their forehead!) and allowing me to ignore them (and the unfolded laundry) for hours or days at a time as I created these stories. I love you so very much Steve, Fiona, and Finn, and your love and support is at the center of everything I do.

To my sisters for whom this book is dedicated—thank you Sharon and Coco for always being my BFs. You mean the world to me, and I feel so lucky that my best friends are also obligated to spend major holidays with me.

I am so thankful to belong to several supportive writing communities. Writing is at first glance a solitary venture, but if you dig a little deeper, you find a connected web of cheerleaders, commiseraters, and guides. My home base is the Emerald City

Romance Writers which has been a part of my writing from the beginning. I'm also indebted to the members of Romancelandia on social media who spill the tea, shout from the rafters, and share their news both good and bad...as well as their favorite lines in #FridayKiss. And I love being a part of the Dragonblade author community, where all the writers I've met so far have been supportive, kind, and effusive in their love of historical romance.

To my writing pals—Nicole Knightley, Priscilla Cook, Catherine Chase, Joanne Machin, Christina Braver, Lynne Pearson, and Maggie Menane—thank you for being awesome.

A big shout out to author extraordinaire Maisey Yates who did a workshop for the Emerald City Romance Writers on writing with dictation a couple of years ago. Using her generous advice, I drafted this manuscript with Dragon, saving my wrists and hands from a world of hurt. Apologies to anyone who may have inadvertently heard me dictating the word *moist* into my headphones.

My editor, Cynthia Blackburn is as eagle-eyed as they come, finding my many errors and suggesting the perfect fixes with patience and good cheer. Thank you, Cynthia. It's been such a pleasure to work on this trilogy with you. And I promise to be mindful of independently acting eyeballs in the future!

And to Kathryn Le Veque, Shawn Morrison, Evelyn Adams, and the rest of the team at Dragonblade, thank you so much for embracing The Ladies Covert Academy series and for all your help and support.

About the Author

Jenny Hartwell has a confession–she loves People magazine as much as Pride and Prejudice. Her fun, pop culture adoring side shines in her contemporary rom-com set in a gourmet chocolate factory while Jenny's Regency romances feature strong damsels and swoony lords. Her writing has won or finaled in numerous contests including the Golden Heart, The Emily, Four Seasons, Fool for Love, and The Catherine. Jenny lives with her family in the verdant Pacific Northwest. She loves movies, travel, and staying up late with a good book. And, of course, chocolate. Jenny is represented by Lesley Sabga of The Seymour Agency.